...THAN LIVING ON MY KNEES

PART II

The Cleansing Begins

HARALD ZIEGER

Brilliant Books Literary
137 Forest Park Lane Thomasville
North Carolina 27360 USA

If you can't tolerate evil,
you have to walk the road to the end

—Harald Zieger

CONTENTS

What Has Happened so Far

The Old Guard, the communists who, under the umbrella of the power of the Soviet Red Army and with the support of the Communist Party of the Soviet Union, installed the communist system of power and control over that part of Germany that was still Germany yet under their control, had become old. Most of them were in their late seventies or early eighties and had no comprehension that the style they ruled the country with was no longer working.

All over the country, the people rebelled, and large demonstrations began to disturb the order of the communist system. Fearing that the whole system could collapse any moment, a group of influential, second in line of power comrades decided they had to take over to earn at least a piece of the pie for themselves in late March. They conspired behind the leaders, which they called the Old Guard; voted them out of the Polit Bureau, the highest commanding entity in the nation; dissolved the existing Central Committee of the Communist Party SUP; and sent the Old Guard into retirement, as they called it.

They formed a new Central Committee, the sole decision-maker entity of the new structure of the party. In a first public announcement, they declared their intention to correct the mistakes of the past, to clean all organizations of corrupt people, and to call for a new party congress as soon as the preparation was finalized. They appalled the citizens to help the party correct mistakes and trust the new leadership until they could see the results of their efforts. Later, they installed a new agency, realizing that most of the already existing anti-corruption tools inside the organization had been compromised over the years, with an enormous power second to the Central Committee as a group. That new agency's only objective was to be the secret weapon against corruption inside the party and outside of it.

Open demonstrations every Monday in more and more cities indicated the people's discontent. On top of that, a secret underground resistance was forming throughout the nation that the leaders had no clue about. The most attention was placed on what was brewing for a long time inside the party, and the new agency, just being established, had some severe incidents right at the start. While collecting the first most critical files from the northern region on his way to his new home, the former county secretary for Agitation and Propaganda, in short CS-AG, now appointed commander of the Office of Investigation and Recovery, had to order the State Security Police, in short SSP, to arrest one First District Secretary, in short FDS, one First County Secretary and killed in a shoot-out, in which he was slightly wounded, another FDS.

The sudden discovery of his hated brother, a traitor, and enemy of the cause of communism, being in Neubrandenburg instead at work in Stralsund initiated a lightning of thoughts and suspicions. Still, the day's actions buried those suspicions for the time being.

When he was finally on his way to his new home, he was so exhausted that he even forgot to check in on the results of the surveillance he had initiated on his brother in the morning.

CHAPTER 1

Transferring the First Communicators to Friends and Trusted Members of the Resistance Movement

With a paper bag, where he placed two sets of his communication systems and topped it with some older versions of the journals *Funkamateur* and *Radio Fernsehen Elektronik*, in one hand, Fritz moved slowly away from the parking lot, stopping from time to time to look into one of the few shop windows, as if he was interested in their presentations. In reality, he was paying close attention to the mirroring people visible and how they behave. Was there somebody who suddenly stopped walking and turned himself toward a shop window? Since not many of those were there, it would be awkward to see someone turning and not knowing where to look. He crossed the street several times, just as if he wanted to see what the other shops had to present, and non*e* of his attempts revealed any tail he might have. Sure, now that he was not followed, he went straight to the small coffee shop on the opposite and entered.

Although it wasn't really cold outside, the wet weather and low temperature were still uncomfortable, so the warm air greeting him inside the small coffee shop was a welcome relief. Fritz looked around and walked to the table in the corner where the wall connected with the large windows on the street side. Fritz sat down and placed the paper bag under the table, pushing it to the other side with his foot. Just in case something happened, he could claim it wasn't his. The waitress, the only employee visible, came over to his table and asked what he wanted to order. He ordered a coffee, and she walked over to the counter. She was about to place the cup on his table when another guest asked for the receipt. She confirmed and walked over to him when the door opened, and a man, Fritz's age, walked in.

He looked around and saw Fritz. He walked straight over to him.

"Hi, is it you, the guy who wants to sell some electronic journals?"

"Yes, that's me, but I have only four, and there should be a second guy I am waiting for."

He sat down and smiled and said, "Great to meet you finally in person. I got a message that we will have awesome communication tools?" his voice just above whispering.

"Let's wait for the other guy. I guess we are too exposed here to be able to train you on using it."

"That shouldn't be a problem. I will take you both to my home, and we can go through the instruction there. I am Michael, by the way, #3 here in Neubrandenburg."

"Do you know the guy from SUR?"

"Yes, we had several meetings in the past, and he is an excellent electronic tinkerer. That doesn't mean he would be able to do things like what you have, but he has helped us with alarm systems, which has saved two of our guys from being arrested two years ago. They could escape and go underground in Berlin. Unfortunately, we have had no way to connect again ever since."

"Okay, I would say we will leave the coffee shop when he enters, and since he knows you, will he follow?"

"Yes, let's pay, and we will just walk out when he comes. He will know what to do."

They called the waitress, and Fritz paid for his coffee. While he was taking one of the journals out of the bag, the door of the coffee shop opened. The guy walking in recognized *Michael* immediately. With a short nod, he confirmed that. Fritz and Michael stood up. Fritz grabbed the bag from under the table, and they left the coffee shop. Michael turned to the right, opposite the parking lot where Fritz had his car, and they walked down the street until the corner of *Glink Street*.

They turned into the street where the central police station was located, and there was almost no pedestrian traffic. Any tail would have been easily discovered. They turned right into Darrenstreet and walked to turn left into Second Ringstreet. After about two hundred yards, Michael stopped in front of the entrance to a multifamily apartment and unlocked the door with his key. They walked up three flights of stairs where Michaels's apartment was to the left side. He chose another key from his ring and opened the apartment door, letting Fritz go first and locked the door after he had entered.

"My wife is at work, and the kids are in school, so we can talk without interruption."

"Does Felix know where we are?"

"Sure, but he is even more careful than I am. He will take some sideways and ensure he doesn't have a tail."

Fritz was unsure that they were walking to Michaels's apartment, doing a lot of diverting potential tails. "You call that careful how we walked almost directly to your apartment?"

"Oh, we had Felix about thirty meters behind us, and if we had had a tail, he would have started to run and pass us, turning right into the Ring Park. I would have known we have a tail and would have told you to get lost in the park. He will be here in a few."

When he said it, the bell rang, and Michael went to the door and hit the opener for the house door. Shortly after that, he opened the apartment door, letting Felix in, and locked the door after him. Felix walked over to Fritz and said, "Hi, I am Felix."

"Nice meeting you, Felix. Okay, guys, let's get to it because I have to get to Berlin after this, and I really don't want to hit the rush hour. Fritz took the communicators and the programmers out of the paper bag and placed them on the table.

"The black box is the communication system, and that thing that looks like a calculator is the programming device. The communicator is powered by a 9V battery and has 64kb of storage for programming and 128kb for data storage. That might not tell you much, but it is necessary to remember, at least for the second number. This number tells you that the communicator stores roughly 128 thousand characters, a little less, but that's unimportant. And I believe it is more than we will ever need.

The programmer has a display with five lines and twenty-five characters each. The communicator is activated with a small magnet because it has an internal reed switch. The unit is turned on by holding the magnet on the small side with the red dot for three seconds. The unit switches off when you hold the magnet for about six seconds."

"Wait for a second," interrupted Felix. "There is no indication whether the communicator is on or off."

Fritz smiled and answered, "Great observation, Felix, and thank you for bringing that up. Let me demonstrate how that works because we are at the point where I will show how to enter messages into the unit."

Fritz took out his small pocket Bible and explained that this was the best book to code a message for the beginning. "Later it would be necessary to agree with all further connected groups to establish a standard list of books and give it a five-number code. Here in the example, we use the Bible, and I will give it the code 5 1 0 0 0. Let's say a second book is Schiller's *Don Carlos*, and we would give it the code 5 2 0 0 0. In our example here, my first five-number group would be 5 1 0 0 0. That tells the receiver of the message that he needs to take his Bible to decipher the message. Since there are several different translations, we must ensure everyone uses the 1916 translation from Martin Luther." Fritz looked around again to see if he was still followed and saw his new friends looking at him with great interest. He continued, "As a first step, we have to tell the calculator that it now functions as a programming unit. The reason is that if a STASI officer gets his hands on one of the devices, he has a standard calculator, and all it does is calculate." Looking around the room, Fritz said, "Do you have a paperclip or a darning needle?"

Michael went to the other room and came back with a paperclip, and handed it to Fritz.

Fritz continued the instruction, pointing to a small hole at the bottom of the calculator and pushing the paperclip in the hole. "Now, it is a programmer. And when you type numbers, the software enters into a specific programming mode, configuring the numbers into five sequencing groups."

Michael was amazed and expressed amazement by saying, "Man, that is genial. They will never figure that one out."

Fritz went on. "I will now make a complete transmission of a message and then show you how to read that message out.

"First, we have established the source for the code: 5 1 0 00. Now we have to tell what book and chapter in the Bible, or when it is just a book, it is only the chapter. Since working with five-number groups, we have four groups in a line and as many rows as needed. Let's say we chose the 2 Kings, book number 12 in the Bible. Our first group would look like this. To get all the characters we need, we chose chapter 4, verse 16. And the second group would look like this: 5 1 0 0 120 4 0 0 16.

"Now the message text itself. We want to let the message receiver know we want to organize a meeting of all #1 officers at the Designer Outlet Berlin McDonald. We would shorten the sentence to 'meeting at Mac d berlin design center d1204 t1500 L1.' To make it easier for us to code the text, here is an example of how you could do it:

And he said, About this season,
1 2 3 4 5 6 7 8 9   10 11 12 13 14 15 16 17 18 19 20 21 22 23 24

Accord I ng to the time of life, thou shalt
25 26 27 28 29 30 31 32 33 34 35 36 37 38 39 40 41 42 43 44 45 46 47 48 49 50 51 52

embrace a son. And she said, Nay, my lord, *thou* man of God, do not lie unto thine handmaid."

Fritz numbered the characters of the text until 52 and said, "That should do it. I don't think we need more. If we need more, we can go and number more characters. One of the rules for good coding is to use different numbers for the same character if available within the text you have chosen. It makes it more difficult to break the code. And we won't use the same verse again. The Bible has sixty-six books, so sticking with one is unnecessary. The more you variate, the more complicated it is for the SSP to break the code."

And after a second of thinking, he added, "They shouldn't ever be able to get their hands on the message if you play it safe.

"We would code it like this:

5 1 0 0 12	0 4 0 0 16	41 42 5 15 17	32 33 10 39 41
21 26 9 11 20	29 45 8 24 3	38 19 8 33 24	27 5 24 14 5
29 0 0 0 0	3 12 04 0 0	15 0 0 0 0	45 1 0 0 0

"We must also remember that the last three of the five-number groups we program are first, the date; second, the time; and third, the addressee, either L1 for the #1 or L2 for #2, the security or even ALL, which means the message must be transferred to all known communicators.

"We have an eight-bit data bus, so we need to tell the unit when a number is complete and when a group is complete. The programmer always shows the last four rows of data. The unit automatically recognizes when a fourth group is complete and switches to the next row."

Fritz continued with the demonstration and said, "We have the message now coded, and now we need it to be written into the memory of the communicator. We can't know the status of the communicator because there is no indication. You remember I activated the communicator several minutes ago when I kept the magnet at the red dot for about three seconds. Since then, the communicator has been in receiving mode for sixty seconds and went to sleep mode for ten minutes. And that is on purpose. It wakes up after ten minutes, listens for sixty seconds, and falls back into sleep mode again."

"But our programmer, 'calculator,' can stay on for much longer. We will now write our code to the programmer's memory. It has the same memory size as the communicator. To tell the programmer the completion of the number, we use the comma key [,], and for the end of a group, we use the dot key [.]. With an equals key [=], we signal the end of the message. When we have written all the five-number groups into the programmer's memory, we hit the [M+], the command to transmit the message to the communicator. It is necessary to tell the communicator that the transmission is complete, and the communicator can go back into sleep mode, therefore, the equals key [=]. Suppose the communicator is awake and in receiving mode. In that case, the transmission starts, and you can see it on the programmer's display, line by line, disappearing. With the transmission complete, the communicator sends the number **10-123** back to the programmer, which stands for A and means acknowledged with the ID number of the communicator.

That tells you that the transmission was successful. You must repeat the transmission if you don't get the number **10-123** back. If a transmission fails multiple times, meaning no response from the communicator, the battery must be replaced."

Fritz hit the **[M+]** key, and Felix and Michael leaned over to see the display of the programmer. Line after line disappeared, and the number **10-015** appeared on display within less than a second. Michael was just amazed, and all he could say was "Wow!"

Felix, though, with at least some understanding of the functionality, his primary college studies were high voltage and energy, said, "That solves one of the most significant problems underground organizations have, secure communications. Most organizations get destroyed because of tracking their exchange of messages. It is just fantastic, Fritz. But how do I get a message out of this thing, uh, communicator?"

"That is really easy, Felix," Fritz answered. "The programmer has a **[M-]** key. And Let's say this communicator is hidden in a tree hole at an Autobahn Raststtte. And all you know, it is near the parking area's center. You drive to that parking lot and find a spot close to the center. You take your programmer, switch it on, push the paperclip into the hole, and hit the **[M-]** key. Then you leave your car, lock it, and go to the restroom, restaurant, kiosk, or whatever is there to spend ten-plus minutes. Remember the ten-minute interval of check mode of the communicator. When you come back, you check the programmer, and when you see the message in the display, you can scroll up and down with the [+] and [-] keys and drive off. Nobody, even the most suspicious SSP officer on your heels, will have the slightest idea that you just received a secret message."

Fritz said, "Okay, let's download the message we just transmitted to the communicator a few minutes ago. Saying that, Fritz hit the **[M-]** key, and nothing happened. "Remember the sleep mode cycle," Fritz repeated.

Every eye was on the display of the calculator-like-looking programmer, and it was total silence in the room. The only noise was the sizzling of the electric night-storage heater. Then after about a minute and a half, suddenly, numbers appeared on display, and line by line, the message was transmitted to the programmer.

5 1 0 0 12   0 4 0 0 16   41 42 5 15 17   32 33 10 39 41
21 26 9 11 20   29 45 8 24 3   38 19 8 33 24   27 5 24 14 5
29 0 0 0 0   3 12 04 0 0   15 0 0 0 0   45 1 0 0 0

Felix and Michael talked simultaneously, "Awesome! Almost a miracle"—and with astonishment—"It works!"

Fritz waited a minute to get the excitement cooled off and said1, "Before I leave, I need to get with you, guys, over the possible books I have selected so far. First, as I said, the Bible. Since most people in the UR movement are Christians, it should not be an issue. Then as 52000 Schillers 'Don Carlos,' 53000 Schiller 'Mary Stuart,' 54000 Schiller 'The Robbers,' and 55000 Schiller 'Wilhelm Tell.'

"Please ensure that you, as the CO of the groups, have those books handy at any given time. I recommend—actually, I insist that you use different books for each message and disordered. And you are the only ones in your group who know about the communicator and have access to the programmer. We are working on a regimen to send and receive central messages, but for now, it is the job of the different group's COs to place the units and let the geographical next group know what station it can be read and programmed. To let the others know where it is, you only need to get it close enough for a transceiving distance of approximately one hundred yards. The best way to inform those who need to know where it is, take a *photo*. Have the photographer's shop make a picture postcard and send it out with a text like, 'Here is where I waited for my wife for two hours,' 'My car broke down,' or something like that."

And thinking briefly about how to say it best, Fritz added, "Something additional came up last time at a local meeting. We plan to begin training for a group of six to eight unique fighters based on a trainer crew with Speznaz training and war experience. Please try to select interested members of your groups and scan them carefully. Please be extra careful with this. We could barely get those brothers to safety."

Michael looked at Felix, and both nodded because they immediately knew whom he was talking about. Nothing else needed to be said. Felix said, "I think we are okay so far. If we have any questions, we will use the system and let you know. That might also be a good chance to test the system out." He closed with a smile.

Michael stood and walked to the kitchen window, looking down at the street in front of the house and over to the tree line of the Ring Park, where he suspected an SSP officer would hide to watch his house.

"I think that's it. If you don't have any questions about the programming and receiving messages, I am on my way."

Returning to the living room, he said, "Fritz, all clear outside. You are safe to leave the house. I suggest turning left and turning left again when you hit Treptower Street. You will end at the southern corner of the parking area where your car is parked."

Fritz was baffled. "How do you know where my car is parked?"

"Our group had you in sight from the moment you left the car," Michael said with a smile. Our security officer did not want me to run into a situation where you may have a tail since you don't know our city very well. I was following you, but you were too conscious, and I lost you after the second stop at the shoe shop window. I had to enter a house entrance, and you disappeared among the people."

Fritz, smiling, said, "You must be pretty good, though, because I never recognized you following me. Okay, guys, have fun with the toys and play with them for a while, but don't forget to shut down the communicator until you place it at the point of access."

They said goodbye, and Fritz left the house, turning left as Michael suggested. Just a short distance down the road, he saw an opening at the Ring Park wall and crossed the street to enter the park. Walking inside the parklike area, which appeared to be a part of the former city wall, he felt a little more relaxed and was almost discouraged when the sign for the Treptow Street exit came into view.

He turned into Treptow Street, and after about 250 meters, the parking area opened to his left, exactly as Michael had described. Since it was later in the morning, he wasn't surprised that many more cars were parked. Walking along the rows toward his car, Fritz thought about his trip to his next stop, visiting his friend Reinhard. Being in his thoughts already on the road, he did not register the Lada limousine parked just two rows behind him with two young men sitting in, one of which was just lifting a camera to get some excellent pictures of Fritz.

He started his car, and since he could leave the parking lot driving just out into the street in front, he never realized that the other Lada, also occupied by two young men, was turning right after him into Stargarder Street and following him. He had decided to use the 96 because that would give him several opportunities to get to Reinhard's place based on the situation. Fritz had to enter the left-turning lanes while driving toward the Ring along Große Wollstreet. Looking into the mirror, he saw just one dark-blue Lada behind him that seemed to drive straight. Setting his turn light, he switched to the left lane and wondered as he realized that the dark-blue Lada suddenly did the same.

The hair on his neck suddenly stood up, and his gut told him something was brewing behind him. The traffic light turned green, and he proceeded as he had planned in the direction of hitting the 96. He knew there were a lot of possibilities to get rid of his tail, and all he needed was to stay focused and not get panicky. He used the opportunity of the four-lane road to change the lane twice, and the dark-blue Lada changed three cars behind him the same way he did. Now Fritz was sure he had a tail, and this dark-blue Lada was only one of possible two or even three. He decided to use Neustrelitzer Street to get off of the Ring and try to use multiple traffic lights to escape the surveillance.

With his right turn lights on, he switched to the right-turn lane into Neustrelitz Street. Looking into his mirror, he saw another Lada, this one light green about six or seven cars behind, acting as if the driver had just now decided to change direction. The usual race began on the way to the next traffic light, only five hundred to six hundred meters after the turn. Every driver tried to get in the front row and maybe, even maybe, outrun the cycle and get through at the end of the yellow light phase. That precisely was what Fritz had based on his decision to change direction instead of going the Ringway to 96, using the more congested Nuestrelitz Street. Again, a look into the mirror confirmed his suspicion because now the light-green Lada had accelerated so much that it was only one car behind yet in the second lane. The dark-blue Lada was far behind, almost invisible, about seven or eight rows back.

The situation was similar at the next two traffic lights, just that the light-green Lada was now in the same lane as Fritz was, yet three cars were between Fritz and them, and Fritz was in the first position. That was what he wanted to get them to be. Fritz could see the traffic lights of the crossing street, which would give him a decisive advantage into an early start. Now, when the traffic light at the crossroad lights turned yellow, he started to count 1001, 1002, 1003, and hit the accelerator. He was already halfway across the crossing when the traffic lights in his direction turned green, and the colon slowly started to accelerate.

He accelerated, not paying attention to the speed limit, and got through the next traffic light just before it switched to yellow. Fritz was now far ahead of the colon, which had started entering Neustrelitz Street; he had crossed a second traffic light, and the traffic from the crossing roads entered Neustrelitz Street, blocking any attempt of the two Lada to close up on him again. But to be sure, he stayed slightly over the speed limit, and when he turned into the south direction of the 96, there was nothing to see in the mirror of any of the two SSP cars.

Thanking his Lord in silent prayer, he drove ahead in the direction Nuestrelitz just a little bit above the speed limit, which everyone knew the police would tolerate. He considered the possibility that the SSP would contact the police in Neustrelitz to look out for his car, but he would stop at the next parking area and throw mud onto his license plate. There were so many Skoda with the same color on the road that he knew that no police officer would waste his time to find out if he was among them. And he also believed that these guys, having his number, would rather believe that he was driving north, not south.

CHAPTER 2

Moving into the New Home and Experiencing the Headquarters Office

After an uneventful drive, Gunther finally hit the opener for the property gate to Bodo's new home. He said somewhat louder, "Comrade Zipper, we have arrived."

"Bodo startled out of his dreamless sleep, wiping his eyes with the back of his hands, and stretched. "Are we finally there? I guess I slept several hours."

"Yes, comrade Zipper, you slept almost two hours, and even when I had to fuel, I let you sleep because the fuel station on the Autobahn did not need your confirmation. The ID card you gave me is like money."

"Did you get a copy of the receipt? It is your only proof," Bodo answered. When Gunther confirmed that, Bodo got out of the car and saw only one of the moving trucks at the front of the house, and he wondered what had happened to the other one. Concerned that they may have a defect lying somewhere on the road, he walked through the door held open with the automatic door closer locked and called out for the movers. The group leader came out of the kitchen and was visibly pleased to see Bodo.

Before Bodo could ask what happened to the second truck, the mover said, "We had made excellent progress. We arrived earlier than I had thought, and we had already emptied the other truck, so I could send it away. We are done with the master bedroom and the kids" bedroom. All the living room furniture is already in the house. I was just placing some dishes and silverware in the kitchen and am on my way. I will be back tomorrow at about 10:00 to 11:00 AM with a four-man crew to move the rest in and place everything according to your wife's wishes."

"That sounds great. I will see that my wife is here when you, guys, come back and leave it to her to arrange everything."

The mover walked out to his truck, where the other two had waited already. Bodo followed and watched them driving out of the property. He walked over to his car, where Gunther was standing after carrying Bodo's luggage to the house entrance, and said, "Gunther, I think you can get home now. Leave the boxes in your car, but make sure the car is locked. You are still living at the SSP headquarters?"

"Yes, comrade Zipper."

"Pick up my wife and son and bring them here tomorrow morning. But not too early. Actually, I have not tried the phone in the house yet. I will call them better now and let them know. Please wait for a moment." Bodo walked back into the house, into his new home office, again amazed by the office furniture left by the former owner, and picked up the handset of the very sophisticated phone. Knowing it was on a highly encrypted line with a direct connection to the CC switchboard, he dialed zero and waited.

After the second tone, a woman answered, "Switchboard, how can I serve you, comrade?"

Bodo responded, "This is a connection test since the line was connected. Many thanks."

"Certainly, comrade. Have a good night." Knowing that the phone was working, he went outside and told Gunther that he could leave and should pick up his wife at the guest house of the CC at around 11:00 AM. Gunther confirmed and drove out onto the road, and Bodo hit the button next to the door to close the gate. He walked back into the house, still in amazement about where he was and barely able to comprehend that this was his family's home now. He walked through the house, took all the greatness in, and felt for the first time that he had arrived.

That he had arrived, in a sense, that he was, where he believed he needed to be. He had arrived, not at a finishing line, but at the starting block of a new journey. The starting block of an operation that could occupy his whole waketime for years to consume every hour he was awake and steal time from his family in a way he had never envisioned. Yet he would not stall for a second. He knew he had to sacrifice everything to fulfill the order of the party leadership to the completion.

He returned to his office, where many boxes with office stuff, papers, files, and books waited to be unpacked and sorted. He picked up the phone and called the guesthouse of the Central Committee, which he had written down when he was staying there the week before. The switchboard answered, and he told his name and wanted to talk to his wife. He was immediately connected and sighted joyfully when his wife answered, "Yes, hello? Who is there?"

"Hello, love, it's me," Bodo answered.

"Great to hear your voice," Sarina said. "How are you, and more importantly, where are you now?"

"I am in our new home. I just arrived about forty minutes ago. I am a little tired, but otherwise, I am okay." This wasn't entirely true, but he did not want to tell her about the shooting and the grazing over the phone to get her all excited and unable to sleep.

"Do you want to come us out there tonight? You could probably arrange that, right?"

"I could, but it is actually late, and I would need to get Gunther to bring you out here, and I don't want to do that to him since I just sent him home. He was driving all day long. I told him to pick you both up at the guest house at about 11:00 AM tomorrow, giving you time to get a good breakfast and sleep in a bit."

"Yeah, you're right. We had two incredible days, and Nick really enjoyed the attention we got here from all the comrades. I believe he said twenty thousand times how his friends would be jealous if they knew. Nick has been totally exhausted and asleep for almost an hour now. Otherwise, he would tell you himself. But that has time till tomorrow. I look forward to seeing our new home, and I hope it will be too hard for Nick to change schools in the middle of the year."

"Yeah, it won't be easy, but he is smart and has great human skills, and that shouldn't be too challenging to adapt and find new friends. Good night, honey. See you tomorrow."

"Good night."

Bodo hung up, ensured the heavy wooden house door was correctly closed and locked, and walked up the stairs to the master bedroom. He was delighted that the bedroom furniture was assembled entirely and placed where it would probably be if he had placed them, but he wasn't sure that Sarina would be. But for now, it was all he needed. He went to the bathroom, through his usual hygiene, and was asleep before he had his second leg in the bed.

While Bodo went to bed to get his well-deserved rest after an unbelievable day, a day he had never dreamed would happen to him, the two teams of the Neubrandenburg SSP officers who had failed to surveil Fritz for more than twenty-five minutes, tried to write a report who would not cost them their position in that department of the SSP. When they returned to the office and reported to the lieutenant in charge that they had lost the trail, they did not think about much. It had happened before and would happen again because traffic was always an issue, especially if they had only two cars.

Even though they were sucking on the pens and formulating sentences backward and forward, there wasn't really much they could say other than that they had been unable to hide well enough because they were only with two cars. The lieutenant had destroyed their indifference in a few sentences, explaining that this order had come from the most powerful man in the country, the commander of the new OIR. They had better some excellent reasons in their report, which he had to send directly to comrade Picker. He was sure they would be on foot patrol within the next twenty-four hours or, worse, opening envelopes in the basement.

When the report was finally on the desk of the officer in charge, now at about 9:30 PM, he immediately called the headquarter of the SSP and said that he had a report that he was ordered to have in front of the general when received. The switchboard asked back several times if that was the case, and after he confirmed it every single time, they said he should send it via Teletext. He said okay, noted it in his guard book, and typed the report into the Teletext machine. He clipped the code strip to the report, placed it in a tube, and sent it to the lieutenant's office via the air tube system. That was all he could do, and the case was closed for him if he had only known.

The following day, it was about 7:30 AM when General Pieker, head of the SSP, entered his office as usual. He went to his desk and took out the messages prepared for him during the night with the incidents from all over the nation, which the regional offices considered noteworthy for the general. He reviewed the combined reports about the demonstrations, the persons involved, and any new findings. Then he took the following report: a Teletext print with the code strip attached. And he almost exploded. He yelled after his secretary in a loud voice, ignoring the intercom. With a bright, red face, she stormed through the door and asked, "Comrade General, what happened?"

Still very angry but with a reduced voice, Pieker said, "Who was on guard at communications yesterday's second shift? I want to get the communications chief in my office within fifteen minutes. But keep him out there until I call."

"Yes, comrade General, yes." She answered, completely shocked still. She had not seen him that angered since he had taken over from his predecessor, who was choleric, and everyone in his environment was used to him losing his temper. But comrade Pieker? That was the first time ever! Carefully closing the door, she walked to her desk and called the communication center. "The general *wants* to have the chief communication officer in his office within the next fifteen minutes. Make it happen because he is so angry. I have not seen him in fifteen years."

In the meantime, Jürgen Pieker had found his countenance and called her over the intercom, "Please connect me with comrade Zipper. He should be available at his home office now. Do you have his number?"

"Yes, comrade Pieker, I got it yesterday right after the technicians were done with installation and testing. I will call him now, comrade."

When the phone rang, Jürgen picked it up immediately. After the secretary had announced that comrade Zipper was on and had hung up, he said, "Good morning, Bodo. I see you made it to your new home in time to be at your office that early."

"Good morning, Jürgen. Yes, I was home. It still sounds a little strange, late at night yesterday. I believe it was about nine thirty or so. But I went to bed almost immediately, so I was up early to adjust my office. My home office, I have to say. My actual office, I haven't seen yet.

I am curious about what has been done over the last week. But I guess that's not the reason why you are calling."

"No, Bodo, that's not the reason. I just came into my office, and the first thing I saw among the reports, which came in after office hours was the report about the surveillance you had ordered on your brother."

"Great, what have they found out? Did we catch him meeting somebody?"

"Unfortunately, they lost him about ten minutes after he drove off of the parking lot. They had two teams on him with Ladas, upgraded Ladas, I should say, and they lost him anyway. I am not only furious about that, but nobody informed me and just sent a Teletext and placed it in my in-basket. I ordered them to inform me immediately about the results. I am sorry."

"Jürgen, I understand your frustration and am shocked that that happened. But it shows how much work you must do to better train your officers. I guarantee you that the reason is that he outran them from traffic light to traffic light because your officer did not want to go over the speed limit. I have heard that more than I can count. But the real issue is that we now have no clue where he went and what he did in Neubrandenburg. There is no family or work connection to that city. Here is what I think is best. I will start a case group on that because that stinks too much. I would like you to get information to your offices to keep an eye out if that car appears in any of the cities. And I mean across the nation. I smell that he is up to something."

"Bodo, I could order the officers in his hometown and the shipyard to check around and see if we can find out what he was doing there?"

"Better not, Jürgen. He is too intelligent and would immediately smell that we are behind those questions. That would get him into sleep mode, and we would start at zero. He must have been in a restaurant in Neubrandenburg or a coffee shop to meet someone. Maybe you can have somebody check if some of the waitpersons or salespersons remember having him seen."

"Yes, Bodo, I can initiate that. Before I forget, I have a list of eighteen potential candidates for your officer positions. Of whom are three very experienced investigators. The rest is brand new from officer school, all with three with infantry NCO service. My secretary will send a courier over to you before noon."

"Great, many thanks, Jürgen. Talk to you." And Bodo hung up.

Bodo was starting to sort all the stuff he had brought that he considered staying at his home office and placed the books and files in the appropriate places. While doing that, he was again amazed about how well thought out the whole design of that home office was. It pointed to somebody who was able to have an organized work environment. When he was done, he went to the kitchen for another cup of coffee. He enjoyed the look again out of the kitchen window into the garden area. He imagined the different vegetables and herbs growing there during the season. He worked back into his office.

Bodo never understood why people would place their desks so they would face the door with the back. He had changed the position of the massive desk so that he had a good look out onto the front yard, gate, and driveway. All was completely visible because of the large *French* doors leading out onto a small terrace with a waist-high balustrade of professional set clinker bricks.

While taking out the first file concerning the reports about the corruption of his former boss and first county secretary of the party on the island, he prepared himself for the worse of corruption. Not only because of what he had seen already and what had caused him to get the man arrested immediately but because of what might come behind the first three pages he had seen so far and because he knew there had to be more. During the few years he had worked at the county leadership, he had always had a bad feeling about the man, especially when they were sitting in a meeting. He wished the complaints of people Bodo had daily contact with aside. He was digging into the file and started to make notes for the dictation to his secretary for the case he would bring in front of the members of the CC. He noted evidence, part of the file, and witnesses needing interrogation.

He was about an hour into the file analysis when suddenly the phone rang with a strange noise. He looked at it and realized that the number 9 key light blinked. He looked at the instruction manual for that somewhat unusual phone. He read that this meant that somebody had hit the intercom. Pressing the button, he said, "Who is there?"

"Hello, comrade Zipper, I am a currier from SSP headquarters, and I have a package for you personally only."

"I'm opening the gate."

The gate opened, and the courier drove up to the house. Bodo went out, and he handed him a package and a clipboard where he had to sign that he had received the package. While he was signing, a strange thought went through his mind. The courier was satisfied, and Bodo hit the gate button next to the house door to close the gate. He stood at the open house door, and that thought that had just crossed his mind came back with might. What if this was someone attempting to harm him? What if he wasn't home and some bad people tried to get to his family? He needed to know who was at the gate before Sarina, Nick, or he hit the opening button. Walking back into his office, he placed the package on the desk, grabbed the paper knife, and opened the package. As promised by Jürgen, there were eighteen files with the data files of the potential officers for the OIR. That reminded him of the situation with the gate and that Jürgen was the best person to help. He grabbed the handset and looked for the button with that name. It was the second next to Bodo's. No coincidence; as a smile crossed his face, he hit the button.

"Comrade Pieker here" came even before a ringtone.

"Hello, Jürgen. Sorry for interrupting your work, but I just received the package with the officer's files."

"Something wrong with those?"

"No, no, not at all. It was just that while I hit the gate opener and had the courier drive up to my house, I thought that was dangerous because I could not, under any circumstances, know if he was really the courier you sent. I wondered if there is something like a camera that would show me or Sarina or Nick, who is at the gate. And I don't want to have any of those monsters you have at the headquarters gates mounted," Bodo said, laughing.

"I understand entirely, and no, you don't need to have such a monster," Jürgen answered and laughed too. When we met, we had so many things on our plate about the technical stuff for your new offices. These house intercoms are leading technology brought in by our CoCo organization. We have camera-integrated intercoms, and I will have our technical department get you one mounted immediately. We had actually decided to have those ready for all of your office facilities, and I wonder why we forgot to do that for your house. It must have escaped my mind."

"Thanks, Jürgen. Have a nice day."

About half an hour later, the gate's intercom buzzed again. Bodo hit the button and asked, "Who is there?"

"Comrade Zipper, here is the technical team from SSP for replacing the gate intercom."

"Hold on. I'll come out." Bodo was perplexed about the incredible speed with which the SSP technical team responded to just a question, not even a demand uttered. He ensured his Glock 19 was concealed under his light sweater and walked to the gate to be safe.

He opened the small person gate, and one of the technicians got out of the car and greeted him, "Comrade Zipper, we were at the office facility at Adlergestell and got the call to install the camera intercom at your house. We thought we install yours and pick up another set when we returned to the office tonight. Since we already had the other one for the RON in the car, we plan on driving up tomorrow morning to install phones and all the other technical stuff.

"Wow, that is fast thinking, comrade."

Oh, by the way, I had no idea that the RON facility was that far developed already. It wasn't even a week since the location was chosen."

"I don't know about that, comrade Zipper. All that I know is that we shall be there tomorrow and start the installation. Can we go ahead and replace this one?"

"Sure, go ahead. Do you mind if I stay and watch because I am not an electrician or electronic expert, just a mechanic, but I am always interested in things like that?"

"No problem, comrade Zipper."

In the meantime, the second technician brought the tools and replacement parts out of the car, and both went to work. It took them only about twenty-five minutes to change the device. Bodo walked into this office and called the gate intercom. Immediately, the display on his phone changed and showed a wide-angle image of the area in front of his gate. He could see the technicians as they packed their tools and loaded them back into the car. One of the technicians returned to the gate and hit the button, saying, "One, two, three, voice check."

Bodo responded immediately, "All clear here, and I have your image on my phone too. But what about the house intercom?"

"I will be right there, comrade Zipper. A monitor module is already in that system and is covered."

The technician came up the driveway, entered the entrance area, and removed a small metal cover in the upper area of the intercom module. A little screen became visible, and when the technician hit the button, the sound from the street area and the image were visible. Bodo was visibly relieved. Now, he could be sure that whenever the gate bell signaled someone at the gate, Sarina and Nick would know who had rung the bell before they decided to hit the opener. He thanked the technicians and wished them a safe trip to the north, and after he was sure that the gate was closed and secured again, he returned to his office.

He hit the hands-free button and the key for Karls's direct call, and when Karl answered the phone, he said, "Good morning, Karl. Can you tell me who is organizing all the actions around the new offices of the OIR?"

"Good morning, Bodo, it is me. Did I make a mistake? Is something wrong?"

"No, not at all, Karl. I just wanted to meet and go over the progress so far. I just had some technicians here at my house. They told me they are already installing communications technology at the RON tomorrow. I am amazed about the speed with all of it going on."

"I am glad that you are surprised because that is what I wanted to achieve, surprise you with the success of setting up your work environment. Comrade Bruno ordered me to drop everything and be at your disposal to get all the facilities operational as soon as even humanly possible. The CC decided to pull all stops after you left because they understand that your new organization is worth nothing until you have a working environment."

"That is awesome. I would like to review the locations status, get updated, and see where we stand. Can you come to the headquarters office at 2:30 PM?"

"Shure, Bodo. I will be there at 2:30 PM. See you then."

Bodo hung up and was about to go back to the file analysis when the buzzer on the phone signaled someone at the gate. Hitting the button, he saw his car at the gate and hit the button twice. The gate opened for the car to drive in and up the driveway. Bodo walked out and stood on the entrance stairs to receive his wife and son into their new home. Nick came running and hugged him fiercely while brabbling away about all the noteworthy things to tell him in a millisecond. Sarina walked up to him, joint the hugging, kissed Bodo, and said, "I am speechless. Is this our new home, or are we here just until something else is found?"

"No," Bodo answered. "This is our new home and whatever you can make from it."

Gunther had taken their luggage out of the trunk and had placed it on the upper one of the three stairs in front of the entrance door. Bodo turned to him and said, "Gunther, I have a meeting with comrade Karl at the office at 2:30 PM. Please be here in time to drive me over. Until then, you are free."

"Thanks, comrade Zipper. I wanted to get back to headquarters and see if our housing department can get me an apartment closer to here, maybe Eichwalde, Bohnsdorf, or Grünau. I will be back in time." With that, he got into the car and drove down the driveway, and the gate, which had been closed automatically after their entrance, opened up to let him drive out. While he was going through the gate, the movers with the last truck and trailer with their furniture arrived, just in time for Bodo to hit the opener again before the gate closed.

"Sarina, let's bring the luggage in, and then I need you to take care of the furniture the movers have already unloaded and those they still have on the truck and trailer. I will show Nick his room and the outside, and then he can tell the movers where he wants to have his furniture in his room. They are four guys, and that should take care of getting everything done today."

"Bodo, don't run away. I am lost for words here. I have no idea what to do or to say, and this is the most amazing house I have seen in my whole life."

Bodo laughed and said, "Okay, let me tell the movers where to start, and then we will make a tour." Bodo went out to the movers, which stood at the back of the trailer, and said, "I will show my wife and son around since they just arrived so that they get an idea what is where."

"No problem, comrade Zipper. We will sort out how to start in the meantime."

Bodo grabbed the arm of Sarina on one side and Nick's on the other and marched through the first floor with them. He showed them the laundry room with the extended mudroom and door to the garden area, went back with them into the dining area where the large table with the twelve chairs was still in place, and finished at the living space with the movable window-style doors covering the whole wall toward the riverside.

Sarina was too occupied with being astounded about the kitchen appliances, which were somewhat out of a different world, to say a word. Nick couldn't get the refrigerator and freezer, both full-sized from floor to ceiling, opening and closing often enough. He was thrilled about all the lemonade they could store there and would never run out of it.

Then he led them up to the second floor, and the amazement went to another level. Nick discovered the two rooms with separate bathrooms and was torn about which one he should choose. After a few times back and force, he said, "I would like to take this one, Dad, can I?"

"You can, Nick, and it is the best choice because you have a direct view of the river and a small balcony which the other doesn't. However, the other one is a few square feet larger."

"Oh, Dad, the size difference isn't really a point here. Both of the rooms are twice as large as your bedroom was at home. I said at home, but this is our home now, right?"

"You are right, Nick, this is now our home, and I hope you soon feel like it and find new friends here too."

"That's what I might miss most, Dad, my friends. Can I use the phone in your office occasionally and call Peter?"

Bodo realized how difficult it really was for an eleven-year-old boy to be ripped out of his known environment and thrown into a completely unknown situation. Adding to that, he was probably under special attention by that new environment because his position wouldn't be a secret long in this small village-styled town.

"Nick, you may not have noticed among all the overwhelming new stuff, but we have a phone in each room. We have three direct lines, one of which is blocked for my office use only since it is encrypted and has to be locked when I am not in the house. The other two are free for you both to use at any time. But think about the cost. This new house is much more expensive than our house on the isle. We had to pay only the operation cost there because we owned it. The SUP owns this house, which we rent with a particular contract. The contract allows me to pay more than the rent, and I can pay off the house over several years. Nick, please do me a favor and go down to the movers and tell them where you want to have your furniture placed. I will show Mom our bedroom, and then we will be down too."

Nick ran down the stair, and Bodo took Sarina by the hand and guided her to the master bedroom. He opened the door and stood there while she walked into the room. Their bedroom furniture was already placed, and Bodo had slept there the night. With that, it was furnished as much as they had furniture to do it. Sarina stood there, looked from one side to the other, and was still. After a few seconds of complete motionlessness, she turned to Bodo, and he could see the teardrops forming in her eyes. "Bodo, I can't comprehend what I see. I have difficulties processing that we are about to live in that beautiful house."

Bodo walked to her, embraced her, and said, "Sarina, we have arrived. All the years of rejection, the many times I was ridiculed for my stand and harassed for the betrayal my brother did to the party, all that is history. The comrades who are leading the nation into a new era of further development of the communist society recognized my capabilities and my relentless drive to do what is necessary to reach that objective. This house is a start for us into a new future. But it comes with high costs. I will be away a lot, working all day long, and will be gone during the week for days, but I will make sure that most of the weekends our ours."

Sarina freed herself from his embracement, looked him in the eye, and said, "Bodo, I will be with you. I will support you as much as possible and use this opportunity for our best at any time."

She walked through the bathrooms and the walk-in closets and started to talk about the arrangement she wanted to make. Bodo reminded her that the mover was waiting downstairs, and they both went down. They walked down, and Sarina immediately took command of the furniture placement.

Bodo entered his office, closed the doors behind him, and was again very impressed by how solid all doors were made. Even with the large glass inserts in his office doors, the noise was barely audible, although the movers were calling back and forth about the work. While working on the analysis of the R-Case, as he called it, the Rostock case of corruption because it was the district in which all the corruption was committed, he suddenly realized that all his notes had to be rewritten by his secretary.

Remembering that his agency had a hard currency budget, he wrote down what he thought should be added to the desktop computer list. Things like pocket memos and extremely small recorders would allow one to record impressions immediately and have the secretary type them directly into the computer. And those small transportable computers, he remembered HP had them presented last year at the international fair in Leipzig. There should be one for each officer to make work much more efficient.

The buzzer on the phone for the main gate buzzed, and Bodo hit the key and said, "Hello, who is there?"

"It's me, comrade Zipper, Gunther's voice returned. I just hit the opener and wanted to alert you I am here to pick you up."

"Oh, it's already that time. I will be out when you are at the stairs."

Bodo grabbed his Glock 19 out of the drawer, placed it in an inside holster he carried in his three-o'clock position, and closed the office doors behind him. He never had to lock his office at home because Sarina and Nick wouldn't enter when he was not in. They never did after he explained why he did not want them to enter in his absence.

Sarina was in the entrance hall, and he told her he would be back for dinner around 7:00 PM. He walked out, got in the car, and Gunther drove off. The gate had not yet closed entirely, and he noted to call the technicians to reduce the waiting time. They arrived at the headquarters facility, and the opener worked to open the main gate, so Gunther drove right in and parked in front of the office's main entrance.

Bodo was surprised at how great that building looked on the outside with the new coat of paint and walked in to be even more surprised to see that the office was ready for work. They walked over to his office, and since all doors were open, he could see that all the offices were fully furnished and ready to receive the workers. He noticed his office door was thicker than the others, with three lockbolts on each side. Bodo walked to his desk, lifted the phone's handset, and listened to the ready tone. Obviously, everything was ready to get to work.

He walked out of the building and waved at Gunther to follow him to the barn building. Several masons were busy finishing the changes they had discussed during their visit. Bodo was again surprised that all was done as they had discussed during their initial visit. The wall separating the holding cells from the workshop was finished, and the safety door, which looked almost like his office door but with no wood covers, was in place. Walking through the door, he entered the holding area. He saw that all the cells were finished, even furnished, and the sanitary systems were installed. The only work left was the soundproof insulation for the ceilings and locks that needed to be installed.

"Na, Gunther, what do you think? It looks like we are ready to get the first guests invited?"

"Yes, comrade Bodo, it seems to be the case. Do you want to transfer the two guys from the north to the facility?"

Before Bodo could answer, he heard a car driving into the yard, and they walked out to see who had arrived. Although Bodo knew it could only be Karl for their meeting, it could also have been a worker of material delivery. But his first thought was correct. Karl was just getting out of his car when they exited the Barn. He turned to Gunther and said, "I have a meeting now for about two hours, maybe less. Keep around, and I will call when I need you."

"Hello, Karl, how was your day so far? Uh, what, why do I even ask? Your day must have been gorgeous because you look relaxed," Bodo said, laughing at Karls's baffled face.

"Bodo, if I wouldn't know better, I would consider that a compliment," Karl responded.

Both laughed and walked into the office building to Bodo's office. They closed the door and sat at the conference table, a remnant of the forest organization that could easily seat twelve people. Karl opened a rather large briefcase, took out a box, and placed it before Bodo. "I thought you might be interested in these items for your active crew?"

Bodo was too perplexed to say anything but took the notepad from his smaller briefcase and placed it before Karl. "Slowly, but just slowly,

Karl, I believe you can read my mind. And that scares me. Look at my notes I made about an hour ago."

Karl started to laugh, and then, looking at the notepad Bodo had placed in front of him, he startled and said, "Bodo, I am at a loss for words. I thought while I was coordinating the activities around the two locations we have so far decided for your offices, It would be great if the officers could write their reports to a certain degree themselves instead of loading their handwritten, mostly unreadable, notes onto the secretaries, of which you may never have enough." And bowing down to the briefcase, he took out another smaller box and placed it next to the HP box. While Bodo, with uncontrollable curiosity, opened the HP box, Karl grabbed a red pen. He marked the two words on Bodo's notepad.

"Man, Karl, that's HP's latest version of the OmniBook." And opening the other box, with "Philips" written on it, he took the pocked memo out and was amazed too. "How were you, guys, able to get your hands on these devices? Aren't those under an embargo for export to us?"

"I am not 100 percent sure, and I don't care. But I learned that since I work directly for comrade Bruno, there are certain connections into the NSW. We have export companies in some countries that can get stuff for us. Most of it comes through CoCo, which means comercial coordination. And these guys are really tied-lipped, as you can imagine."

"I thought that since we have a lot of convertible currency assigned to our budget, we may be able to buy this stuff as we need, but the money seems not to be the issue, at least not totally?" Bodo said. He unpacked the devices and carried them to the desk to plug them in to fully charge the batteries. At that exact moment, the phone rang, and when he looked at it, a button on the direct-call section blinked. He looked closer and saw that the name Tauscher was written on the label. Wondering what could cause the SG to call him directly, he picked up the phone. A friendly soft voice of a woman said, "Comrade Zipper, can you take a short call from comrade secretary-general?" Bodo was a little perplexed by the question. How could he refuse to take a call from the head of the power players in the nation? "Sure, please patch me through."

A few seconds later, the distinctive and expressive voice of the secretary-general sounded through the handset, "Comrade Zipper, I would like to invite you to our four PM meeting of the CC today. I know it is a short time, but I believe you should be there if you can make it happen. I would also see that you get regular invitations to our meetings since many issues we are debating may relate to your assignments. You may decide whether or not it is beneficial for all of us if you participate or not, depending on the agenda."

"Comrade Secretary-General, it is an honor for me, and I will make it possible to attend the meeting today."

"Thanks a lot, comrade Zipper," the SG answered and hung up before Bodo could even say a word.

"Did you get this, Karl?" Bodo looked over to Karl.

"Yes," and with a smirk, he said, "I probably have to call you comrade now again since you are now honored to sit at the power table."

"Don't be silly, Karl. If you start calling me with 'comrade' again, I will find a way to create a case about you. You and Bruno are close, and he and Jürgen had already switched to the first name basis."

"Oh, that would be scary," Karl answered, laughing. He turned to his notes on his own OmniBook. He went on to explain the situation about the RON. When they looked at the area, Bodo suggested establishing the Regional Office North (RON); they discovered a facility that belonged to the navy and was used for the Kampfschwimmer, an equivalent of the US Navy Seals. It was abandoned about fifteen months ago when the new training station at the Baltic Sea was finished, giving them the necessary environment for the special training for what they had used that facility at the lake.

Karl had driven out there on Friday afternoon and had found a perfect property with all the buildings necessary. There were even quarters for the potential officers who were unmarried. He showed Bodo the exact location on the map. Although it was on the other side of the lake, it was as easily accessible as Bodo's chosen location. The photographs he showed Bodo made it easy to envision it as a perfect place for his northern office.

"Changing the subject, Karl. I need you to do some more things for me. I need to get a single-family home rented in Wittstock, which is the nearest town large enough to keep the identity of my office head secret. For that reason, it should be the ICC central, meaning you, to get that rented, or if necessary, we will buy it with the OIR budget, and he will pay it back with the rent. Next, my COO is one of my most trusted friends and needs an apartment near the headquarters. And I need an apartment for the second secretary I hired from the regional headquarters in Rostock. You remember the woman you gave your business card to?"

"Oh, yes, unfortunately, I never asked her name."

"It's Maria Hafler. She is single, and with that, a nice one-room apartment somewhere in Grünau would be great. Maybe near where Giesela lives, allowing them to drive together to work. And considering all of it, they need to be moved. Can you get all of that arranged for me, Karl?"

"Bodo, I am happy to help you start the new agency as soon as possible. It was about time. Every day we could spare to get it running would benefit us. That's the reason why Bruno told me to skip everything else and get you settled in and started. I will move every asset I have to and pull every rank necessary to get your people settled in within this week. Do you have a specific order in case I have to set priorities based on recourses?"

"Let's say, Peter Wille, who will be my COO, should be first, and the house and moving Reiner Worser and family to Wittstock is second. He needs to be there asap because he already has two cases with arrested people on hand and one with a dead FSD. So he needs to get going within the week."

Karl had typed all of the information in his OmniBook and, looking up to Bodo, who stood at the front of his desk, said, "Consider it done, Bodo. And before I tell you that you have to call your driver because you have to leave now if you want to be in time there for the CC meeting, I admire your unwavering belief that the party and, with that, the country can be saved, your faithfulness to the cause and your strength you have to use the force of that position to make it happen. Not to schmooze you, but to let you know, that I am right behind you, always ready to be your second hand."

"I am really thankful for you telling me that, Karl. I know I have the complete support of the CC right now, but it might come a time when even those who made it possible to install this agency don't want to face the consequences of their decision. Then I need all support I can get within the party from those who still believe in the cause and are willing to step over dead bodies when it comes to that," saying that,

Bodo turned to the phone and hit the button for his mobile. Gunther answered immediately, and Bodo told him to prepare for the trip to the CC office. Karl packed his stuff, and they walked out to the front of the office building where Gunther had already waited, having the car door open for Bodo. Bodo waved at Karl, entered the car, and said, "Let's get going, Gunther. I have to be at the meeting at four."

"No problem, comrade Zipper. I will get you there in time."

Bodo used the time and called his secretary, Giesela, and told her that standard office time would start the next day at 8:00 AM at the HQ office. After she noted the exact address, she confirmed, and Bodo hung up and called Reiner. He told him to stay in touch with Karl, this guy who, suddenly, out of nowhere, called him just a little over a week ago. He told him Karl would take care of the Wittstock house and move him probably within the week. Then he called Peter. Bodo was surprised that Peter was joyful and excited to hear that Peter would get a great apartment near the new office where he should move in before the end of the week. Bodo thought Peter would start again to argue that he is too old, that he is not the right person for it, and that he never accepted a higher position in the party because there are better than him. Bodo hung up and called the woman in Rostock, Maria, and told her to get ready to be moved within the next day or two depending on available resources. She was extremely excited and said she would sit on packed luggage and have everything ready to be loaded.

When Bodo hung up on that call, they were already at the gate for the CC building. After showing their ID cards, Gunther drove into the underground garage and stopped at the elevator. Bodo went to the elevator and hit the passcode for the top floor where the conference room was when he entered. Just as the elevator doors were about to close, he saw Bruno's car entering the garage, so he held the doors open for him.

"Thanks, Bodo. Great to see you again. What about your wound?"

"You know, Bruno, if you wouldn't have asked, I would even know I have it. I have completely forgotten about it. Not even tell Sarina about all that was going on yesterday. She might eat me alive when I finally tell her that I was shot at and got a gaze."

Bruno laughed, saying, "You better tell her when you get home. This meeting should not take long, and you might stop by the med station downstairs before you drive home. They can look at it and make sure it is okay."

While they exited the elevator on the top floor and walked toward the still-open conference room door, he answered Bruno, "I'll do that."

Taking their seats after they had greeted all the other members of the Central Committee, Bodo looked at the piece of paper in front of him with the agenda, and there was only one point, the arrest and death of FSDs in the north region. "Oh, oh, that will be nice (I don't think)."

The SG called the secretaries to order and opened the meeting, saying, "Comrades, this meeting is only about the agenda you see on the paper in front of you, and we can keep it short after we get the explanation of comrade Zipper what has happened. Comrade Zipper, please."

"Comrades, after I had your confirming vote last week, I drove home and finalized the packing for moving my family to our new home. Before we even had the meeting on Friday, comrade Bruno had ordered all DS-ICC to pack the ten most incriminating cases for OIR investigation and have them ready to be picked up. When he told me about it on my way to the north, I told him that was great, and I could just make a cross trip and pick them up myself. So on Monday morning, my first stop was at the office where I worked for several years, and I picked up the package from there. Although not a DS-ICC officer, I have knowledge of extreme irregularities, which were never acted on because of the suppression by the FSC. I thought it would be helpful to have those cases too.

"We had just driven out of the city when my first looks into the file about the FCS revealed a preponderance of the evidence, and I mean evidence, not just rumors or gossip, of corruption beyond any imagination. That was why I immediately called comrade Jürgen and asked him to arrest the FCS. And because there was as much evidence in the file that the FDS was part of the whole corruption and defalcation, I told him to do the same for the FSD in Rostock too.

"Comrades, I can confirm every word comrade Bodo is saying. And without anticipation of comrade Bodo's further investigation, we already have a comprehensive protocol of statements from the FCS and the FDS, accusing each other of being the driving force behind their criminal acts. Excuse me, comrade Bodo. I just wanted to let everyone know that we have something more already besides the files. And before I give the word back to comrade Bodo, I have to add that the criminal FDS of Schwerin, who actually tried to kill comrade Bodo who was able to react faster and was therefore only slightly wounded, Was even worse. The interrogation of his wife revealed that they have not only several bank accounts where they hide the money they cashed in for their corrupt actions, but they also have obviously hard currency accounts in Switzerland and Sweden. But as I said, I don't want to anticipate the investigation of comrade Bodo. I just had no possibility of letting him know about it.

"Comrades, all of this and an incredible amount of evidence those collected boxes contain prove that we do not have much time to solve those issues. The corrupt members of the party are a danger to our bare existence, and the attack on my life is the best proof.

"If I had had more time to prepare my statements here today, I would have laid out a suggestion on paper that all current first county secretaries (FCS) and all first district secretaries (FDS) are immediately placed under specific surveillance 24-7 because of that immediate suspicion, that many of them are already hard at work to destroy evidence. It won't help them because their attempt to suppress any kind of investigation over several years, in some cases, has produced an enormous amount of evidence and witnesses."

There was silence in the conference room, and only the breathing of some of the comrades was audible. Then comrade Pieker said, "We have the capacity to the surveillance, but I need some time to get the teams together and instructed. As you know, comrades, even the SSP is not clean and has to fight corruption. We are not complete with the background checks yet. Maybe comrade Bruno can give us an update on the status. I know he placed a high priority on armed institutions."

"Yes, comrade Jürgen, based on the latest report from this morning, we have checked and cleared about 73 percent of your officers and so far declared twenty-eight unfit for service based on suspicion of corruption. The files of these officers are all prepared for the final investigation by the OIR. When we are done, we will transfer them over to you, comrade Bodo. So no fear of running out of work soon," Bruno said with a sarcastic tone.

Jürgen jumped back in and said, "Great news. We will have all the necessary teams ready by the end of the week. How long do you believe, comrade Bodo, will we need that surveillance?"

"Comrade Pieker, as soon as I have the OIR HQ fully staffed and the systems installed, we need to scan all the files, at least cursory. We can perhaps take the surveillance teams off. I guess about a week, two weeks for some at the most."

"That sounds reasonable," comrade Jürgen said and leaned back in his chair, visibly relieved.

"Great, comrades," Werner Taucher jumped in. "We have the temporary replacements in charge right now. Comrade Kreuger has prepared the specific message for the evening news. In our next meeting on Wednesday, comrade Tecker will present two candidates to replace these criminal elements. Comrade Bodo, my thanks and appreciation for the courage you showed facing this criminal, and I am sure I speak in the name of all the members of the Central Committee. The meeting is closed."

The secretaries stood, walked over to Bodo, and patted him on the shoulder. Some shook his hand and expressed their hope that the actions he had in mind would secure the power of the party and secure the nation.

On the way out, Bruno reminded Bodo to stop at the med station, and he did so. There was actually a doctor who had served in the military and looked at the gaze. He said putting a new bandage on would not be necessary and sprayed what he called a liquid Band-Aid.

Gunther was ready with the car, and they were on the road to his home in no time.

CHAPTER 3

Discovering the New Home, Great Neighbors Assigning Positions and the First Steps of the Operation

t was already after 6:00 PM when Gunther hit the opener for the gate at Bodo's home. *Home?* Bodo thought. It was still overwhelming when he thought that this huge house was the new home for him and his family.

While driving up to the entrance, three wide curved stairs lead up to the impressive entrance door, which in turn opens into a large entrance hall with the monumental stairs to the second floor in the center, and his home office on the left side and an open living room going around the corner on the right. That was something he had never dreamed of living. And there was so much more to it he hadn't even seen yet. He told Gunther to be at the house the following day at 8:00 AM and that they would drive up to the new RON facility and wished him a good night.

He exited the car and walked up the stairs where Sarina awaited him. Bodo turned around and watched Gunther drive off the property to time the gate closing delay. It took almost two minutes after the car was through the gate before it started to close. "Uh, shit, I did forget about that," he said to himself. Then turning around, he kissed Sarina, and putting his arm around her, they walked into the house with her, saying, "Let me see what our new home looks like after my honey worked all day long to get the furniture in."

"Oh, Bodo, there is so much to do, and I need a lot more time and stuff to decorate and to make it our home. Until now, it is just a home, barely ours. You know what I mean?"

He laughed and said, "You can get whatever you can find to buy and place it here, but first, we need to find a way to make you mobile. I need to talk with Bruno about some arrangements. And I believe you will love it. But first things first." Bodo walked into his office and removed his Glock 19 with the IWB from his belt; and Sarina, seeing that, asked, "Do you have to carry that gun all the time? We have an eleven-year-old in the house."

Bodo remembered that he had not yet told her about the shoot-out with that crazy FDS of Schwerin and thought that would be the best way to get it done with the least amount of damage for being late. He took off the jacket and shirt and showed her the gaze wound on his left upper arm, which was covered by the spay and had already begun to slough. "Yesterday, when I was trying to converse with the FDS of Schwerin and had two SSP officers with me, we discovered that he was about to destroy evidence. After I knocked on the terrace doors, he pulled his gun and shot at me. Thanks to my excellent training with this Glock 19 last week for many hours, I was fast enough to respond and shoot him dead before he could kill me. It all happened so quickly that the SSP officer who stood just a few feet away didn't even have his gun drawn when all was over."

Sarina listened to him without a word, tears forming in her eyes, and she started to say something but could not get the words out. She walked over to him, embraced him, and finally sobbing, she asked, "Why would he do such a thing? Is your work really that dangerous? You were lucky that he was such a bad shot."

Holding her tight, Bodo answered, "I have accepted the assignment to cleanse the nation, especially the party we both love, from all the filth and dirt that has developed over several years of blowsy leadership. These people have much to lose and may try things like that for our family and me. That's why I stood there and timed the gate closing, which is much too long. That's why I want you to get the same training I got and be armed when you leave the house. And we will explain to Nick why we have those weapons and that they are no toys, and when he wants to hold them, he can only touch them when one of us is with him. And he is smart enough to understand and obedient enough to follow those instructions."

He let go of Sarina, put his shirt back on, and both walked out into the living area. Looking through the glass doors toward the river, he saw Nick sitting at the end of the dock.

"Sarina, I will go out to Nick and talk with him about that stuff. We will be back soon because I have not seen the basement."

"Okay, Bodo, I will see what I can scrape together for dinner since I have only the stuff we bought yesterday at that unique grocery store Karl showed us."

Bodo walked out to the dock and sat down next to his son. "Hi, Nick, how was your day? It was a very nice evening after the day had been unusually warm for mid-April. Did they set up your room as you like it?"

"Yes, Dad, all is set up as I like it. But the room is so much larger than the one I had. I would like to get a larger desk, which would improve my efficiency in doing homework."

"We can surely do something about that. It might take some days, but we can surely increase the furniture in your room and reduce the enormous space to what you are used to," Bodo said with a smirk on his face. "But I wanted to talk about something else with you. I know you are eleven years old, and many things that happened last week may be overwhelming. But I know you're much more developed than the years tell, and therefore, I will tell you to stuff you usually would not get told. You are listening to Mom and me often discussing things other parents do not discuss in front of their children.

"I have to carry a handgun most of the time I am awake because the new work the leaders of our country assigned to me can be dangerous. It can be dangerous because those stealing from and betraying our country don't want to be caught and might try to kill me to get away. Mom will get a handgun soon for the same reason and will be trained to use it efficiently, and with that, she will be able to secure you and herself if necessary. I wanted you to know all this because you may see one gun lying somewhere when we removed it from where it was, on our belts, pockets, or the drawer. I want you to know that there is no reason, under no circumstances, to touch those guns.

"If you want to handle it or have an idea how it feels, ask Mom or me, and we will ensure the gun is safe, and we are here to help you understand how it works. Do you understand all of this?"

"That is a lot to take in, Dad. Yes, I understand. Although I don't like it, I know it is necessary. I have often listened to you and Mom talking about the country's status and that somebody needs to do something about it. I will obey your instructions, Dad, as I most always did."

Bodo laid his arm around his son, pulled him close, and kissed him on his curly hair. "Let's go back to the house. It's getting dark, and Mom should have something to bite ready."

They stood and walked back to the house, where the sun was settling behind, throwing long shades of the house. When they arrived, Sarina was on the intercom in the kitchen area, talking to someone, probably at the gate. Bodo walked over and got the last few words, "I'll hit the buzzer. Just pull the gate."

"Sarina, who are you buzzing in at the gate?"

"It seems to be comrade Bruno had an idea to surprise us. He said he lived just two houses over down the road and wanted to welcome us into the neighborhood."

Bodo was surprised, to say the least, and walked through the house, opened the entrance door, and during the dimmer getting light of the setting sun, saw Bruno with his wife and, as it appeared, his two children walking toward the house. Sarina and Nick joined him in waiting for their guests, and when they arrived at the stairs, they wished them a good evening and welcomed them at their new home.

"Bodo, I apologize for not telling you in the afternoon about our invasion because, for one easy reason, I did not know about it. Annabel had that great idea to walk over to your place and welcome you with a little gift, and since she thought Sarina might not have had much chance to buy groceries, we thought we would bring some dinner." With that, he handed a large picnic basket to Sarina, which she almost dropped because it was really heavy.

They entered the house, and the women immediately went to work to arrange the dinner. Bodo let Bruno out onto the terrace, and they sat down at the outside seating area where they had a fantastic view of the riverside of the property, which was glowing in some parts in the light of the setting sun, and Bruno, with a deep sigh said, "I repent now not having moved over here after the house became available. Too late now, and I hope you, guys, enjoy it for a very long time. I am happy for you and Sarina, Bodo, and I wish you both growing old right here with many grandchildren."

"Thanks a lot, Bruno. I am still working on a way even to start to deserve it, though."

"If what we have heard today, and I am sure it is just the tip of the iceberg, is true, you have more than deserved this."

The women came out and put plates on the table and the prepared sandwiches on a massive platter in the center of the table. Sarina called the children, which were in Nick's room, to come for dinner. They came running down the stairs from the second floor, apparently starting a friendship already.

Nick could not hold back his excitement and stated, "Dad, Willi is just a week younger than me, and we can probably go to the same class. He also likes water, and even though it's just the river, they have a sailing club here nearby. Can I get to the same school, Dad?"

"Nick, slow down, sit down, and get something to eat. We can definitely talk about all of it when it is time."

Willi and Nick high-fived each other and then touched Lisa's high-raised hands. Sarina and Annabel looked at each other and smiled, happy that the kids seemed to like each other at the get-go. While they ate and talked, it became really dark, and suddenly, the lights at the posts of the terrace railing switched on and bathed the whole terrace with a soft light. After dinner, the kids returned to Nick's room, and the adults took another glass of wine Bruno had brought. They talked about the situations Bodo had experienced.

Bodo said he had talked with Sarina about getting a training course at the SSP headquarters. Annabel said she had done the same and would probably need a refreshing session. So with that, Sarina and Annabel agreed to do a class together as soon as possible, and Bodo would arrange that. He promised to arrange that the following day. While they talked about the arrangement for Nick to get to school and Sarina to the gun course, they came to the point of how to move around. Bruno jumped into the discussion and said, "You have the right and the resources to get a car with a security-trained driver for Sarina, the same as I have for Annabel. But I guess, the same way Annabel sometimes just despises the security and drives by herself, Sarina might be the same."

Both women laughed, and Sarina answered, "I am not a helpless old lady that needs a chauffeur to get to town. I can drive myself, I will learn to use a handgun sufficiently, and I am secure by myself."

"Yeah, you are right on that, Sarina, but sometimes it is just great to have a very well-trained driver with a registered license plate who can get you faster to the place you need to go than you can say the address," Annabel added.

Sarina thought for a moment, remembering the traffic the days before in Berlin, and said, "You might be right. But I don't want to call whenever I want to drive somewhere and wait till the guy arrives."

"That's not how that works," Bruno answered. "If we assign a car with a driver to you, Bodo can do that with a written order to the SSP. You have a car 24-7 if you want. We assume that you will sleep at night and with that one driver should be enough, but I agree, you should also have your own car. Uh, Bodo, by the way, have you ever checked the additional garages? I have never looked at them."

"I have not seen any garages other than the empty ones attached to the house here at the property," Bodo answered. "Where would those be?"

"I believe they are behind the conifers at the right side of the driveway on the way out. Let's go and have a look. The keys must be in that key cabinet, which is recessed in the wall next to the door."

They all entered the entrance hall, and Bodo found the key cabinet. Among several keys, he had no idea which ones were, so he took all that could fit. When they arrived at that conifers hedge, they walked around, and Bodo switched on the flashlight since the property lights did not reach around the hedge. Considering the highly well-thought-out architecture and amenities of the whole property, he was sure there must be lights too. But for now, they used flashlights. And there they were. Three large garage doors indicated that there was enough room to park a car. Bodo went ahead of the others, and it took him three trials to get the right key. He opened the door and was just as stunned as any man could be.

The garage contained one brilliant blue metallic Lada, one dark-golden Volvo 760, and a mechanical workplace as if it was copied from an NSW catalog. Bodo turned to the others, still a few meters away, talking about the thoroughly-thought-out design of the house's front yard that kept the whole, relatively large garage building hidden, and said, "Bruno, have the SSP officers never looked into this garage? I can't believe what I see here!"

"What is it that gets you so excited? I hope there is not a bag with money lying around in there?" Bruno answered, and walking through the open garage door, he stopped and stood in awe next to Bodo. The women, becoming curious because of the sudden silence of their men, came into the garage too. Looking around, Sarina said, without uncertainty, "See, Bodo, the question about me getting a car is solved."

"I am not sure what the legal situation is, but Bruno should be able to clarify that. Am I correct, Bruno?"

Bruno had to get his own mind to stop from running on 120 miles a minute about how that happened that the garage had been obviously completely overseen. Turning to Bodo, he said, "As much as I hate to say, just joking, Bodo, I actually love to say it, these cars belong to the house, and since the house was sold to you *as is*, these cars are part of the package and belong to you. I have no idea how that could happen, that the garage was completely overlooked, maybe because the attached garages let them think that there is nothing else. But here we are, and you own one heck of two cars together with the house."

Bodo was already thinking ahead and thought about practicality. The Volvo was too noticeable for them to use and would only catch unintended attention to them and this place. With that thought in mind, he said, "Bruno, I would like to suggest something you may need to discuss with the members. I want to give the Volvo 760 to the Central Committee in exchange for a Lada. In addition, I want both Lada up-tuned to the power of the Lada I have for the service. I know that the SSP mechanics can do that in no time."

"I don't need to talk to anyone. This deal is a no-brainer for the CC. That's like getting a priceless gift three times. Are you sure? You are losing with this deal."

"Bodo, what are you doing? Giving away a Volvo 760 for a Lada? Have you lost your mind?" Sarina was protesting, even agitated.

"Think about it, Sarina, how many people, even in Berlin, are driving a Volvo 760? And who are those people? The members of the Central Committee, and that pretty much is it. Do you want to draw that attention to yourself, Nick, and this place here, especially since it will be only a question of time? The cleansing of the party structure will have my name in public?" Bodo answered with a convincing tone.

After a little moment of thinking about it, Sarina nodded a couple of times and said, "You are right, Bodo. It's just such a great car to give up."

Bruno looked at Sarina and said, "You are right, Sarina, it is a nice car, and since it is my company car, I know it. But Bodo's careful consideration of the circumstances is correct."

Bodo started both cars, which ran smoothly, with less than 1,000 km on the odometer. They walked through the garage, checking everything. The mechanical workshop area had almost everything a mechanic could dream about. Bodo asked Bruno, "I wonder what a micro surgeon wanted to do with a mechanic workshop equipped like that? He couldn't work on a car engine on Sunday and go into the surgery on Monday."

Bruno thought about it for a moment, recalling the protocols he had read about the issue. While walking back to the house, he said, "I believe it was about the need to have the cars available at any given time in case of an emergency, and the regular repair shops are notoriously unreliable, as you surely know. And being the general MD for several members of the Old Guard, he got approved for whatever he asked. One thing is the 380VAC/400A electrical house service. Absolutely unheard of for a single house. Not even my house has more than the maximum 200A service. Okay, I wasn't the secretary ICC at the time when we bought the house from my uncle, but anyway, that is a lot of power."

"Yes, it is," Bodo answered, entering the house and closing the door behind them. "But what did he need that much energy for?"

"Haven't you been in the basement yet, Bodo?

"No, I am barely a few hours in here and continuously drawn away or harassed by visitors," he said, smiling. "Let's go down. We finished the garage and now the basement. Let's see what surprises await us there."

They walked down the stairs, which were also unusually wide and comfortable to step down, and Bodo opened the door at the end of the stairs. A sizeable general room with a seating area, a large TV, and a third open fireplace gave the room a comforting and cozy feeling.

"Ha, that's the third open fireplace, one in the family room, one in the Master Bedroom, and now one in the basement." Sarina was positively surprised.

"As you can see, we did not remove all the furniture because only what we thought some officer or secretary was lacking," Bruno explained. And he continued, "Here, to the left are the utilities, and to the right is a small bedroom, actually more like a small apartment with kitchen and bathroom included."

They all walked through the more than spacious "small" apartment, which could easily house a couple for weeks, and went over to the side where the utilities were installed. Bodo opened the door to the area, and there was a small hallway with stairs up to the back of the house and two doors with signs on them. One read "Electric," and the other read "Heating/Water." They first entered the heating/water room, and a substantial one-thousand-liter water boiler dominated it. Next to it was a very sophisticated water filter system with seven stages and a separately installed reverse osmosis system usually found only in hospitals. Bruno was surprised to see that the water filter system was actually built and installed by a local company. He noted the data and said, "I was unaware of that company here in our town. I am very interested in getting something like that for our house too. The water comes from the river, and sometimes the waterworks isn't doing well."

On the other side of the room were many manifolds installed. Each had a line of blue and red hoses connected. There were twelve water circuits in total, meaning every functional room or section of the house had its own heating circuit. Each circuit had its own water pump mounted next to the manifolds. Each pump was fed via a three-way valve, which was electrically controlled. Following the water lines for those pumps, Bodo found that those were connected to a large divider for hot water and the other to one for cold water. Currently, the three-way valve was pushed into the position for the hot water.

Walking over to the door with the sign "Electrical" on it, Bodo was keyed up on what he would encounter. They opened the door, switched on the lights, and froze in astonishment. The electrical installation was the best you could buy for the money. It was a commercial grate switchboard installed. It comprised a 400A main switch and a second breaker field where the different main feeder breakers were mounted. Each room had its own breaker panel, and all breakers were meticulously named. The communication panel, including the safety systems, had a separate feeder supported by a backup battery. Bodo looked at the data and quickly calculated that the battery would power the communication system for over a month.

With their thoughts still on the technology they had just seen, they walked silently upstairs, and after bringing the wine glasses into the living room, they sat down. Bodo said, "Bruno, are you sure that the party made the right decision to sell the house to me as we have agreed under the condition 'AS IS'?"

"Bodo, you need to stop doubting your worth to the cause and the survival of the party and even this nation. When you first presented your general structure of the OIR, and we sent you out to discuss your proposal, we all had your file in front of us. All CC members unanimously agreed that you are the only comrade we can trust to pull that assignment through. And consider what we know about just the two cases you looked into. With that, you have already recovered ten times the money for the cause than this house may have brought in an auction."

"Okay, Bruno, I understand and will shut up about it. But here is my condition for the car exchange. I want the new Lada in exchange for the Volvo with no more than 100 km on the odometer. I want a lifetime service agreement with the SSP workshop for both cars. Even if I replace those later with others, I may own two cars under lifetime service with the SPP car workshop. And that Lada has all the bells and whistles you can place in it. Suppose somebody brings Lada with the special license plates already mounted and the title in my front yard. In that case, he can drive off with the Volvo and that title for it."

Bruno laughed and said, "Bodo, consider it done. I will gladly accept the worst deal you have ever made in your life for the benefit of the party." Looking at his watch, he jumped out of the chair and said,

"Wow, I had no idea how late it was. We need to leave and get the kids in bed. They have school tomorrow."

"Thanks for coming over, Bruno and Annabel, especially for the great sandwiches. Sarina was trying to throw something together for dinner, and your package saved the evening."

While the women went upstairs to get the kids, Bruno thanked Bodo for the hospitality and the excellent gift for the party. The women came down with the kids, who weren't happy that they had to leave. Still, they all said good night, and the Tecker family walked to the small side gate. Nick was eager to hit the button to buzz the door open. With a last waving of their hands, they disappeared into the dark while the gate slowly closed behind them.

Bodo sighed with satisfaction, closed the house door, and locked it. Turning to Sarina and Nick, he said, "That was a surprising closing of a somewhat crazy day. What do you both think?"

"I like them very much," Nick stated firmly, not explaining in more detail what he meant. But Bodo and Sarina looked at each other and were sure he meant the kids. So Sarina asked, "Nick, what did you three do up there all the time?"

"Ah, Mom, nothing special. I pulled out some of my games, and we played three. All three were unknown to Lisa and Billy, and we had a lot of fun. Dad, can I attend the same school where Lisa and Billy go? That would be really nice to know at least somebody in a new school."

Bodo looked at Sarina and hesitatingly said, "I am on the road tomorrow and won't be back before later in the afternoon. So you need to wait until the next day if you want me to go to his new school with you. Or I could call Karl on my way out of town and ask him to pick you both up and drive you there. But I would rather be there with you and Nick."

Sarina answered immediately, "No, Bodo, we will wait. That one day isn't a big deal, and it is better when the teachers see you too."

Since they were all tired after a very exhausting day, they tucked Nick in and went to bed. On their first night in their new and fantastic bedroom, they were both too tired to kiss, and Bodo, holding Sarina in his arms, fell asleep within a few minutes. Sarina followed shortly.

CHAPTER 4

Meeting the First of Old Friends and a Shock in the Morning Turning into a Great Surprise

After Fritz had successfully lost his SSP tail, driving south on 96 toward Neustrelitz, he used the first opportunity to stop at a parking area, which was probably thought to be a rest stop but is nothing more than a piece of dirt road bending off of highway 96 and back to it about two hundred meters later. Since a small hedgerow separated it visually from highway 96, it provided some privacy, and based on the smell from the strip of trees on the outside, people seemed to use it for natural requirements.

Fritz drove to the edge where the dirt road was about to enter the highway again and stopped. It was a relatively warm day for mid-April, and since it had rained a lot during the last week, he could easily find a small chunk of clays that was wet enough to use to smear a part of the license plate so that it wasn't completely readable but could still look like it happened by chance. After he looked at it from different angles, he was satisfied, got in the car, and drove on.

He passed through Neustrelitz without any unusual situations or ostentatious movements of police or other civil cars. He stopped at a small fuel station on highway 96 about one hour after passing Neustrelitz to fuel the car. The station had just two gas pumps, one for gasoline and one for diesel, and with that, it was easy to ensure that there was no tail. It took him two more hours to reach the ring Autobahn around Berlin.

Then he had to drive another forty-five minutes to get to the exit for Reinhard's home because the rush hour had already started. Fritz often wondered how it was even possible to have such a thing as rush hour in a country lacking everything. But it happened, and it probably was because people get inventive when they want to improve their situation desperately enough. Circling around some construction holes in the side street, probably already a year or more open, because the parts to repair the underground pipe or line correctly weren't available, and the provisory repair had to hold for the time being the holes stayed open, he finally arrived at Reinhard's driveway at about 5:00 PM.

He parked his car at the side of the driveway, not knowing if Reinhard was home yet, and did not want to block the way into the garage. He left the car, walked to the house entrance door, hit the bell, and nothing happened. He decided to knock, waited a while, and knocked again a little bit heftier.

"Do you have to brake my door because an old man can run fast enough around the house to greet you, 'Oll fishhead?'" Reinhard yelled, coming around the house, laughing like crazy, joyfully taking Fritz in a man hug. "Man, great you made it this time. How many times did we talk about it and never get it done?" He was obviously delighted to have Fritz as his guest. "Come in, Lupo, I have to introduce you to the better half of mine, and we have to get a beer. You must be dried out like a fish on land, oll fishhead."

They walked into the house where a young woman, definitely some years less than Reinhard, was tending to a little boy who was visibly delighted to see Reinhard, raising both of his little arms to get out of the high chair. Reinhard introduced Fritz to his wife Katarina and his boy Bernd and took him on his arm.

"I knew you would screw up his dinner again," Katarina objurgated Reinhard with a defeated smile and placed the spoon into the uneaten bowl of baby food.

"Look at my boy Lupo. Look at him. Do you think he needs more to eat?" If I do not interrupt Katarina sometimes, she will feed him into a little ball." Reinhard made a real show from the presentation, and Fritz was immediately reminded of their time at the university. He had a particular way of making a fun show out of any situation he ran into.

Still laughing, Katarina took the boy from him and said, "Hello, Friz, welcome to our modest home. I wonder how he got through university, not being even a little serious about anything. He is always making fun of situations where I would actually be angry. Then I just can't." She walked out of the kitchen area to bring little Bernd to bed. Reinhard grabbed two cold beers from the refrigerator and said, "Come on, let's sit down and have a beer, and then we can get you settled in the empty bedroom upstairs. It is not much, but it has a toilet, and the bathroom will be shared with us."

They walked into a rather large living room, which was nicely furnished and sat down on comfortable chairs. "So tell me, Lupo, what happened to you that they threw you out of the navy base? Did you try to capture one of their super modern, highly sophisticated technology of tomorrow, high-speed rocket boats, and deliver it to the class enemy? Hahaha." He could barely stop laughing about his joke. Fritz laughed with him, and he knew that there were probably a lot of documents collected about him; therefore, his fun about the joke wasn't as great as Reinhard's. He suspected his children would have to pay a heavy price for his decision to choose God and Jesus Christ before men and the Communist Party.

They would be stigmatized, and their way through life would always be lined up with his decision to abandon a satanic organization with only the destruction of people in mind. They drank the beer while slowly Katarina was back in the kitchen area and preparing a dinner of several sandwiches with different cold cuts. She placed the large plate with the sandwiches on the table, and they sat around and began eating while Fritz wondered where she got all the different types of cold cuts. She must have read Fritz's thoughts because she looked at him and said, "Reinhard had just recently discovered that a former member of his navy crew, who had finished his education as a master butcher, lives in a small village to the north of here, in Schönerlinde. Now, once a week, we can go there and buy almost any type of meat and cuts we like and afford.

"And the best thing is that he joined my group last month. After a sudden rash of anger about the communist swine in his village who wanted to shut down his butcher shop because he was getting better by the week at organizing animals for his butchery, I asked him if that was all he was about to do," Rainer stated. And continuing, "He looked at me and said that if I still had my Kalashnikov and a battalion of like-minded people, that communist spook would be over in no time.

"We were in his walk-in freezer, and we were sure nobody could hear us. So that was my opportunity to get him to his cards. He told me that he was fed up with the communists and could bite himself in the ass for serving three years of his life, believing their lies for much too long." When Reinhard told him to join the protesters on Mondays to express his frustration with the bastards in power, his friend looked at him and asked if he had lost his mind. He said he wouldn't risk his existence for these losers. So Reinhard confronted him directly and said, "Let's assume for a moment, just as a hypothetical possibility, there is such a movement, an underground resistance that despises these Monday marchers and works on an actual insurrection. Would you be willing to join those? Would you swear a blood oath to keep silent until your death? Would you really take a rifle and start shooting when the time is ripe?"

"You know that you have risked your own organization by doing so?" Fritz asked.

But Reinhard smiled and said, "No, Lupo, he will never betray me. I saved his life when we were in the navy. And he was really about to die. We were out in the Baltic Sea, on patrol, and had terrible weather. From your experience, you know how these waves in the Baltic Sea are short and create sudden jumps. Every MSR had a smoker area at the stern, but at night it was forbidden. The class enemy could see the cigarette glue for miles on end and all that garbage. My friend was on engine room watch, and I had the radio watch. When I walked back to the smoking area, I thought I would hear a call for help, but I wasn't sure about the wind, the engine sound, and the waves. I went on, lit my cigarette, and then I heard it again, clearly now: 'HELP.'

"I am bending over and would have fallen overboard myself if it wasn't for the railing post on which the stupid shirt hung. There, my friend, was, hanging with one hand on the missing railing chain, which somehow—and I would say by the mercy of the Lord—was caught at the superstructure of the MSR stern. You surely remember from your time there were these self-closing clamps. That was where the chain had been caught. He was hanging in the water. The waves washed over him now and then, and he could not hold much longer. I grabbed the lifesaver, made sure the rope was fixed, and precisely circled it. I can't explain till today, right over his head. He could get his free arm through it and let go of the chain and was still strong enough to get the second arm through before the line went stiff. That ripped him out of the water, and I went and hit the man-overboard alarm. That rip strained both his shoulder ligaments. I got three days of arrest for smoking at night and leaving my post, he was hospitalized for four weeks. Then they had to discharge him with invalidity payment, which allowed him later to build his butcher business."

"Man, Sarge," Fritz said, using Reinhard's nickname first time because he was so drawn into the story. "That is something to live after. I have been on board fishing trawlers long enough to know that the changes are zero when a man is overboard. I witnessed one loss personally. But how did he get paid and not punished for violating an order and causing that much trouble?

"Turned out, the railing eyes, where the chain was snapped into, that is, the chain we must remove to roll the water bombs out, was rusted through. My friend said he was just up there to get some fresh air and leaned backward on the chain. That was the last thing he did before hitting the water. His parents had a good lawyer at hand, and the rest is history."

"Wow, what a story. How come you never talked about it?"

"Nothing to brag about. You know me well enough, Lupo. I try to turn everything terrible into a joke so I don't get a heart attack or drive crazy. And honestly, until I walked the first time into that butcher shop two years ago and saw him there, I had almost forgotten about it."

At this time, Katarina stood, took the plates and the big plate on which only one sandwich was left, and walked out into the kitchen, saying, "I know what you, guys, are doing from a bird's view, and that is all I should. Early on, our group decided to keep the details away from the wives for their own security. Have fun, Reinhard. I will drive over to Nia. The room for Fritz, or should I say, Lupo," she said with a smirk, "is ready."

While she was packing some sewing stuff together, Reinhard and Fritz walked out to his car and took all the stuff he needed out. Then he locked the car and went back into the house. Reinhard led him up the stairs and showed Fritz the small bedroom built out under the roof. Reinhard apologized for it, but Fritz was more than happy to stay there for the two nights they had planned.

Fritz took one communicator and a programmer and went down where Reinhard had just switched on the TV. When Fritz looked at his watch, he realized that it was already time for the NewsLie broadcast, as they called it.

He sat in the chair beside Reinhard, and the lying session began. But to their astonishment, it sounded so different that Reinhard immediately checked the channel believing it was the West Berling channel RIAS. But it was GDR, the *Current Camera*'s signature tune and the physiognomy of the speaker were unmistakable. The speaker began to read the news in the usual stoic manner of better propaganda lines from the paper. Yet this time, it was different, not so much by the tone but rather by the content.

"The secretary for information of the newly elected Central Committee has issued the following statement about the extraordinary circumstances concerning the incidence in the northern region of the nation:

1. The arrest of two leading members of the Socialist United Party, the First District secretary of Rostock and the First County secretary of Rügen is based on the discovery of enormous amounts of misappropriation, corruption, and blackmailing of comrades.

2. A third leading member, the First District secretary of Schwerin, resisted his arrest by the State Security Police and opened fire at the comrade using his legally owned handgun. In that shootout, he suffered deadly wounds and died on the way to the hospital.

3. Both incidents are still under investigation. The member of the Central Committee and the secretary for Information want to ensure all citizens and comrades support the new Office of Investigation and Recovery in its assignment to clean out the swamp that is hindering the improvement of the lives of all citizens."

Then he went on to report the successful panting of potatoes at another fighting agricultural collective, and Reinhard and Fritz did not pay more attention to the babbling.

"This new organization they have installed seems to be really aggressive. Have you heard anything about them here in Berlin?" Fritz asked Reinhard, breaking the silence they had sat in for a few minutes.

"No, all I know is that they created this new agency and that all idiots, uh, I am sorry, I meant law-abiding citizens, should let them know if they know something. Or something like that. But it seems that they mean it. I am not sure, but have you ever heard that one of the bigwigs has been arrested, let alone being shot dead?" Reinhard was evidently baffled by what he had just heard in the news broadcast. "Just that they report it this way is a 180-degree turnaround of their information policy. Normally they would just cover it up and would instruct and threaten everyone who was even in a fifty-mile circuit to the events to keep their mouth shut or else."

Fritz was still processing what he had just heard from a news broadcast that was known, even by the most devout comrades, as a notorious lying propaganda machine. He was sure there was much more behind it than they openly confessed. But on the other hand, maybe Reinhard was correct. It could be that the new Central Committee wanted to clean up the mess their predecessors had created or accepted for forty years.

"I am not sure, Reinhard. This sudden honesty doesn't smell right. Somehow it suggests that the comrades suddenly became honest and won't allow themselves to stay above the people. And that precisely is what I do not believe. These power-hungry bastards will never stay away from total control. That is their lifeblood. Without total control, there is now socialism/communism in a country. Total and absolute dominion is the basis for the power of the Communist Party. I was part of it, I learned it in detail, and I know they can't let go. If they do, they are out within a few weeks or months."

Reinhard looked at him doubtfully and said, "Aren't you a little too harsh on them? They have been in power for over a week, and you hear they arrested two of their leading comrades. That should have their critics and the demonstrators to stop and think and say to themselves, and maybe they are changing things."

That was the key-phrase Fritz needed to get his thoughts in oder and to finalize the processing of what was really going on. That was it! "Reinhard, you are right."

"See, that's what I meant. You are always too critical. Give them the benefit of the doubt and wait for what happens next," Reinhard said with conviction.

"No, Reinhard, you got me wrong. Let me explain. Here is what I think they did. They installed this new agency with the power to crush the remainder of the Old Guard based on their known corruption and misappropriation of finances for their benefit. By doing so, they show the flat-thinking average citizen that they are really cleaning up the mess, exactly as you thought they would yourself." Seeing the protesting expression on Reinhard's face, he held up his hand and said, "Hold on for a moment, Reinhard. Let me finish explaining how I see what they are doing, and then you can respond."

Nodding his head, Reinhard said, "Okay, go ahead. I will be silent."

Starting with a rhetorical question, Fritz continued to express his thoughts about what was behind all of that. "What would be the outcome of an extension of those actions? What would happen when the newly created OIR arrests another of the First District secretaries, maybe one of the more powerful ones, let's say, Dresden? I can tell you what will happen: the Monday demonstrations will crumble and disappear within less than a month. That is what they want. Getting rid of the remainder of the Old Guard is a convenient byproduct.

"I knew you have a different opinion on this, Fritz, but I also know that you have a much better inside look into their mindset, and with that, I can follow your analysis. But why not just remove all of the Old Guard from power and set their own cronies in?"

Fritz had the answer already on his lips, "They can't because too many comrades have become friends of those in power and have done their own little here and there under the big umbrella. It would create a hell of a shitstorm they cannot handle right now."

While Fritz had answered Reinhard's question, Katarina returned from her friend, checked on little Bernd, sat beside Reinhard on the couch, and asked, "So what do you think will happen next?"

"This new OIR agency appears to have enormous power, apparently equal to the members of the Central Committee of the SUP. The OIR has not been created solemnly to clean corruption but to crush any activities that could endanger the power of the leaders of the SUP. And I mean just their power. They wanted to have total control over the party, and the SSP was to corrupt itself. It would not be flexible and coherent enough to obey any order of that group. Understanding their mindset, I assume that the OIR is a small organization ordered to investigate all suspects and prepare a case file with all documents necessary to convict and execute the guilty and recover whatever they had misappropriated or is left.

Reinhard and Katarina were now sitting at the edge of the couch, listening more intently to Fritz's analysis. Fritz did not even recognize that they looked at him like children at a Christmas tree for the first time.

Collecting his thoughts about the subsequent statements, he continued, "We will see more of those leading comrades being arrested or, sometimes, more conveniently shot. We will also experience a collapse of many of the Monday demonstrations because the less critical people will say, see, the new leadership is honest. They clean up the mess, report about it as it happens, and next, we will have free elections. What will be left in opposition are those who have opposed the indisputable power of the Communist Party since the beginning of this misconstructs of a country. Two or three Monday demonstrations will hold out throughout the year until the CC finishes the internal cleanup. Then they will use any kind of force necessary to crush the remaining opposition, even the military if necessary."

"You believe the average soldier will shoot at the citizens, peacefully demonstrating for a change?" Reinhard asked, doubting Fritz's statement.

"No, Reinhard, not the average soldier. They will use their special troops, such as the paratroopers, who are highly indoctrinated and will follow orders. The reasoning will be these people can't be talked with. And the masses will accept it. The masses will accept it because they are tired of the demonstrations. The news broadcast will tell them it is no longer necessary because the party has understood what is wrong and is working on improving the situation. All that is needed is time and patience." Fritz disagreed. "This whole campaign against corruption in and outside of the party, the appearance that there are suddenly only decent and upright persons in power, has three major objectives."

Reinhard let out a deep sigh and asked, "And those are in your opinion?"

Fritz thought about formulating his opinion best and answered, "The first objective is, as stated before, to get rid of the remainder of the Old Guard. Including the potential of regaining some of the values they have misappropriated. And don't doubt for a second that we will hear sooner or later that there were even western currencies included."

"The second objective is to take the wind out of the sails of the Monday demonstration movement, so to speak."

When Fritz stopped there and seemed deep in his thoughts again, Katarina looked at him and said, "Fritz, you said three objectives. That was just two."

"I am unsure how to say it, but I will try. Over the last two years, a slowly but steadily growing underground resistance has formed nationwide. Small groups, such as yours, Reinhard, are spread out all over the nation. Most of them don't know each other because communication is highly complicated if you can use mail or phones. But they exist, and it is the actual resistance movement. The members of those groups are ready to take the country by force when the time comes and get rid of the communists, install a free provisional government and organize free and secret elections. And the people in power know that. Although the SSP failed over the two years to discover them, they know that we exist. And that is the third objective of the Office for Investigation and Recovery. To uncover and destroy the resistance, the only real danger to their power. That means that we all have to be very careful how we recruit or even accept new members and how we can check them thoroughly."

"I can see that now," Reinhard answered Fritz's lengthy explanation. "That means the most crucial point right now is to solve the communication issue and coordinate actions?"

"Yes and no. No, we are not at the point where we can coordinate any actions. We can't coordinate anything until we have a solid coordinated structure of leaders who communicate and then coordinate the different functions of the specific groups. Yes, we must fix the communication issue, and that's why I am here."

Fritz used this point in their discussion to take out the communicator and the programmer and demonstrate how those work. He then had Reinhard program send and receive several messages to ensure he had it all. At that point, Reinhard told him that they would meet with the comm officer of his group the next day and that it would be a thing to call it a day. They said good night to each other and went to bed.

CHAPTER 5

A Navy Special Forces Training Property Becomes the Regional Office North of the Office for Investigation and Recovery

Bodo woke up earlier than the wake-up call was set, was silent, and slowly walked into the bathroom. His bathroom. Still in awe that there was a separate bathroom for him and her. And rightly connected to it was the walk-in closet where Sarina had placed all of his clothes yesterday while he was at the new headquarters. With astonishment, he realized that he had only two suits of the quality he would need in the future. He was sure he could not run around all the time just with trousers and wearing a shirt and a sweater in summer, just a shirt. At the same time, his mind told him not to go further down that road because it would mean endless hours of dressing and undressing in men's shops under Sarina's watchful and critical eyes and Nick's joyful tittering. After choosing the trouser, shirt, and light sweater for the day, he returned to the bathroom. He had a long relaxing shower enjoying the comfortable large shower area. Closed and ready for the day, he walked out into the bedroom and saw that Sarina had left. He went downstairs and found her in the kitchen, preparing breakfast for them.

"Good morning, honey. Is Nick still asleep?"

"Good morning, love. Yes, he is, and I thought I would let him sleep in because, other than having a huge shopping tour today with Annabel is not programmed, which will wear him out for sure."

Bodo looked at his watch and said, "I'll go to the gate and check if the newspaper is already there. And then, I have a good hour for breakfast and get ready and prepare myself for the surprises of the day."

He opened the impressive, solid, wooden house door and, again, wondered how fast his life had changed and walked down the nice split-covered driveway to the gate. Unsurprisingly, the *New Germany* newspaper was already delivered to this new address under his name. He suspected that was the work of the incredibly efficient Karl. Walking back to the house, enjoying the fresh air and cool but not so cold temperature as some of the April days could be, especially in the week before Easter, he stopped halfway and looked around.

To his right, he had a relatively good view of the river on the back of his property and was pleased to register the many large and small trees covering the area, which would give a greatly appreciated shade on hot summer days. When he looked to his left, he saw that decoratively arranged conifers covering the three-car garage. With a smile, he remembered the big surprise for him and even more for Bruno about the treasures they had found there the night before.

When he entered the house, he smelled the coffee and bacon. Within a few minutes, Sarina and he sat at the smaller table in the kitchen area and enjoyed breakfast. Reading the *New Germany* newspaper by separating them between them as they did for years whenever the rear occasions happened that they had time to sit together.

"Bodo, do you think we can have breakfast together like that and maybe even lunch since you are working so close to home now?" Sarina asked, looking over the top of the newspaper at him.

"I think that could be arranged. I plan on starting my office time at 9 AM, which means Gunther doesn't need to be here not earlier than 8:50 AM. And I can come home for lunch when I am in the office at the headquarters. Now, there will be many days when that is impossible, especially in the near future. But whenever possible, we will know before you have to cook lunch," Bodo answered with a smile looking back at her while laying the newspaper down to get a draft of coffee.

At that moment, Sarina had turned to the front page of the part she had taken from the newspaper. She always started with the first part of the newspaper. In contrast, Bodo started with the reader's letters and commentaries in the second part of *New Germany*. He did so because he found the best information for his position as the secretary for Agit Prop in people's reactions to what happened in their daily lives.

"Bodo, you need to see this!" Sarina almost yelled over the table at Bodo.

"What is so exciting that you start to yell as if the moon fell down to earth?" Bodo asked back, and she pushed the front page to him, saying, "Read this!"

Bodo grabbed the paper and read the article, describing in detail the actions that led to the arrest of one First District and one First County secretaries and the death of another First District secretary and referred to the current news broadcast from the night before. After he was done reading, he lowered the newspaper. He said, primarily to himself, with an astounded expression, "They really mean it."

Sarina looked at him. "Did you doubt that they really mean to change all the policies of the Old Guard? Did you not trust them 100 percent? And if so, why did you take the job?"

Bodo looked back at Sarina and said, "Let me think. How I would answer that question without sounding insane? Let me say it this way. I witnessed after we had a long meeting with all members of the Central Committee explaining and discussing the content of the assignment to this new organization and the delivery of an extended written structure and strategy paper that one of the members caved and refused to support the consequences of the organization's discoveries. He was removed from the position by a majority vote, and you remember that they said he resigned for health reasons in the news, which was a lie. I thought they would lie about the arrest of the FDS also. I wonder what is the difference?"

"I think I know," Sarina said without looking up from her reading. "This guy was one of them, meaning the new leadership. The others, the FDS and the FCS, are from the former leadership pool. If your work shall have any impact on the situation of the party and, to a larger extent, the country, they all need to be replaced."

"Sarina, I would be blown away if I did not know how smart you are. And you are entirely correct. That is why I asked Bruno to bring that up to the agenda, and we discussed that yesterday in the surprisingly called meeting. And since I know you are not talking about things, I tell you the SSP has several of those already under surveillance. We will start investigating them over the coming weeks, and I guarantee we will leave no stone unturned in their lives. And many others will be on my list. I will take no rest until the traitors are eliminated, and corruption is erased."

"You have a lot of work in front of you, Bodo," Sarina uttered with a deep sigh.

Just at that moment, the ring buzzed, and a voice from the intercom said, "Good morning, comrade Zipper. I am coming in."

"Okay, my love, I am out and won't be back before tonight, maybe even tomorrow. I have all I need to be packed, and I will call occasionally and give you an update."

She kissed him, and he grabbed his duffel bag and walked out to the car, dropping it into the trunk. He returned to his office and grabbed his briefcase with the OmniBook and packet memo. He turned at the car, waving Sarina goodbye and told Gunther to stop at headquarters before he got them to the place of the new Regional Office North or RON for short.

At the headquarters, he immediately registered that some shipments must have arrived. Several large boxes with furniture parts stood around the office building entrance. Several workers were busy unpacking and carrying them into the different offices. Bodo entered the building, squeezing by a worker carrying a cabinet piece that needed to be in a different room. When he reached his office, he was glad to see Giesela in full commanding mode, directing the workers where to place which part.

"Good morning, Giesela. Good to see you heavy at work," Bodo greeted his senior secretary with a smile.

"Good morning, comrade Zipper. The furniture came in yesterday late in the afternoon, and since nobody was here, they left all the parts out in the open in front of the property. I can't even imagine what would have happened if it had rained overnight, or worse, someone had taken them. I called Karin already and talked to her because I did not know who else, and I did not want to bother you with this chicken feed."

"Thanks a lot for taking action, Gisela. But I want you to write this following into your brain with a hot iron. You can call me for any chicken feed at any given time. And I really mean that. You might think that is nothing I need to be bothered with, but I might see it from a different perspective. You work for an organization for which even the slightest information might lead to an enormous discovery."

"I am sorry, comrade Zipper. I really thought I didn't need to bother you with the furniture stuff," Giesela was visibly concerned that she had made a mistake and wasn't sure about the consequences. So Bodo immediately took her by the shoulder, led her to a chair, and slightly encouraged her to sit down.

"Giesela, I understand entirely that you are trying to shield me from things you consider unimportant. And I know that is how you have been trained and how you feel about shielding your boss from negligible issues. And that's completely okay with me, as long as it doesn't affect the office's work. By office, I mean the organization as a whole. Let me give you an example. The furniture. If the furniture had been damaged by rain or stolen because someone thought it was okay to leave them outside of the property, the work of our office would have been disrupted and the start of operation postponed. If, on the other hand, the car of one of our future officers has a flat tire, that would interrupt his ability to travel. Still, it would not affect the whole office operation, right?"

Her posture changed. She pulled her shoulders back, looked Bodo in the eye, and said, "Comrade Zipper, for a moment, I feared you would send me back to comrade Bruno's office. I understand now what you mean by our different work and the circumstances connected. And I will learn to be more attentive to the difference between what you need to know and what not."

"Excellent, Gisela. That's the mindset I need. Let's get to your office because I see it is already completed, and let's go over some stuff." With that, they walked to her office, and Bodo closed the door behind them and started his instructions.

"I need you to start handling my schedule of standard daily work. Official work starts for all office work at 8:00 AM. I will be here shortly before 9:00 AM and want to get a day overview briefing from you. Calculate about fifteen minutes maximal. At 10:00 AM, we will have an officer meeting in the conference room, mandatory for all on the property. That meeting should take no more than thirty minutes and is a kind of recount of the day before and what is on the agenda for the current day. This is probably not an immediate fix point but will become one over time. And your main task is to transfer all the files from paper to the computer. I see that your main desktop is already set up, which is excellent. Karl has organized somebody from the justice department to come out and install a software package they use to sort legal cases in a specific way. They will train you and the other secretary on how to use it."

"What other secretary, comrade Zipper? I am excited that I am not alone with all that seems to come up."

"Yeah, sorry, Giesela. I forgot to tell you that we will have a second secretary, and I do use the number second on purpose in a few days. Her name is Maria Hafler, and she worked at the office in Rostock as a general secretary for whatever came up. She should start before the week is over. Karl is looking for an apartment close to yours, and she is approximately as young as you."

"Wow, I am looking forward to meeting her." Gisela was visibly excited to hear about getting support.

"We should also get equipment for every officer containing a small computer called OmniBook. Here is mine, and a pocket memo called dictaphone for each one. You should get a desk version of the dictaphone so you can type the spoke report directly into the computer and attach the document to the case it belongs to. Like this one, Bodo showed her what the devices looked like.

The next is preparing the office for the chief operation officer, Peter Wille. Comrade Wille has my 100 percent trust in anything. He will organize the day-to-day operation of the whole organization and has his office on the other side of mine. "With that, I have you both next to my office, and we can connect quickly when needed. He might also arrive before the end of this week. You have my mobile number programmed and can call when necessary. I think that's all for now. I will be back sometime tomorrow afternoon."

Bode grabbed his briefcase and walked out of her office, throwing a brief look into his office where just a few additional pieces of furniture were necessary to be set up since the forest company had left the boss room furniture almost entirely behind as they did with the conference room. Gunther was in the car, and when Bodo entered, he started the engine. Looking in the internal back mirror, he asked, "RON, comrade Zipper?"

"Yes, and see if we can make good of some of the time we used her at the office."

Gunther smiled and said, "My pleasure, comrade Zipper." And with that, they were on the road. Bodo waited until they reached the Autobahn before he pulled down the table from the back of the front seat, took out his OmniBook, and was about to start making some notes for the next steps for the week when the phone rang. He picked up and had the cheerful voice of Karl in his ear. "Good morning, Bodo. How are you today?"

"I am actually feeling very well, and I reckon you can say the same, considering your cheerful voice," Bodo answered. "What is it that makes you so excited in the morning of a day in April?"

"What? Do you mean I must be sad and unhappy only because it is April?" Karl laughed and continued, "I have some excellent news for you, and you may need something to write and tell Gunther to slow down a bit."

"Gunther is the best driver I have ever experienced, besides me, of course," Bodo answered with a smirk in the direction of the mirror where he could see Gunther's questioning expression. "Okay, what do you have for me, Karl?"

"I have the movers organized for your COO and the secretary from Rostock for tomorrow. They will be at their doors no later than 8:00 AM. Please let them know. Now, hold on. The rocket starts. I have three newly finished single homes with garages attached, which were built for the officers of the navy training camp and are now available. We have them blocked until the end of the week. The homes are at Liebenthaler Weg 10A, 10B, 10C. I have five apartments in an apartment block at Käthe-Kollwitz Strasse 21 for your officers. Those have been empty for a few weeks and renovated by the navy to return them to the city. Still, I convinced the apartment manager to let us have them since the whole block has become available for the city. You must get your RON manager to Wittstock tomorrow morning to choose the home and sign the contract with the navy guy. Otherwise, those go to the city too."

"You are one great worker, Karl. Can you move completely over to OIR and work for me?" Bodo said and laughed because he knew that the answer would be a clear no. And it came like a bullet; without hesitation, Karl answered, "No way, Bodo. As much as I feel responsible for you being in that very challenging position you are in now, I would not destroy my chance of being in the future position to replace comrade Bruno. Have a great day, Bodo. See you soon." And with these words, he hung up.

He called Giesela's office number and wondered again how easy he had her within seconds on the phone. "Giesela, I need you to find a good hotel in Wittstock/Dosse and reserve a room for a couple for two nights, arriving today. Then call comrade Reiner Worser. His number should be already programmed in the phone system. Then get a hold of the secretary from Rostock and let her know that the mover truck will be at her place at 8:00 AM tomorrow. Karl found a nice two-room apartment in the same block where you are on the second floor."

"That is awesome, comrade Zipper. Do you know the exact number?"

"Unfortunately, I did not ask Karl for it."

"Oh, no problem, I will call him, and even if I have to pull his teeth, I will get it out of him. I can do that, correct? It is not affecting the organization." When she had hung up after Bodo confirmed, shaking his head and smiling, he dialed the number for Reiner. Finally, he got him on the phone after several trials. "Reiner, I need you to get packed up for a two-day trip with your wife to Wittstock. Giesela will call you in a few minutes. She getting your reservations. There are three homes available to choose from for you, and you need to get it done soon. The responsible guy is meeting with you tomorrow morning at ten at Liebenthaler Weg 10. I will see if I can stay and meet you there tomorrow. I am on my way to the new office place, which I will show you after you choose the house."

"Is Sarina with you?" Reinhard asked.

"No. She is still busy getting us settled in at the new house, and there is just too much she wants to do. All clear? I'll see you tomorrow." And instead of hanging up, Bodo told him to connect him to Peter. After a few seconds, the voice of Peter came up, and Bodo said, "Hello, old fellow, how are you today? Are you busy packing?"

"Bodo, I was just thinking of you. I somehow had the feeling that things may be rolling faster than we thought at first."

"That's correct. I have the mover at your house tomorrow morning at 8:00 AM. Be ready to throw in your belongings, and you are on the road. We have a nice apartment about fifteen minutes by bus from the office."

"Okay, Bodo, I will be ready. Oh, before I forget. Whoever decided about the replacement for the FCS is a genius. This guy is great, at least from our perspective. Straight to the point and consequent on implementing the rules of the communist revolution."

"Great to hear that, Peter. I was hoping the CC is going in that direction and you confirm once more that they mean business. I'll see you soon in the office." Bodo hung up, and when he focused on the road they were driving on, he asked Gunther how far they were.

Gunther answered, "We are about to exit the Autobahn at exit 21 in a few minutes, comrade Zipper."

"Thanks, Gunther."

Bodo considered taking the OmniBook out and starting notes for future meetings. Still, he considered it better to focus on the environment to better understand the new RON area. Shortly after, they left the Autobahn, and turning west, they drove down the L18 for about two kilometers. There, on the right-hand side, a small connection road to L14, and they turned on it. After another two kilometers, they turned right into a more or less gravel-covered forest track. After another two and a half kilometers, a very high fence, crowned with barbed wires and barbed wire, rolled on the bottom from the densely wooded forest to the left, touched the forest track, and ran along it.

A few hundred feet later, a relatively solid gate, wide open, showed the entry to the property. Gunther turned onto the property and drove along a reasonably well-maintained gravel road for a couple hundred feet. Two buildings appeared next to the lake, which spread out behind them to both sides. Bodo directed Gunther to turn to the left side, where several marked parking spots on the concrete pad were visible in front of the smaller building. Getting out of the car, Bodo was approached by a man who was obviously surprised to see a new car on the property and asked Bodo, "Who are you, if I may ask?"

"I don't know if you have the need to know who I am, but to settle the question of authority once and for all. I am Commander Zipper, and I am the head of the Office of Investigation and Recovery. This property is under my jurisdiction, and I wonder why the gate to a secret property is wide open and not even secured?"

The man, turning out to be one of the technicians to do the final touches on the upgraded communications and security systems, was appealed. With a significant scare in his voice, he answered, "I am sorry, comrade Commander. I had no idea that you were arriving today. But we are in the final touches to get everything tested, and we will be out of here within two to three hours."

"Comrade, that is not my concern. My concern is that a secured facility has a secure fence and gate, and the gate is gaping wide open with no guard at it. Where is the SSSP security guard?"

"Uh, they left about an hour ago to get some lunch. They were under the command of a sergeant if I am not mistaken. They said nothing could happen since we were here, and nobody knew what was happening at this place."

"Okay, comrade, go back to get your work done, and let me know when we can execute a test of all of the security and communications systems."

Bodo turned back to the car and looked at Gunther, who was grinning, and Bodo had to contain himself not to explode into his grinning face. "What do you think you need to be happy about, Gunther?" Bodo asked with a slightly threatening tune in his voice.

Gunther turned immediately severe and said, "I am sorry, comrade Zipper, but did you not notice that this guy almost peed his pants?"

"There was nothing funny about it, and you should know better. This property is still not secured, and we are here in the open anyone from the neighboring village or even an undercover agent from the enemy can walk in and look around. As a graduate of the SSP officer academy, I expected a bit more seriousness from you in situations like this. I may have to talk to comrade Pieker if he has someone more inclined to have situational awareness." Bodo was angry about the apparent incompetence of the danger for the new organization. Yet he immediately realized that it was partly his own fault.

He entered the car, grabbed the phone, and called the direct line for Jürgen Pieker. When he heard his voice, "Hello, comrade Pieker, whom am I speaking with?" Bodo was already calmed down and answered the phone with his usually calm and collected voice, "Hello, Jürgen. I need you to take immediate action to secure the property at Black Lake in Herzsprung. You know the facility we took over from the navy last week. Sorry for being so formal, but I don't like this unsecured property and the gate wide open. And by the way, how are you today?"

"Hello, Bodo, no reason to apologize if there is a break of protocol. I need to know firsthand. And yes, until your call, I was fine, I actually thought, finally a morning without any complaints about our failing force of the 'Shield and Sword' of the party," he said ironically. "As far as I know, there should be a team of eight SSP officers under the command of a sergeant guarding the property. Aren't they there?"

"The main technician told me that there was a group of armed SSP officers when they arrived, and they were there until an hour ago or so, and then they went to get lunch."

"They did what?" Jürgen answered with an angry, surprised voice. "Can't believe that we still have officers in the field acting like that. I need to make some phone calls, Bodo. I will get back to you in a few minutes."

"Thanks, Jürgen, appreciated," Jürgen responded. "Not for that. Will be back soon."

Bodo exited the car and called, "Gunther, I want you to go up to the gate, close it, lock it, and not let anyone enter without my personal confirmation. Understood?"

"Yes, yes, comrade Zipper," came his prompt answer, still scared that he might return to the barracks instead of having a dream job driving the most powerful man in the nation he knew. Nobody would get through it without his boss' confirmation. He would rather die than lose his job. He turned on his heels, ran to the gate, closed it, locked it using the sophisticated locking system, and pocketed the controller.

CHAPTER 6

The Regional Office North: Breach of Security and a Grievous Degradation

Meanwhile, Bodo checked with the senior technician the state of the work and was pleased to get already shown the security camera system, which was reporting several life camera images from around the property back to the control room. He could see the four directions along the fence lines, and two cameras showed the gate from both sides. He smiled at the intention of Gunther to iron out his mistake and now, taking the security at the gate to an entirely new level.

"We might have all the high voltage safety systems on the lake fences ready for testing in about one hour. The communication systems should be done a little later," the senior technician explained to Bodo. He thanked him for the demonstration and left the office building to look at the other two-story building. It had standard living room windows on the first and second floor on half of the building and more like workshop windows on the rest. When he entered the building through the entrance door, there was a short hallway with stairs going up to the second floor and a door to both sides. He opened the right door and looked into a relatively spacious workshop and garage area with several excellent, solid-looking workbenches. Closing that door, he went to the left side door. When he entered the room, he discovered a fairly large, comfortable, well-equipped mixed dining and living room with space for eight to ten people. Walking further into the room, he discovered to the right side a kitchen built underneath the stairs going upstairs. It was also wholly equipped and could start cooking meals at any moment.

Remembering that Jürgen would call him back any moment, he went back to the car and unlocked and took out the brick as he had begun to call the mobile phone. While walking back to the living quarters, the phone rang. When he picked up, the voice of Jürgen was definitely more joyous than when he had told him about the security breach before, "Bodo, I have a squad on the move from Pritzwalk, which should be there within the next ten minutes. According to his file, the commanding sergeant is very experienced and someone who would have made it into your unit if he had not been married and had four children. He will take care of the lost sheep also and take them under his command. With that, you have eighteen officers for the property, which is appropriate to secure it considering the large lake on its west side."

"Many thanks, Jürgen, that takes a lot of anxiety off my mind. This commanding sergeant who went to lunch with his troops without a care in the world for the security of this property needs to get corrected, though!"

"Yes, he will be degraded to the rank of a private right in front of his squad and escorted back to his barracks. The sergeant who relieves him has the order with him. You, as the highest-ranking officer, have to execute that order. Are you ready to do so?"

"You can bet your life on it," Bodo answered, his voice loaded with certainty. He ended the phone call and returned to examine the building that seemed to have been the soldier's quarters and would certainly be used the same way for his office. This time, Bodo went upstairs and discovered a total of ten bedrooms with two beds each and a huge bathroom area entirely sufficient for ten soldiers' hygiene requirements. On his way down and walking out into the yard, he decided not to stay overnight at the property to give the coming soldiers a little privacy after what they would endure when they arrived. He took the handset from the brick and called Giesela. "Giesela, can you do me a favor and make a reservation for me too at the same hotel you reserved the room for comrade Worser? I need to stay there."

"Sure, comrade Zipper, I will do it now and call back with the confirmation." A few minutes later, Giesela called back and confirmed the reservation at Röbler Tor Hotel. He had just finished the call with Giesela when he heard Gunther yelling for him and soon after saw him running toward him, coming around the trees that covered the view at the gate from where he stood between the two buildings.

"What is the matter that you are so agitated, Gunther?"

"Comrade Zipper, there are a lot of uniformed SSP officers at the gate, and some pointing their rifles at the other, and they are yelling, and I thought you better come to the gate before something happens," Gunther spluttered, still short-breathed from running and yelling at the same time.

"Okay, okay, calm down, Gunther. We will get it solved before they kill each other."

Together Gunther and Bodo walked back to the gate, and Bodo noticed that Gunther had his hand on the spot where he carried his concealed gun. When they reached the gate, the situation was somewhat under control. Yet it still looked like two opposing parties would get at each other's throats at any given moment.

Bodo introduced himself and asked who was in charge of the undisciplined, weapons-toting horde of a disgrace in uniform. Both sergeants answered simultaneously that they were. Bodo orders them to take down the rifles and keep them safe. When that was done, he told Gunther to unlock the gate. Bodo asked who Sergeant Weber was. Although it was evident who of the two Sergeants it was, he needed to keep the command structure clear for all officers. He then ordered Sergeant Weber to command and muster the troops at the yard in front of the living quarters. Sergeant Weber did so, and although hesitantly following the order, the officers, including Sergeant Kapers, fell in and marched down the driveway toward the yard.

While Bodo, with Gunther on his heels, walked behind the column of twenty officers, he thought about the task at hand. Considering his age, he had to degrade a sergeant who was probably ten years with the SSP and might have served three years with the military. And all that because the people, even in such an essential service as the SSP, have become corrupted in their ability to understand the danger of the current situation in the country. But he realized that there needed to be made an example. He was determined to do whatever was necessary to build a strong, determined, and secure the Office of Investigation and Recovery for the sake of the communist ideals he admired so much.

The troops reached the yard, mustered in front of the living quarters, and Sergeant Weber commanded, "Attention! Right dress! Eyes ahead!" Sergeant Weber made an about-turn and saluted Bodo, stating, "Commander Zipper, twenty men, including two NCOs, mustered to receive your orders!"

Bodo did not return the salute since he did not wear a uniform and answered, "Thank you, sergeant, let them stay at ease!"

"Comrades, at first, I have to execute an unfortunate order, which came direct from your commanding comrade General Pieker. Sergeant Weber, please hand the written order to me." Bodo took the folded page from the sergeant's hand, broke the seal, and opened it.

"Sergeant Kapers, step up!" The sergeant stepped forward and made an about-turn, as military training had drilled into him for several years.

"Sergeant Kapers, on the order of the commanding general of the State Security Police, under whose jurisdiction you are, do I herewith degrade you to the rank of a private of the SSP and command that all of your medals and all awards are revoked! You will be guarded back to the barracks where you are stationed and serve a ten-day arrest punishment."

Statements of Ground for this decision. Sergeant Kapers left, on his own decision, without authorization by higher ranking officers and without informing his commanding officer at the barracks about his intentions, a critical property classified as critical for the defense system of the GDR, with all subordinated officers. In doing so, the property he was ordered to secure and protect for several hours was unprotected, and the object's security was severely breached. Such conduct is absolutely incongruous with the sense of duty of a commanding officer of the state security police. The pronounced punishment is, therefore, "justified and irrevocable on the order of the commanding General of the SSP."

While Bodo finished reading the order, he walked over to Sergeant Kapers. He removed his insignia together with some reward badges. It was clearly visible that Sergeant Kapers was emotionally stressed by that action. With a low voice so that only Kapers could hear it, Bodo said, "I am sorry, but you should not have become complacent."

Bodo returned to where he stood and ordered, "Sergeant Weber, take command, secure the property, and schedule security service. Order three of your officers to guard Private Kapers back to the barracks. Have them dismissed."

Talking to Weber directly, he said, "When you are done with the organization of the security, please see me in the office." And while turning and walking already toward the office building, he said over his shoulder, "Make sure you are not sending Kapers's friends as guards. I don't need dead officers and a refugee with loaded rifles on top of this dilemma."

"Understood, comrade Commander."

About twenty minutes later, Weber entered the office building, and Bodo heard him asking one of the technicians where he could find him since the door to the office he used was open. It was the only office completely furnished with high-quality furniture, so Bodo thought it was probably the office of the commanding officer of the navy and would become the office for Reiner. He called out to the sergeant, "I'm back here. Come in." When Weber walked through the door, he added, "Close the door please and sit down."

"Sergeant Weber, how long are you with the SSP? Do you know Kapers, and what is your background at all? I need to know a little about you, and then I will explain why the punishment for Kapers is the minimum he could receive."

Weber swallowed hard, and after a moment of collecting his thoughts, he answered, "I have been with the service for twelve years now, and Kapers started about ten years ago. That is how long I had known him, right when he left the academy and was assigned to our battalion in Pritzwalk. And honestly, I never understood why he joined the SSP."

"Why so?" Bodo responded, now getting curious.

"He always had a, how shall I say, he had some kind of inattentiveness no matter what Kapers was ordered to do, not taking anything seriously. Once I pointed it out to him, he said I should shut up because it was none of my business. I told him I would talk to his CO, and he laughed at me and said 'Go ahead.' When I did, his CO looked at me and said that he appreciated my concerns, but I should stay on my side of the fence."

"Is the CO still there?" Bodo asked.

"Sure, he is now the CO of the whole battalion. That is why I do not have the three officers sent away yet with Kapers because I wanted to make sure you want to send him back." Bodo became even more attentive. "Why is that such a bad thing to send him back to the barracks?"

"Kapers and the now battalion CO are close. They are very close friends, far above traditional association. I don't believe the battalion commander will have Kapers arrested for a minute, even though he received the order from General Pieker by Teletext and handed it to my CO with the order to secure the property and execute the order."

"Thank you a lot, Sergeant Weber, for your openness. I will later have a statement to the troops. I want you to find a way to hold Kapers in solitary confinement. Make sure that he is treated correctly."

"Yes, comrade Commander."

When Weber was out of the office and had the door closed behind him, Bodo took the handset from the "Brick" and called Jürgen's number. "Hello Jürgen, I am sorry to interrupt your work-loaded day again, but I just got informed about some interesting details which I am not sure are known outside of the SSP station in Pritzwalk."

"Bodo, stop apologizing for calling me. I am sure you will never call me for unimportant reasons. What is it that you think that I don't know about the garrison in Pritzwalk? And by the way, until this morning, I did not know that we had a whole battalion of SSP troops stationed in Pritzwalk."

"You need to get someone you really trust to look into the CO of that battalion. The sergeant sent to bring your order for the degradation of the guy who thought lunch was more important than security for a critical property is best friend with the battalion CO. So I decided, based on that information, to keep that guy, whose name is Kapers, under my jurisdiction for now."

"Oh, my Bodo, believe more and more you have been chosen because your pure presence drives the rats out of their holes. But thank you so much, and keep this guy there until you hear from me. I will immediately get my internal reevaluation team to work and check that battalion. Thanks for letting me know, Bodo." With that, he hung up.

Bodo grabbed the brick-mobile and walked out of the office, running directly into the senior technician. "Comrade Zipper, can I show you the final status of the systems? I have technicians at all the points to demonstrate how it works."

Bodo, sighing because it wasn't really his primary interest to get all the gimmicks, but he understood the technicians' eagerness to show their accomplishments, said, "Sure, let's see what you got." They walked into the central security office, and the technician demonstrated the communication system by calling different rooms in the office, the outside speakers, and the living quarters for the troops. He then went to the security system, pointing out the monitors and explaining which property sector was covered. By hitting certain buttons on a large operator's console, he activated a communication line with the technician at that specific camera spot, with his microphone connected to the camera's pole.

"Very impressive, comrade. Very impressive. I am happy that at least someone understands the importance of the work here. I have to tell you before you can leave, you must train Sergeant Weber and his troops in operating the systems. I will send him over in a few minutes."

Bodo walked out of the security office and to the living quarters, where he found three officers reading and Sergeant Weber writing something that looked like a report. Seeing him entering the building, one officer called out, "Attention!"

Bodo immediately responded with, "As you are!" so they relaxed and returned to what they were doing. He walked over to Weber and told him he needed to get himself comfortable with the security and comm systems.

Bodo told him Kapers would remain under his watch and in solitary confinement as ordered. If there was helpful work for him, cleaning and things like that, he should let him get to work.

"I am leaving now, and I will be back tomorrow before lunch with the new chief commanding officer for this property to whom he would report in the future. We will have another muster when I come, and I will address the troops then."

"Yes, comrade Commander, I will take care of everything."

Bodo walked out of the building and looked for Gunther until he finally saw him sitting at the lake on a small steg for boots. He walked down to the steg, and Gunther must have heard his steps and jumped to his feed turning to him simultaneously, almost losing his balance and falling into the lake.

"Whoa, Gunther, it's not the time to bathe now," Bodo called out to him. Gunther got his balance and answered with a questioning, insecure voice, "Are you sending me back to the SSP reserves, comrade Zipper? I really didn't mean to be unreliable. I find it strange that an experienced sergeant prefers lunch over responsibility."

"No, Gunther, I will not send you back, at least not yet. It is one of my essential principles that everyone has a second chance. The only exception is security. Broken security can lead to death. There is no second chance when you are dead. I am out for the day. I want you to stay here, be my eyes and ears, and be comfortable with the security and comm systems. We will have something similar at headquarters soon. I will be with the new property commander tomorrow at lunchtime. And then we may drive back home."

Yes, comrade Zipper, and thank you for the second chance. I will make sure I don't need a third one."

Bodo, now smiling, answered, "You better do. There is no third one." With that, Bodo turned around, walked to the car, ensured the mobile was secure in its place, and started the engine. At the moment, he was about to drive off, he remembered that Gunther may have his luggage in the trunk. Bodo got out, and Gunther was already at the back of the car. He opened the trunk, removed his duffle bag, and closed the lid. Bodo went back in the car and slowly drove toward the closed gate. The guard saw him coming and hit the button to open the gate. Bodo drove out and turned left.

After about eight hundred feet, he turned right onto another well-maintained gravel road. A little more than a quarter mile away, he entered the L14, turning right. After a short drive of about fifteen minutes, he entered the parking lot of the hotel Röper Thor and parked his car. Taking out his luggage and mobile, as well as his briefcase, he felt himself loaded like a tourist, walked into the hotel, and found himself in a very nicely arranged reception hall.

"Hello, my name is Bodo Zipper, and I should have a room reservation."

"Uh, hmm, yes, I have you here for a single room for one night. Is that correct, Mr. Zipper?"

"Yes, that's correct. And I am awaiting friends of mine arriving soon, Mr. Worser and his wife. Please let him know I am here and what room I am in."

"Surely, Mr. Zipper, I can do that," the receptionist said while filling out the paperwork, collecting his personal ID document, and handing him the key to the room. Bodo grabbed the key, loaded himself up again with all his stuff, and since the room was on the first floor with no elevator, he walked up the stairs. On the first floor, he oriented himself in what direction his room was. When he arrived, he used the somewhat archaic key attached to a large piece of wood to open the door. The room wasn't large but had a practicable desk with a chair, and the room itself and the bathroom were clean and well-tempered. Bodo placed his luggage on the shelf next to the door and his mobile and briefcase on the desk and decided to shower and refresh. When he was done, feeling like new, freshly clothed, he hit the button for his home phone and, within a few seconds, heard Sarina's voice. "Hello?"

"Hello, my love, it is me. Did you pick up the phone in my office?"

"Hello, Bodo. Great to hear your voice. No, I am in the kitchen area with Annabel. We just returned from shopping, and I have to tell you, unbelievable those shops they have here. I have bought so much stuff that I will be busy decorating the house for the next three weeks like I imagine it should be. And these fabrics for the curtains and—"

"Sarina, I can't imagine how happy you are, but I don't have much time. I just wanted to let you know I am not coming home tonight. I am staying overnight in Wittstocka and meeting with Reiner and Corinna. They are on their way because they have to select a house for them to move in. I will be back tomorrow afternoon, and you can show all you have."

"I am sorry, Bodo. I know you are busy. Call me tomorrow when you are on your way back. I am just sooo excited about what I can do.

Love you." And she hangs up. *Great*, Bodo thought that went better than I thought. *At least she is happy with all the stuff she got and will be busy for weeks to come.*

He took the OmniBook out of the case and started it up. Choosing the text-writing software, he created some letterheads for memos and orders he would need in the future and began to line out some of the bullet points for the next three to four months the organization needed to get solved to get it to a perfectly oiled machinery. He was about to close up and leaned back in the chair to marvel at the amazing technology of that little computer OmniBook, considering briefly why their own engineers weren't able to develop something like that, yet rebuking himself for such defeatist thought, knowing very well that they could, if the evil capitalists would not cut them off of the international electronic markets. A sudden knock on the door yanked him out of his thoughts. He got up and opened the door where Reiner and Corinna stood in the hallway smiling, simultaneously yelling a joyful hello at him.

"We just arrived and get told that this is your room. After being refreshed, we thought we would rip you out of your dreams. We are just three rooms down the hallway from you," Reiner explained.

"Have you, guys, eaten something on the road?" Bodo asked, recognizing that he had not eaten anything since breakfast. He was reminded of that fact by the grumbling sound of his stomach.

They looked at him as if he was not fully awake, and Corinna said, "What do you think we had to do to get here in time? Getting the kids to the in-laws and packing stuff, and you know, there was no way we could stop somewhere on those back country roads on the shortest way over here to have lunch."

"Oh, sure, sorry, did not think clearly. Let's see what we can find because I have not eaten either." Bodo returned to the room, grabbed his jacket and the room key, and locked the door behind him. They walked downstairs to the receptionist, "Can you refer an excellent restaurant for us to get a decent dinner?" Bodo asked.

"There are two really excellent restaurants in town," she answered. "One is brand-new. It just opened a week ago and is very highly frequented. But the chef there is a cousin of mine. Let me call him and see if I can get a reservation for you, Mr. Zipper." She said the handset was already in her hand, dialing a number. After a few rings, the phone was answered, and she made her request to the person on the other end. Looking up at Bodo, she asked, "Four people?" and he shook his head.

After a few more words and a friendly *tschhüß*, she hung up and said, "You are all set. There is usually enough parking at the *markt* in front of the *rathaus*, and the restaurant markstübchen is right there at the corner, across the street from the markt. When you leave the parking, turn left onto Gröper Wall and turn right when you hit the Königstraße."

Bodo drove them there within a few minutes with that precise description and the short distance. They entered the restaurant and were asked friendly by a waitress if they had a reservation. Bodo confirmed his name. They were led to a table in the back of the room in a corner where they had some kind of privacy. After they sat down, Bodo said that as a first rule for tonight, there were no work discussions. He explained that he was unsure it was safe to talk about their work publicly because the old rule that walls have ears was not a myth. And secondly, he would like to enjoy dinner with friends because he had not the slightest idea when that could be repeated.

The waitress came with the menu, and when she saw the prices on the menu, Corinna's eyes went wide, and she bent forward over the table and said, "Bodo, have you seen what that costs to eat here?"

Bodo smiled and said, "Sure, if you would rather eat a Bockwurst outside on the market, I won't stop you. But joking aside, you are my guests, and we can easily afford that with my budget for the OIR. Choose wisely because the cost doesn't count today. Whatever you think you would like, order it."

They had a great dinner and were most assuredly satisfied when they returned to the hotel.

He told them to be at the breakfast area at 9:00 AM and wished them a good night. Back in his room, he checked if anyone had called the mobile. That wasn't the case, so he made himself bed ready and was asleep immediately.

CHAPTER 7

Building a Nationwide Resistance Network Sometimes Comes with Strange Surprises

The day after Fritz arrived at Reinhard's place, they woke up later than usual because Reinhard had taken the week off. The only reason they were up a little before seven was little Bernd, standing in his crib singing with all the might of his young voice the only text he knew, "Lala, lala."

Although Fritz was in the room upstairs, the cheerful voice of the little boy filling the whole house was audible. He went downstairs, found the bathroom empty, did his hygiene, and was downstairs a few minutes later to find Katarina in the kitchen having a great breakfast, almost ready. She filled a cup of coffee and, not even asking, handed it to him without sugar or milk.

"How do you know I take my coffee black?" Fritz asked, sipping at the hot cup and enjoying the impact of the caffeine.

"You worked on a vessel, and Reinhard was on a vessel. I assumed you are all the same, coffee, hot and black" was her answer, looking at Fritz and smiling. "You are men, easy to read but difficult to understand."

"Wow, Katarina, it seems as if you have a philosophical streak in you. But you know we men have the same issue with you, women?" Fritz returned.

"I know, I know. I just have to let it out occasionally and love to tease Reinhard's friends."

"What are you doing again with my friends?" Reinhard's voice sounded from the hallway. He was on his way from the bathroom back to the bedroom and must have heard the chatting between Katarina and Fritz. Both looked at each other and started laughing loudly, which caused Reinhard to look out of the bedroom, yelling, "I can hear ya!"

A few minutes later, he came out, and they sat down to have breakfast together, joking around and having fun by watching little Bernd eating a piece of bread, stuffing it with both hands in his mouth and half of it over his whole face. When he was done, he held his hands toward his dad. With a wide grin, he said, "Dada." Fritz enjoyed the joyful environment of his friend's family and was again deep into thoughts about the country's future when Reinhard startled him out of the thought world.

"Hey, Fritz, where are you?

"It's okay, I am here. I just thought about something. What did I miss?"

"I said that we were driving over to the comm officer of our group. He took a few days off and wanted to meet you too. We will use my car because it's better when we are not driving around so much with your license plate after your street race with the SSP yesterday."

"Great, how far is it?"

"About twenty minutes, depending on the traffic, but it shouldn't be more than thirty-five."

"Okay, let me get another comm set, and we can go. Buy, Katarina, see you later." Fritz went to his room and grabbed two more comm sets out of the box. When he came out of the house, Reinhard was already out of the garage with the car, Fritz jumped in, and they were on their way. They did not talk much, and Fritz was looking at the buildings and the area they were driving through. During his time at the university in Berlin, he had been at Reinhard's house several times, which belonged to his parents, who both had died in a car accident when he was in the navy. Since he was an only child, he inherited the house. But Fritz had never paid much attention to the environment because they were using public traffic at that time, which was a totally different story.

When they arrived at the house of the comm officer of Reinhard's group, Fritz was astounded by the large and great-looking building, which indicated that this guy must have been in a relatively high-level position in the economic hierarchy or even government. Even before they had left the car, the door opened, and a man exited the house with a friendly grin, yet Fritz froze in his seat, with his mouth open and in shock. Turning to Reinhard, he saw an even wider grin on his face. Finding his voice again, he said, "Are you out of your mind, bringing me to one of the greatest comrades the university had ever had among students?"

In the meantime, Manfred had reached the car, and Reinhard had gotten out and man-hugged Manfred, greeting him as if they were old friends and had not seen each other in years. The first was right, the second not so much. Fritz came slowly out of his consolidation and opened the car to get out, looking at both of them, pointing fingers at him and laughing their asses off. Fritz finally got out of the car and, with great hesitation, took the stretched-out hand of Manfred to greet him.

"I don't know yet what the game is you are playing with me, but I hope for the sake of both of you, I can laugh as much as you, guys, did when it is all clear," Fritz said, somewhat angry and still not convinced that he was on safe territory. Manfred led them into his house and living room, which was much more extensive than Reinhard's whole house. Still the little bag with the two comm systems in his hand, Fritz sat on the edge of a comfortable chair and, looking at Reinhard, said, "What is going on? Manfred was surely the last one on my list I would dream of having in a group like yours."

"May I jump in and explain?" Manfred said, and Reinhard immediately, already a little uncomfortable by Fritz's rejective reaction, said, "Go ahead, Manne, no one else can explain why we are here better than you." And Manfred began to tell a story that immediately reminded Fritz of what Leo went through. Manfred was the genius in the seminar group at the university. Straight A+ in all subjects. He had stopped pursuing a doctorate study because his wife gave birth to a child with Down syndrome. And not only that, he was the party's student representative. And the party used the fact that he had a genial mind throughout his time at the university to pressure not so well doing students to work harder. Several classmates were "exmatriculated" because of his assessment that they could not fulfill the requirements after graduation because of their mediocre attention and intellect.

After graduation, the party hired him for an extraordinary top-secret project at an Army R&D laboratory where he could put his genius to work. A year into the fascinating and successful work, his daughter with Down syndrome died suddenly. That was a shock for his wife, but she had just finished her medical exams for becoming an eye doctor and buried herself in her work at the clinic. Manfred had to pause a second. He was obviously emotionally touched again by telling this.

"We both earned good money, and I worked for that nonexisting military lab. And my wife was an accomplished emergency station eye doctor. We had the income and decided to buy a piece of land and build a home, hoping we would have children again sometime down the road. We had just finished the house and lived there for a few months when I got a call from the clinic that she had collapsed on the floor and was in the intensive care unit.

"Turned out that one of her kidneys had failed completely. Just shut down. Typically, one kidney is sufficient, but the problem was the other kidney was inflamed too, and the medication available did not work. The chief physician told me there was a method to regenerate a dysfunctional kidney developed by a team of specialists. When I asked who they were and when they would be in the clinic, he said that they were in West Berlin and would definitely not come to this clinic. I told him, 'Okay, what do you do to get her there? What can I do to help?' And he started to fill out the paperwork for a temporary patient transfer for emergency surgery.

"When it came to my occupation and employer, I could not tell him. I told him it was top secret. He said, 'No problem, we have a form for that too.' I grabbed that form and drove to my boss. It was already after 8:00 PM. He looked at the form, listened to my pleading, and said no. Quite simply, no. I went home and wrote a petition to the party group of my lab and a copy to the FDS, who was, and still is, a really high-up guy in the party structure, to sign the paper to get my wife the surgery that would save her life. It was declined. I wrote to the secretary-general that heartless swine of a devil in human skin, and I was jumping up and down when I had his answer in the mail. With some lapidary words, he thanked me for my unwavering bond to the cause, my excellent work at the lab to benefit a great nation, and my additions to the outstanding accomplishments of the paradise of the worker's class. But he denied my wife's transfer for life-saving surgery because of the danger of the state security because of my job. I was about to vomit when I read it.

"I drove to the hospital to see my wife, and she was in a horrible condition then, so I am not sure that she even heard that I told her that I would quit the job and she could be transferred. The following day I dropped my immediate resignation from my position and all my id cards on my boss's desk. I walked out of that facility believing she would get the transfer approved.

"But no, at the clinic, in her room were two guys with these awful leather-imitating coats, and they told me that I would now have to wait five years to be clear from my top-secret clearance. They told me that in the presence of my wife, whom they had just told, in those few minutes a day when she was fully conscious, I had stupidly terminated my employment and that she should try to get me to go back and withdraw it. She wanted to say something, but it was all too much. I could barely hold myself back not to knock that asshole of an SSP officer out. My wife died the same day.

"I canceled my party membership and found an excellent job at the EAW in Treptow, developing some stupid industrial computers for applications, such as generator controllers and load-shedding systems. We thought about how Reinhard should tell you the background and why I am in his group and that he fully trusts me with his life, but then we considered it better you hear it from me direct. If Reinhard told you about me, I thought you would not come here, and you would probably no longer have complete trust in Reinhard.

"I have to apologize, Manfred, because, in the same way, I changed from being a wholly brainwashed communist. I should accept that others can change too. And we can definitely have a different opinion about the stupid industrial computers you are developing now. I am setting them up at the shipyard in Stralsund. There are several lines in the program I have figured out to be changed so that we avoid generator shutdowns. I wonder how I could return information about programming errors to the developers. But we can talk about that later."

"Apology accepted, Fritz. And I would be more than happy to talk with you about the program of the application. Maybe I can convince my boss to request your attendance at our monthly meetings for application feedback. If you can, get me some of the program lines or commands you must change. That would convince him that you know what you are talking about. But now, let's get into my little workshop and see what gifts Fritz has brought us."

Manfred led them downstairs and opened the door to the right of the stairs. What they walked into took Fritz's breath away. A huge workplace in the form of a countertop was mounted along three walls. The fourth wall was filled with breaker cabinets, climate simulation cabinets, and what looked like a radio wave-isolated chamber. It was the dream of any decent electronic engineer tinkering around with new ideas and inventions and bringing fantasies to reality. Fritz needed some minutes to recover from his surprise and said, "Manfred, this is an engineer's paradise."

Manfred turned around with a grin and said, "Not that fast. We are not there yet. But yes, being down here and doing some exciting experiments is excellent. It helps me forget what is happening to my wife and daughter, find a reason to live, and help those joining us fight this evil, satanic system. But what did you bring for us that made Reinhard so curious that he was talking for hours on a row about what it could be and if I would have an idea?"

Fritz opened the bag and placed the two comm systems on the countertop. He placed one communicator and programmer together in front of Reinhard and one set in front of Manfred. Fritz encouraged them both to actively execute the steps. At the same time, he explained the technical details, the programming and encryption of a message, and the sending and receiving of messages from the communicator using the programmer. They programmed, sent, and received several messages, felt comfortable using the devices, and finally shut them off.

"Wow, I am incredibly impressed, Fritz," Manfred uttered, still in awe about the ease with which the system could be used and how Fritz had designed and built those systems with his limited tools and resources. "And all you had was the multimeter and an oscilloscope? I can't believe you get the transceiver adjustment done without a frequency analyzer. And the AD/DA converter circuits, how did you do that without a logic analyzer?"

Fritz, a little overwhelmed by the chorus of praises by a guy who had always placed light years ahead of himself, being the genius he was, swallowed and said, his voice a bit tight, "I just calculated the circuits according to the data books I got from the TI guys at the exhibition and corrected two or three resistors and capacitors when I realized that the signal was capped out. But I am sure that using the park of instruments you have here, the communicator can be optimized to be at least 30 to 40 percent more efficient. I would like to increase the range without killing the battery prematurely. It works for at least two or maybe even three years, with one daily transmission. Optimizing the writing and reading of the RAM and improving the output and the antenna circuitry could reduce power consumption significantly. My dream would be to have a communicator near every member's place so we can coordinate actions as needed without deadly time delays."

"Can you get the circuit diagrams and calculations to me? I will work really hard on getting them optimized. I have all the tools I need for that, and if I need something else, I can just take it from the laboratory I am working now. My boss is a brilliant theoretical but has two left hands. Half of the time, he doesn't understand what I am doing with all those instruments. How many communicators do you have built so far?"

"I had twenty-five, plus two, in test stations in Sassnitz. I have already delivered four and have all the others with me. I have these two here. The rest is in my luggage at Reinhard's. Why are you asking?"

"I would like to open one up, and we could do some measurements and see what we can find out in a hurry. Look at my instrumental collection here. A radio engineer would like to have nothing missing and some more because we are working on combining analog and digital. Again, Fritz, I am genuinely amazed at what you have accomplished without the instruments I am used to."

"It's actually no big deal to open the communicator. I had to design it to replace the battery without breaking the unit. Do you have a heat gun?"

Manfred took out the heat gun. When it was heated up, Fritz used a PCB vice, clamped the communicator so that approximately only a third of its thickness was in the clamp, and slowly moved the heat gun around the middle of the device. Within a few seconds, a black, greasy liquid started to drop. Fritz immediately took a piece of paper and said, "You don't want that stuff on your countertop. It is like ever-glue."

With a small screwdriver and ever so slightly moving around the circumference of the device, Fritz opened it and removed one-half of the case. The groove where the greasy stuff was in was empty after a few more seconds. He explained that the main issue with the battery was the maximal size he could get into the case, which was one of the commercially available soap boxes, people used when traveling to pack their block of soap. To fit the PCB in, he needed to use those with edged corners, not rounded corners. But he could only get a limited number and was forced to integrate the battery into the box.

"What would you have done differently if you had an unlimited supply of these soap boxes?" Reinhard asked. "Reinhard, come on. You can't be that stupid," Manfred threw in. "He would have stacked the soap boxes and had enough space for many more batteries. Am I right, Fritz?"

"Exactly. Suppose I could get one hundred of those soap boxes. In that case, I could stack fifty communicators with a dramatic increase in transceiving power when activated by keeping the same lifetime of the battery. I have one test system running in Sassnitz. I sealed the boxes the same way as this one, but because the wires penetrated the case walls, I used a shrink tube and shrunk both cases together. It has been out there now for almost a year, and the farthest away I established stable communication was 28 km. The best is that the unity is hidden above the doorpost of a little shop."

"Fritz, I had just something like a brainwave. But I have to chew on that for some time. Can you stop here on your way back for two days?" Manfred asked.

Hesitating momentarily, Fritz answered, "I have to see how I can rearrange my trip. I could shorten two visits by having them on the same day and be back on Thursday night. That would allow me to stay till Sunday morning, but not longer. I want to have at least Easter Monday with my family."

"That would be wonderful, Fritz. I am already working in my mind on some basics. I believe I could have my thoughts sorted out until then, and we can review some drafts I will have."

Looking at his watch, Reinhard reminded them that it was already after 6:00 PM, and all were shocked at how the time had flown by without them even recon it. The SSP wasn't keen anymore on watching his property. Manfred suggested that Fritz stays in his home when he returned because it was enough room. They all agreed and said goodbye.

On the way back to Reinhard's place, Fritz was already thinking about the phenomenal advantage of having the genius as part of the resistance movement. His enormous theoretical knowledge and brilliant mind, combined with Fritz's ability to transfer even the slightest idea into practical usage, was a combination that could mean winning the communication and information war against the communist power structure.

Since Reinhard had to get up early the following day to return to work again and Fritz wanted to start south also not too late, they were not chatting too long into the night. Katarina was curious about how it went with Manfred. She laughed until she hurt listening to Reinhhard's somewhat dramatized version of the first encounter with Manfred as a movement member. When she asked Fritz if they told him how it came that Manfred joined the movement, Reinhard began to hum and haw and finally said that they did not come to that. It was apparent that he did not want to talk about it. So Katarina started to tell the story, and as more, she spoke about Reinhard became uncomfortable.

"Turned out that when Manfred quit his job at the secret company, which isn't so secret to us anymore, but it is Manfred's decision to tell you," she said, "he had no idea how evil the communist system would attack him. He still had that somewhat rosy idealism about the great communist philosophy in his mind when they struck him to revenge for his betrayal, as they said. They froze his bank account with the accusation that he had misappropriated money and corrupted companies to use materials determined for projects at the company for his house. They dragged him from one court hearing to the next, only to withdraw their accusations at the exact moment when he could present the invoices and orders to the judge.

"One day, Reinhard used the car; usually, he goes by train to work. There was a rerouting on the way home, and suddenly a guy jumped out of the dark in front of his car. Since the opposite direction was free, Reinhard could avoid running over him, just gazing and throwing him into the ditch on the side of the road. Turned out he recognized Manfred as the guy, dragged him into the car, and brought him home. He was knee-walking drunk and just lightly hurt. I cleaned the abrasions while he wasn't even able to talk. We placed him on the couch and had a long confession morning with him the following day. He broke down entirely and cried like a baby."

"Stop it, Katarina. What shall Fritz think about the genius when you tell things like that." Reinhard threw in suddenly, fully alert, and both looked at him with questioning impressions. Then Reinhard laughed and said, "Fritz, you have no idea how much I enjoyed that moment and, simultaneously, was ashamed for feeling like that as a Christian. The genius to whom even the professors at the university looked up, who had mocked you and me and many others for being too stupid to follow his thought process, this guy was now sitting in my living room and crying his soul out. But I immediately realized more was behind his collapse and was even more ashamed. He explained the whole drama he had gone through over the last fifteen months and that he was at the end of his rope and could not live any longer in a nation based on a complete lie and stepping over dead bodies. We both told him that there is a reason to live, and we led him to Christ, and within a week, he was ready to go for another job, and that is the story."

"I would never have thought that the genius could lose it. Drinking, had you ever thought he could even through a beer?"

With that, Reinhard said goodbye to Fritz and, with a huge bearhug, sent him with God's blessings on his way because he would be long gone when Fritz got up in the morning.

Fritz slowly woke up, smelling a wave of coffee aroma seeping into the room. He went to the bathroom, got his hygiene done, and was in the kitchen quickly. Katarina placed a cup of coffee before him and said, "Good morning, Fritz. Did you sleep well?"

Fritz confirmed that he felt rested and ready for the trip to add two of the remaining visits to the day and end at night at his last stop before returning to Manfred's place. After an excellent breakfast, Katarina outdid herself again. They bid farewell to each other, and Fritz was on his way.

CHAPTER 8

The New Chief of the Regional Office Reiner Chooses a New Home

Bodo woke up early. Over the last several years, he had developed the ability to wake up at a certain time, mainly by telling himself that he had to get up at that specific time when he went to bed the night before. It was just after dawn, and the sky seemed to be only partly cloudy. He got up and opened the windows wide. He inhaled the fresh April air deeply into his lungs. He had a great view over the pond behind the hotel with a clearly noisy fountain now with open windows. He could see the river Dosse, part of the town's name to his left and behind the pond.

After getting his hygiene done and dressed, he reviewed the notes he had made the night before on his OmniBook. Then he grabbed the pocket memo and dictated a general security rules statement for Giesela to write up. Some of those rules seemed to be rather extreme, but he knew he had to make it that way to avoid a situation with his own officers as he had experienced the day before. His idea was to make it a part of the service oath for the officers serving with the OIR.

From the first day on, he would imprint into their brains that they were something special. They had an assignment that set them above all regular law enforcement and made the SSP a support unit for them. But this specialty did not give them rights to arbitrariness. And based on the objectives, they were predestined to be targets of those who were corrupt and treasonous yet still in powerful positions until those people were removed from their positions of power. Their job was to make that happen, and that put a target on their back.

He looked at his watch, and even though it was still a little early, he decided to go down and start his breakfast. Since he loved to read his leading newspaper, the *New Germany*, at breakfast, he always needed more time than others. The breakfast room was almost empty, and he learned that the breakfast in that hotel was served. This was in the German Democratic Republic, only done in exclusive hotels, such as the International hotels in Berlin or Rügen-Hotel in Saßnitz, where he had stayed just a few days ago. At that moment, he realized what a tremendous and action-packed few days he had behind him.

He got the newspaper and ordered his breakfast, with fried eggs over-easy and bacon as he liked it, and Sarina always complained about it. While reading about the critical messages about the increasing demonstrations in some cities, he noticed that there were other cities where the number of demonstrators had reduced. In Bodo's opinion, the commentator inferred logically that this was the first proof of increasing trust in the new leadership. The commentary concluded that the new style of honest reporting about discovered corruption, especially the *Current Camera* report on the shoot-out and justifying the killing of a member of the top leadership structure of the SUP, had demonstrated to the people that the new leadership was severe in its attempt to clean the mess. To his astoundment, he also read that the letters to the new organization OIR had increased to a point where additional ways needed to be established to handle them promptly. He needed to call Karl to get detail about that.

He laid the newspaper aside when the waitress brought his breakfast and a small pot of coffee, usually two cups. He began enjoying the fresh eggs and the great coffee, which he considered was the brand you could only buy in the newly opened specialty shops. The goods sold there were much better quality, often overstock production for the NSW Nicht-Sozialistischer Wirtschaftraum (not socialistic economies). Bodo thought for a moment why it wasn't possible to have all products produced with such quality but immediately blamed the capitalists for the misery because they blocked so many raw materials needed from being able to import.

He had just filled his second cup of coffee when Reiner and Corinna entered the hotel's breakfast area and waved them over to sit with him at his table.

"I told you, Corinna, Bodo will be down already," Reiner said, wishing Bodo a good morning and sitting down. A few minutes later, the waitress appeared and took their orders. Bodo finished his eggs, and after preparing a slice of delicious rye bread with a homemade blueberry spread, he said to Reiner, "Did you see the headline in *New Germany*?"

"No, I have not had the newspaper in hand yet," Reiner answered and continued, "I can read yours, but what is the specific you ask?"

"I would rather not tell you because I would like your unbiased opinion," Bodo answered.

"Okay, let's have breakfast, and I will read it later," Reiner said the moment the waitress brought the breakfast for Reiner and Corinna. They ate and made small talk and finally had to hurry up to meet with the guy to see the home they would choose from. Bodo grabbed all his already-packed stuff from his room and walked down to the receptionist. He asked her if she had a list of government accounts. She confirmed that they had just opened a few months ago after a significant renovation, based on their proximity to the Autobahn connection to Lübeck and, on the other side, the still operational Monastery Heiligengrabe.

Bodo gave her his account number, which he had memorized in the meantime, told her to put his and Reiner's rooms on the bill, and signed it off. The receptionist compared his signature with the signature probe on the account sheet and said, "Mr. Zipper, may I see your ID, please, since you are here for the first time, and I don't want to get into trouble for not being careful."

Bodo smiled at her, placed his ID card on the counter, and said, "I appreciate the thoroughness with what you are making sure that all is in order. Nothing to apologize for."

She checked it out, confirmed the transfer was okay and gave him his ID card back.

Bodo walked to his car, placed his luggage in the trunk, and put the mobile into the snap holder. He heard steps behind him and, turning around, saw Reinhard and Corinna walking toward him. Bodo stopped them as they came close and said, "I think it is a good idea when you take your own car. I would like to start from the house you chose to the Regional Office North (RON) with Reiner as soon as you have made up your mind. I will sign the contract for your choice, and Corinna can drive back to the hotel or use the time however she likes. What do you think?"

"That's an excellent idea," Corinna said. "I like that. I will fill my mind with the new home I have to decorate and go shopping for things I know we don't have."

"We have to talk, Bodo," Reiner said, throwing an angry look at him and walking to his car. Bodo laughed out loud and got into his car and slowly drove off the parking lot of the hotel, ensuring that Reinhard was following. They arrived at the address just about ten minutes later and parked at the side of the road. The man responsible for the house transfer to the city and the manager of the city housing management was already there, and they greeted each other.

Reiner introduced himself and Corinna as the interested persons. Although in civil clothing, the navy officer was immediately recognizable as such, explaining that all three homes, numbered 10D, 10E, and 10F, were identical. Since they had the chance to select one of them, they should feel free to check every one of them. Bodo joined Reiner and Corinna on their extended and intensive investigation of the three homes. He was amazed about the quality of the materials and the work the renovation contractors had done to prepare the homes to transfer them to the city.

After intensively investigating all three homes, Reiner and Corinna stood at the corner property 10D discussing the cons and pros of that particular property. Bodo walked over to the navy officer and the city guy. The officer looked at his watch, indicating that his time was running short, and asked Bodo, "How much longer do you think they might need, comrade Zipper? I must leave soon to return to Stralsund for a meeting." The moment Bodo started to answer, that they should be done any second, Reiner and Corinna crossed the street and walked to them. With great joy in their voice, they announce, both speaking simultaneously, "We decided to take the corner property 10D." Then they looked at each other and laughed loudly, and Corinna moved over to Bodo and hugged him. The officer handed them the second set of keys and a package of papers to Bodo and another two packages to the city manager and said, "Please have those papers authorized and signed and send the original back to my office. The address is there. Keep the copies for your own records." And turning to Reiner and Corinna, extending his hand, he said, "All the best in your new home and the new job."

Then he turned and walked to his car, where the driver had already started the engine. *He must really be in a hurry*, Bodo thought, turning back to the group of Reiner, Corinna, and the city housing manager. They were already discussing getting the utilities turned over to the new owners. The city manager explained that the city would probably use the other two homes for high-ranking city employees to avoid any potential concerns about what kind of people would be their new neighbors. The city manager left, and all three went back into the new home of the family Worser, where Corinna, taking over the presentation, started to explain all the details of the future arrangements. Reiner began nervously looking at Bodo, and Bodo shrugged his shoulders and grinned. Corinna did not notice anything going on behind her back. She was in her own world of living the dream of decorating their own house, a whole house for them alone.

Bodo finally had mercy on Reiner and said, "Corinna, I don't want to destroy your lively presentation of the future decoration of your home, but I have to steal Reiner and take him to work. Since he is already on the payroll at my agency, I need him to work for the money he needs to fulfill your buying dreams."

Corinna paused for a second, interrupted in her speech, and then walked over to Bodo, hugging him again, and said with a very moved voice, "Bodo, you will never realize what you have done for us. I can put it in words"—looking over to Reiner with a smirk in her eyes—"he surely never."

"Corinna, Reiner, and I have known each other for a long time, and we have been friends since we first met. You both know how frustrated I looked at the destruction of the tremendous socialistic experiment on German soil by the increasing corruption among our own ranks. When I was offered the chance to be the correction factor, the force to turn the development around, I immediately thought of Reiner as one of my office leaders."

"We all, including the wives of our officers, have a tough time in front of us. We have to make decisions that will be at the limit of our human conscience. Still, we have to execute them for the sake of the victory of socialism. Remember the number one rule W. I. Lenin placed in the heart of the revolutionaries: Who is not for us is against us! And there is nothing in between. I appreciate you both, Corinna, and I hope you are strong enough to support Reiner in his demanding job. Sometimes, he might look like he is somewhere in space and pays no attention to the family—that is, when Reiner is fighting with those decisions that may crush a man's mind and when he needs you the most."

"I promise you, Bodo, and even more you, Reiner, I will be there for you. Outspoken or not. I will always be there for you," Corinna said with a lump in her throat, blinking a tear away; she began to smile, looked at Bodo, and said, "You almost made me cry."

Reiner and Bodo said goodbye and walked out to his car. Bodo started the engine, turned, and drove down the road. While driving, Bodo told Reiner the whole experience of the day before and reminded him that they were in a different type of game now, working for the OIR. He told Reiner that this would be the best way to get to the property daily without bringing attention to his travel. They left Wittstock behind and, shortly after, reached the Autobahn's underpass. Behind that, it was just another few miles, and Bodo turned left into the forest road, which, after another left turn, brought them in front of the gate. This time it was closed and guarded.

There were two guards, confirming his first good impression of Sergeant Weber. One of the guards came to the car on the driver's side, and Bodo lowered the window. The guard immediately recognized Bodo yet asked to see an ID for Reiner. Bodo told the guard that Reiner is the head of this property and starts to work today. The guard hesitated for a second then signaled to open the gate. Bodo drove in, and the gate closed behind him. Bodo stopped the car, and the guard came over, asking if everything was okay. Bodo answered, "All is clear, comrade, and thanks for being careful. I wondered momentarily why you hesitated to let me in. I realized that we had not agreed upon a distress code. I recommend you for that and will let Sergeant Weber know about it. When the buildings came into view, they discovered two large trucks and workers carrying office furniture into the office building."

They walked into the office building, and Bodo went straight to the future Reiner's office, whose door was wide open. One of the workers was just finishing the last tasks to fix the furniture and excused himself and went out. Bodo looked out into the hallway and, seeing that the security office door was open, said, "Come on, Reiner, I will show you the security center of your property." While they were walking down the hallway, the main door opened, and Sergeant Weber walked in. "Good morning, comrade Zipper."

"Good morning, sergeant. May I introduce you to your future boss, comrade Worser?" Comrade Worser will be in command of this property and is a colonel of the SSP." I was about to show him the security center, but you can do that later. I need to see that I get back on the road, but I must address the guards before leaving. Please get them mustered."

"Yes, comrade Zipper!"

Bodo gave him a few minutes, and then he walked to the front of the living quarters with Reiner, where the troops had lined up. They went through the salute ceremony, and Bodo began to address them. "Comrades, I have the honor to present to you the commander of this property, comrade Colonel Worser. From this moment on, he is in charge of everything concerning this property. But before I have him say a few words, I want to use the opportunity to make the specialty under which you serve your country at this property evident to you. This is not your ordinary barracks or office object to which you are ordered to provide security. This property is used to investigate the political and economic corruption among our country's organizations, up to the highest levels of leadership in the northern part. Those who are targets of our investigation will try to stop our investigative officers from finding the evidence and will do everything, including initiate attacks on this property. You will later be asked to swear an additional oath to hold whatever you may experience at this property as the most profound secret you have ever held. Not even the location can be known to people not sworn to the same oath. I am the newly formed agency commander, and comrade Colonel Worser reports directly to me. Make no mistake, any traitor who believes that what happens here is worth bragging about among friends, family, or relatives will experience the full power of my position. Comrade Worther may say now some words to you, and then you are dismissed."

Reiner stepped forward and walked along the line of the nineteen officers in uniform and the one guy without one, Gunther, who caught his attention. "Who are you, comrade, that you are in line without properly dressed?" Bodo was about to say that Gunther was his driver. Still, Gunther quickly answered, "Comrade Worser, I don't have my uniform with me since I am ordered not to wear uniform when I drive my boss through the nation."

Reiner looked over his shoulder at Bodo, who had already turned to look at the lake and saw from the corner of his eye the look from Reiner. With that, Reiner turned back to face Gunther, "And who would that mysterious boss be, comrade?"

"Comrade Commander Zipper, Comrade Colonel Worser."

Now Reiner turned fully to Bodo, smiling at him, and Bodo said, "I can confirm that I ordered him not to wear a uniform when he is on the road with me."

"Let them be dismissed, Sergeant," Reiner ordered, and walking over to Bodo, he said, "You could have said something, you scalawag." Whereon Bodo laughed and said, "You learned fast, Reiner. I will leave you alone with your troops here. But one thing before I leave. You need to deal with the guy who was degraded yesterday. To do so, we need to call Jürgen, which means I have to call and see what he got arranged."

Bodo walked to his car, and hearing steps behind, he turned around seeing Gunther running toward him. They walked to the car silently, and Bodo told him to get ready because they would be on their way in a few minutes. Gunther walked back to the living quarters to get his stuff, and Bodo got into the car and hit the button for Jürgen's direct number. "Jürgen here. Bodo, what took you so long? I was expecting your call shortly after midnight. But jokes aside. Are you okay out there?"

"Yes, Jürgen, everything is fine. I just brought my new office manager over here, and he addressed the troops. Please don't forget to get his credential to send over ASAP because I want to ensure he is not harassed by the local law enforcement."

"That stuff should be there by latest tomorrow by courier. I signed it yesterday. Here is what we do with that idiot we had to degrade. I have had a team of my internal security check at the barracks in Pritzwalk, and they are 100 percent sure that the current battalion commander is absolutely clean. Yes, he supported that guy years ago when he was his company CO. Still, he was young and inexperienced. He wanted to learn from the experienced NCOs. He had no idea which squad was ordered to secure the property. He just gave the order to the company CO as usual."

"Okay, Jürgen, that's sufficient for me. So I will get an escort to transfer the guy to his barracks, and they will handle the rest?"

"Exactly, Bodo, get it done, and you are safe. Give your office manager my direct number, please. No need to go through you for bites and pieces if he can handle them."

"Sure, Jürgen, thanks for that short line for him, have a nice day. Talk to you later." Bodo hung up and walked back to the office building, finding Reiner and Sergeant Weber deeply discussing the ins and outs of the security and communication systems of the property.

"Sorry to interrupt you. Reiner, here is the direct number of comrade Pieker. Call this number whenever there is a need to get an issue with the SSP cleared quickly, and you are in the best hands."

"Comrade Pieker, THE Pieker? Wow, that's high up the line. I am not sure that I can handle that. I will try you first."

"Reiner, he asked me to give you his direct number for a reason. He is cleaning up the mess inside the SSP he had inherited, and if you have an issue that can't wait, he wants to know immediately."

"Okay, get it. I will use it wisely."

"Now to you, Sergeant Weber. Your battalion CO has been cleared of all suspicions. You have the order to send private Kapers with three men escort under arms to the barracks in Pritzwalk. Be careful whom you choose, and make clear that they are ordered to use any force to ensure he gets there. Are we clear?"

"Yes, Commander Zipper, very clear."

"Please make sure that comrade Worser gets transportation as needed. I hope you have some well-trained drivers? And before I leave, I want you to create road blockades here, here, and here," pointing them out on the large-scale map of the property environment at the wall.

"Reiner, I will call Karl on my way home and see that I can arrange your moving trucks for this weekend or maybe earlier. How far are you, guys, with packing? Are you necessarily need to go back with Corinna, or can she get it done with the help of the movers? They are total professionals and fast. And I have to tell you, we barely touched anything. I would rather have you here at the RON and may need you at headquarters on Friday. If I am not mistaken, the carpool for the office shall arrive tomorrow, and I want you to take over personally. I know that I ask a lot, but we have to get things rolling. After what happened on Monday, the rats are smelling the flames."

Reiner answered without any hesitation, "Bodo, I understand entirely. Corinna is a strong woman, and she will understand and can handle it. I am ready."

"Great. Sergeant, keep an eye on the colonel and make sure the delinquent get secure to the barracks. See you all soon again." With that, Bodo was out of the office building and walked to the car, where Gunther held the back passenger door open for him. Bodo got in the car, and when Gunther started the engine, he told him, "Gunther get us to headquarters as fast as possible. It is now 1:30 PM. I want to be there no later than 3:00 PM. Can we make it?"

"I will do my best, comrade Zipper. We may have a tail of police cars every now and then."

"Yeah, but when they notice the license plate, that should turn them off. Let's go."

As soon as they were on the Autobahn, Bodo grabbed the phone and called Karl. "Karl, how is your day going so far? I thought I would give you some work so you don't fall asleep."

"You are a joker, Bodo. If I wouldn't know better, I would think you mean it and would be angry," Karl said, laughing on the phone. "I have your guys for Berlin on the road. They should be finishing moving into their new apartments tonight."

"That is great because I need to return them to Rügen to move the Reiners family to Wittstock ASAP. Can you arrange that?"

"Shouldn't be a problem. I could have them there Thursday night and start packing. That would bring them to Wittstock on Saturday afternoon. Would it be two trucks enough, one with a trailer for their household?"

"Excellent, Karl. Another thing I thought about, do you know anyone I could use as the southern office's manager? Maybe I have to talk with Bruno about that."

"Yeah, Bodo, I think it is better to talk with Bruno. They are pretty far with collecting the complaints files from about the last ten years for your agency, and he might have an idea for a candidate."

"Great, I will do that. Have a nice rest of the day. Talk to you later."

Bodo hung up and dialed the direct for Jürgen again. "Hi, Jürgen. Sorry for bothering you again so soon. I thought it might be a better way to interview the candidates for my agency at the SSP academy instead of driving them to the headquarters at Karolinenhof. Could you arrange that for me, starting tomorrow morning, let's say at 10:00 AM?"

"Bodo, that's a great idea. I was always thinking about how we could drive them around efficiently. I will have a room and some service arranged for you at the academy, and since I have a meeting there in the afternoon, maybe we can find the time to have lunch together."

"Sounds like a plan. I will be there at 10:00 AM. See you possibly at lunch."

CHAPTER 9

Meeting the Next Friend Who Has a Great Surprise and Some Armoring News

The months of April in middle Germany were always great for surprising weather changes. It was again a fairly lovely day for mid of April, and Fritz, on his way out of the Berlin district of Pankow, knew it could change any second. He could drive with an open window, enjoying the fresh air coming in after he had left the city area behind, and was driving around the east side of the Moloch to avoid the many construction areas and traffic lights, which often didn't work, causing endless traffic jams. But he enjoyed the great spring day and had the window on his car half down because of the Autobahn speed limit of 100 km per hour.

Although it was an extra 60 km to drive, it would be much faster this way. And even passing by Bernd's place just a few kilometers to the west, he wanted to get the other two contacts Theo in Hermsdorf and Robert in Karl-Marx-Stadt meet first and stay overnight at Bernd's place. It was a long drive, but he wanted to know what idea had shot through Manfred's brain when they looked at his communicator's specifics. To make that possible, he had to be back at Manfred's place the following evening, and so, he bit the bullet and drove through, mile after mile, with no break. When he reached Hermsdorf at about 1:00 PM, he was forced to stop to get fuel and used the chance to get to the phone and call Robert. After a few transfers, he got him on the phone. He explained that he would be at his apartment at about 5:00 PM or shortly after because things had changed, and he needed to return north today. Robert confirmed and said it would not be an issue.

Fritz drove the rest distance to the apartment address where Theo lived. It was one of these twenty-story concrete slab constructions with as many as fifteen entrances where you were lost when you came home at night, and the streetlights did not work. Driving slowly down the front of the colossus, he finally discovered the number and parked his car. Fritz grabbed his briefcase, loaded with two comm systems and programmers, and first walked to the wrong entrance. The entrance was locked, and he hit a bell just so. A woman answered, asking who was there. Locking left and right all the time to see if somebody was watching him, he said he was looking for a woman named Meier. The woman on the intercom answered that she did not know anyone named Meier, and that was all he needed. He apologized and returned to the correct entrance, stopping once to bind his leashes, another opportunity to check for tails. No one was on the street, and he went to the entrance, ringing the right bell this time. Theo answered and asked, "Is it you?"

Fritz answered, "Me."

The buzzer worked, and Fritz went into the hallway. The elevator was a few steps up and around the corner, and to his frustration, yet not surprisingly, the elevator was out of order. He walked up the ten stories to Theo's apartment, where he found the door ajar and walked into the apartment, announcing that he had arrived, and closed the door.

Theo came out of the kitchen, greeted him, smiling with a bear hug, and said, "Sit down, Fritz, you must be hungry. I have prepared lunch, and as you know, I love to cook, so you will enjoy it."

Fritz knew that Theo was living alone after a somewhat nasty divorce after discovering that his wife, his girlfriend since high school, had started sleeping with the city's first secretary. He had punched the guy unconscious in the highest-level restaurant in the city. He was only still in his job because he was the only one who could read the schematics the guys from Commercial Coordination, the unofficial smuggling organization of the GDR, brought into the country through their spy networks from the West. Based on his extraordinary abilities, he was indispensable. In a rare case of power-poker, his department head, a double PhD and internationally renowned expert in CMOS technology, had accomplished that Theo stayed in the department with all the security clearances he needed to work.

They ate an excellent lunch proving that Theo was a great cook. At the same time, Fritz explained the function of the communicator and the idea behind building a communication network that would connect the resistance's separate groups. Theo loved sending photographs to the other nearby resistance groups to tell them where they could connect to a communicator. He improved the idea by taking a photo of the part of a map, showing the parking lot with a cross marking where the car broke down. One had to wait two hours until a friend came to tow him to the car repair. Fritz was excited by this great idea and angry at himself for not having thought about that.

"And I have a great gift for you, Fritz," Theo finally came out with what was tangible on his mind all the time. "About three months ago, I broke through a secret in the drawings the spies had brought in last year, and we started to produce EEPROM in series last month. Now, since I am the 'genius' who broke the code, I have to make sure they are all functioning, and I have control over the test labor. Here is a package of thoroughly tested EEPROM in CMOS technology without serial number and not counted." Saying that, he handed a large package over to Fritz, whose mouth stood agape. Fritz realized immediately what that meant for their future development of communication systems. Low-power CMOS was their most significant advantage in the otherwise lagging East German digital microelectronic industry.

"That must be a huge number of chips, Theo. You do not think that someone may notice?"

"Nee, I am the responsible engineer for ensuring that all functioning chips are registered, serialized, and counted. The 180 chips in this package are all defective and have been destroyed during the last two weeks."

"Wow, Theo, that's fantastic. I am speechless. I really hope that you are not getting in trouble because of this. We need you. The movement needs you. Please be extremely careful. What you do is dangerous. The SSP can get to others through you."

Theo laughed and said, "Wait for a second. I will show you what will happen if these idiots come for me." He walked into the bedroom, returned just a few seconds later, and showed Fritz a semiautomatic pistol.

"You know how to handle that thing? Where did you get it? Is it a reliable source?" Fritz said, taking the pistol, Theo had made safe, taking the magazine out, and ejecting the cartridge. It was a Soviet-style pistol, type Makarow produced under license in the GDR. It was manufactured and assembled in their country. The factory had redesigned the Makarow to have a double-stagged magazine using the more common nine-by-nineteen luger cartridge.

"So here is the story." Theo started to explain how he got this equalizer, as he called it several times, in his hands. "I was hiking, and it was a very nice Saturday in late August last year. I still had much to deal with after the separation and the divorce. Although the forest surrounding our town here is incredible with all the remarkable points you can see over the valleys, my mind was not in nature. At least for the first several kilometers, that changed slowly. I began to listen to the birds and tried to determine what kind I heard.

"I had done that many times with my dad when I was a kid, and we were hiking together. My mind started to focus on nature and began to wander away from all the nasty scenes I had experienced in the weeks before when I suddenly heard a voice, very weak it seemed to be far off. Then I realized it wasn't far off. It was close and feeble, like exhausted. I oriented myself, determined where the voice came from and walked off the way into the undergrow. The voice became more apparent, but not much louder, and finally, when I broke through the undergrow, I almost fell off the cliff.

"I grabbed a small tree to keep myself from going over, and there he was, hanging on a small trunk of a young tree, similar to the one I had grabbed to keep me from falling. But he was about six to seven feet down below the ridge of the cliff and was barely hanging on. As I had learned in my childhood expeditions with my dad, I always had a backpack with two water bottles, some bread, a twenty-foot rope, and other valuable things. It is so ingrained into my nature that I never leave home without it.

"He was definitely at his last end of holding on, and I took out my rope, made a loop, and told him that I would lower the loop over his body, and he needed to get his arms through it, one by one. It took all my strength to lift him over the edge, and we were lying in the grass for a while before he even could speak."

"Man, Theo, that's a story. You saved a life. You should get a medal being in the newspapers. But what has that to do with owning an illegal weapon?"

"You won't believe it. But it is a real thing. This guy is now a member of my resistance group. He is the weapons master at the WIEGA manufacturing plant in Gera. He is responsible for test firing and stamping every weapon, rifle, pistol, special weapon, you name it. He test-fires them and stamps them."

Fritz was now on the edge of the chair he was sitting in, "Are you out of your mind to get someone like that into your group? I never considered you to be lightheaded. He could be a spy for the SSP, and your whole group could be in prison tomorrow."

"Calm down, Fritz, calm down. He was extremely thankful, as you can imagine, and when I was about to leave and walk my way, he held on to me and said I needed to listen to him. He has been the primary test senior weapon master in that facility for eight years. He loved his job and always agreed with the party in power, although he never became a member.

"He held the first in-house designed and manufactured weapons about two years ago. He was proud of what they had designed and the quality with which it was manufactured. It was named WIGA, and he learned shortly after that it was tested in several areas around the world, to his horror, not by states for the legal military weaponry, but by so-called revolutionary forces to get adequate weaponry to fight their oppressors. He had experienced those freedom fighters on many occasions at the test shooting range of the facility, and he was shocked this type of weapon would be sold to these gangsters, as he called them. Then last year, they had their first unique silencers in the test. They were outstanding in holding up the stress of selective fire, magazine after magazine.

"A few weeks later, a high-ranking SSP officer had been invited to test-shoot the smaller version of the redesigned Makarov pistol produced under license at their factory. He was extremely arrogant and bragged about how he would enjoy killing the enemy with this fantastic silencer more effortlessly than without. While they were driving back from the range, my contact, I will keep his name secret, was sitting in the back of the car, and that SSP office was bragging about how he had killed at least eight, what he called traitors, with a headshot from behind in a facility in Leipzig.

"This guy didn't even consider my friend as being present. He said it was as if he did not exist. The breaking point came when he saw the guys from an African rebel organization with the nickname 'Blood Diamond' throwing a briefcase full of diamonds in all sizes on the accountant's table and said that the shipment of the 5k WIGA was expected within two months. He wasn't even supposed to be in the office when that happened, but again, in their arrogance, these people acted as if my friend didn't exist. He was later called into the office of security. He had to sign an additional nondisclosure paper that notified him that he would be shot if he mentioned anything to anyone. That's the whole story. And he is willing to get us more weapons than we can handle if the time is ripe. He is starting to place weapons and ammunition aside with the remark nonfunctional and reserved for rework. Most of the time, they are forgotten until he reminds the remanufacturing master about it."

"Wow, I am baffled. I can only say that you have to be even more careful. This guy may do more than he can hide just to show off."

"I know, and I have already talked with him about it. He is careful because he said he wants to be in action when the day comes to repay these bastards."

Fritz returned the pistol to Theo, saying, "I have to leave, unfortunately. I have a long trip in front of me. We will be in touch. I am working on getting the nationwide communication network set up. Then we will organize a meeting with all group leaders."

They hugged, and Fritz grabbed his briefcase and left Theo behind in his apartment. The elevator was still out of order, so he walked down the stair, much easier than up. He used the large glass windows in the door to look for any suspicious person lingering around but could see none. A few minutes later, Fritz was on his way to Karl-Marx-Stadt.

CHAPTER 10

Occupying the New Headquarters Offices a Wide-ranging Decision: The First Directive

It was just a few minutes before 3:00 PM when they arrived at the headquarters. Bodo was astounded by the enormous progress all the installations and construction efforts had developed. The construction workers cleaned machines and prepared leftover materials and tools to move out. When he entered the office building, he waved at Giesela through her open door and walked into his office. Again, surprised at how much it had changed in those one and a half days he was away. He placed his briefcase on a small side cabinet next to the desk, and when he turned around, she was already at his door.

"Hello, comrade Zipper. Great that you made it back," she greeted him with a smile, and Bodo answered friendly, "Yes, I am happy to be back. Who made these nice decorations? It looks like an office now, not just a room."

"Thank you, comrade Zipper. I thought I would just try to make the offices a little more comfortable because I guess we all will spend many hours here for the next several months. I spent some decent money to get all the decorations, and I hope I did not overstep my competencies?"

"Oh no, not at all. I should have thought about that before I left. I will arrange a particular expense account for you, and all you have to do is to get the invoices signed by me. As with all other invoices, I want you to take responsibility and collect them and send them once a month to the accounting office for special affairs at the Department of

Finance. There is a specific accounting code, and that's what we have to do. Within the first week of the following month, I will get a statement about our financial affairs status. That will become a standard procedure, and we will have control over how we spend our budgeted money. What is the status of our equipment? Karl said to me that all stuff should be delivered."

"Yes, comrade Zipper, we have all the equipment received. We have, and I have already equipped the offices accordingly. We have here at HQ five offices for the officers, your office, comrade Wille's office, and my office. Each of the five offices can easily accommodate three officers, and one is large enough to accommodate four. We have three bathrooms. One is attached to your office and has a small shower. There is a smaller bathroom with a sink, which I designated a women's room, and there is a large one, which the construction guys turned into a men's room."

Bodo was stunned momentarily and then answered her very appreciatively, "Giesela, you have earned yourself the unchallengeable position of my forever principal secretary. I am amazed at what you have accomplished here in these few hours. And I mean it."

"Oh, you make me nervous, comrade Zipper. All I did was think about how we would use the facility over the coming years, and I thought it might be helpful for you to have that little bathroom for yourself."

"No, really, Giesela. This is more than a secretary usually is asked to do. I am happy you have that mindset. I can see you and comrade Wille working very well together to keep this HQ running smoothly. Comrade Renner informed me just a few hours ago that he has the movers for comrade Wille and our second secretary Maria Hafler at their places tonight. With that, they could start working on Friday or Monday next week. Another good news is that he got an apartment for Maria on the same block and even the same entrance where you are living since she is by herself and got a lovely two-room apartment."

Then he explained to Gisela the papers he had drafted for the additional oaths any member of the OIR had to take. He told her to review it, clean up the spelling and get thirty copies for his meetings tomorrow. He also handed her the pocket memo cassette on which he had memorized his thoughts about the organizational actions that needed to be done within the next two weeks. Those were mainly notes and instructions for Peter. She left his office and closed the door; and he sat at his desk, leaned back, closed his eyes, and recapitulated what had happened over the last week and a half. It appeared simply incomprehensible to him what had happened and at what neck-breaking speed.

At that exact moment, Bodo realized that his first thought about being the head of the headquarter's office or placing that function together with the assignment of the COO would not work. He could not load Peter with the daily organizational agenda of the whole organization and is responsible for the headquarters' actions. The other thought he had early on in his imagination for the organization, to run the headquarters active cases by himself, was a no-go also because he had to be much too flexible in his position to oversee the whole Office of Investigation and Recovery and keep all balls in the air at any given time. He needed to see if there was one potential leader in the officer pool he would interview the next day.

Using the intercom system, he called Gunther to his office, and when he appeared, he told him about the planes for the following day. Gunther guessed they would need about one hour to be at the academy. So they agreed to be at the house at 8:00 AM, stop short at the office, and be on their way in time. Then as if a sudden lightning hit Bodo, there had never been thought about where Gunther would be while Bodo was at the office, and he did not need to drive. On the one hand, he would be available to drive for other office's general needs if it was sure that Bodo would not need him.

On the other hand, there might be assignments with the interrogators or case officers where he could lend a hand to help with their assignments. Considering all this and talking it through with Gunther, Bodo hit the intercom button for Giesela and asked her to his office.

"Giesela, I just discussed the general situation of Gunther. Being my driver doesn't mean he always sits in the car waiting for me to jump in and drive. Do you think we could have a place for him in the office of the interrogators where you said is plenty of room for four, and we start with only three? At least for now."

"Comrade Zipper, I don't think that would be an issue. The room is huge enough for four officers. Since Gunther won't be in there all the time and may have to wash all the cars of HQ twice a week"—she threw in with a smirk in the direction of Gunther—"I think it will work just fine."

Bodo laughed and looked at Gunther, saying, "There you have it, Gunther, another regular assignment." And when Gunther made a face that did not express much excitement, Bodo added, "You surely won't drive your boss around in a dirty car, right?"

"I would never dare do such horrible things to you, comrade Zipper. I love my job too much."

"Okay, I have another idea. We have five offices which have comfortable space for four officers. At least for now, We need only offices for the teams. Yet we will need another office for Maria because I want her to be close to the teams being the secretary mainly working for them. Gunther can share the office with her, and since he needs not much space, Maria has enough space for the office furniture she needs. To keep his job, he will see to an immaculate car at any given time." Bodo completed the discussion with a smile and sent them both out of his office.

He looked over the direct dials on his desk phone to familiarize himself with all the dials. He noticed that all of the members of the Central Committee were on a particular button. Again, that nasty thought about the inability of the tremendous socialistic economy of the GDR to produce such marvels of technology, which he pushed aside with the excuse of the rotten capitalist hindrance because of the boycotts, crossed his mind.

He hit the button for Jürgen, and Jürgen answered immediately, "Bodo, what can I do for you this time? I have heard that Karl is done with the preselection of the officers for your agency. Will you interview them tomorrow at the academy?"

"Ye, that's the plan. I will be there by 10:00 AM and hope to be through by 5:00 PM, taking a lunch break with Karl since he might be there too."

"Sound's good to me. I am scheduled to hold the graduation ceremony next week. I told you I would be there tomorrow but can't do it. It doesn't look good when the commanding general appears before the time unofficial. I won't be able to come out, sorry."

"That's okay. I am really curious about what my brother had to do in Neubrandenburg on a Monday morning. But I don't want, as we talked already, to wake up to any suspicions that he is watched and, therefore, again, no actions at his workplace or home. Do you have any news about the lost trail in Neubrandenburg?"

"I personally don't. But I have instructed the officer in charge of the office in Neubrandenburg to give you a comprehensive report. I am just too busy, Bodo, to handle such things myself, and I guess you shouldn't do either. But since it is your brother and you know his history best, I guess you can easily place the case on your OIR. Nobody would have anything against it. You need to be careful about being biased, though. But that you know without saying."

"Be assured, Jürgen, my bias goes in the opposite direction. In my world, he is considered a traitor and a subversive element that needs to be watched closely. I believe that he is up to something. Your office has removed him from the possibility of interfering with the defense systems of our NAVY. But I am not sure that it quieted his thirst for revenge."

"Understood, Bodo, you know the danger to our cause better than anyone else, and that's why we chose you to be at the assignment you are. We trust you 100 percent. The officer from Naubrandenburg reported yesterday that he can comprehensively report all the discoveries tomorrow. I told him that you would contact him directly. Is that okay for you?"

"That is great, Jürgen. Thanks for the information. We will see then on Monday at the CC meeting, and I will give a first comprehensive report about the status of the OIR becoming operational."

"See you then, Bodo." And Jürgen hung up.

Bodo hit the intercom for Giesela and told her to connect him with the officer in charge of the SSP in Neubrandenburg. A few minutes later, his phone rang, and Giesela said that she had the officer on the phone.

"Commander Zipper, whom am I talking to?"

"Major Enzim, the commanding officer in charge of the SSP office for the district of Neubrandenburg. Good afternoon, Commander Zipper. What can I do for you?"

"Comrade Major, General Pieker informed me that you are almost done preparing a comprehensive report concerning the appearance of a particular car in Neubrandenburg, the followed failed surveillance, and the additional findings in the aftermath. Is that correct?"

"Yes, comrade commander. I was planning on seeing General Pieker personally to report on the case, but he said that somebody else would contact me, and I guess that is you, Commander Zipper?"

"Ye, comrade Enzim. That's correct. I would like to connect you back to my secretary to arrange a meeting here at my place on Friday, preferably in the morning. I am looking forward to meeting you in person, comrade Major."

Bodo hit the connect button for Giesela and instructed her to arrange all the details with the major for his visit on Friday morning. She should schedule the meeting for a maximum of one hour.

Bodo began working through the files of the two comrades he had arrested the first day in command of the Office for Investigation and Recovery. Reading through the files of serious accusations, he wondered if he could have those cases handled by the regional offices. And right then, he decided that all cases of treason and corruption involving the first secretaries of a district (FSD) or county (FSC) had to be handled exclusively at HQ.

He hit the intercom and told Giesela to come to his office for a quick dictate and bring Gunther with her.

A few minutes later, a knock on the door, and both entered his office after being called in.

"Gunther, can you go and check the status of the holding cells, please? And let me know what needs to be done to use them."

"Yes, comrade Zipper. I believe the construction workers said those were ready, but they also said that their boss would come back on Friday and go through with you to see if there is anything you want to have changed. I will go check and let you know." With that, Gunther left Bodo's office. He turned to Giesela, who had sat in the comfortable seating area with her notebook and was ready to take notes.

"Directive 001-1989, date of today. Effective immediately. I, commander of the Office for Investigation and Recovery, order that,

1. All cases concerning the involvement or the suspicion of the involvement of persons with the following listed positions are exclusively handled by the officers of the OIR Headquarters under the direct supervision of the CO-HQ, or the commander, comrade Zipper.

2. Any such person in functions or positions listed below has to be immediately separated from each of their peers and kept in solitary confinement.

3. No visitation from whatever person, which ranks or functions ever, is allowed without the approval exclusively of Commander Zipper.

4. If the holding capacity is exhausted, the COO, comrade Peter Wille or Commander has to decide on external detention in agreement with General SSP, comrade Jürgen Pieker.

5. Persons who are considered in this category are the following:

    a) First Secretary of Districts

    b) First Secretary of County

    c) Director General of Combined Production Corporations

    d) Director of Production Corporations

    e) Heads of Ministerial Departments

    f) Commanding Officers of the Armed Forces (rank of Major and above

    g) Commanding Officers of the Police or Customs (rank of Major and above)

"Any violation of this order causes immediate suspension, arrest, and indictment for treason with all consequences of the specific OIR law.

"Signed and the date and that would be it, Giesela."

"Comrade Zipper, how do you want me to circulate this? I could add it to each employee's instruction folder together with the instruction of operation you gave me earlier."

"That is actually a great idea. In addition to that, I want it to be sent to all members of the CC and add the distribution list to avoid mistakes. And declare it APO."

"Yes, comrade Zipper, I will have it done for your signature in a few minutes. May I ask whom that secrecy level APO actually includes? I know all levels, but I have never heard of this one."

"It is the 'Authorized Persons Only,' meaning the highest security clearance level. That is the security clearance level you and all members of the OIR received when you were assigned, background-checked, and sworn to an additional oath of office which you signed before you started. Everyone else signs the same starts to work for us."

Giesela walked to the office door to get out, the door opened, and Gunther entered, holding the door for her and closing it after Giesela. "Comrade Zipper, all the holding cells are in ready condition. They all have the furniture and a small sanitary corner with a toilet and sink. They smell after fresh paint and mortar, but I don't think that is an issue."

"You are right, Gunther. It doesn't matter how the holding cells smell. These people we must lock up there are enemies of the tremendous socialistic accomplishments. They have stolen from the people and demoralized builders of the workers' paradise on German soil and made it a joke. They don't even deserve a cell so comfortable. They should have to use an outhouse. But I am going ahead of myself. Many thanks, Gunther, that solves some issues." Gunther turned and walked out of the office.

As soon as the door was closed, Bodo hit the direct dial button for Jürgen and immediately had him on the phone, "Bodo, what can I do this time?" Jürgen asked.

"I just issued a directive ordering that a specific type of delinquent has to be handled exclusively here at the HQ. A copy is coming by courier within the hour to all members. We have the facility to handle them, and I would like you to transfer the two Frostock traitors to my HQ as soon as possible."

"Nulla problema, as they say, Bodo. I will send the order out immediately. I have to transport them separately, though. That would take a little preparation. But they can be at your place by tomorrow night."

"Great, Jürgen. Appreciated. And thanks for keeping them for the time. By the way, you sound much more relaxed than a few hours ago?"

"Yeah, you know, Bodo, I received the confirmation that we have finished our internal safety and security checks. We have just ninety-two suspects we have arrested and dug deeper into their past. I feared that the SSP was much worse after being misused for so many years by my predecessor. But it turned out that the lower officer ranks did an excellent job filtering who wanted to join and who did not. We will transfer the cases to you as soon as we dig deeper and find relations to external crimes. As long as it concerns internal issues, we will handle it in-house. Is that okay with you, Bodo?"

"Excellent, Jürgen. I really like it. That would keep the unnecessary load off of my organization, and we can really focus on treason and corruption."

"That's what I thought, Bodo. I will ensure you get your 'Spezies' tomorrow afternoon, and have a good night."

"You too, Jürgen."

Bodo hit the direct dial button for Bruno. Not sure he was even available, Bruno replied, "Hello, Bodo."

"Hello, Bruno, you seem to be in a good mood as Jürgen is, with whom I just talked before I called you."

"Yes, I am, and the reason is the same as he might have told you. As the control organization over the SSP, you know that my department was deeply involved in the investigation, using the same system as we did in the late seventies, talking about the exchange of documents. And it worked because none of the ninety-two suspects even thought that they might be caught, which ensured that there weren't any rumors going around to give others a chance to hide their crimes. There might be some cases with far-reaching treason and/or corruption included, but I guess you won't get ninety-plus cases from the SPP. My guess is about forty to fifty."

"That is really comforting, Bruno. Only forty to fifty additional cases. But we will see and treat every case with the same diligence. But that wasn't the reason I wanted to talk to you." And looking at the watch on the wall, Bodo realized it was already five forty-five, and he hadn't even called Sarina yet. So concentrating on his call with Bruno, he asked, "Do you think I could come over tonight for a while to talk with you? I am chewing an idea, and I need to throw it at you and see what you can come up with?"

"Nothing to ask for, Bodo. The wives have already decided that we will have dinner tonight at our place, and I am sure you won't interfere with that."

"Oh, I hope that gets me out of trouble. I haven't even called Sarina since I am back from Wittstock. She will rip me apart in the air."

"Don't worry too much. They have been busy shopping and decorating your house the last two days. They have been bosom buddies from the first second they met. I called her today for lunch because I knew they were in town, and Annabela just said she had no time to meet me and hung up. So don't worry. Sarina will probably say, ah, there you are. Nice that you're back because we're going to dinner at the Tecker's."

Bodo laughed and said, "Okay, see you tonight, Bruno." And hung up. He hit the intercom to call Gunther. At that moment, Giesela came in. She presented the directive for him to sign the copies for the CC members. He signed them, and when Gunther looked through the door, he told him they would leave in a few minutes. He told Giesela to call the courier to deliver the envelopes, and then she could get home.

Bodo placed the file folder into the safe, locked it, and walked to the car. Gunther was already in and had the engine running, and within seconds, they were on the short way to his home.

CHAPTER 11

The Next Friend of the Resistance Movement and Another Surprising Gift

Fritz was about two hours on the road when he stopped at the Autobahn Raststätte at the intersection with Highway 95. He needed fuel, and he wanted to try to get Robert to meet him there. Robert was not living far away. Because of his position at the Research and Development Center for Machine Tools, the most export-oriented manufacturing company with an export rate of more than 80 percent into the NSW, he had a fully functional phone connection in his apartment. After a few rings, Robert picked up the phone. "Robert Klein here, whom am I speaking to?"

"Hi, Robert, it's me. Can you meet me at the Autobahn Raststätte at Hwgh 95 south side, east direction?"

"Sure. When will you be there?"

"I just arrived. How long will you need?"

"I need about ten to fifteen minutes."

"Great, that means I don't need to take a nap," Fitz said, laughing.

"Not really. Only if you're getting old and need your rest, old man. See you in a bit."

Fritz went into the restaurant, studied the menu, and did not see much he would want to eat, so he just went with the travelers' traditional food in East Germany, a wiener with a roll. He sat at a table in the corner, having both doors to the parking lot in sight, and slowly ate his afternoon meal while looking around and trying to evaluate every guest.

Since he was past the Autobahn 4 Kreuz with Autobahn 9, which was a transit route from West Germany to West Berlin, he did not consider that there would any of the guests be an SSP in civil clothing, but he did check everyone anyway.

As projected, Robert arrived just about twelve minutes after their call. When he entered the restaurant, he went to the counter and bought a lemonade. Slowly he moved through the rows of tables, of whom most were occupied, which made it even more normal to come to the table where Fitz sat, and he seated himself. Taking a nip of the lemonade, which caused him to squinch his face, and said, "Hi, Fritz. It's a long time since we met. How are you, and how is your family?"

"Hi, Robert, good to see you. Yeah, it has been a long time. The kids are fine. The move to my in-law was actually something they appreciated. But my wife doesn't like to hang around in that small village where she grew up, and all the communist idiots are still there and asking stupid questions. So she avoids being in the village, and since we have a large garden, she has much to do there. And she enjoys it."

Robert looked around, repositioned himself to oversee the room, and said, "You seem to have changed plans. You said you would probably stay overnight in your letter, but now you are just passing through?"

"Yeah, change of plans. I have to be back in Berlin tomorrow. I have a gift for your group in my car. But I can't explain the operation here in the restaurant, and since I need to be at Bernd's before 6:00 PM tonight, I can't even go with you to your apartment. I know your wife would not let me go without eating dinner, and as much as I love to do so, it is just not possible this time. Can you contact Theo, and he can explain it to you?"

"Sure, Fritz. I have planned a meeting with Theo for next weekend anyway. He called me last week and said he had a big surprise. Didn't say a peep about what it could be, but it must be exceptional because of how he talked. We will meet in the area where we usually have our hiking tours, making it easier to do some stuff."

Fritz smiled and said, "I can confirm it is something special, but I cannot reveal what it is. Walls have ears, as you know."

"I get it, Fritz. Any general information about the situation? What about these Monday demos? I am avoiding them because they are a magnet for the SSP officers. And I can't really have a note in my files."

"You are doing the right thing. No, we have to stay away. We all have to stay away from these dreamers. They believe they can move the heart of the communist bastards that ruin our lives and don't understand that they don't have a heart. These are no humans. These are animals with human skin. Their heart is not from flesh but from stone. It won't take long, and these new members of the Central Committee will crush this movement with all their might. And it will be a bloodbath," Fritz said in a low voice but determined to ensure Robert understood the danger connected with the demonstration crowd for the resistance movement.

"I get it, Fritz," Robert answered. Fritz stood and walked out of the restaurant, and when he saw that Robert followed in the distance, he went straight to the restroom. He washed his hands and very slowly dried them while he listened to if there was anyone in the stalls. But there were all empty. After a few minutes, he entered the parking lot and saw Robert imitating a tire check. He walked over to Robert, and Robert opened the trunk. Both bent a little into it to cover themselves from potential onlookers. After looking around again, seeing nothing suspicious, Robert turned a little and sat on the back side of his Wartburg Kombi. Looking at Fritz, he explained the surprise he had for him.

"Several weeks ago, we received a delivery of long-awaited oscillation crystals from the COCO idiots. A total of eighty pieces. We needed only forty, but everyone was happy anyway because we thought we could use them for the following projects. To the great disappointment of my group, they had a completely wrong frequency. We needed 3.2MHz, and they sent us 32MHz quartz. I guess the idiot who had to organize them in the West thought 32MHz was better than 3.2MHz, right? It is more, for sure.

"But as you know, Fritz, we aren't developing radios. We are developing machine controllers based on programmable logic computers. Now, the boss knows I am a big fan of building copies of the famous Hammond Organs, and he asked me if I could use them. I immediately confirmed, not knowing what to do with this stuff at that moment. But I knew this was top quality, the best fabricated and ground for the US military. I got them for one hundred East Mark dedicated junk by the head of the department. Fritz, you know I am greedy, so I kept ten pieces for myself and packed the rest for you." Robert closed his explanation with a smirk and handed a small package to Fritz.

Fritz's mind had already started churning on the possibility of using the 32MHz crystals for a new generation of transceivers. He wasn't paying much attention to Robert handing him the crystals, so the small package almost dropped to the ground. He grabbed it a the last second and said, "Robert, this is fantastic. I am already thinking about a new development running through my mind. But I guess it is time to leave. We may already draw more attention than we need. Come with me to my car. I will give you the communicators and programmers and head out of here. Theo can explain all the ins and out of the system to you." They walked over to Fritz's car, which stood on the other side of the more or less filled parking lot, using this the same time as a way to scan the environment for anything suspicious.

Fritz handed the package with the two communicators and programmers to Robert, they said goodbye, and Fritz was on his way out of the parking lot, hitting the Autobahn in the east direction. Robert returned to his car, placed the package in it, and locked it. Then he walked back into the restaurant as if going into the restaurant room but turned right in front of it and went to the restroom. Any SSP tail he may have had would have been completely caught off guard by that and would have been revealed. But there was none. Robert finished his business, returned to his car, and drove home.

Curious about these things, what Fritz called communicator and programmer, he immediately went to his little craft corner. He unpacked the gifts, ignoring his wife's questions. Robert was amazed about the small dimensions of the transceiver, and his curiosity peaked even more to see how all of that worked. He packed it all back together, placed it in the cabinet, and went to the kitchen, where his wife was waiting with tons of questions and the delate lunch.

"No, my love, I could not convince him to come over for dinner. It would have been too much stress, as you know. He is in a hurry to see Bernd and must be back in Berlin tomorrow. He promised next time he would stay at our place.

In the meantime, Fritz had made it to the Autobahn Abzweig Nossen and turned toward Leipzig. This part of the Autobahn was much more frequented than the others because it connected the two industry molochs, Dresden and Leipzig. With the speed restrictions of 100 km/h for cars and 80 km/h for trucks, he needed almost two and a half hours to get to the exit for Taucha. Turning east and driving in the direction of Eilenburg, he arrived at the home of Bernd's parents just after 5:00 PM.

As always, Bernd's mom was delighted to see Fritz, whom she saw as a positive influence on her very often mood-driven son Bernd, the youngest of her children. Bernd's dad was a more grounded and taciturn man who had just a few months ago retired from hard work at the local sawmill. He considered Fritz a more accomplished man than his son. He lost no chance of pointing that out to Bernd whenever the opportunity occurred. This, in turn, made Bernd even more depressed to the point where he would just leave the room to avoid arguing with his parents.

Although Bernd suffered under the constant, even unuttered, reproach of not being as successful as his siblings, he loved his parents dearly. He had decided not to move out because he saw that it became increasingly difficult for them to handle the small farmstead. Bernd had told Fritz once that he had absolutely no ambitions to be "somebody," as his father always presented his siblings as an example he should follow. He hated that. His whole personality was that of a dreamer. That was one of the reasons why he spent every Pfennig and minute he could spare for his trips to Romania. There, in the mountains of the settlements of the formal German settlers, he found his rest.

"Man, Fritz, I am so happy to see you again. How long is it since you were here? Two years? I can't believe it."

"Yeah, Bernd, two years almost to the day. Great to see you are healthy and in a good mood. How is the job going? Any news from Romania? I heard that it is simmering there too. Do you think they can topple Ceausescu?"

"I am fine at work. You know, after all the years, I don't complain anymore. I have been promoted, which brought a decent increase in salary, and made my parents a little more proud of my accomplishments, which are actually nothing. I now have a team of engineers who I control writing down data in a logbook every hour, which is recorded by electronic systems anyway. Instead of controlling computers recording data by writing them down into a logbook, I now control engineers who control computers recording data by writing those data into a logbook. Seems an exciting job, right?"

"Bernd, you must understand, that this is necessary for a communist worker's paradise. Where would all these engineers, including you, be if the powers to be would consider economic laws of demand and supply?" Fritz responded ironically to Bernd's ironic explanation of his new job position.

At that moment, his mother called them to come to the dinner, and when they entered the eating area of the traditionally large kitchen, Fritz could smell the incredible smell of the excellent cooking skills of Bernd's mother, which was actually a very normal thing for that generation. Women of that generation had learned to cook when women were still considered honored to be mothers, raise well-behaving and respectful children, and manage the family's household.

Bernd's dad said with a considerable portion of pride in his voice, "I did butcher a duck for us for tonight to honor the visit of a friend and brother in Christ." Then he said the blessings over the food and thanked the Lord for the safe travel of Fritz.

They talked about the things concerning every East German citizen then, the demonstrations and the demonstrators, and speculated about the organizers.

"Do you think, Fritz, are the communist bastards in the Central Committee serious about cleaning up the corruption?" Bernd's dad asked. Using the word *bastards* brought him a disappointing look from Bernd's mom, "You should not use such words for these people. Somebody will hear it one day, and you will disappear," she said.

"I have a definite opinion on that issue with the sudden openness of the communist leaders of this country," Fritz answered, looking at the friends and Christians around the table. "I will try to explain it to you. I hope you can agree and avoid any activities these demonstrator organizers are initiating."

"So you believe they are actually undercover agents from the SSP to lure people into unlawful actions to get them arrested and thrown into jail?" Bernd asked.

"No, not at all. But to be more precise, some or maybe all of these organizations leading those demonstrations are infiltrated. That's a given, in my opinion. But that is not the real danger," Fritz said. Then he began to elaborate on his analysis of the situation since the takeover of the control of the SUP, and with that, the whole country by the younger generation of communists. Fritz pointed out that the elimination of the Politüro and the integration of the responsibilities of the different ministries of the government in the functional positions of the members of the Central Committee created practically an oligarchical control system that wholly followed the lines of Lenin's literature of a successful revolution. Then he repeated his analysis of the status he had given at Reinhard's house in the evening when the *Current Camera* news announced the arrest of two and the killing of another top leader of the SUP."

There was silence for several minutes at the table. Everyone was holding onto their thoughts, processing what Fritz had just explained. Finally, Bernd's mom said, "That doesn't look as great as what they try to indoctrinate the people with. But I believe Fritz has given us a good alternative to what they are saying, and we experienced throughout our life that there is a 100 percent difference between what they are saying and what they are doing."

"I am no prophet and have no insides into what is happening. All that I said is based on my observations and the education and training I received while I was on the path to becoming a top leader in the communist system. I know how they think, and I know that they have a general rule: Who is not with us is against us, and who is against us must be eliminated! These people don't know mercy!" Fitz said with definitiveness.

Again, there was silence in the room, and after a while, Bernd's dad finished dinner with a prayer, thanking the Lord for keeping them informed and guiding them on the right path.

Bernd and Fritz went downstairs to a workshop room that Bernd had built in the old basement. Fritz was surprised at the room's comfort, even though it was clearly an electronic workshop. "This is my little fiefdom," Bernd said after they sat down on two very comfortable chairs, and Fritz was wondering where he got those chairs from. Bernd opened a small refrigerator and took out two bottles of Radeberger Bier, a rarity in East Germany. Although produced in the town of Radeberg, because of its top quality, it was mainly exported for the dime on the dollar, in millions of bottles into the NSW for hard currency.

And as if Bernd had guessed Fritz's thoughts, he said, "I got those chairs from one of the compressor stations in my district. The company rerouted the pipeline when they renewed it and built a new compressor station a few kilometers north. As with all these compressor stations, it is built by an Austrian company that delivers the compressor turbines. They provide a turnkey operational compressor station; all my guys have to do is push the button. But you know, never did one of my engineers or I push a button to start a new station. It was always a big-wig event with TV and all the fat cats. And the last station they built, at least in my region, was a year ago."

Fritz nocked his head, knowing precisely what Bernd was talking about. He took a swig from his beer and said, "Okay, but that doesn't explain how you could confiscate the chairs for your kingdom down here?"

"Oh, that was easy. The most challenging part was to get 100 percent confirmation that they—meaning our company—were shutting down that compressor station. When I was sure it would happen on a particular day, I borrowed the Barkas from my brother GmbH drove there, and loaded up what I thought I could use. These chairs, some nice oscilloscopes, several digital multimeters, channel analyzers toolboxes, and the four of these nice chairs."

Two questions came up. Fritz said, "Why would nobody complain about the missing material? There was surely an inventory list, and where did you leave the two other chairs?"

Bernd laughed and answered, "Fritz, you sound now almost like an SSP officer. But it is easy to answer the first question. This specific station was the station where I started my job after graduation for the company at that time. Almost nine years ago, it was just opened. I worked there for nearly seven years, and when I was promoted to regional head of Services, the station was already considered to be replaced. The construction project for the new station had started. I knew every single nail in the wall at that station. Why has nobody complained about the missing parts and equipment? That's easy. Nobody knows about it. And the two additional chairs? Those were the payment for my brother for the Barkas."

Now, Fritz's curiosity was piqued. He could barely sit in his chair, "Come on, Bernd, nobody knows about the missing of all of that?" Waving his hand around the room, Fritz pointed out all the stuff Bernd had gotten from his former workplace.

"They can't. There is no way they will ever know other than by going back and digging a deep hole where the station once was," Bernd said, grinning from ear to ear.

"You are telling me they just filled that underground compressor station with dirt, and that was it?"

Now, Bernd got serious and said, "Here is how it is done. All the machines are removed. That usually happens weeks before the closing, meaning filling the whole. That is actually the term on the project plan as the last step. I was there two days before and cleaned out what I could and what I thought was useful for me.

"They prepped the whole underground facility with explosives and blow it down so that the cover plate falls onto the installation in one piece. That crashes everything in there. That cover plate is about 1.5 meters thick of reinforced concrete and covered by about 5 meters of soil. That is to make sure if the compressor or the turbine fails, you wouldn't even notice the explosion beside a little grumble. Then they fill the hole with dirt, cover it with topsoil, and the farmers come and use it as if nothing was ever there."

"I can't believe that is happening," Fritz said, almost speechless and searching for words. "They are wasting hundreds of thousands of hard currency, which they are always short of, and nobody seems to care?"

"Fritz, do you have a clue what my work is?" Bernd asked.

"Not really. I think you are ensuring that the compressor-turbine combination at the LNG compressor stations, pumping the LNG from the Soviet Union supplied through the pipelines in our country for the different manufacturing facilities and cities to get it."

"No, Fritz, that is an entirely different company you are talking about. My company manages and maintains the pipelines that deliver several different technical gases to West German customers. Such as nitrogen, helium, hydrogen, carbon dioxide—you name it, we deliver. That's the reason why we have the money to buy new compressor-turbine stations without even thinking twice. Suppose one of the corporations producing the gas, mainly the Leuna Werke in Buna and Schkopau, gets a supply contract secured for more than five years and the appropriate quantity per month. In that case, we build a pipeline and the necessary compressor stations because it is cheaper than train transport. The contract usually includes at least part of the compressor station costs paid by the customers. They want to make sure the compressor-turbine combination is of top quality. And our negotiators are pretty good."

Fritz was baffled. They had finished their beer in the meantime, and Fritz unpacked the two communicators and programmers he had brought for Bernd's group. He explained the programming, sending, and receiving process and handed him the list of books with their specific codes. He reminded him that these book codes needed to be memorized and the list to be burned.

At the end of the training session, where Bernd had programmed, transmitted, and received a complete message twice without mistakes, Fritz let out a deep sigh and said, "Okay, Bernd, you are now ready to receive and transmit encrypted messages for the movement and can communicate with everyone who knows the area where your communicators are positioned. To make those areas known in our movement by photographing that parking lot, resting place, or whatever it is, and sending it around with a sentence on the back. Something like here is where I had my car broken down and waited for three hours. Or if it is a park, here is where I warted for my girlfriend, and she never came. You get what I mean. And please, Bernd, memorize these books and the codes and burn the paper. That is the only weak point in our communication system. If the SSP gets their hands on the book list, they can use modern computer technology to decode our messages."

"I get it, Fritz. I know it is dangerous, but man, with this system, we can start to communicate safely, allowing our movement to coordinate and finally start actions. And I am all for small actions first until we are strong enough."

"Great, Bernd. Let's close her, and I am drained. Thanks for the beer. I always wonder how people get their hands on rarities like this."

"I have a whole box for you in the garage, and we will load you up before you leave tomorrow. By the way, what time do you want to leave?"

"Not later than 10:00 AM. I have a stop in Berlin and will drive home on Friday."

They walked upstairs, where Bernd and his siblings had their bedrooms, and Fritz was placed in one of them, which had been turned into a guest room some years ago. They wished each other good night, and Fritz was in bed quickly. And as his wife always wondered, he was asleep before the second leg was under the cover.

The following morning, Fritz woke up to the sound of a rooster announcing the new day with a loud crow. Fritz looked at his watch and wondered why the rooster waited until 8:00 AM to crow. He opened the window and enjoyed the fresh chilly air of the April morning. It had rained during the night, and the temperature had dropped, but it wasn't frigid. He went about his hygiene, clothing with a long sleeve shirt and a light sweater, packed all his stuff, and went downstairs with his luggage. When he entered the kitchen, he was overwhelmed by the scent of freshly brewed coffee and what smelled like fresh rolls and bread. He was warmly greeted by Bernd's mom, and his dad, with his nose in the newspaper, said hello without even looking up. For this, he received a disappointed "Would you please?" from her, but he was too long married to even react to it. He looked over the paper while Fritz took a seat, and with a smirk, he said, "Fritz is a man. He knows things." Fritz was happy that Bernd wasn't in at this moment because that would have led to another argument between them, and he did not want to be again in between both.

When Bernd appeared, he had taken care of the animals, they all started to eat, and there was a lively discussion about all the ins and out of the next few days, meaning Easter festivities, which were still somewhat a center point of the village where Bernd lived. He was highly active in church activities on such occasions.

When they were done, Bernd's mom and dad loaded all kinds of sausages, smoked meat, and other stuff into his car, all from their own butchering at the end of the last year. Long ago, Fritz learned that protests would only lead to more stuff loaded. Hence, he expressed his gratefulness, which was really from the bottom of his heart, because it helped the family dramatically save money. The supply situation in their village wasn't really good either.

That done, he said his goodbyes, got hugged by all of them, and was on his way.

He had decided to avoid the morning traffic around Leipzig and drove north, catching the 183 and the 107 in Bad Düben. From there, he was almost in no time in Coswig, where he hit the Autobahn direction north to Berlin. After about two hours, he reached the Berliner Ring, followed the Autobahn for about forty-five kilometers, and turned north at the Autobahn Keuz Schünefeld. Hitting the Treptower Schnellstrasse, he was soon in the center of Berlin-East. The traffic was horrible, and he had to stand at some traffic lights for three, sometimes for cycles, but after passing the center, he was on his way to the district of Pankow. At about 4:00 PM, he was at the gate of Manfred's home. He honked the horn and did not wonder that the gate opened automatically. Manfred stood at the house's entrance, pointed to the two-car garage where the door opened, and Fritz drove into it. He stopped the engine, and Manfred entered the garage from the house when he exited the car. He greeted Fritz with an excited hello and said, "Come in, Fritz. This house is yours as long as you are here."

CHAPTER 12

A Great Evening with New Friends and a Revelation That Was Not Expected

When Bodo entered his home, he was not greeted by Sarina nor saw her on the first floor. Curious about what was going on, after the notification that the two women had been busy for two days, he walked upstairs, and when he walked toward the half-closed door of the master's bedroom, he heard voices. He opened the ajar door completely, and there they were. Sarina and Annabela working at the huge panorama balcony doors, hanging curtains.

"Hello, ladies. Can I come in or wait downstairs until you are done?"

Sarina half turned, looking over her shoulder said, "Hi, love, great you are back. We have much more women's work to do, and you are just in the way. Since we were unsure when exactly you would be back, we decided to have dinner at Bruno and Annabela's tonight. Bruno is grilling some steaks for all of us. We come down when we are done."

"Okay, I have some stuff to prepare for tomorrow anyway," Bodo answered, somewhat astounded about the rather cool reception after being away for two days. On the other hand, he was satisfied that he could go into his office and prepare himself for the interviews he would have the following day. He walked downstairs and, looking out over the terrace, saw Nick playing with his ball. He walked out and called, "Hi, Nick, how are you, son?"

Nick looked up and came running toward him. Hugging Bodo, he said, "Great, you're back, Dad. Can I ride my bike over to Willi? I asked

Mom, but she said it might be dangerous, and you are not home. But there is nothing dangerous about riding my bike a few hundred meters down a cul de sac."

"I know," Bodo answered, "come in and let's call them if they even have time for you to get on their nerves. And as I just learned from Mom, comrade Tecker is grilling tonight for all of us. So it might be a good idea if you get there and keep Willi busy."

They went back into the house, and Bodo hit the home number button for Bruno on his office phone and, after a few rings, had Bruno on the line. "Bodo, what can I do for you? Did the girls eat you alive, or are they still busy?"

"Hi, Bruno, they are still busy. But I called because Nick asked if you could come over now to play with Willi, and he wanted to ride his bike to you, guys."

"Oh, sure. No problem. I believe Willi is already bored. I'll let him know, and he will get Nick at the gate. See you later."

"Okay, Nick, you can get your bike and get over to Willi. He is awaiting you at their gate."

"Super!" Nick yelled out with a loud cry and ran into the attached Garage, where he took his bike and was through the small gate in no time.

Bodo went back into his office and took out his OmniBook. Happy about the fact that Giesela had used the two days he was out to scan all the personal files of the SSP officers and investigators into computer files. She had loaded them onto his OmniBook when he returned from his trip. Now he could quickly go through them and read the different evaluations and reviews of their steps through life from kindergarten through school, the trade or college education, military service, and how they ended with the SSP academy. Reading through those reports, he wondered what his report would look like and if he could get his hands on that. Smiling, he thought for himself to ask Bruno tonight was curious about the face he would make.

The carrier of all six potential interrogators Jürgen had selected from his pool was terrific. All six had solved high-ranked cases of treason in support of illegal border crossing. By seeing this, he realized that his comrades at the Central Committee took his assignment seriously. The officers were all accomplished three-year veterans of the armed forces and some with special training. One had actually been a Kampfschwimmer (an underwater fighter) comparable to the NAVY SEALS. It would be interesting to know if he was at the facility at Black Lake.

He made some notes on each of the personal files, and he was just about to close when Sarina put her head through the door and asked how much time he would need to get ready.

"I just want to have a few minutes to refresh, and I am ready to go," Bodo said. Getting up from his desk, he walked to her, kissed her, and continued, "Are you girls done with the decoration, or do I have to get onto another business trip?"

Sarina laughed and said, "No need for that, even though we may have another two or three days for the house to finish. And then I might not be finished because I have so many more ideas, but that will be step by step."

"Great. I will be down in about ten to fifteen minutes."

"Oh, Bodo, don't hurry. Take your time. I'll walk over to Annabel's with her and Nick, and you can follow when you are done."

"Nick is already there. I asked Bruno if it would be okay, and he said indeed, so I sent Nick to play with Willi."

"Oh, okay. See you later then." And with that, Sarina and Annabel walked out the door and were gone. Bodo went upstairs and got undressed, and after a shower, he redressed more comfortably with just some pants. And a warmer sweater because he assumed it would get a little chilly later. Just when he was about to lock the house door, he heard the buzzer from the gate. He returned and hit the button to see a large truck in front of his gate. He checked his watch, and it was just a little after 6:00 PM, so he hit the intercom and asked who was there. The co-driver walked to the intercom and said, "I am Sergeant Miller from the headquarters, and we are here to pick up two cars. We bring one in exchange for one of them. And we have an order for the second car to be brought to the HQ Motorfleet Service station." By expressing that repair in a certain way, Bodo knew immediately what he meant. "Here is my ID." He held his SSP ID into the camera so that Bodo could clearly identify it was him. He hit the opener and walked out to the driveway to direct them to the garage.

The driver stopped at the gate and came out to investigate the property and to decide how best to drive up with the task of unloading and loading.

When Bodo reached him, he greeted Bodo respectfully and said, "Commander Zipper?" Stretching out his hand, which Bodo took and shook, he said, "Wanted to make sure I don't damage your lawn. I will turn around outside and back up into the driveway directly in front of the garage." He walked back to his truck, and the co-driver directed him to back up on the driveway to the garage.

They unloaded the Lada car using ramps hooked to the truck. They professionally drove the more extensive Volvo limousine onto it first, then the Lada, which would be tuned to the SSP follow and escape standard. It took about fifteen minutes, Bodo signed the paperwork, and they were back on the road. Bodo drove the Lada into the garage and used the remote in the car to close the garage door, testing its functionality simultaneously by starting the process and stopping it, then restarting the closing process again.

He finally closed the garage door for good and walked out of his property through the private gate. Walking down the road toward Bruno's home, he turned around and looked back. Again, his thoughts went to the unbelievable fact of how dramatically his life had changed within just a little over ten days. He was 100 percent convinced that his unwavering belief in the cause of the international victory of the communist revolution was the reason for this change. He would do whatever was necessary to make that happen, or at least put his part of the work to it.

He arrived at Bruno's house in just a few minutes' walk. He rang the bell, and the gates lock snared. Pushing the gate open, he walked through. He realized how close he really lived to a member of the Central Committee, the governing power of the nation. He walked toward the house on a small walkway that appeared to be lined by a lovely flower bed with roses and other flowers, which all were still in their winter status. The property seemed a little smaller, but that could be an optical illusion because the daylight was already gone, and twilight covered the house and lawn.

Reaching the house, the door opened, and Bruno was standing at the door with large barbecue tongs, smiling and saying, "You must have a seventh sense, Bodo. I just finished the steaks, and we were about to call you."

"Bruno, you won't believe it, but I just received the first fantastic car and lost another one for it."

"Why, that's excellent news. And that excuses you for being late. Just come in, sit down, and have fun with all of us. The others are all around the table and waiting to get started."

They walked into the large eating area, which was similar to Bodo's home, next to a large kitchen, but a little smaller. Everybody said hello and greeted Bodo as if he had been away for a month, and he sat down next to Sarina, where a place was kept for him. After the hellos and the excitement had faded away, he said, "Just for all to know, we now have a very nicely tuned car, and Sarina can drive wherever and whenever she wants." This caused another storm of yay and yahoos. Bruno used the time of the additional excitement to place a huge plate with grilled steaks in the center of the table. He added a plate with skinned potatoes and a big salad bowl.

They all chose one of the large juicy steaks, potatoes, and salad and placed it on their plates. All that was, again, accompanied by a lot of chatting and laughter because they crosse each other's paths and stuck their forks into the same piece of the meal. "Bruno, where did you get the idea to grill steaks, and where did you learn about barbecue? Bodo asked. "Isn't that an American tradition, not really German?"

"You won't believe it, Bodo, but I once worked at the Ministry of Foreign Affairs after graduating from the SUP Academy. The SUP Internal Control Commission (ICC) had hired me from the Academie as their executive at the Ministry. I guess that happened because one of the professors at the Academie was a former ICC executive and must have seen something in me. But the main reason was I always had a hunch for languages. I am fluent in Russian. That's a given. And English, Italian, and French are languages I can speak almost accentless and read and write in as if it is German."

"Wow, I had no idea. Did you learn that independently or go to school for that?" Bodo was amazed because he had always struggled with learning a language. He had often desperately tried to improve his proficiency in Russian because he wanted to read Lenin in the original language.

"Most of it. But when the school realized I had a talent for it, they organized me to participate in the international school for the diplomatic missions, which was just awesome."

"That's where you learned about barbecue?" Lisa, his daughter, asked with her mouthful of meat chewing and the juice running down her chin.

Bruno laughed and said, "No, my love, as I said, I worked for a while at the Ministry of Foreign Affairs. On the day, the department where I had my office was invited by the American Embassy to a celebration of Independence Day. Since not all in that department had foreign contact clearance, they needed to fill out the six invitations and ask me. Based on my position, I was considered a good addition but had no knowledge about state secrets, so I went. We arrived a little early, and the other guys were familiar with some Americans because of work contacts with their economy division. I was all by myself. Suddenly a tall guy approached me and asked if I ever grilled steaks. I said never, and he pulled me over to his barbecue stand, and the rest is history."

Bodo had just finished chewing the last bite, swallowed, and said, "Wow, that is quite a story, Bruno. I had no idea that you are such a multi-talent. But why did you take the position of the ICC instead of becoming the secretary of Foreign Affairs or Economy, which also controls the trade departments?"

Bruno had finished his steak, and when he looked over to Bodo and saw that he was finished too, he said, "Bodo, why don't we go over to my office and keep the work away from the women and the kids?"

Annabel exchanged a knowing and approving look with Bruno. He stood and walked to his office room, followed by Bodo closely. When Bodo entered the office, he was immediately blown away. They took a seat in the very comfortable chairs next to a small table. Bruno enjoyed the astonishment of Bodo looking around the room with all the solid wooden bookshelves and the hundreds of books. It was more like an old stylish British library than an office.

"Wow, Bruno, that is an excellent library. An office would be a horrible understatement for this room."

"Bodo, do you realize your office is even larger than this one? I am sure, if you check around, I wouldn't wonder if the former owner hadn't already arranged something to that point. I believe the existing furniture and shelving were just some high-level standard stuff he could import from the other side until he had time for a professional carpenter to make it more exclusive. I can give you the phone number of the GmbH, which did my office two years ago. You can get a very nice library set up in there," Bruno explained while getting up and walking over to a section of a built-in cabinet next to the window, which went from floor to ceiling, just like in Bodo's office. Bruno opened the cabinet, revealing a small but well-equipped house bar. He took out a bottle of Nordhäuser Doppelkorn and two glasses and returned. He placed the glasses on the small table and filled each with a good portion.

He took one of them, Bodo took the other one, and Bruno lifted his glass and said, "To a great and well-organized future of our great socialistic nation! A nation without corruption and no traitors alive!"

"I drink to that with all my heart!" Bodo said, and they touched their glasses and emptied them. Then Bodo continued their conversation from before when they left the dining area. "Why didn't you take the position of the Secretary for Economy? You have had the experience and maybe connections."

"You know, Bodo, I thought for a moment that I could, and maybe I should do it. But only for a moment. We had several meetings when Werner approached me about the movement to expel the Old Guard. All in deep secret because we knew we would be dead if they got the slightest idea that we were about to cook something. Jürgen and Frank were included in those meetings. We discussed how we could clean this mess of a nation, and the only solution was to remove the Old Guard and completely restructure the whole government. We decided early on to abolish the whole party structure and have just one decision-making caucus with a limited number of members.

"That was when the list of members of the Central Committee was created, and the different ministries were subordinated to those secretariates. Werner asked if I would take the secretary of Economy because of my stint in the Ministry of Foreign Affairs. I hesitated briefly and thought I would be better at taking the ICC. I explained it to Werner and the others, and they all understood. My stint in the MFA was much too short, and my experience inside the ICC was much more vulnerable to restructuring the party. And so far, it turned out to be the right decision."

"I am tempted to agree," said Bodo, laughing and pointing the finger at himself. "I am the best proof so far. Who knows if anyone else than Karl would have come up with the general idea of an OIR and then gone out and found the right leader within two days. And yes, I agree, you are doing an excellent job with the party membership renewal. By the way, Karl said you, guys, are almost done?"

"Yes, we are nearly at 92 percent of the verification of the members, and we are done with the SSP, and we should finish that within the next week or two. We have a lot of potential cases for your offices, and I can see you busy as a horse for the next several years."

"Do you have a rough estimate of how many potential cases of corruption and treason you have so far?" Bodo asked, not sure if he even wanted to know upfront.

"As you can imagine, Bodo, we have established several specialized workgroups in each district, and they are supervised by the regional assistants of my secretariate. We have scheduled a meeting with my regional assistants for Friday morning. Each has to give a brief report on the development so far. I should know more by the time after lunch. Maybe you want to come to my office, it's scheduled for 9:00 AM, and you can get a first count."

"Bruno, that's a great idea, but I have already scheduled a complete OIR meeting for Friday. I consider it a constitutional meeting since I will have all the selected members, meaning the whole team. We will have a day-long instruction to get to know each other and everything. But, Bruno, what do you think about sending Karl over, let's say at 2:00 PM, to present the work of ICC in general and the findings you have so far?"

"Great idea, Bodo. Let me organize that for you, and we will make it happen. As far as I have seen data, we have about seven FDS and their families, about nineteen FCS and family members where we have profound evidence that they are somehow involved in corruption activities, maybe even more. I have seen the names of CEOs and presidents of renowned corporations with direct or indirect export licenses. I can't tell how many indications I have seen or heard about COs and NCOs of the armed forces, the police, and not to forget the SSP. As I indicated before, you will be busy for years to come. You need to focus on the top traitors to eliminate them immediately. That is one of the reasons why I was surprised and happy when I saw your directive."

"I agree, Bruno. We can't tinker around the corners. That was my concern last week when Gerd Hollorek started to imply justice and court. Who knows what kind of legalistic shit he would have come up with to pretend these pigs, which have almost completely destroyed the people's trust in the communist cause and the party, that these traitors have any legal rights. That time is gone. I was relieved when you all agreed to eliminate him from the Central Committee because you would have trouble with each tough decision for years. What happens with him actually? Not that I need to know. I am just curious."

Bruno laughed a short and devilish-sounding laugh and said, "Just so you know, we will not publish all things that happen with traitors among the comrades. He is not more."

"What? Was he executed? Isn't that a little too much for having a disagreement? After all, he helped to get the Old Guard out and restructure the decision-making system to be more effective."

Now, Bruno laughed loudly, and after he caught his breath, he said, "No, Bodo, that's not how it happened. He was really a traitor, and we had no idea how deep he was in on it. He was caught with falsified documents trying to cross the border in Salzwedel. He thought his contact in the west would have given him an absolute save false passport.

"But he did not know right after we took over that Jürgen ordered the replacement of visas with new ones and that all confirmation stamps of the SSP pass control were replaced. So his Italian passport had an expired visa, and the confirmation stamp from the entrance border crossing in Bebra was almost six years old, even though he had scribbled the date from two days before.

"When the officers asked him to leave the car, he panicked and tried to break through the fortifications. The concrete walls on bearings and shot to close the street was much faster. He jumped out of the car and tried to run, but as you know from your service, we have the best marksmen at the border. He was dead before he hit the street. I actually think it was the best solution. The nice Volvo car was undamaged and is back in the motor pool."

"That's good news. Those cars are expensive. And we don't have a chance to arrange daily meetings between the atomic powers," Bodo commented and continued, "But you said it was best for him. What do you mean by that?"

"He was actually recruited by the Italian AISE about eight years ago. He delivered documents from our justice department, where he was a deputy to the minister. Mainly statistics and analytical documentation about the resistance. That gave the west names and potential points of contact. Very nasty what the comrades from SSP found when they raided his house. He wasn't married and had no relatives, which makes it a little easier. We will probably announce his dead next week. You know, about a long and severe illness and all that crap. But it's over, and we have a new start."

Bodo nodded in approval and said, "So the comrades at the Central Committee already have a replacement for him?"

"Not really, we have two or three potential candidates in mind and discussed a bit, but nothing has been decided yet," Bruno answered. "We don't want to hurry on that. It is not really necessary. Werner controls Justice as a second assignment at the moment. There are some experienced deputies, and he has little trouble there."

"I like that you have a replacement soon anyway," Bodo said, "because, at the moment, you have eight members. That might create stalemate situations when a vote needs to be made that may not convince all members in the same direction. That can lead to trying to coerce one of the members to vote differently, and I don't want to have a decision made based on coercion."

"Oh, Bodo, you entirely misunderstand your position. You are an extraordinary member of the Central Committee, and as such, you have voting rights. Now, we understand that you don't want to execute those voting rights when you present a case for a decision for capital punishment. But it is your decision to brake a stalemate if it comes to that or let the case go." Bruno explained the particular Bodo's situation concerning the CC.

"Wow, I did not see it this way," Bodo answered, and after a moment of consideration, he said, "I would rather not be in the situation because I might be biased, which can lead to conflicts of consciousness."

"I completely understand that, Bodo. That's why I put a lot of pressure on the members to come to a conclusion and vote on the matter. Since you were not aware of the matter, I will send you the profiles of the candidates and ask you to prepare yourself for a statement and vote on Monday."

"I appreciate that, Bruno. I will make sure I am ready. But there is something else I need your help with."

"You need my help? I have only half of the workforce of Karl right now. Isn't that enough help from me?" Bruno, grinning, asked.

"Yeah, I did not mean that, Bruno. I need you to help me find a chief operation officer for the southern office, which we named Regional Office South (ROS). I also thought about the situation at headquarters. I decided not to run the office because that would take too much attention from the overall control of the whole operation of the OIR. And loading that function on Peter Wille, my COO, would be unfair since he has to take care of the whole operational issues of the organization. So it makes sense to have a chief officer for each office. That means I need your help to find these two officers. I just don't know anyone from that area whom I could trust with having the right mindset and a great leadership personality."

Bruno thought for a moment, and slowly nodding, he said, "I believe I know someone who could be a good candidate. Do you remember that young man with me at dinner after last week's shooting training?"

"Was that really only a week ago? I can't believe it. It seems like some years ago. So many things happened in such a short time. It seems that can only happen in years. But yes, I remember him, relatively young, for being in your office as a regional assistant. So you need to get rid of him?' Bodo said, grinning back at Bruno.

"Oh no. Not at all. He is one of the coming stars in my department, and I see him growing in the position of Karl when I sometimes should decide to retire and get Karl into my position. No, he is a perfect choice for you because he has all the characteristics you need for that position. He young, yes, and he might need some close guidance for the next few years, but he is all you can ask for in that position."

"You would just let him go with no fight and discussion? Bodo asked with doubts in his voice, expecting some request for compensation, still suspecting the old attitude in leaders always acting like, "I give you this, what is in for me?"

"Bodo, you really need to get some trust into your brain that we are a new type of leaders. This old style is gone. We want the same as you, so you have been selected for that position. If it helps to get your organization operational asap, I give you Joachim without hesitation. I will find a replacement for him easier, then you can find another Joachim. That is a given."

"Thank you so much, Bruno. I really appreciate the support I get from all the members of the CC. Can you organize for him to come out to my office on Friday at noon? We will have the whole officers crew there, and I will take time to talk with him and see if he wants to be with the OIR and if he fits in."

"Sure, I will have him there on Friday. He can come over with Karl after they have presented their findings. The other thing about the CO for your headquarters I am not sure. I have to think about it."

Bodo looked at the grandfather clock, which gave the library office a very outstanding appearance, and said, "I think it is time to get going, and thank you so much for the great dinner and the conversation. It is very helpful to exchange thoughts with someone like-minded."

"I enjoyed it too, Bodo. Since we are close neighbors, we can do that at any given time. And be advised, I might come over to your place more often than you think because I appreciate your deep knowledge and conviction of the cause of our communist revolution, which many comrades have completely missed or forgotten."

They stood and walked out of Bruno's amazing library office. The women were in the living room talking about decorations they thought may be great for Bodo's and Sarina's new home and said they would call it a day. Sarina said goodbye to Annabel and walked to the stairs to call Nick. They all said their good nights, and the Teckers stood at the house door until the Zippers were out and the gate closed.

On the way to their home, just a few hundred yards down the street, Nick was talking like an overwound clock about their great time playing all kinds of dice games, which the Tecker children seem to have an uncountable number. After a short walk, they arrived at the place, and Bodo enjoyed testing both Sarina and Nick about the code for the electronic lock at the men's gate. Both had it immediately opened, and he ensured it locked back correctly when they were through.

Sarina brought Nick to bed, and Bodo was using the time to organize all the information for his interviews with the officer the next day by checking the profile files for each of them on his OmniBook. Again he marveled at the technology and was happy that he did not have to carry a ton of paper-printed binders around. When all was done, he leaned back in his chair and looked around the office. For the first time, he realized that his office was probably as large as his living room in the house on the Island.

Since the office had no blinding ceiling light mounted, but somewhat very comforting three small table lights connected to a three-circuit switch, the office was illuminated by soft light from the three different places, yet everything necessary was clearly visible. Bodo turned the desk light down and looked around the room, wondering how it would look if he got some wooden walnut shelves for his many books and some decent cabinets to replace the existing ones looking less impressive than what Bruno had. Deep in his imagination, he was startled by Sarina's voice, "Are you dreaming or sleeping already, my love?" She walked into the office to one of the very comfortable leather chairs next to one of the small tables and sat down.

"Actually, I am dreaming. I am so amazed by how Bruno's office looks that he noticed it and said that I have a larger room for my office, which could be an impressive combination library office too. So I am sitting here and imagining what it could look like."

"I saw it yesterday afternoon when Anabell and I returned from our first shopping tour. Yes, Bodo, that is a really nice environment to work in, especially when the work you have to do, is to deal with the scum of our nation, trying to destroy the socialistic achievements."

"Bruno said he would connect me with his cabinet maker, who understands his trade well, and see where I can get the wood I want. I thought first on walnut, but now, looking at the room with only a few lights, I believe cherrywood might be better. What do you think, Sarina?"

"Cherrywood it is. It is much better, looks warmer, and isn't too dark. With the gorgeous trees out there, you will have shad most of the day, and with walnut, you would feel too dark, even in bright daylight."

Yes, that's what I thought. Thanks for your advice, my dear. Let's call it a day, I have a tough day in front of me tomorrow, and I would like to be rested."

They left the office, closed the doors behind and walked, holding hands, upstairs and turned without even thinking about both at the same time toward Nick's room. They walked out and to their bedroom. Bodo silently opened the door to Nick's room, and both smiled at him lying in bed with his stuffed animal deep in sleep. After a short shower and cleaning their teeth, they went to bed and enjoyed each other in a way they had not done for a long time. After that, they were both asleep fast.

CHAPTER 13

Interviews, Decisions, and a Fleet of Cars, the New Headquarters Getting Busy

When Bodo woke up earlier than the clock was set as it was custom to him for a long time, he set it only as a security not to oversleep when he was too exhausted; Sarina was already out of the bedroom. After the morning hygiene, he entered the walk-in closet and chose a dark-blue suit and a red tie with deep blue stripes for the white shirt. Walking down the stairs, he could already smell the bacon and coffee.

Hugging his wife from behind, he kissed her on the neck and said, "That's a great way to wake up in the morning after a night like the last one."

She kissed him back, smiled, and said, "Sit down, dear. I have the breakfast ready in a few minutes."

"Sure, but first, I'll go for the newspaper," Bodo answered.

He walked out of the house and was surprised that the whole yard was wet and some little puddles were still on the walkway here and there. At the gate, he took the newspaper, opened the gate, and walked out into the street to see what the neighborhood looked like at 7:00 AM. It was quiet. It appeared as if all neighbors were already out for work. When he was about to turn around and work back into his place, a bus stopped at the corner with the Rehfeldtstrasse. Just then, the Tecker children ran out of their gate, waving at the bus, and entered after the bus driver had opened the door for them again.

Bodo walked into his yard, closed the small men's gate behind him, and returned to the house. He thought that this would be great for Nick to catch that bus in the morning instead of Sarina driving him to school every day. As it became a new ritual for them, they sat at the breakfast area table at the large floor-to-ceiling French terrace doors with an incredible river view. They enjoyed their breakfast, splitting the *New Germany* newspaper between them.

"Sarina, I just saw the Tecker children entering the bus for the school. I think it is a good way to get Nick there, too, instead of you driving him there every day?"

"Yeah, that sounds reasonable. If the Tecker kids can use the bus, it would also be secure for Nick. But we should drive him there the first day and talk with the teacher and principal. I know you have a lot of stuff right now going on, so I decided to drive over there later today. Annabel said she would introduce me to the teachers and principal because both boys will be in the same class."

"Super, my dear, I like your initiative in this since I am really buried in work today and tomorrow. I have noted that I will be available on Monday morning, and we can drive to the school together."

At that moment, the doorbell rang. The voice of Gunther was heard through the intercom from the gate, "Good morning, comrade Zipper, I am coming in." A few moments later, Bodo heard the gravel crunch under the tires of the car as Gunther turned around to be ready to drive out.

Bodo went to his office, grabbed his briefcase and a light trench coat—just in case it rained again, it was still April—and walked out to the car after he had kissed Sarina goodbye for the day. Entering the car, Bodo said, "Good morning, Gunther. Let's stop at the office and go straight to the academy."

"Good morning, comrade Zipper. Yes, first the office and then the academy." Driving out of the property, Bodo noticed the delay of the gate closing again and thought about reminding Jürgen of his promise to take care of that. Yet he thought differently after a second and memorized to tell Giesela to take care of it. It took them only a few minutes to get to the headquarters, and he told Gunther to stay around because they would go on soon.

When he entered his office, he noticed that all the plants were watered and some fresh flowers were on the side table at the wall. He placed his briefcase on the desk and sat down when Giesela knocked on the open door and said, "Good morning, comrade Zipper. I have a cup of freshly brewed coffee for you. Do you want it now?"

"That's great. Coffee all the time. Thanks, Giesela. And then I have some things for you to do."

"Yes, comrade." A few minutes later, she entered Bodo's office and placed the coffee before him. She sat down with a notebook and pencil in her hand and waited for his instructions.

Bodo looked up from his OmniBook and said, "First, I need you to call comrade Pieker and remind him of the gate-closing issue we discussed on Monday. Secondly, the second secretary should arrive with her household this afternoon. I want you to see if you could be there and ensure that everything is best for her to feel at home asap. Thirdly, check in with comrade Wille, who should arrive this afternoon too, and let him know that we are ready for him to start working yesterday." Bodo laughed at her shocked look and said, "He knows me too well to be surprised. Don't worry; he is an old Grumbler with a communist heart of gold."

Now, Giesela laughed and answered, "For a moment, I thought he was late to work and you would reprimand him before he even started."

"How is the preparation for the big meeting tomorrow going forward?" Bodo asked next.

"We are almost ready. I and awaiting some additional folding tables and chairs from the SSP centrale, and other than that, I think we are ready."

"Great to hear. We have to leave now. I hope to be back by about 2:00 or 3:00 PM and should be able to give you a list with all team officers by then."

Bodo grabbed his briefcase and walked out of the building, astounded that a crew of gardeners planted bushes and flowers to create a great-looking yard between the two buildings and along the driveway toward the entrance gate.

Gunther was at the car, and he asked him about the gardeners, and he said that he heard that comrade Renner had organized that. Shaking his head, Bodo entered the car and told Gunther to get them to the academy. They were on the road for about ten minutes when the mobile rang, and he picked up the handset to hear that it was Karl. "Hi, Karl, did your ears ring? I just talked about you.

Karl laughed and said, "No, Bodo, I just wanted to let you know that I have a potential place for the ROS. And since you somehow were lucky to talk Bruno into giving you Joachim, it might be best to plan a trip there on Monday or Tuesday and check it out. And on a side note, Joachim will be forever in your debt because he was yearning to get back south. He is definitely not made for Berlin and the Berliner's attitude."

"Monday is impossible, we have CC meetings on Mondays, and I am now officially required to participate. But Tuesday would be fine. Did Bruno tell you I want Joachim and you to attend our meeting at Headquarters on Friday?"

"Yes, and that is already arranged. I will bring Joachim with me when I come over to present the ICC and the result overview of our investigation to your team?"

"Okay, I will send all the information about the location and the property to your office. You can get familiar with it and let me know what you think. It is again a former military property, and Secretary Bode was extremely helpful in getting this one. Maybe you can tell him how much you appreciate his help on Monday. These guys are under extreme pressure right now and will help him stay focused."

"Thanks for that information, Karl. I will definitely do that. Do I see you later today for lunch, as indicated earlier?"

"No, I am sorry, Bodo, but there is too much on my desk right now. We are in the final stages of the renewal of the party documents. There are a lot of personal files I need to get through. Make sure nothing is missing before we turn them over to your office. I would love to sit down with you and chat. There has been a whirlwind of exciting things accomplished during the last ten days, and I love to be stressed out when it goes in a positive direction. So yeah, we will find some time soon."

"You are the man, Karl. When we have reached a steady state with the OIR, I invite you and Bruno to dinner at my house, and we will have a nice evening."

"I am looking forward to it, Bodo. Have a great day. See you soon." And Karl hung up.

Meanwhile, they were closing in on the SSP academy, and Gunther informed Bodo of that. A few minutes later, they reached the guarded gate.

They were stopped by a guard armed with the standard military rifle AK74, who walked toward the car's driver's side. A second guard professional kept a clear line of fire and stood at the guard house, holding his rifle at the low ready.

Bodo handed his ID to Gunther, who handed his and Bodo's IDs to the guard. The guard thanked and walked back to the guard house and, after a short time, returned, and while saluting, the gate opened, and Guther drove into the academy. Knowing his way around since he had graduated from the academy the year before, he drove straight to the commander's office building, stopping at a parking area for guests. Bodo got out of the car, and right at that moment, the main door of the building opened, and an officer came down the five staircases to greet Bodo. Although he had no uniform jacket, the red stripes on his trousers betrayed his rank as a general. He saluted Bodo, who, in turn, not wearing a uniform, just stood in attention. At the same time, the general greeted him, "Comrade Commander Zipper, I welcome you to the State Security Police Academy. It is an honor for the academy to have you as our guest today. The commanding officers wish you success selecting the candidates."

Bodo was surprised and felt a little insecure for a second. But he immediately remembered his status as an extraordinary member of the CC, took the honorable greeting with a friendly expression, and answered, "Thank you for the warm welcome, comrade General. Let's get to work."

With that, they both walked up the stairs and into the building, where several high-ranking officers stood at attention. Bodo was almost shocked about the honor they presented to him because he was conscious that he had an official rank of a reserve sergeant. But again, that was just for a second or even less. He had a completely different position now. He had to get used to this. After a brief attention posture and a thank you to the officers, the general led him down the hallway into a larger room which appeared to be a conference room and had been turned into a room for his interviews.

"Comrade Bodo, we have prepared everything here for you. This phone here is directly connected to the secretary ordered to serve you. Your candidates are ready when you are, and the secretary will send them in once you let her know."

"Thank you so much, comrade general. This is really great. I will contact you when I am ready for lunch, probably around one thirty.

"Of course, comrade Zipper, it will be an honor. We will inform the officers' mess about the time and are glad to have you as our guest." With that, the general saluted and left the room. Bodo arranged the desk for himself, placed the OmniBook, and started it up. He walked over to the small side table where some cups and a thermos with coffee were placed, filled himself a cup, and sat down behind the desk.

He hit the button on the intercom unit of the phone, and the secretary answered immediately, "Yes, Commander, you wish to get the first officer sent in?" Bodo confirmed, and a few minutes later, the first young officer entered the room, saluted, and waited for Bodo to address him. That was appreciated by Bodo, who considered it one of his tests with new subordinates. He read again through his file and stopped at the place where he had made some notes. Looking up at the officer, who still stood at attention, he said with a friendly voice, "Please sit down, Officer. I hope you're not too nervous, and I'll try to make it as short as possible. You grew up in a foster home?"

"Yes, comrade Commandant, I never knew my biological parents, and the foster home could not find parents to adopt me. They said I was a problematic kid. And to a certain degree, they were right from the point of view I have now. But that is past."

"What made you a problematic kid? Did you have any therapies?"

"I remember two or three times being at a doctor's office and getting asked all kinds of questions, which I did not answer because I did not know what to say. I knew whatever I would say would only upset them, so I decided to say nothing. I knew all the questions he asked. Within a few months, I had read all the books these people had studied for years."

"Wow, why did you read those books?" Bodo got curious. This guy was something different. He felt that this officer could be a star in his office.

That foster home had a vast library. I was told it was a former mansion, and the squire was a very well-educated man. While all the kids would run around in the large park, I would love to read. I read many classical books, and at nine, I was through with the Roman, Greek, and German heroic stories. I could debate the meaning of ancient literature for our time, and some teachers believed I was a genius. I read psychoanalysis books when I heard they would ask for a psychic. Some thought I needed to be in an asylum."

"How did you end up at the academy after being almost disposed of in an asylum?"

"When I graduated, I started a trade school as a librarian. I love books. In the army, I was assigned to the cartographic department of the division because they realized my photographic memory. And when my service time ended, the SSP interviewed me and said I could really serve the nation that made sure that I grew up in peace. I love this country, and the SUP is the best guarantee for the ideology of peace. I always wanted to serve where my abilities, which I understand now better, are exceptional and can produce the best results."

Bodo had listened with increasing attention, and his brain was already thinking through different scenarios where this office's special abilities could be the game changer.

"Comrade Mueller, I thank you for your time and willingness to join our team, and I assure you we can use your specialties. In your screening interview, you signed a Top-Security Agreement (TSA) with comrade Renner. You are bound by that, and I decided to ask you if you are still willing to join our office, you need to sign a special agreement in addition, which contains capital punishment without court trial in case of proven treason. Are you ready for that?"

"Yes, Commander, I am ready to serve, even with my life."

"Wellcome to the team, Officer Mueller. Get ready to be picked up tomorrow morning with the other members. You are dismissed."

Officer Mueller had just left the room when the secretary called and asked to send in the next one. Knowing he had many candidates to interview, he confirmed and thought to shorten the time with the officers. They were all prescreened and had signed the TSA. All he needed was to get that personal feeling that they would fit.

CHAPTER 14

The Genius and the Practitioner and the Development of a Long-Range Communication System for the Resistance

Fritz took the luggage and his briefcase out of the car and walked over to Manfred, standing at the door to the house. "Hey, genius, thanks for receiving me back into your gorgeous home. Do you have a broom closet where I could stay for two days?" Fritz greeted Manfred, laughing.

"Unfortunately, Fritz, you have to do with the guest room. The broom closet is already occupied," Manfred responded and joined Fritz in laughing while he gave him a friendly slap on the shoulder. Then he guided him through the mud room and the small hallway, passing the open living area to the opposite area of the house and into the guest bedroom. Manfred showed him the connected bathroom and everything he would need for hygiene. He told him he would be in the living area when Fritz had refreshed himself.

Fritz took the opportunity to shower quickly and replace the slightly sweated cloth. When he came out into the living area, which was open toward the kitchen cooking area building a combination of it that he barely remembered from the visit a few days ago since they had spent most of their time in the workshop in the basement, he found Manfred finishing a large portion of sandwiches. He had some lemonade ready for them both. Manfred placed the large plate of sandwiches in the middle of the breakfast bar and pointed to the chairs for Fritz to take a seat.

Seated across the breakfast bar, Manfred said a short prayer, thanking the Lord for the safe travel of Fritz and the food and the ability to work together on a solution for long-range communication. He looked up at Fritz and, pointing to the lemonade, said, "Sorry, but I have no alcoholic beverages in the house. I have been an alcoholic after my world collapsed, and only by the grace of God and the help of Reinhard was it possible for me to get away from the stuff that was about to kill me. I can't even stand the smell of beer anymore."

"Nothing to apologize for, Manfred. I drink only occasionally beer and hard liquor rarely. Lemonade is very welcome. I had a stepdad who was a drunkard and terrorized the family when he was drunk," Fritz answered, already a sandwich in his hand and smiling at Manfred. "Are you harassing the same butcher as Reinhard is doing? These cold cuts are delicious. I guess it has the same source."

Smiling back at Fritz, Manfred said, "You have to support your friends, right? Especially when they are considered an enemy of the state and are constantly attacked by the wimps of the SUP in the village because they are actually serving the people. Yeah, we usually try to go together, with one car, since it is still a decent distance and fuel has its price. I usually have two or sometimes three shopping lists from colleagues, but those are not long because the meat there is not cheap."

When they had finished the sandwiches and felt satisfied, they were ready to go to work. Manfred led the way down to his workshop in the basement and led Fritz directly to the large drawing table in the center of the room. "I have started to draw up some circuits based on your basic design and added some of my ideas. Look here, you see this component?" Manfred pointed to a symbol of a component that seemed to indicate a watch but with an antenna.

"I see," Fritz answered, "but I have no idea what that symbol means? It looks like a watch?"

"You almost got it. You can't know it because, until now, it is unknown to most of the engineers in the GDR. It is the symbol for a clock synchronizing receiver. It receives the time signal from a transmitter of the PTB Braunschweig of the Cäsium Atom Clock. It is a complete component with everything needed; you only need to connect the power supply and the antenna."

Fritz was totally at a loss for words for some seconds, then barely able to speak, he said, "Manfred, how do you know about it, and how would you get one of these if it is even unknown to most of the engineers in our country? And I must confess, I had no idea that something like that existed."

Manfred looked at Fritz for a moment, and Fritz could see that he was thinking hard about how he would answer Fritz's question. Then, taking in a deep breath, he said, "Some years ago, the team I worked with at the secret military laboratory that doesn't exist was questioned to develop a rocket-guiding system that could not be disturbed by the known systems, such as frequency blocking, or radar pulse deflecting staff and so on. We went through several different ideas and designs. One of them was to use the PTB's timer signal to control a specifically required synchronization. The idea was insufficient, and the three hundred receiver chips the COCO organization had smuggled in were obsolete. At that time, I was still at the top of my career and was the team leader for the frequency circuit calculation. After the decision to abandon the time synchronization idea, I asked if I could buy these chips. If I remember correctly, I paid about 50 GDR Mark, and here they are."

By saying that, Manfred opened a drawer in his cabinet. On top of the antistatic matt lay the chips, nicely lined up row by row and column by column. Still, in awe, Fritz was thinking a mile a second and realized that this was the solution to a nationwide unrestricted communication network. He turned toward Manfred and said, "If we can securely and with high precision synchronize the wakeup cycles of the communicators, we can build a nationwide communication network. It will be utterly undetectable because nobody actually needs to know where these transceivers are."

"You are correct, and that's what shot through my mind when you were here with Reinhard. The general idea is to have time-synchronized transceivers, which would wake up at precisely the same time because the clock generator would be corrected at any time they are awake. With that, we can build a network with a primary transceiver to collect all information from the connected transceivers, send the new message to those, and then send the received messages to the next main transceiver."

"Okay, Manfred, let's get the terminology right here before we get confused. Let us name them Master and Slave transceiver. And we need to program so that the latest message from each slave is recognized and the determined receiver of that message is identified. We could have the slave transceivers at any group leader's home or nearby. The master transceiver boosted in power for 100 km or more with the larger batteries."

"You are right, Fritz. And if we use the data compression sequence we had developed at that nonexisting military laboratory, nobody would ever know that a radio message was transmitted. The only issue might be the limited memory space for the program."

"Oh, wait a minute, that's no longer an issue. I have many EEPROMs in my luggage, which we can use for the program, allowing us to reallocate the most significant part of the internal RAM for the messages. We would need only a few kB for the wake-up program."

"Where did you get that stuff from?" Now it was on Manfred to be astounded. "We would love to have EEPROMs for our controllers instead of EPROMS to make out programs a little more secure from external IR-Light. We have many reclamations about erased software when people use light sources with high levels of IR near the controllers."

"I hear you," Fritz said, "I regularly suffered from that effect until we had all the welders understand to cover the controller windows before the weld in the control room. These are a gift from the tremendous socialistic, worldwide leading manufacturer of computer chips. I guess your company should be able to get some soon. The bad examples were sorted out for destruction, have fallen into my hands, and miraculously began functioning again," Fritz added with a smirk.

Manfred laughed until he had tears in his eyes, and finally catching his breath, he said, "I guess I have to convince my boss to hire you so that we can use your magic hands to repair the defective device we get shipped back every week."

Frith looked at Manfred, trying to make a very concerned face, and said, imitating the voice of the new secretary general, "We cannot afford to allow any activity that would benefit the class enemy."

Now both laughed and had to sit down to catch their breath. Then they focused back on developing the general design of the master and slave transceivers. After that was lined out, Manfred looked at the watch and said, "Fritz, I'd say we call it a day. It is already ten thirty. We can finalize the design and finetune tomorrow. Let's get to bed and start early tomorrow morning. What do you think?"

Fritz yawned and said, "You are right. I did not realize how late it already is. I am tired enough. We would only make mistakes in our calculations if we went ahead tonight."

They cleaned up what they had used on paper and threw what was not needed into a shredder, which Manfred had gotten from his nonexisting military laboratory employer and had kept; nobody ever asked him after his fall from grace. They walked upstairs, and after eating another sandwich, they were ready for bed. They wished each other good night. Fritz went to his guest bedroom, where he was again amazed by the comfortable arrangement of the bedroom and bath together. He cleaned up, brushed his teeth, and within a few minutes after laying down, he was sound asleep.

The following morning, he woke up to the sun shining through the window directly into his eyes. He went through his hygiene activities, closed light with pants and a shirt, and walked into the living-kitchen area where Manfred was already working on a decent breakfast with eggs, bacon, and toast. He said hello, which was answered with a friendly question if he had slept well, and soon they were sitting down, eating and drinking a delicious coffee. When Fritz asked where Manfred got coffee from, Manfred explained that one of the assemblers at his work was from Ethiopia.

Soon after he had started working there, he discovered that one of the issues with defective units was caused by an assembly mistake. He went to the factory floor, and after he got pointed to the guy who did that work, he discovered that it was an Ethiopian. He had been in an apprenticeship program for the communist revolution in Ethiopia, and after he finished, he stayed there. He earned little money but was happy not being back in that war-torn country. They started discussing the mistakes, and Manfred explained what he needed to do differently. While doing that, they ended up talking about coffee. Manfred told him he would like to taste it, which was the beginning of a semi-illegal trade. Manfred paid him a reasonable price for the excellent coffee. The guy could buy stuff unavailable in Ethiopia and send it home.

After breakfast, they went down to Manfred's fantastic electronic workshop. They fine-tuned the design for both the master and the slave transceiver. Actually, the only difference was that the master had a much higher transmission power and transmitted at a different frequency, which would guarantee a more significant distance. Programming the master with Manfred's data compression software; after all, he was a math genius and solved a mathematical theorem as a student, transmitting a midsized message measured in just a few microseconds.

When they were done with all the calculations and design and double-checked everything, it was about 11:00 AM, and they decided to have a short break. They walked upstairs, and since it had become a really nice and warmer April day, they decided to sit on his terrace while having a lemonade and talking about the general political situation and how far the new leadership would go to keep their newly gained power. Fritz explained his analysis of the situation and the potential consequences to Manfred as he had done with Reinhard and Bernd's family.

Manfred was impressed by Fritz's deep understanding and foresightedness and, standing finally, said, "Fritz, you should take over the movement's leadership. This movement needs a leader who can combine the potential force of all the groups and make it a fighting force with a chance to win. Right now, it is a loose bond of like-minded people who understand that this system needs to be erased. That communism must be wiped off of the face of the earth for mankind to have a chance to survive."

After a long moment of thinking, Fritz took a deep breath and answered, "Manfred, you are not the only one who told me that, and my answer was, I don't want to be that man. I am a former communist, and many in the movement would not trust me."

"I think you are entirely wrong, Fritz. Do you know how I learned that you have abounded the Communist Party and have become an outspoken Christian, criticizing the Communist Party wherever possible? You don't know? Reinhard did not tell you? Okay, I will tell you. After I gave my life to Christ and joined the movement, we had a Sunday service with our group and a guy from another group who happens to be an ordained pastor. I don't know what group, and I have no idea what he looks like because we take security as seriously as all groups in the movement.

"He told us about a guy who was the star of the communist youth organization in the northern region. He told us about this guy's steep career before him and that he threw it all away when confronted with God's word. He continued telling us that this guy did not just leave that evil satanic organization. He told them he was a disciple of Jesus Christ, his Lord and Savior, and he did that right there during a SUP party meeting. This guy said to all the members sitting there that they did not believe the lies they told the people themselves, and if they had a little brain functioning, they would follow him. And then he left the meeting."

Then the pastor placed two front pages of the newspaper "*Young World* on the table and asked everyone to look at them. One was from some years ago, showing you in an interview about your great success in forming youth brigades throughout the National Fishing Corporation with over 450 members.

"The second one was from a year ago. If I not would have known that the picture showed the same person, you, I would not have believed that the two articles were about the same person. This article was short of asking for your execution, and it had a statement from your brother included, who was interviewed for the article. He said that you are an unthankful piece of s——t, a traitor, and if it were for him, he would see that you get lined up and shot for the damage you have done to the cause."

Fritz was deeply moved by Manfred's explanation of the situation and how he learned about Fritz's fall. After a while, he said, "Manfred, you are the second person who told me that my confession to be a believer in Jesus Christ went through the underground movement like wildfire. I had no idea. I always believed that the fact is unknown to most, and I am mainly approached with suspicion."

Manfred thought for a moment, looked at Fritz, and said, "Fritz, I am now, more than ever, convinced that you are the guy who can unite and lead this underground movement. Let us finish the transceivers and build enough of them. Get them placed and call a central meeting. One of my uncles has his own group of almost forty members in Havelberg and has a restaurant with a cellar room large enough to meet with the leaders of all groups we can contact."

"Let us get the work done, get the systems out, and the friends know how to use them, and when that is done, we can look into organizing the meeting. Then, at the meeting, we will see what happens. There might be several potential leaders with more experience than I have, and I am more than happy if that is the case. If not, and the members vote unanimously that I should lead the movement, I will humbly accept that burden." With that statement, Fritz considered the discussion closed and indicated that fact by standing and walking toward the guest room without turning his head to Manfred and saying over his shoulder, "Wake me latest at 8:00 AM if I am not up. We have a lot of work, and I want to be on the road latest at 4:00 PM."

About thirty minutes later, he was sound asleep.

CHAPTER 15

An Interesting Lunch Experience the Arrival of the COO and the Arrival of the First Detainees

Bodo had just released the twelfth officer from his interview, making some notes in OmniBook at the officer's file when the intercom buzzed. The secretary said, "Comrade Commander Zipper, the comrade general asks if you would be ready for lunch now? The chef at the officer's mess has everything ready for lunch."

Bodo looked at his watch and was astounded that it was already past one thirty and answered, "Sure, I am ready. I will be out in a minute." He saved the files, locked the OmniBook, and left the office. The general talked with *another* officer in the hallway close to the exit. When Bodo closed in on them, he turned and addressed Bodo, "Comrade Commander Zipper, may I introduce to you, comrade Colonel Seiter. He teaches interrogation techniques and the philosophical rules behind the successful techniques."

Bodo extended his hand, and the colonel took it and shook with a firm handshake. "Great to meet you, comrade Colonel. We can definitely use some of your best students for the future challenges we have. I may even ask you, occasionally, to assist us if that is possible?"

The colonel laughed and said, "Sure, comrade Commander, if you have a hard nut to crack, I will see if what I teach the students here is working in praxis." Now, that all aught about the statement, and Bodo thought, if he could joke about himself, he might be the right guy if needed. They walked out of the building into a light mid-April sprinkle.

The general stopped at the top of the wide stairs and said, "Should we call for a car?"

Bodo answered immediately, "Comrade General, I don't think it is necessary, we are soldiers, and that means any weather is our friend. A little sprinkle won't dissolve us." They all laughed and moved on.

The officer's mess hall was only a few hundred yards across the large parking and parade ground. They were not even noticeably wet when they arrived at the mess hall entrance. Bodo was surprised by the elegant outfit of the officer's mess and the comfortable tables and chairs. Each table could sit comfortably six people. Bodo noticed that at the corner near the now-closed bar, two of those tables moved together, and several officers stood in groups, talking. After the general introduced Bodo, without mentioning his specific assignment, the officers, leading teachers at the Academy with many years of experience in the field as case officers, took place.

The waiters appeared immediately, serving lemonades and water, and the soup was served within a few minutes. The whole lunch was excellent, and Bodo asked the officer next to him if that was always the case. He confirmed and explained that the meals were the same for the personnel of the academy as well as for the students. It was a separate mess hall for the teaching officers, all ranked major and above. The main reason was to avoid any opportunity for fraternization between the teaching officers and students, and support staff at the academy.

Bodo agreed that that was needed. They talked about the nation's difficulties, their work, and the responsibility as teachers of the future members of the "Shield and Sword" of the party to ensure that the eternal power of the party is not broken. After a while, Bodo looked at his watch and saw that it was nearly two thirty, and when he looked at the general, he confirmed with a nod that he understood that it was time to end the lunch.

After Bodo bid the officers farewell, the general and Bodo returned to the administration building. The rain had stopped, but it had appreciably cooled down, and Bodo was glad when they entered the building. The general bid his farewell, excusing himself with a lot of preparation work for the next week's graduation ceremony. Bodo went to the conference room office to finish the interviews. It was almost

4:00 PM when he dismissed the last of the officers, and he felt it was worth every minute. Not only had he gained a great understanding of the personality of his future officers, but he had also chosen to eliminate two of the candidates from the pool because he was not sure they had a comprehensive understanding of the assignment they were about to accept. Both uttered remarks, such as "No problem, easy to do, will do with my left hand."

Bodo packed all his belongings. He said goodbye to the secretary helping him through the day, thanked her for her outstanding support, and walked to the parking area. To his relief, Gunther was at the car and was waiting for him. Gunther opened the door, Bodo went in, and they left.

While driving to the headquarters office, Bodo asked, "Gunther, how was your day? Were you able to meet with some officers you knew?"

"Yes, comrade Zipper, I met with some friends who stayed and accepted special supporting positions. One of them is actually the driver for the commanding general. Yeah, I had a good time."

"Glad to hear, Gunther. I felt bad about having you wait for a long time, and I am glad you could use it that way."

Then Bodo thought about transferring the two traitors from the north to the headquarters holding and that they would need a guard detail there. He picked up the phone and called Jürgen, who answered the phone. "Hello, Bodo. How was your day at the academy?"

"It was successful because I could confirm all but two candidates. The two I declined were a little too agitated to get their hands on the tools to, as they called it, squeeze the ball of the traitors. I have the impression they are more sadistic-oriented, not so much on getting out the truth by using specific methods. And don't get me wrong, Jürgen, I believe that we have to use those tools if necessary, not because we have fun to see them suffer, but because we need them to get to the truth."

"I agree, Bodo. Sometimes it is necessary, and we must have the guts to do it. Send me these two names, and I will interrogate them to see if we should release them from the SSP."

"Sure, will do. But there is something else I wanted to talk to you about. Since we will have the highest-ranking traitors at the OIR Headquarters facility, I thought about having a guard detail there for security. I wanted to ask you if you can arrange that. We have no accommodation there as we have at the RON, so I don't know how this practice can be handled, and I'll leave it to your organization. The only rule I would ask is that the squad on duty would be subordinated to the CO there."

Jürgen thought momentarily and answered, "I think it should be easy to handle this request via the barracks at Schönefeld. That is close enough to drive the officers back and forth to have a 24-7 security squad. I will arrange that now because they are scheduled to arrive tonight. I will call you soon and give you the name of the commanding sergeant."

"Thanks a lot, Jürgen, for helping on such short notice."

"No problem, Bodo. That's what we are here for. That's why we a called the Shield and Sword of the party." With that, he hung up, and Bodo placed the handle back.

They arrived at the headquarters at about 5:00 PM, and to Bodo's surprise, it was bubbling with activities of all sorts. The backside of the property was filled with cars, all types of Lada with different colors. And there were also 6 SUVs of the Soviet type Lada Niva. Bodo got out of the car and walked over to the parking area, and he wondered how they got them all there so fast. While he walked around the parking lot and looked at the cars, he recognized three cars with the same color and three colors, dark blue, dark red, and dark brown, and four in black, in total, thirteen cars. The six Lada Niva came in dark blue and dark red. With that, his OIR had three cars for each office area plus the cars for the COs of the offices and one for Peter as his COO.

He was startled out of his thought by his secretary Giesela, "Comrade Zipper, I saw you walking over here. I thought I needed to tell you that the documents and keys for all the cars are in your office."

"Hello, Giesela. Thank you for letting me know." And after a few more minutes of looking at the enormous fleet of cars, which was something really seldom to see in this nation of usual shortage of everything needed at any given time, he said, "Let's get back to the office, and you can update me on what happened during the day."

Bodo went into his office and took out the OmniBook of the briefcase, and copied the files of the officers he had interviewed to a 3.5-

inch floppy disk to be transferred to Giesela's computer. After a short time, she knocked at his door, although he had let it open, and he called her in.

"Giesela, I need you to take the files on this disk and transfer them to your computer. Ensure you have a personal file for each officer, but I marked the two as failed. I want you to keep track of each of them, and we have to hold them current at any given time."

"Yes, comrade Zipper. The IT team from the SSP has already installed the Personendaten software on my computer. With that, I can hold all files current and give you any information about each if needed."

"That is excellent, Giesela. So the cars were delivered. What else did happen while I was out?"

"Okay, where do I start. With the beginning, as best," Giesela said and smiled. "At about 10:00 AM, we received a call from the SSP prison in Rostock that the two requested criminals were on the way in two different transporters. They should arrive shortly after 5:00 PM." She looked at the clock on the wall, clapped her hand over her mouth, and said nervously, "Oh my, I had almost forgotten about that. I am sorry, comrade Zipper, but they can arrive any minute now."

"Don't worry, Giesela. They will arrive, and we are prepared. Please do me a favor and call comrade General Pieker and let him know that we need to have the security detail for this object now."

"Yes, comrade Zipper. I will do that now." Giesela left Bodo's office and closed the door behind her.

Bodo used the chance to test out his personal bathroom and refresh himself. As he came out, he heard the intercom speaker calling his name, and he hit the button to answer. Giesela was telling him that the two transporters from Rostock had just arrived and that a guy, Peter Wille, was at the gate. But the just-arrived security guard did not let him in because he had no credentials.

Bodo walked out of the office, and when he entered the front yard of the building, the two transporters had just stopped in front of the barn where Gunther had them directed. He talked with the transport officers and waved for Bodo to come over. Bodo walked over there and introduced himself, "I am Commander Zipper. I guess you have the two criminals from Rostock transferred?"

"Yes, Commander Zipper, here is the transport order you must sign for receiving the delinquents."

Bodo turned to Gunther and said, "Gunther, please go to the gate and get your future COO in the property. The new security guards don't know who he is and won't let him in. His name is Peter Wille, and he is my most trusted comrade and friend. So tried him accordingly." And while Gunther was already on his way to the gate, Bodo called after him' "Bring him over to the barn."

The transport officers walked to the back of the cars, and after removing the safety locks, they opened the doors. When the two delinquents were helped out from the cars by the officers inside the transporters, Peter arrived with Gunther, both in an excited discussion about something. Bodo was astounded because it appeared the two knew each other, but he focused on the two traitors, which would be their primary focus for the next several weeks. He went ahead and signed the paperwork for the reception of the two traitors.

Turning to Peter, he said, "Peter, welcome to your new place of action, and it is great that you made it over here when our old friend arrived. We can talk about everything later in the office."

Peter approached Bodo, gave him a big bear hug, and said, "I am so happy to see this piece of shit with human skin in chains. I could forget the twenty years of agony I experienced under his corrupt leadership." And in confirming his statement, he spits at the shoes of the former FCS of the island.

Bodo looked at both of them, and all he saw in their eyes was distastefulness. He had to use his strength to avoid exploding into their face. He restrained himself, saying, "You two may still have the idea that this is all a mistake, and your friends will come over and reprimand me, set your free, and you can go ahead and wreck the party and me entirely. But you are deadly mistaken if you think that would happen. This is the end of you. We will spend the following days and weeks finding all your hidden treasures, and then you will be toast."

He turned to Gunther and said, "Comrade Gunther, show the officers where the hotel rooms are for these. How did you call them Peter? Uh, yes, pieces of shit are where they will enjoy our company for the next foreseeable future."

Bodo grabbed Peter's arm and, turning around, said, "Let's go to the office and get you a nice cup of coffee before I have to vomit when I see these POS any longer today."

When they entered the office building, Giesela stood at the entrance to her office and asked, "Commander Zipper, would you like me to serve a cup of coffee for you and your guest?"

Bodo used the opportunity to introduce Peter with the words, "Giesela, this is comrade Peter Wille. He is the COO of the organization, and his job is to keep this organization always running at 110 percent. You must work together like a well-oiled machine to make that happen. I trust your ability to do so as my senior secretary, and now, please bring us some coffee."

Entering Bodo's office, Bodo directed Peter to the small coffee table with a comfortable double-seater and two chairs and said, "Peter, sit down and get a little rest. You must be tired of getting moved here today and now coming over here immediately."

Peter smiled, looked at Bodo, then around the office, and finally said, "Yeah, I am a little tired. But you know, I am all alone, and there is not much to move. All it took was one of those large moving trucks. When I arrived here, the movers had already moved most of my stuff into the apartment, so I walked through the rooms. When I saw the telephone on the floor in the room, I was thinking about what I would place where I would make my living room. I picked it up, and since I still had the number of that Karl, the guy who moved me, I called him. He was pleased I had arrived and friendly asked if I had any complaints. I told him to the contrary and asked if he could give me the office's address, which he did. And here I am."

Bodo laughed and said, "I know you are a workhorse, and I can trust you with my life. And that might not be just a saying. I am glad you joined us and took my offer to run the organizational issues because I know you are the best. I could think of doing that exactly as I would like."

Peter was listening to Bodo's praises with a smile and then, getting severe, answered, "Bodo, we have known each other for many years. I remember your reaction when the SSP told you that your brother betrayed the party and you could not go to the academy. I remember your angry outburst in my office when you read the *Young World* article about the show he staged at the party meeting. I knew him, watched him climb the party hierarchy ladder, and saw him as a potential top leader. And I mean really the top of the top. And I was shocked by his betrayal."

There was a knock on the door. After Bodo's call to come in, Giesela opened the door and balanced a tablet with freshly brewed coffee and some sandwiches, and placed it on the small table they were sitting at.

"I thought comrade Wille might be hungry and made sandwiches," Giesela explained.

"This is an excellent idea. Thank you so much, Giesela," Bodo answered. While filling the cups with the coffee from the can, he told her, "Please tell Gunther to come to the office when he is done with the detainees."

"Yes, comrade Zipper, but I think I will give comrade Wille a few more minutes to eat some before I send him in."

"That's okay, Giesela. Thanks for your care."

After he had taken a sip of the coffee, Giesela left the room. Bodo asked Peter, "Peter, you have to tell me how you know Gunther so well that you both were immediately conversing as if you have been friends for years?"

Shewing on the bite he had just taken from his sandwich, swallowing it down, he used the time to formulate his thoughts. Then he answered, "You remember that assignment I had several years ago to be present at the paratrooper barracks to look into the background of that incident with the general getting physically attacked by his son? Although the military has its own party organization, since he was a member of the local party group, we thought it would be good to understand what was going on there."

Bodo set down his cup and said, "Oh, yes, I remember very well. It was discussed at several meetings at the office in Bergen. But I can't remember what came out of it or the details." And seeing that Peter had just taken another bit from his sandwich, he continued, "Please, Peter, eat your sandwiches, and I'm sorry that I interrupted you with my stupid question."

They sat for a while, Bodo drinking his coffee and Peter eating the last sandwich and drinking some coffee in between. When Peter had finished, he took a napkin, cleaned his lips, and said, "Wow, Bodo, I guess I have to come into the office hungry every day. These sandwiches are just too good. But back to your question."

"I was integrated into the paratrooper's officer corps for about four weeks and interviewed them all. I needed to get around since they were often at different places for training sessions with their troops. The general—who, by the way, was completely cleared of all suspicions—lent me his jeep with his driver. That was Gunther at that time. So we spent many hours together, and he was a good source of background information."

"So the general had no issues with you investigating him in his own command area?"

"No, it turned out that he has not just the total trust of his officer. They admire him. I spoke with several of them, who said they would blindly follow his orders. They said they had absolute trust in the total devotion to the cause of the international communist agenda. They would not question his judgment if he ordered them to attack the enemy, no matter whom he defined as the enemy. During all that time, Gunther drove me around, and we built some kind of connection. When I was done with the investigation, we agreed to stay in touch, but somehow when he ended his service, we lost contact. So I was gladly surprised when I saw him walking toward the gate to get me in."

Bodo was thinking about the travel to the island with Gunther as his driver and realized Peter had never seen him. He said, "You know, as strange as it sounds, but Gunther was driving me around when I was moving off the island, and yet, you never saw him."

At that moment, there was a knock on the door, and after Bodo called, "Come in," Gunther entered the office.

"Gunther, since you have known comrade Wille for a long time, I need to remind you that we have rules," Bodo addressed Gunther in a more official tune. "How you two communicate in private is not of my concern, but I have to ensure that the official interaction is accordingly to the position of comrade Wille as your superior. As the Office of Investigation and Recovery's COO, he will be in charge of the day-to-day activities and his orders as if they come directly from me. Is that understood?"

"Yes, comrade Zipper."

"Now, I want you to go out with comrade Wille and have him choose one of the black Ladas for his personal car, get it cleaned as if it were mine, and ensure he has all the paperwork at Giesela's office."

Bodo turned to Peter and said, "Peter, be sure you choose the best black one because you will be stuck with it for a while."

With a smile, Peter answered, already standing up and walking toward the door, "I have never had something like a personal car, so anything called a car is an improvement. But I will take your word seriously and check them out. Maybe there is one where our Soviet brothers forgot to put an engine in?" Laughing, he clapped Gunther on the shoulder, and they both left the office.

Bodo needed a few seconds to process the defeatist sentence he had just heard from Peter. A small doubt entered his mind for a few seconds. Did he make a mistake? Did his eternal gratefulness for Peter pull him out of a depressed status cloud his discernment? No, that could not be. Peter was as solid as he himself was. It must be a kind of momentary form of cynicism because of the situation the Communist Party and the nation were in.

Shaking off those dark thoughts, he looked at the clock and realized that it was already almost six PM again. He wondered if this would become a regularity, being late at the office. He hit the intercom button for Giesela and was not really surprised when she answered, "What can I do for you, comrade Zipper?"

"I was hoping you were still here, but I don't want you to always be as late in the office. You have family that needs you too. But can you come over for a few minutes so we can go through the day's event tomorrow?"

"I will be right there."

When Giesela entered the office, she was accompanied by Peter with a big smile about the great car he had now at his disposal any time. They both sat in front of his desk. Bodo started the list of what was going on the next day. I know it gets a little stressful, but I need you both to arrive at 8:00 AM. We have a massive agenda for tomorrow, and it will be a long day.

The officers should arrive at 9:00 AM and be instructed to sign the additional oath. The officers have been assigned me during the interviews at which office they will work. They must team up two by two, and the cars must be assigned. Headquarters members must choose the offices and prepare to start work. The officers for the RON will participate in the general meeting. They will drive there after the end, using the cars for the office. The officers assigned to the ROS need to be advised to share the headquarters offices until the office facility for the ROS section is ready, probably at the end of next week. I will drive down there with the new CO, Joachim Lehmann, on Tuesday, and according to Karl, they should have all the restructuration on the building done by the end of the week.

"Giesela, I guess that the cafeteria area in the Barn—I think we will just stay with that name for the building until something better comes up—is already arranged for the meeting tomorrow?"

"Yes, comrade Zipper. I wanted to show you when you came back, but it wasn't possible because so many things happened at that time at once."

"That's okay, Giesela. At 2:00 PM, comrade Karl Renner will be here to present the completed investigation and the potential cases, meaning the OIR has to investigate starting Monday. Uh, and I had almost forgotten, I have the officer in charge from Neubrandenburg here at 10:00 AM. Peter, that means you need to take over from there, which I believe is good because they should realize ASAP that you are in charge and I am not the to-go guy for anything. And since it is Friday, and the RON officers have a long drive and need to get situated there, we will try to close out at 3:00 PM. I believe that's it for today. Anything to add, Peter, Giesela?"

Both looked at each other then back to Bodo and shook their heads.

"Okay, then, let's close the day, and I'll see you both and all the others tomorrow at 8:00 AM. One last thing, Giesela, could you look at Maria Hafler? She should have arrived today and may not know how to contact us yet, and I had no free time to look after her."

"Yes, comrade Zipper, I will definitely do that since Karl said she would move into the empty apartment in the same house I am living in."

When Peter and Giesela said goodbye and were about to leave the office, Gunther walked in. He said the car for comrade Wille was ready to roll. He handed him the keys, and Peter said, "Giesela, aren't you living in the same building where I just moved in?"

"Yes, comrade Wille, that is correct. Looking back at Bodo, she explained, "Karl tried to get us all as close together as possible. I know some two-room units were empty in my block, but how he did that to get them in there is a miracle."

"Great," Peter answered, "that means we can drive together home and tomorrow to the office without waiting for the bus and having a side-seeing tour trip before we arrive here."

Bodo laughed and said, "Okay, comrades, get out here so I can get home."

Bodo placed all the documents in his safe and closed and secured them. He grabbed his briefcase with the small OmniBook computer and left the office. He saw the backlights of Peter's car disappearing through the gate where the security guard was closing it after him and looked for Gunther. He did not see him in the yard, so he walked over to the barn and opened the door to the completed cafeteria. He was positively impressed by how much it had changed and how inviting the room looked. The tables were all lined up in five rows, with enough chairs placed for the whole team.

A kind of kitchen was built at the end of the room, and the light there went just out when he entered. Gunther exited the kitchen and, seeing Bodo, he said, "Comrade Zipper, I was just double-checking that everything was in order."

"That is very mindful of you, Gunther. Let us have a last look at the detainees for today, and then I need to get home."

They crossed the small hallway separating the holding area from the cafeteria. Bodo was surprised to see the same security board he had in his home at the wall next to the door without a door handle. He pushed the button and said, "This is Commander Zipper. Please open." He noticed a snapping noise, and the door sprang open just a gap.

Bodo grabbed the door rim and opened it, and both walked through. The officer closed the door behind Bodo and Gunther and saluted Bodo, "Commander Zipper, I report four officers on duty inside and five outside. I am Sergeant Heller, and commanding the night shift detail. Thank you, Sergeant." The not-so-small room was equipped with comfortable furniture to comfort the SSP security guard when they were off duty.

"How are our guests? Any complaints?"

"Yes, commander. They tried to argue with the officers who brought them the dinner several times. When those did not respond, as they were all instructed, they started to thread them with all kinds of consequences, including execution. So I went in and had to rough them a little bit. I was told by my lieutenant that I was allowed to silence them if things like that would happen."

Bodo could not hinder from laughing loudly and said, "Okay, Sergeant Heller, let us go in and look at their injuries." Emphasizing the word in a mockery version. They walked into the holding area with the secured eight holding cells on each side and the special interrogation room at the end of the barn. The sergeant hit a button next to the door, which led into the holding area. The face of an officer appeared at the small window in the door. After recognizing his commanding sergeant, he opened the door. The sergeant introduced the commander to the officer. After a brief salute, the officer explained that the detainees were quiet.

Bodo walked to the first cell on the left side, where he was told the former first district secretary was. A small door was closing the window, and Bodo asked the officer to open it. Looking in the cell, he saw the FDS lying on the bed, and when he recognized that Bodo was looking at him, he sprang up and walked to the door. Bodo could not hear what he was saying and was satisfied that the noise reduction was that good.

"Can we communicate with the detainees without opening the door?"

"Yes, commander," he answered, pointing to a small device in the wall beside the door.

Bodo pressed the button and immediately could hear the agitated voice of the former FDS. "Bodo, I know you ordered my arrest, and I have no idea why the SSP would even follow that, but the consequences for you and whoever is supporting this insanity are severe. You have only one chance to survive this and get away with some years in prison. Let out now!" Bodo thought for a second and then answered with the coldness of ice in his voice, which came directly from his heart that changed in a heartbeat from flesh to stone just by listening to him.

"You are one of many who will pay the price for their betrayal of the Communist Party. You and that other piece of shit in the cell across the floor are my number one case until II see you both in front of a firing squad. We will interrogate you until we have all the information about where you are hiding the stolen money and with whom you conspired."

The FDS spat on the floor and said, "Never! I won't tell you anything. You are the traitor. If comrade Haecker would know what the new leadership is doing, you would all be toast by tomorrow."

Bodo laughed and said, "Keep dreaming, traitor. We will see how far your bravery goes." Bodo hit the button on the wall again, shutting off the intercom, and closed the door over the window. He turned around and walked out of the holding area, the sergeant and Gunther following. In the guard room, he said, "I guess you have visual at the cells too?"

"Yes, commander Zipper. Over here." He pointed to a desk where a set of monitors showed the inside of the cells and the holding area outside of the cells. The technical department of the SSP had really not spared anything to make his operation as successful as possible. Bodo was delighted and now fully convinced that he would succeed with his operation as he thought and needed to save the party's power.

He said goodbye to the sergeant and thanked him, and turning to Gunther, he said, "Gunther, drive me home. I am done for today."

"Yes, Commander," was the straight answer, and within minutes they were on their short way.

At his home, he told Gunther to be at his place a quarter to eight the following morning. He left the car and watched Gunther driving out. He registered that the gate closed much faster than before, and the waiting time was also reduced. He had completely forgotten to ask Giesela if she had called Jürgen about it.

Turning around, he found Sarina standing atop the stairs, smiling and waiting for him to approach her. He hugged her, remaining slightly longer than usual, and said, "I am done today. It was a loaden day with all kinds of things, and it really drained me. I think I will have some shorter days when we have finished this week and get the ROS next week."

Sarina, extending her arms and holding him at arm's length, said, "You look tired, Bodo. I can see that the last two weeks have taken a toll on you. Maybe after next week, you can take some days off?"

Bodo laid his arm around her. Walking together into the house, he said, "Maybe not immediately after next week, but soon." He placed his briefcase on the desk in his office, took Sarina's hand, and went upstairs together. After briefly looking into Nick's room, deep in his dreams, they went to their bedroom.

Bodo went through his hygiene routine and closed with a wormer set of nightwear and a bathrobe. He walked out into the bedroom, and to his surprise, Sarina had fired up the fireplace. The smell of burning wood and the flames flickering made him relaxed. He went over to the chairs in front of the fireplace, and just as he was about to sit down, Sarina came in with a bottle of wine and two glasses. He went to the door and closed it behind her.

After he had opened the bottle and filled the glasses for them, he sat down, and both sighted simultaneously. They laughed and clung to the glasses, and Sarina said, "To your great day tomorrow and a good start to the operation." They said for a while, enjoying the warmth from the fireplace and exchanging their thoughts about the unbelievable changes and gorgeous house they called their own. Then Bodo reminded her of his demanding workday tomorrow, they went to bed, and Bodo was soon in a deep, dreamless sleep.

CHAPTER 16

The Constitution of the Team of the Office of Investigation and Recovery and a Not-so-big Surprise for Bodo

Bodo woke up to the rattle of the bell of the alarm clock, and it took him a few seconds to get it shut off. He was relieved to see that Sarina was already up and he had not rattled her out of sleep. Bodo hated it when that happened. She wasn't working, and he wasn't sure she ever should again. For that, she did not need to be ripped out of her sleep at 6:30 AM by that ugly tune of that old-fashioned bell.

He went into the bathroom. When he was done, he decided to wear a suit with a tie today because it was a special day, and he wanted to show that with his appearance. When satisfied with the serious look he presented to his floor-to-ceiling mirror, he walked downstairs, where Sarina was already finishing breakfast for them. He kissed her good morning and went to the gate to see if the newspaper was already there. It was, and he thought I needed to ask why the critical information for comrades was never delivered before 10:00 AM at his former places wherever he lived.

Coming back inside, Sarina had the breakfast table ready, and coffee was filled in his cup. All he needed was to sit down and enjoy breakfast with her. Reading and slurping coffee and eating the eggs, today boiled as he noticed with a smile, no bacon. They talked about the demonstrations as a never-ending interruption of normal socialistic society's life because there was an article that several so-called Christian organizations had announced to remain with the peace demonstrations.

Bodo set down the cup hard, and Sarina feared it would break by pouring the coffee all over his trousers. Bodo swallowed the bite of toast and said, "What do they call for a peace demonstration? Do we have war in the country? We have mercy and let them destroy the minds of children and youth, and they are attacking us as if we have war? Are these dumb Christians totally out of their mind? They can have war. If they really mean there is a need for peace demonstrations, we must give them a reason, right?"

Surprised by his angry outbreak, Sarina looked at him. She said, "Bodo, you have all the power to go after these seditious people. Have you not?"

Bodo took another sip of the coffee and answered briefly, leaning back in his chair, "Actually, you just got me an idea. The nasty agreement the party leadership under the old guard made in 1978 was the greatest mistake. And these people think we will back down? They're mistaken. I can tell you that."

They finished breakfast, talking about the day's events Bodo had in front of him, and he promised that the weekend would be for the family. Just at the moment when Nick walked down the stairs half asleep still and barefoot, the intercom came to life, and Gunther was announcing his arrival. Bodo turned toward Nick, scooped him up from the floor, and hugged him. "Good morning, son. It looks like you slept very well."

"Yes, Dad, I missed you yesterday night. Mama said you would come in and say good night, but I can't remember that you did."

"I am sorry, Nick. I came home late, and you were already asleep when I came to your room. And it appears right now that this will be the same tonight. But as I just promised Mom, we will spend the whole weekend together, and Mom and I will bring you to your school on Monday. How does that sound?"

"That sounds awesome, Dad, and I hope you can keep that promise. I know. With your new job, we sometimes must accept that you have no time for us. Mom explained that to me yesterday. I just hope the new job does not require this situation for too long." He jumped off Bodo's lap and ran to Sarina, where he claimed onto her lap and started looking at the rest of her breakfast, stating that he was hungry.

Bodo kissed Sarina goodbye, walked to his office, grabbed his briefcase, and was out the door. At the back passenger door, Gunther greeted him friendly, "Good morning, comrade Zipper. I hope you had a restful sleep." Bodo entered the car, and while Gunther started, he answered, saying, "Gunther, I can confirm that I am well rested and ready for the day's challenges. I hope you can say the same."

"Why, comrade Zipper, I hope so too. But I guess there is not much driving for me today?"

"No, I guess not. But since you are some kind of a joker in the affairs of the day, I may use you here and there for different assignments, which may keep other officers from things they need to hear or do."

They arrived at the HQ a few minutes before 8:00 AM, and to no surprise, Peter's car was already at the reserved parking place. Gunther parked at Bodo's space, and they entered the office building together. In the hallway was a small group of people assembled and talking to each other most of them holding a cup of coffee. They all turned their attention to Bodo and greeted him with a joyful "Good morning, Commander Zipper," which he returned. He was satisfied that the second secretary had arrived too. He greeted her separately, welcoming her, "Welcome, Maria, to our team. I hope your moving to the new place wasn't too stressful?"

"No. Commander Zipper, I am delighted to get a new start and to be part of something the party should have started years ago. The new apartment is excellent, especially in the same block entrance as Giesela. She came over yesterday night for a while and helped me unpack stuff."

"That's great to hear. We have to expect the officers from the SSP academy at any moment. Gunther, when they arrive, please settle them at the Barn and make sure they have coffee ready. Giesela, please show Maria around, show her the office she will work in, and I want all of you in my office in ten minutes."

They all confirmed with a "Yes, Commander." Bodo entered his office, sat at his desk, opened and started the OmniBook, and prepared himself for the many issues on the agenda for the day. One was the visit and reporting of the officer in charge from Neubrandenburg. He was extremely curious about the findings on the issue of his brother's visit there. He was reading the notes he had made for his introduction speech to the officers when the knock on the door reminded him that his team would come in for a brief update and instructions about the day's agenda.

Bodo called them to enter, and they all sat at the conference table. Bodo took his OmniBook and took place at the top of the table. Looking around the group, he was pleased with their eagerness to hear his instructions. He began, "You all know that today is the official opening of the Office for Investigation and Recovery operation, in short, OIR. From Monday on, we must be 100 percent on the target, getting the traitors on the cause of communism identified, investigated, and eliminated as a threat to the nation. And by eliminating them, I mean that we have to build the case for their execution. Those cases must be persuasive to convince the Central Committee to vote for the death sentence." Looking at each of them, they all nodded in agreement with Bodo.

He continued assigning tasks, "Giesela will be at my availability during the day. Maria, I want you to ensure that all officers are treated well and that the organized food supply and beverage are handled correctly. Peter, please handle the organizational issues with the officers assigned to the different offices. They all were told yesterday where they will serve after I had interviewed them, and all you need to do is to get them set up. The ROS officers must stay at the headquarters for the next week or two, so it might get crowded. I will give a short greeting speech and meet with an external SSP officer at 10:00 AM. After that, we will have lunch and have some Q&A, and then it's time for Karl to present the prescan and the results of all members."

Peter looked up from his notes and asked, "What time will Karl be expected to arrive? And do we have a CO for the ROS yet?"

"Good that you asked, Peter. Karl will be here at 2:00 PM. He will be accompanied by the future CO of the ROS." Just at that moment was a knock on the door, and when Bodo called, "Come in." The door opened, and Gunther entered, followed by Reiner. Gunther announced that the bus with the officers had arrived and that he had led them all into the barn cafeteria. While Bodo thanked him and waved him to sit down, Reiner was standing at the door, his mouth agape and a grinning look on his face.

"Do you want to grow roots there, or can you come in, close the door and sit down?" Bodo asked Reiner. He startled out of his stare at Peter, walked to the next chair, and sat.

"Giesela and Maria, please go over to the cafeteria and get everything started with the officers. Peter will be over soon." The secretaries left the office to look after the officer.

Reiner slapped Peter on the back with a grin and said, "Peter, old fellow, how did Bodo get you uprooted from the Island? I am surprised you are even alive five minutes after not breathing in the Baltic sea air!"

Before Bodo could react, Peter answered, "Reiner, you know better than me. Bodo would screw up everything without me and then blame me for not agreeing to help him." He laughed out loud about his own joke.

Still fighting his own laughing, Bodo jumped in, "He had less a chance to say no, than you had, Reiner. I virtually highjacked him. So here he is, and he is your direct boss. Make sure you do not make him angry about you." Now it was on Bodo to laugh about Reiner's baffled look, and he ended the whole fun series with the instruction for both to follow him over to the barn.

When they entered the Barn, Gunther called out, "Attention!" All officers turned toward Bodo and sprang to attention. Gunther reported. "Commander Zipper, all officers are ready for the event."

Bodo thanked Gunther and commanded them at ease and to sit. He walked up to the front of the row of tables with Peter and Reiner following. He greeted all officers at the headquarters of their new agency and introduced Peter as their chief operations officer and second in command of the agency. Then Reiner, as the RON's commanding officer.

After that, Bodo explained the importance and uniqueness of the Office for Investigation and Recovery. He became increasingly more intense in describing the extreme responsibility extensively to them and the complex task set before the agency. He reminded them that they had signed an oath of secrecy and a separate paper stating that they had committed suicide because they had betrayed their agency and could not live with that fact on their conscience.

Bodo finished his opening speech by saying, "Make no mistake, officers, I have sworn an oath the same as you and some. I will die fulfilling that oath and expect the same from you. I will not tolerate any misguided sympathy with the enemies of the party. For example, the two traitors behind that door on the other side will be the first to experience the wrath of the party I will bring down on them and their families involved in their betrayal. And we all, as a team, will do so by pretending to work for the individual's freedom, only to enslave the worker's class again into capitalist slavery. These are liars and counterrevolutionists and need to be treated that way. Our guidance is 'NO MERVCY' and no tolerance."

Bodo ended his opening speech with these words, and the assembly of former SSP officers and graduates from the highly valued SSP Academy chanted, "NO MERCY."

Then Peter took over and briefly instructed them about the agenda and timeline of the day. When he was done, Reiner took over for his assigned officer, and they grouped with him while the others grouped with Peter. Bodo answered a few rather personal questions. Peter caught his attention, and he walked over to him.

"Bodo, I have been asked about accommodation for the officers not assigned to the RON."

"I had a short phone call with comrade Pieker yesterday. He said they would have rooms at the SSP barracks in Schönefeld for the time being until Karl can squeeze some more apartments out of the army resources and Grünau. That's for both the headquarters and the ROS officers."

Peter nodded, thanked Bodo, and returned to talk with the officers. At that moment, Giesela appeared at the door and waved at Bodo, who went over and followed her out of the barn. "Comrade Zipper, the OIC of the Neubrandenburg SSP, just arrived. I have him in the lobby with a coffee and said I would get you."

"Many thanks, Giesela. Let's go and see what he has for me." They walked back to the office building, and when they entered, a man in uniform with the rank of a captain stood. Bodo stretched out his hand, which he took, and said, "Welcome, Captain. Let's go to my office and get to it. I am curious what you have got for me."

They went into Bodo's office. Before he closed the door, he told Giesela to bring a can of coffee and no interruptions if no emergency was required.

Bodo pointed to the comfortable chairs at the small coffee table in the office, "Please sit down, Captain. It's more convenient to sit here than on the conference table."

The door opened after a knock, and Giesela placed a can of coffee on the table, filled a cup for Bodo, and left the office.

The OIC of the Neubrandenburg SSP section opened his briefcase and took out two relatively small folders, of whom he handed one to Bodo. He opened his and began to explain the results of what they had found out so far. To Bodo's disappointment, not much.

"Commander Zipper. Your brother was approximately three hours in Neubrandenburg. We have witnesses who saw him parking the car and walking away. Using the photograph we got from his file from the comrades in Sassnitz, we could find a small coffee shop where the waitress recognized him. He was there only for about ten minutes. When another man, unknown to the waitress, entered the coffeeshop and sat at the same table. They talked for a few minutes and left together."

Bodo listened and, when the captain stopped, asked, "Did she say that she did not know the man or that she did not recognize him? Could she describe the man?"

"Commander Zipper, our comrades brought her in and, with her help, created a graphic image of the man. The officer then walked through every shop in our town to find someone who had seen this guy without success. We believe your brother met someone from outside of Neubrandenburg. Therefore, nobody recognized the man in the image."

"Not that I want to downplay the skills of your officers, but have you considered that the waitress may have given you a falls description to get over it and left alone, or she might even be a sympathizer of the counterrevolutionaries?"

"Yes, Commander, we thought about that after the first round of investigations through the nearby shops was fruitless. We brought her back into the SSP and interrogated her again. Still, she stood with the description, even after we pointed out that she, a single mother, could lose custody of her child. That usually breaks women in our experience."

"Yes, that's correct. This guy must be in SSP files somewhere. Did you find anything that could give us an idea why he was meeting this guy, whoever that was?

"No, Commander Zipper. We tried anything we could with the resources we had. I concluded that your brother was meeting a man outside our operation area. In my investigation summary, I suggested sending a nationwide request to all SSP stations or forming a special task force. Both are outside of my authority to initiate. But you definitely have that authority and even the resources to do that."

"Thank you so much for the report, and please, let the officer know that I appreciate the intense research they have done in this case. You may not have the resources, but you did a great job eliminating your area of operations as a potential center of counterrevolutionary activities."

"Thank you, Commander Zipper. I would have liked to find out why he was in our city. Suppose we could have nailed him connected to the organizers of the Monday demonstrations. Those Monday demonstrations are disturbing, and many comrades ask when we will finally stop the insanity. In that case, we may have a reason to open additional investigations with added resources."

Bodo thought of acting against his treasonous brother differently and answered, "You did a great job there with your officers, and I understand your limitations. Unfortunately, the officers lost track of him driving out of the city. But I know him well enough to not be mad at them. They probably need a little more training, and please encourage them to be more aggressive when they realize that a suspect has detected their surveillance. Many thanks again, and have a safe trip back home."

With that, Bodo stood and, shaking hands, escorted the captain out of his office, using the opportunity to take a breath of fresh air. He watched the SSP officer driving out of the property and walking over to the barn to see how things were developing. When Bodo entered the cafeteria, Bodo found only Reiner with his new officers sitting in a circle they had built with some of the chairs and talking. He recognized that they discussed the assignment, experiences, and tactical surveillance issues. Bodo thought that was great timing to explain to them the mistakes the SSP officers had made in Neubrandenburg losing contact with his brother's car.

He walked closer to the group. One of them noticed his presence and called them to attention. Bodo waved his hand and said, "At easy." He then said he would like to join the discussion and give them an example from a recent event. All of them, even Reiner, looked at him, curious about what story he had to reveal.

"A few days ago, I was in Neubrandenburg to receive the ten worst cases of treason against the party when I noticed that my brother's car was parked at the main parking lot of the city," Bodo began to explain to them the incident of surveillance failure by SSP officers. I told them how his brother used the sudden and irregular change of traffic lanes to detect the following SSP car because of the inexperienced panic reaction of the driver, fearing losing contact.

"You see," he continued, "our enemies are not stupid. We shall never underestimate them. The first order is never to panic. The second is to use your tools. You have radios and very powerful engines. If the suspect detects you, the second car must take over but avoid sudden actions. My brother used the fact that the SSP officer would not follow the average citizen's play, trying to be in the front row at the next traffic light. That was their mistake. What do you think it told him?" Bodo asked the officers.

"Commander Zipper, are you saying that the average citizen consciously breaks the law to race from traffic light to traffic light only to be the first on the next one?"

"Oh," Bodo was astounded for a second until he realized that most of them, just in their early twenties, may have never driven a personal car and even made their driver's license at the academy. He answered, "Yes, comrade, that's a rampant kind of game drivers play, especially in larger cities with numerous traffic lights in short distances."

Another officer jumped in, saying, "Now I understand your advice with the radios and powerful engines, Commander Zipper. We can avoid being detected by using the radio to call the second car to come forward instead of jumping lanes behind the suspect. Then the second car can participate in the race, and the suspect would not realize of being under surveillance."

Another officer joined the discussion, stating, "But now you have only one car on the suspect and might lose him in the traffic, especially when you have rush hour."

"Great observation there, comrade. But again, think about the engine your car has. There is no civil car in the nation that is even close.

Do you think the officer know their city well? Sure, they do. They have to. And so are you. You have to learn and memorize every street and corner of the area where you are sent to work a surveillance job. If the second car had accelerated at max speed and had turned the next street to his right, they could have been at the street cross two traffic lights down, where they finally lost my brother because the cross traffic blocked their view."

At that point, Reiner took a deep breath and said, "I think we have some decent training in front of us, comrades. Thanks a lot, Commander Zipper. We really appreciate your insides."

Bodo stood and pointed out the time, saying that the lunch prepared by the Schönefeld barracks would arrive in a few minutes; he walked out of the barn. Entering the office building, he turned toward the officer's office area, and seeing one door open, he went there. The office was one for the interrogators, and he was glad to see that the officer assigned to the headquarters and the ROS were all sitting and standing there, discussing the ins and outs of their future work regarding bringing information for the interrogators they could use.

"I don't want to interrupt your discussion, comrades. I just wanted to let you know that lunch may arrive soon, and you should prepare for it. Peter, are there any questions that came up during your discussions I need to answer?"

Peter thought momentarily and answered while looking around the group of officers, "No, not that I am aware of."

"Great, I wish you all a great lunchtime, and make sure that the car assignment is finished when Karl arrives."

"No problem, I will see to it."

Bodo turned around and walked into his office. He picked up the phone and called Sabrina at home. "Yes" was her short answer.

"Hi, darling, great that you are at home. I am thinking about coming home for lunch. Can you prepare something in about twenty to thirty minutes?"

"Sure, I will get it done. See you in about thirty minutes. Love you."

Bodo hit the intercom and told Giesela he would drive home in about thirty minutes. No, he would not need Gunther. He would drive that short distance himself. For the remaining time until he left, he went through the investigation findings of the incident with his brother in Neubrandenburg. He was again amazed by the cunning character of Fritz. He felt it in his gut that Fritz had a very specific reason to meet this unknown person in Neubranden burg and that it had to do with his brother's work on the obstruction of the communist system. Still baffled by the extreme swing of Fritz's worldview from communist superstar to an enemy of the state, he decided right there to create a task force just to get his brother's destructive activities discovered and bring him to justice. And it would be a task force reporting directly to him.

Satisfied with his decision, he walked out of the office and looked into the office of Giesela to let her know he was leaving. He jumped into his car and drove home.

Bodo arrived at the office just in time to see Karl and Joachim leaving his car. He walked over to them and greeted them with a bright smile. Since the sun had come out shortly after lunch, the officers had taken some of the tables and chairs outside on the backside of the Barn. Bodo realized that this was a great idea to have some kind of an outside sitting area for the hot summer days. Turning to Karl, he said, "Karl, can you use your enormous organizational skills and get me a pergola build there." Pointing to where the officers had created the small outside seating, he continued, "I think it would be a great place to have lunch on hot summer days for the officers."

"That seems to be a great idea, lifting the mood of your officers when they are loaded with all the shit they encounter from the investigations. I will see what I can do, but the ROS facility down south has priority. At least, I guess," he said, looking back at Bodo.

"Oh, sure, Karl. That facility has absolute priority. And since we are on it, what is the status there?"

"Before we came over, we had a somewhat lengthy conference call with the construction supervisor and architect working on the object. Both said they have it ready for moving all officers in the middle of next week."

Bodo thought about it while they were entering his office and said, "Maybe Joachim and I should not drive down there on Tuesday but wait for Wednesday? What do you think, Joachim?"

Joachim was slightly shocked, being addressed by his boss and commander by his first name, and a little surprised by the unusual familiarity of being addressed this way, hesitated to answer.

Bodo realizing this, added, "I understand, Joachim, you are surprised to be addressed this way. Get over it." Bodo added, laughing. "You are one of three COs in our agency. You will have an enormous amount of responsibility on your shoulders. Probably more than the other two. And I know you are young, but I have been advised that you are an innovative and fast learner. I want you to know that I appreciate you as one of the top leaders in my organization."

Joachim swallowed and said, "Thank you, Commander Zipper, uh, Bodo, for your trust in me. I will do everything and some to be the best CO you have. And to answer your question, yes, I think it is better to wait till Wednesday to visit the facilities. I might be all done and can move in already, saving me an extra trip.

"Is there a place for you to live there permanently? I had no idea."

Karl answered, "Yeah, you haven't seen the property yet. There are several buildings, one of them is a single-family home. It was the home of the group commander, and we had to renovate as we did on all of the buildings since those had been abandoned for almost three years."

"That's great. Excellent that this is not an issue. I was already thinking about how we could find a place for Joachim since it is rather far off from any town there. I just hope you do not get too lonely there in the woods."

They all laughed about that remark, and just then, there was a knock on the door, and Bodo called, "Come in." Giesela entered, balancing a tablet with coffee for all three, and said, "Commander Zipper, it is almost 2:00 PM, and you wanted to be reminded at that time for the presentation by comrade Karl."

"Oh, really, is it already that late? I completely lost track of time. We will be out there in a few minutes. Please let Peter know to get ready for it in about ten."

"Yes, Commander," Giesela answered and left the office.

Bodo, Joachim, and Karl talked a little more about the potential of the facility of the ROS, mainly because of the buildings and the place's remoteness that would allow to use it even for executions necessary. A significant advantage was that it lay in the middle of a vast, restricted military training ground. They finished their coffee and went to the barn, where Karl would address the officers about the intensive investigation, camouflaged as the "exchange of the party documents."

He explained the process and the enormous number of ICC office employees who had worked together without counting the hours they spent, and the results proved them right. A murmur went through the room when he started to list the number of suspects of the different categories. The list shocked the officers who had sworn their lives to the defense of the Communist Party and her eternal right to be the leading force in the nation.

Karl listed them as follows:

1.   7 first district secretaries and some of their family members
2.   19 first county secretaries and some family members
3.   189 general directors (CEOs) of large corporations
4.   218 officers of the armed forces above the rank of major
5.   Numerous commanding police officers
6.   Several commanding SSP officers and NCOs

According to the decision of the Central Committee, all SSP suspects will be handled by an SSP Special Task Force under the direct command and supervision of General Pieker. All suspects of categories 1 through 5 will be handled by the OIR.

Based on the decree of Commander Zipper, all cases categories 1 through 4 will be handled by the OIR Headquarters. He looked at Bodo and added, "It might be that Commander Zipper reevaluates that decree to a certain point because he could not know how many traitors we would discover."

At that point, Bodo walked up to the front and, standing beside Karl, said, "Comrade Renner, I am impressed with the fantastic work the ICC has done in such a short time. In my wildest nightmares, I had not dreamt that so many of the party's former leaders, CEOs, and officers had fallen to betray the cause. I will have to review my decree, and the leadership of the OIR will see that we can handle the cases so that we can finish as many as possible as fast as possible."

Then turning toward the officers hanging on every word, he said, "Comrades, we have a challenging task in front of us. We must collect evidence for each case to nail the traitors without doubt of their guilt. During the following months and even years, we have to spend hours and days in surveillance, interrogations, and analysis of the evidence for each case. Be vigilant, be careful, and always think two steps ahead of the enemy."

The officers clapped and chanted, "Long live the German Democratic Republic!"

Bodo asked Peter, Reiner, and Joachim to follow him to his office. He thanked Karel for his excellent presentation, and they separated, wishing each other a restful weekend. Bodo watched Karl leave the property and was satisfied to see the guards doing a great job ensuring the property was secure.

At his office, they went through some organizational issues. They decided to have an in-person meeting every Friday to coordinate their actions and analyze the week. Since their phone system was integrated with the SSP phone technology, which was the best the country could offer, and was pretty much up to date with international standards, they could connect whenever necessary by phone. Based on the revelations from Karls's presentation, they decided to split the cases differently. Headquarters would still take all of the FDS cases. But the FCS cases and the other categories would be split according to the region they were from.

Since all of the suspects were still under observation by the SSP and had almost certainly no idea that they were suspects, Bodo decided to give everyone a great weekend and have the arrest started on Monday. While the ROS was not operational, he would have Jürgen take over the arrests for the ROS region on Monday by the SSP and deliver them to the ROS later in the week.

They said their goodbyes with great joy that they were finally ready to start cleansing.

Reiner went out, assembled his officers, and after a few minutes of preparation, a convoy of cars and SUVs left the property. Standing beside

Bodo, Peter looked at his watch and said, "Bodo, it is just 3:00 PM. I would like to have a short meeting with one of the interrogators which I want to put in charge of the two criminals we have here. Do you want to participate?"

Bodo thought a minute and said, "No, Peter. I forgot to tell you that I am working on getting a CO for the headquarters because I want you to handle the OIR operation without being consumed with Headquarter's direct actions. You should handle that by yourself to give the guys an idea that you are in command of operations."

"That's great, Bodo. Having a CO here would make a lot of sense too." With that, Peter walked into the office building and started his meeting with the interrogator and his surveillance team.

Bodo looked at Joachim and said, "Joachim, let's go to my office and see what we can find out about the cases you may have to handle soon."

At Bodo's office, he called Giesela via the intercom and asked her to bring the equipment for Joachim. She entered and placed the briefcase with the OmniBook and the recorder in front of Joachim on the conference table. Bodo thanked her, and while she walked out, he explained the little wonder machine to Joachim and showed him the different programs. Giesela had already transferred the cases related to the ROS to his OmniBook, and only the cases of categories 3 through 5 of the region were missing. Calling Giesela back, Gunther explained the changes they had decided. She said she would change the decree for a new issue and copy the files for the ROS onto Joachim's OmniBook.

In the meantime, it was already 4:00 PM when Giesela returned and had everything done. Bodo signed the printed copies of the changed decree and decided that he could have him driven back to his place by Gunther, combined with delivering the revised decree to the members of CC.

Bodo decided to call it a day and informed Giesela to hold Gunther for a moment. He closed the safe, took his briefcase, and walked out. Giesela and Gunther were standing in the hallway waiting for him. He instructed Gunther to drop him off at his home, get Joachim back to his apartment, deliver the new copies of the decree to the members of CC, and then enjoy his weekend. He told Giesela to let Peter know he would return to the office on Monday morning at 8:00 AM. They went in the car, and after the short trip, Bodo entered his home, leaving his job behind for the weekend.

CHAPTER 17

Start of the Power Comm Production and Some Bad News from the Traveling Messenger

When Fritz woke up the following day, he felt well-rested and ready to get home. He missed his family and was sure they were concerned about him. But he would not risk calling them over the phone, especially after his encounter with the SSP on Monday. After he had packed all his stuff, he walked out into the living area, where Manfred was already working on an excellent breakfast for them. They greeted each other.

Fritz said, "I'll drop my luggage in the car and be right back."

"Okay, breakfast is almost done," Manfred answered, and when Fritz returned, it was all on the breakfast bar, and they sat and ate in almost total silence. Then Fitz said, "I am very grateful for your help Manfred. We have designed a system that can be the breakthrough for the movement. I firmly believe that secure communication is the key to our success. Without it, we will never be able to coordinate actions to topple the system and install a real democratic system in this nation."

"Nothing to thank me for, Fritz. I will see that I get as many of the long-range communicators produced as possible. It shouldn't be a big deal since I have all that is needed to mass-produce them. My boss will also request you to come to the company to fix the programming issues. This would allow us to reconnect publicly and discuss more necessary inventions. Thank the Lord for bringing both of us out of the darkness we had fallen into, and we can now use our skills and experience to help the people gain the freedom they deserve."

"You are right, Manfred. See you soon, and now I am on my way. Can't wait to get home after being away from my family for a week now." And seeing the pained expression on Manfred's face, Fritz realized how much the loss he experienced still hurt Manfred. He went over to him, gave him a man's hug, and said, "I can't imagine the pain you have to experience by the losses, but I can guarantee you that they will pay for it. We will make them pay. One at a time or all at once."

"Thanks, Fritz. Even more, I had never thought I would see you again, though calling you a friend and brother in Christ. Have a safe trip home, and we will be in touch."

They walked out in the garage, Manfred opened the door and the gate, and Fritz drove out and was on his way home.

He stopped at the Gardening center where they usually got the white asparagus, but the gardener told him it was too early. They haven't had enough warm days to grow it for harvest. He told him to watch the weather and that he should come by when they had several warm days in the coming two weeks. He would make sure they would have some left for him. Somewhat disappointed, knowing that his in-law would be sad not to get the asparagus she was waiting for, he drove off and, a few hours later, arrived home. The children ran him almost over, and he hugged and kissed Karola passionately, having missed her smile for so many days. His in-law laughed at his sad expression that he couldn't bring the asparagus she had hoped for and said, "No problem. I thought it might be too early since we had just a few sunny days but not enough warming yet. What did he say when you could get back to get some?"

"He said about two weeks. And I think we will all just go together on the weekend two weeks from now."

"Sound good to me. Come in. I have lunch ready for us."

They all walked into the house and had a great lunch. Fritz had to tell them about his trip and told them all the greetings from Reinhard, Bernd, and Robert, who were all well-known because they had been at the place visiting. Then he returned to the car and unloaded the gifts from Bernd's parents, and all the food was received with great joy because it was known well, and the kids loved the hard-smoked small sausages. He drove the car into the garage and locked the doors.

They tucked in the kids, and Fritz read a story from a small biblical-based children's book they had received some years ago from his wife's relatives in West Germany. Later, in bed with Karola, he told her the story of Manfred's losses and his rescue by Reinhard, and she cried and laughed at the change of the story from bad to excellent. Finally, they fell asleep in their arms, happy to be together again.

The following Monday, Fritz used the train to get to the shipyard. He had to get up early and make as less noise as possible to not wake the children. Karola brewed a coffee while he got himself ready. They said goodbye, and he headed to the train station. Arriving at the shipyard in a crowd of many other workers from the train station, he was soon at his place to change into his work close and ready to go to the second vessel he had worked the week before when one of his colleagues told him that the boss wanted to see him.

Fritz wondered what the boss could want from him and went upstairs to his office. He knocked on the door, entered at the "call come in," and found the supervisor for his division at his desk. "Hi, Fritz, great you are back. How was your vacation?"

"Nothing special, just taking care of some stuff that needed to be done after moving to my wife's mother's place."

"Yeah, I understand. It's always some left to be done after moving." Looking up from the paperwork, he continued, "Listen, Fritz, you did a great job before you took off for the week. We were able to get the ship on the trial journey, and that was because you found the defect card and the program issues. It is a shame I can't reward you for it, but you can only blame yourself. You know what I mean. So don't be stupid and increase the pressure on you by acting stupidly. Do you understand what I am saying?"

Fritz looked at him as if he had just learned that the moon shines at night and, after focusing his thoughts, said, "What are you talking about. You know where I stand politically. Everyone knows that, and that hasn't changed, and nothing has been added to that. I have not been contacted by the authorities again. I wouldn't know why they even would care about me, being removed from having even the slightest chance of becoming a danger to the great accomplishments of the greatest communist society that ever existed on German soil."

"Don't be cynical, Fritz. I know you, and I know your views on things politically. But I don't need any additional stress because you are doing something stupid or meeting people under surveillance and getting in trouble. But I have probably already said too much. I just wanted to tell you to be more careful whom you choose as friends."

"I will. What about my work? Am I on number 37 this week, or do you have some other work in mind for me?"

"Willi is on vacation this week, and he would have handled the commissioning of number 34. I want you to take that over for him. The reports are all here. I just went through them. There are only a few items on the punch list for us. It should all be clear, and you should get through with our parts during the week. Good luck, and think about my warning."

"Oh, that was a warning? I did not take it as such. What did you warn me about?"

"Come on now, Fritz. Don't play stupid with me. You had a very subversive exchange with one of the apprentices, and he was bold enough to use your reasoning in school. Can you imagine what almost happened to him? I warn you, stop things like that. You may be unable to handle the results of an official accusation by one of the hardliners. You can be glad that I am taking the pressure off you."

"Thanks, and I will try to be more careful, but it is difficult when it comes to a point where I have to swallow stupidity." With that, Fritz took the folder with the paperwork and walked out of the office. Several of his colleagues were already talking about all the stupid stuff at the crew office and greeted him, some friendly and some just because.

Fritz knew there were at least two SSP officers from the secret program "Officers at a special assignment" among them. He knew this from his time as an electrical engineer on the fishing trawler, where he developed a personal relationship with the captain. For a moment, he thought back then and briefly regretted not staying there but attending university. But it was only a short flashback and ended fast. Drawn back into reality, he looked around and tried to imagine who could be that traitor. But soon, he stopped those thoughts because these people were too well-trained to get discovered. He went to the table where he could sit down and review the paperwork Willi had left behind from his ship, ready to be commissioned. He looked at the punch list and saw only five points in his section. He recognized immediately that two of them needed the replacement of control cards, and he hoped they had those at the material warehouse.

Since the first punch-list meeting was scheduled for 10:00 AM, there was not much time left to check the parts. He walked to the warehouse and was happy to see Billy standing at the large truck gate with a checkboard, checking material that had just arrived. Billy waved at him and mouthed the words, be right with you. Fritz entered his office and sat at the desk, waiting for Billy to arrive.

Billy entered the office a few minutes later and greeted Fritz with a joyful, "Hello, Fritz, great to see you back in one part without scratches."

"Hello, Billy, great to see you too, but why would I not be in one part and have scratches?"

Billy looked around, ensuring nobody else was in the office, and said, "You must have stirred a hornet's nest. I heard about an interrogation of your supervisor about you, indoctrinating an apprentice with subversive ideology, questioning the doctrines of the Communist Party taught in school. So yeah, I thought you might get interrogated too."

"Yeah, I got an earful from my supervisor already. I don't need you to add to that," Fritz said, laughing, and then continued, "This boy was asking me why I had abandoned the party and why I did not believe that communism was the winning ideology in the world. So what should I do? Let him die stupid and brainwashed, or encourage him to use his own ability to think critically and analyze the lies he got told for himself?"

"Although you are right, Fritz, but really I need to ask you to be a little more cautious. We need you and can't get you imprisoned for these teachings. But you are surely not here to get criticized by me. What can I do for you?"

"I need three control-cards replacements for the ship I took over from Willi, who is on vacation, and I shall get it commissioned for our section this week. Here is the list. Can you check if you have some replacements?"

Billy took the list and went to his desk, where he opened his logbook and checked the part numbers. After several minutes of going back and forth between some pages, he began to scribble on a piece of paper and handed it to Fritz. "Go to the warehouse section 7 and talk to the guy there. I have listed the shelf section and location number for each card. He should find them in no time. You're lucky because we got some repairs back last week."

Fritz thanked and was on his way out when Billy stopped him, came close, and whispered, "Tonight at the center place. Leo has some news for us." Fritz nodded and walked out of the office. He got the cards he needed and was on his way to the meeting getting there just in time.

During the meeting, which was led by the production director of the shipyard, several of the managers from the other departments looked over at Fritz from time to time as if to say, what is he doing here. It was widely known why he was at the shipyard, and his history, as far as what positions he had held several years ago, wasn't unknown either.

Looking at Fritz, the production director asked, "You are here for your company taking care of number 34 commissioning? Do you have the list and paperwork you need? And by the way, where is Willi?"

Fritz took a second to sort his thoughts and answered, "Wow, that's a lot of questions at once. But I will try to answer. Willi is on vacation, and my supervisor asked me to take over the commissioning procedure for our company. And yes, I have all the paperwork, including the signed test protocols and the relatively short punch list."

"That is great. Now let's go through your punch list."

Fritz listed at first the three points he could fix immediately. For the remaining two, he needed support from the shipyard. Explaining to get the drive controller for one of the winches replaced would require opening the vessel's side by cutting out the section. The fifth point was the test run of the replaced drive controller with the water resistors as load.

The production director, with the name Werner, thought momentarily and asked, "Why can't you just replace the defective parts in that controller? As far as I understood, several high-current thyristors are burned out. Can't you just replace them? That would save the shipyard a lot of money, cutting the hole, welding it back close, insulation, painting, etc."

"Sir, to replace the thyristor set, we would have to remove one from an existing controller, which may or may not yet be delivered for one of the next trawlers. In doing so, we would violate the warranty for that drive controller. In the same way, we would violate the warranty for the driver, where we took out the defective thyristor set. And then there is the uncertainty that the electronic settings and adaptions made for that defective Thyristor set are identical to the replacement. That would create a considerable complexity of follow-up events, which I highly recommend avoiding."

The room, which had usually been kind of noisy because the managers of the different departments would whisper to each other about details of their own issues, had become totally silent. Everyone looked at Fritz, the discomfort was tangible, and finally, Werner broke the silence, asking Fritz, "You are saying that my suggestion would be more expensive and time-consuming than yours?"

Fritz noticed the tense atmosphere in the room. Not knowing what was going on, he decided to stay with his opinion and said, "I am not sure about the cost, and I am sure that we would need at least four, maybe even five days to finish the exchange of the parts and run the load test with the winches. A result of the exchange of the parts would be the loss of warranty for both winch drive controllers. And as I said before, I am not even sure that the two controllers are compatible in their parts."

Silence again in the room. Then Werner asked, "Why should these not be compatible? Aren't they built following the same design and using the same materials for all of them?"

"They are often not. We have seen the usage of different relays and electronic components. Often, when we changed a defective timer relays, we had to repeat the complete setup procedure to get it to work correctly. So no, these drive controllers are not compatible. They often appear to be scratched together from all kinds of remains lying around just to get them shipped in time for installation. Although these systems should result from a well-thought-out serial production, these seem more likely the result of a series of test systems."

"Are you telling me that our nation's electronic manufacturing industry cannot produce an electronically controlled drive system with repeatable serial quality and in the necessary quantity? Is it that what you just said?"

"I just said that the systems we are getting delivered are anything but a product of a serial manufacturing process." It is outside of my ability to determine If that is based on the ability of the electronic industry in our German Democratic Republic."

Werner looked down at his paper, took a deep breath, and after looking up and at the somewhat scarred faces of the managers sitting around, he said, "I guess that conversation doesn't lead to a conclusion. Led's finish the rest here. And, Mr. Zipper, ensure all the other things are handled. I will get in touch with your company and see what their stand on this is."

"Sure, will do."

After some more back and forth between Werner and the managers from the other departments, the meeting was closed, and all went out of the room as if poison had been spread out. Fritz walked out at the end of the crowd of managers, thinking about how Willi could take in that arrogant POS Werner and keep his cool when he was startled out of his thoughts by the voice of even that same man.

"Mr. Zipper, a word, please, in private."

"Oh, Mr. Werner, excuse me, I was thinking about stuff."

"You know, Mr. Zipper, I have never been challenged that way in a meeting by any of the managers and confronted openly with doubts about the ability of excellent manufacturing qualities of our communist-led industries. Although I found it a little over the top, I wanted to let you know that I appreciate the open description of the reality we are facing more than the cringing of the people without balls in their pants. If we were more honest with ourselves, we would have a much better economic situation."

"Mr. Werner, I thought along the same line years ago and wasted many years before I concluded that failure is inherent in the system. But I try to put all my knowledge and experience into the work because I believe I am required to do that by the only power I report to. Thanks for being honest with me, and I promise you, Mr. Werner, you will never be bullshitted by me."

Fritz looked at a stunned production director, knowing he was actually running the shipyard and was the most powerful man. He smiled, turned around, and walked out of the building. He went on getting the controller cards replaced and updated the records for that. The day was soon gone by, and after writing his workday report and placing it into the basket, he went out of the shipyard to his rented apartment to prepare for the secret meeting tonight. Although he had no idea what it was about, it must be something important that they would have a meeting so soon after their get-together at Leo's.

Using all the tricks to discover a tail and changing the route again to approach the underground meeting place, he arrived shortly after everyone else but Billy. He came a few minutes later, stating that he believed he had a tail. But after the second change and walking through the only department store in the town, he lost it, and here he was.

They asked Fritz to briefly describe his trip, and he did so, not mentioning the discovery of a new brain source for the communication issue yet. He also did not reveal the potential source for getting weapons. He told them that he could spend all of the communicators and that more were in the making.

Then Billy stated why he had called the meeting and asked Ralf to present his information.

Ralf collected his thoughts and began, "Fritz stopped on his way south to visit his friends in a town, where he met two contacts I gave him from other groups. For an unknown reason, a few hours in the afternoon, the SSP started to walk through the town, showing his image to people working in the business. The person in the only coffee shop on that street was taken to the SSP office and requested help to draw an image of the person who was in the coffee shop at the same time and had been seen leaving it with Fritz. She did an excellent job of making it so nobody would ever find the person in that image."

By that time, the color had drained from Fritz's face, and he was asking, "Did they find one of my contacts? Or were they just shooting in the dark."

"No, thanks to the Lord, the waitress in the coffee shop is a sympathizer and was very cooperative with the SSP, they do not suspect her, and they did not find anyone. What I wonder about, though, is why they would, just a few hours after your meeting, run around with your photo. They weren't even aware of the second contact you met."

Fritz thought briefly about how to present the car chase without getting them all scared, "I was done with the contacts and had left them far behind when I entered my car to drive out of the city. I realized I had to turn left and quickly changed the lane at a traffic light. Suddenly, I saw a car behind me changing the lane somewhat strangely. I immediately realized that this had to be the SSP and, after turning, moved to the right turn lane for the next traffic light. That was when I detected the second SSP car. You know the trick with the traffic light racing. So after the second next traffic light, they were invisible far behind me, and I left town without being followed again. I have no idea why they have been watching my car in the parking lot. That is the only place they could have started following me."

There was silence in the room for several minutes, and finally, Leo asked, "Could it be that your brother had something to do with it?"

Fritz and all the others were surprised by that question, and several of them, including Fritz, asked, "How do you get that idea?"

Leo thought for a second and then said, "It seems kind of strange, and I did not give anything at it, but one of the guys at the fleet maintenance shop was at the barricades at the Rügendamm because of our Soviet friends when I drove through and last Friday when I came in for an oil change, he told me that there was a strange story going around in their workers force battalion. It was told that a guy named Bodo Zipper was driven by the driver of the ICC member of the Central Committee in his Volvo to Berlin. But since it was just a rumor, I did not give much to it. But now that looks much different."

Now, Fitz was at 100 percent attention. "Do you know what day that exactly happened?"

Leo thought about it and said, "I am sorry, Fritz, but I don't know. The guy who told me that story wasn't even sure if that wasn't just something somebody wanted to appear important."

Fritz considered several possibilities and said, "Friends, I am sorry this happened. It shows us again that we can't be careful enough. I am working on a powerful communication system that can be used as a transfer beacon and connect the small communicator directly on call.

It will make communication between the many groups that are still separated easy and secure. Until that system is operational, I will stay away from activities other than that, and we will be in contact only at work."

Ralf entered the discussion and said, "Fritz, there is no criticism here about you running into the SSP in that town. You did what was needed, and until we know, if we ever know, why they detected and watched your car, I think it is a good idea to limit the contact."

With that, they ended the meeting with a prayer, thanking the Lord for guidance and security. They left the meeting place with even more attention to potentially dangerous trails than ever.

CHAPTER 18

The Long Dreamed Weekend with the Family and The Discovery of a Talent

Bodo kept the promise he had given his family, and they had a great weekend together. First, they spent several hours in the fenced-in garden area, cleaning out the weed, and by doing so, a large number of beds for planting became recognizable. The former owner must have had a professional gardener working there because everything looked that way. After cleaning, Bodo started to dig each bed over. Nick and Sarina started planting tomatoes and putting seeds in the ground for various vegetables.

They had a short lunch break with just a salad and some sandwiches, and when they finished the work and looked at their work, they were really proud of their accomplishments. Bodo hugged and kissed Sarina, and then they both complimented Nick for his endurance in helping with the hard work. Nick beamed with his dirty face, and only then they realized how dirty they all had become. After a long shower, they sat at the terrace, and Sarina served one of their favorite dinner meals.

They talked about their accomplishments and envisioned the vegetables they might harvest and how great those would taste till late into the night. Sarina started to talk about a small herb area she would like to add, and soon, it was time for bed.

On Sunday, they all slept in and had a late breakfast. In the afternoon, they drove to the sailing club, using Sarina's personal car, which she immediately fell in love with and drove, with that powerful tuned engine, like a pro. At the sailing club, they asked for the manager. They were soon sitting together with a relatively young comrade, who was excited to get Nick into his club. He explained that they had only three children in his age class, and they needed four to participate in club competitions. They would sail the Pirate Class, and if Nick would be willing to take the time necessary to learn to sail the little boat, he could help them to send a team to competitions.

Nick asked if you could try how it would feel being in such a boat, and they walked all down to the river, which was at that place really wide and more like a little lake. The manager took one of the pirate boats off the racks, and Nick was surprised about the boat's lightweight. Bodo and Sarina stood back a little, and without noticing, Nick took over the conversation with the manager. He explained to Nick the specifics of that little boat, that it was the starting boat for many carriers of international very successful competitive sailors, and that there were even international competitions.

Bodo and Sarina found a bench near the landing stage and watched Nick having his first lessons in sailing the Pirate Class boat. And he did exceptionally well, to the surprise of them. He followed the commands of the manager, who was actually the boat class youth teacher, to the point with great joy and was soon circling back and forth along the landing stage. Because of the low wind, it was easy for him to execute the tack almost perfectly by the third tack.

When the manager called him back to the landing stage after about thirty-five minutes, a small crowd of parents and kids had assembled. They were astounded by the newcomer's execution of the maneuvers and even putting the pirate back onto the landing stage without so much as a bump. He had just at the right moment lowered the sail so that the boot had almost no movement when it touched the Landing stage. The crowd was as excited as Bodo and Sarina, and the manager turned to them, saying, "Did your son have had a lot of training and sailing experience with the Pirate Class?"

Sarina answered him while Bodo was holding the boat to the stage for Nick to get out and said, "Not with this small boat, but he has some experience sailing larger boats with five to six men crews on the backwater lakes on the Island Rügen."

"That explains his feel for wind and direction but not the handling of the pirate. He seems to have a special gift for sailing in general." Turning to Nick, who was visibly enjoying the attention from the other kids, the manager asked, "Nick, are you interested in joining our team and sailing with us in competitions?"

Nick looked at his parents and answered, "If my parents agree, I would love to do that. And I understand that there is time to be spent on training, and I need to learn how to handle this nutshell of a boat in stronger winds. This was just a walk in the park."

With a questioning look at Bodo and Sarina, the manager laughed and said, "Now, what do the parents say?"

Bodo and Sarina looked at Nick, and Bodo answered, "It would be up to your mom, Nick because she must drive you to the club. Most of the time, I might not be able to do so. And more importantly, it always depends on your grades at school. As long as you keep school as number one of your objectives, I have no issues with your hobby."

"I promise, Dad, I will pot school first." Then looking at Sarina, he asked, "Mom, would you drive me to the club?"

Sarina looked at the manager and said, "How many days a week is the training, and who is the trainer? Can we meet him today to decide if I will place my son into his hands?"

The manager looked Sarina in the eye and answered, "Mrs. Zipper, I am the trainer for the Pirate Class, and I guarantee you that your son is in good hands. My son is just one year younger and in the same age group. Safety is always number one, and we have training on Tuesdays and Thursdays during summer competitions on most Saturdays, sometimes, mainly during school break, on Sunday too."

Bodo and Sarina looked at each other, and after Bodo slightly nodded, Sarina smiled at Nick and said, "Okay, I will drive you over here, and since I am free, I will most of the time stay for the training time."

Nick yelled a loud "Hurrah" and hugged his mom. They all walked over to the clubhouse into the office. After they had filled out the application for club membership and signed the papers, Bodo paid the membership fee for the whole year, which brought another smile to the face of the manager. "You know that if Nick quits before the year's end, there is no refund?"

Now, all was set, and they walked out of the building. They said their goodbyes, and just as they were about to walk to their car, Bodo turned and asked the trainer-manager, "How many of these Pirate Class boats do you have?"

The trainer's face became sad as he answered, "Unfortunately, we have only three of those, and that has been my whole fight for about two years now. If something happens, we can't even go to a competition because we must register at least three boats to get counted."

Bodo answered, "This is a relatively large club. Money shouldn't be an issue, or are the members not paying their fees?"

"No, it's not the money. But only so many of these boats are built in a year, and there are many more clubs, more significant than ours, with better connections. We may be at position 80 and must wait another five years to get even one additional boat."

Bodo thought about that and said, "Let me see how I can help. Since my family is now a club member, I feel obliged to help the club forward as much as possible. Now, I can't promise anything, but I will try."

He stretched out his hand, and the trainer took it, and with a handshake, they departed. When Bodo turned toward his family, which stood a little further back, toward the parking lot, he saw that Sarina had just removed her hand from Nick's mouth and wondered what that was about. They walked silently to the car, and when they drove off, Bodo asked Sarina, "What was that that you had to cover Nick's mouth while I was talking with the trainer?"

"You saw that? I thought you had not noticed. In his excitement about becoming a competitive sailor, Nick was about to tell you that you should have enough power to get ten Pirate Class boats to the club by tomorrow night. So I had to close his mouth, and he understood that he almost made a big mistake."

Bodo looked back at Nick, who was obviously ashamed of his mistake, and said, "Nick, you understand why you can't run around and brag about the power your dad has with his new positions, right?"

Nick looked up and said, "I am sorry, Dad. I will be more careful. As Mom said, my excitement went ahead of my thinking."

Bodo answered, "Great, Nick." And with that, the issue was solved for him. He knew his son; at over ten years old, he couldn't keep that excitement in control. Soon they arrived home, and since it was already after 5:00 PM, they decided to have an early dinner at the terrace.

Then they went to Nick's room together and prepared all the stuff for his first day at the new school. After a bit of back and forth about the clothes he wanted to wear and which one of the two new backpacks he wanted to use when they were in the city with Annabell, Sarina bought two new backpacks for Nick since they were so cheap that particular store and Nick like a different one more than she and so she ended up with buying both. Now, it turned out that Nick preferred the one she liked to have on his first day of school.

Bodo prepared himself for the next day, knowing that after getting Nick to his new school, he would have a tough day in front of him. He hoped that the interrogation of the two traitors would reveal some of the resources they had hidden somewhere. And then there was the start of the arrests of the next load of these bastards who thought they could steal from the collective.

When he was done, he walked upstairs to their bedroom and discovered that Sarina was already asleep. He made himself bed ready and was soon in dreamland too.

Monday morning started with the alarm clock waking him and Sarina about half an hour earlier than usual, which might be why he did not wake up before the alarm started. He went through his morning routine, which was a standard procedure, having the separation in HIM and HER bathrooms and walk-in closets. When he came to the kitchen area, he started the coffee-making process and the water kettle to boil some eggs. Because Nick did not like fried eggs with bacon, so he made boiled eggs for all.

The coffee was ready, and the eggs, just about so, when Sarina and Nick came down the stairs to the kitchen area and took place at the breakfast bar. Bodo placed the eggs for all of them and filled the coffee cups for him and Sarina. While eating breakfast, Nick fantasized about the new school and how the kids in his class would be. He was less concerned with the potential classmates since he knew his new friend, Willi, was in the same class he would be in.

They were finished with breakfast early enough for Bodo to get over the instructions for Nick to keep the position he had a secret. He told him he would answer any question about his work from the principal or the teachers; I work in a government position. Nick confirmed that that should work because Willi had told him that most school kids have parents in a government position. Nobody wants to discuss the ins and outs of their work. And so should Nick do when classmates would ask him.

The drive to the school was just under thirty minutes. When they arrived, they saw that most of the children were either arriving on foot or by the public traffic system, busses, or walking over from the S-Bahn station. They parked the car and walked toward the entrance when Nick suddenly yelled, "There is Willi and Lisa."

Bodo stopped him short of running to them, saying, "Stay with us, Nick, we want to get to the principal first, and he will get us to the classroom." They entered the school building and were directed to the principal's office. He was already awaiting them and waved them into his office with a smile. They all sat, and the principal introduced himself, saying he had been directing this school for over eight years and believed they had great teachers, resulting in the region's lowest failure rate.

Bodo and Sarina listened, and when he was finished, Bodo said, "Comrade, we really appreciate the introduction, and we hope that the reputation you have so proudly stated is justified. We have heard a lot about your school, and one of our neighbors recommended it. Since his son and we are the same age, we would appreciate your placing them in the same class."

"Who would that be, if I may ask?"

"It's William Tecker. And we would really appreciate it if our son could join that class because they have become friends in the few days since we moved here. It would make the transition from his former school and missing his friends there much easier."

The principal stood and walked over to his desk, saying, "Yes, I agree. I am calling the class teacher for that class because I believe he is not in class at this hour. Such a huge change at this age can load a child's psyche. And having a friendly person around is an excellent help to accustom to the new environment." He spoke on the phone for a few minutes and then hung up. "The class teacher will be here in a minute."

The door opened after a knock, and a very friendly-looking woman in her mid-forties entered. Bodo and Sarina raised shook hands with the teacher, and then all sat again around the small table.

Bodo and Sarina explained what they had discussed with the principal, and smiling at Nick, the teacher said, "I am sure that Nick will feel as if he was always a member of that class. The kids in that class are lovely, and we have no trouble there." She looked at her watch and said, "Nick, why don't we go over to your classroom, and I introduce you to your fellow students and the math teacher who is currently and the next hour teaching your class?"

Nick looked at his parents and then back to the teacher and asked, "When is school ending for my class? Because my Mom needs to pick me up."

Sarina stood and hugged Nick and said, "Don't worry, Nick. I will get your timetable and be here to pick you up."

When Nick and the teacher had left the principal's office, he turned to Bodo. He said, "Comrade Zipper, I have been briefed by the SSP office, which is responsible for our district, and I understand that you have some critical position within the security structure of our government. We, including all teachers, will do whatever is necessary to keep your son safe. We will inform the contact person at the SSP office immediately if we discover any irregularities."

Bodo, his wife, and the principal stood. Bodo shook hands with him and said, "I trust that you and your collective of teachers are aware of the seriousness of the counterrevolutionary activities in our country and appreciate your watchfulness over the children in your responsibility, comrade." The principal walked with them to the exit, and after a brief goodbye, Bodo and Sarina entered the car and drove back home.

"This seems to be a really great school. I am surprised by the professionalism with how they handled our appearance," Sarina said. "I will be here at 2:00 PM to pick up Nick. What is your day looking like, Bodo?"

"I have to check in with the inmates, see how far Reiner has come with the arrests in his area, and the CC meeting in the afternoon. Since I am now considered a nonpermanent member, I have to be there every Monday and Wednesday, I believe it was. Tomorrow I have to be in the south. We have the location for the ROS fixed, and since the construction has been going on for over a week, we should be able to start this week. I am unsure if I will be back Tuesday night or Wednesday."

"Okay, looks like I won't see you much this week," Sarina answered sadly. "But I understand, and we have spoken about this, so don't be disturbed by me complaining."

Bodo laughed while hitting the opener for the gate, "You are right. I won't pay much attention to your ranting until we have the well-oiled machinery for eliminating the traitors and counterrevolutionaries. I will call Gunther and have him pick me up." They kissed, and Sarina walked into the kitchen, saying she had much more work. Bodo went to his office and hit the call button for Giesela. After a few rings, she was on the phone, "Yes, comrade Zipper, what can I do for you?"

"Please send Gunther to my house to get me to the office."

"Yes, comrade Zipper, he will arrive in a few minutes."

And as she said, a few minutes later, the intercom on his desk phone buzzed, and Gunther announced his arrival.

After the short drive to his office, Bodo was still thinking about his son and his first day at the new school he now attended, but the reality of his particular assignment to rescue the Communist Party from being washed away by the oppressed masses, yearning for freedom to live their lives as they saw fit for themselves, caught his attention immediately when he entered the facility.

CHAPTER 19

The First Interrogations, Threats, and a Try Bribery Without Success

Bodo entered the office, and right after him, Giesela entered with a cup of freshly brewed coffee, which she placed on his desk. He took out his OmniBook and started it up, sipping the coffee simultaneously. "Okay, Giesela, what do we have on this morning's priority list?"

"Comrade Zipper, comrade Worser called about thirty minutes ago, and after he learned that you are not in yet, he left the following message for you:

> "I have started the arrests beginning with the highest levels assigned to RON. We have instructed the SSP offices throughout the North region to arrest all levels 1 through 3 and keep them separated in their own arrest facilities. Levels 4 and 5 beginning to be interrogated.

"He asked you to call him when you have time. It was about coordinating the transfer of the Level 1 through 3 delinquents."

"Okay, I will call him as soon as we are done. What else?"

"You have the CC meeting at 4:00 PM, and the transfer of the officers for the ROS needs to be prepared if you find the facility there fit for their arrival tomorrow."

"Giesela, please coordinate that with comrade Karl, and when you are done talking with him, please patch him through to me."

Giesela left Bodo's office and started working on some of his bullet points for the CC meeting in the afternoon. When the phone rang, and he picked it up, he had Karl on the line. "Hi, Karl, how was your weekend?"

"Nothing special. You won't believe how fast time flies by when you are focused on something you had on your mind for years but never had time to do it. I was going back to your suggestion about a training program for the ICC region and county offices and started to work on that."

Bodo laughed and said, "Karl, I believe you. I have been there and done it. And now I am doing it again. But I have something else I would like to talk with you about."

"He, comrade Zipper, what can I do you can't? You can have everything done with the move of your small finger. But seriously, what is it?"

"I have been with Nick at the little sail club we have here in town on the weekend, and he was fascinated sailing the Pirate Class and did very well. The trainer and manager asked if he would like to be a member, and he was so happy when we signed him up. While I was talking with him, he revealed that they have difficulties getting more of those boats because they are listed very far down the waiting list. Can you do me a favor and find out who is building those Pirate Class boats?"

"Bodo, that is easy to answer. I was once a competitive sailor with those boats. These are built by a relatively small shipyard in Rechlin."

"That was easy, Karl. I will call Reiner and ask him to have a visit there. Maybe he can cheat them out of two or three boats out of line delivery."

Karl laughed and asked, "Are you still on for tomorrow's trip to the ROS facility?"

"Sure, I will take Joachim with me, and we will see how it looks. Giesela talked with you about the transfer organization? Most of them drive down there using cars and SUVs, but there might be some personal stuff to transport?"

"Yes, we talked it all through, and you should consider it done. Stop worrying about the small stuff. Bodo, you have a collective now, and they are professionals."

"I know, Karl, it will take some time to realize that I am no longer a soloist in my fight. Thanks for the reminder, though. Have a great day." With that, they hung up.

Sitting silently momentarily, Bodo thought about the next steps and buzzed Giesela to connect her with Reiner. After a few seconds, the phone rang, and Reiner's voice came clear through, "Hello, Bodo, and good morning on this wonderful Monday."

"I don't know about your morning, but mine was okay. How are things up there in the far north?"

Reiner laughed and answered, "We have started to arrest levels 4 and 5 in our area, as agreed and per your directive, but have you seen the list? Oh, sure, you have. We must expand or use the SSP facilities to hold the delinquents."

"I understand, Reiner. But no, no new buildings. We use the SSP holding facilities, which is what those are for, and when we are done with those traitors, there is no need for cells. There are either sentenced to execution or lifelong work in the underground mines."

"Sounds good to me, Bodo. Even though we must deal with the massive number of traitors, I might be ripe for retirement when we are done."

"Something else I wanted to ask you, Reiner. I need you to do me a favor and drive over to the yacht-building factory in Rechlin. They are building the Pirate Class boats, and I need three or four of them for the sailing club Nick joint on the weekend. They have only three, and because it is a small club with no connections, they are very far down the line for delivery. I need you to speed up this week's delivery to that club."

"Did you just say the shipyard company in Rechlin?"

"Yes, that's what I said. Why?"

"We have that guy who runs the show on our list to be arrested. I planned to do so because this factory is one of the major exporting companies for sailing boats and yachts."

"Great. Let me know what is going on when you have the situation under control."

"Sure, Bodo, I will call you when I know what we have there." And Reiner hung up.

Bodo thought for a moment about what he needed to finish for the meeting of the CC in the afternoon, and when he realized that he was pretty much prepared, he thought to have a short meeting with Peter.

Bodo called for Peter via intercom and was told he was at the Barn. He decided to pay the inmates a visit. Bodo entered the holding area and was greeted by the sergeant in charge with a brief report, saying that comrade Peter was in the holding with an interrogator and a guard. Bodo asked him to open the door, and he walked in. He looked briefly through the windows of the two occupied cells and saw that the FDS wasn't in his cell, meaning he was being interrogated. Bodo walked to the interrogation block and entered it.

Peter and the interrogator looked at him, and Bodo nodded at both to continue with their work.

The FDS was seated at the other side of the table. His hands were fastened in clamps on the table, forcing him to sit straight up. Since the recording systems were outside the room in a separate technical cabinet, the room had just two chairs for the interrogators, the fixing chair for the delinquents, and the table. Both were made from stainless steel and fixed solid to the floor.

Bodo asked, "Did he finally come to his senses and realize that he will have no chance but to cooperate?"

The interrogator, Bodo, recognized as Officer Kenner, answered, "Commander Zipper, he seems to realize that we are not joking. Just before you entered, he suggested making a deal. He would inform us where he hid his cash money and inform his foreign money handlers to send us each one thousand West Mark if we would find him not guilty and let him go."

Bodo looked disgusted at the piece of shit that was once the mightiest man in the district and said, "Get that information out of this piece of shit no matter what you have to do. I will personally come back and pull his fingernails piece by piece until he sings like a bird if you can get it out of him before the day is over!" He went around the table to stand at the side of the FDS and smashed his hand flat on it so it vibrated. The shock of realization that Bodo meant what he just said was suddenly visible on the FDS's face, and all the color was gone.

With a low voice, full of fear, the FDS said, "You can't do that. No court would accept your evidence acquired by torture. That would be torture, and that is forbidden by law."

"You piece of shit has not yet realized that there is no court, haven't you? You have no rights. Your rights were gone the exact moment you betrayed the party for your own benefit. The only right you still have to spill the beans without being cut to pieces piece by piece. But only as long as you start to sing immediately. If it wasn't for the money you stole from the party, I would have beaten you into a pulp with a wet towel."

Turning to Peter and the interrogator, he said, "Let me know when he is trying to bribe you again. I will come in, and my threat won't longer be a threat. It will be reality!"

Bodo walked out of the interrogation block, and when he saw the scared expression on the face of the SSP guard sergeant, he addressed him, "Sergeant, do you have anything to say? I am not joking. My threats to this man in there are real. He will physically suffer if he does not speak about the stolen resources' hidings. Do you have a problem with that?"

"No, Commander Zipper. Not in the least. I am astounded that somebody in your position is taking responsibility seriously and acting as promised. Most of the time, the leaders talk, and we must do the work."

Bodo, who had been in an aggressive mood when he saw the expression on the face of the sergeant, relaxed, and with a smile and said, "Sergeant, you can be assured I mean what I say. Always!"

Bodo walked back into his office, and sitting behind his desk, he took a deep breath and then returned to his preparation work. After what seemed to have been just a few minutes, yet in reality, it was almost 2:00 PM, his phone rang, and when he picked it up, Reiner was on the phone.

"You won't believe what we have discovered here, Bodo. We happened to be here just in time to stop the utterly illegal transport of those Pirate Class boats to West Germany. That yacht-building company is a cesspool of corruption, and I had to arrest the whole management, including the accountant. Can you believe this skeleton with human skin wanted to pay me off with an account in my name in West Berlin with ten thousand West Mark? I have to apologize, or actually not, but I knocked him out cold."

Bodo laughed and said, "Rainer, nothing to apologize for. How many people do you have arrested? And what was that with the illegal shipment?"

"So, Bodo, here are some facts. There were sixteen of those boats loaded on a Deutrans truck, ready to leave the property. These are excellent boats of a quality I have never seen before. Sails from a fabric they call Dragon, and I have rewritten the transport order for the Deutrans guy to deliver six boats to the sailing club in Karolinenhof. We found the address in the paperwork here, and we could see that the delivery date to that club had been moved down the list several times over the last three years. Bodo, you must call the manager and tell him to take the boats and be happy. Not that he refuses to take them because he doesn't know if it is legit. And you need to get somebody to the Deutrans headquarters because this transport order with the documents for the export came from somebody in a high enough position to do so."

"Reiner, yo are the best. Thanks again for the catch. I will take care of that immediately and have one of my teams take the Deutrans headquarters apart within the hour. Do you know what the price for these boats is?"

"Hold on a moment." Bodo could hear him talking to somebody in the background. There were some noises as if somebody got slapped around a bit. Reiner returned on the phone, "Bodo, these specific boats for the illegal shipment were priced at four thousand West Mark each. Why do you ask?"

"Please put another one with all the equipment on the truck. I am buying it for my son. Four thousand West Mark is not more than our mark. As you know, it is a scheme of the rotten capitalists to diminish our workers' outstanding achievements. And a last question, before I let you go, did he reveal the data of that West Mark account yet."

"Consider the boat loaded, and I will have your home address with the truck driver. And yes, we have all the data we need to retrieve the money, which is about 2.5 million West Mark."

Bodo was shocked and silent for a moment. After he caught his breath, he said, "So much money for Pirate Class boats. How many years is he doing that?"

"First, it isn't just for Pirate Class boats. They are building really nice sea-worthy yachts here and selling them to rich people worldwide. Most of them were officially exported, but I suspect there are more accounts in other countries, and we might be surprised by how much these gangsters have misappropriated. Secondly, they have been working here for almost twenty years. I need a finance expert to help us review all the paperwork to determine how many they have sold illegally."

"Congratulations, Reiner, for the catch, and tell your collective 'I thank thems' for their determination. And I will have a finance expert at your place by tomorrow. Beat the information about all the hidden places out of these pieces of shit, and don't worry about legal rights. As I just told the FDS a few minutes ago, the exact moment he decided to steal from the Communist Party, he lost all rights. So did these traitors in Rechlin. Let me know what you find out ASAP because I have the CC meeting at 4:00 PM, and they really need some good news." Bodo hung up, and leaning back in his chair, he enjoyed their success momentarily. Then he hit the intercom for Peter but did not get a response. He pressed the button for Giesela and asked her if she could send someone to get Peter to his office. And to let Gunther know to prepare for their drive to the CC meeting. About five minutes later was a knock on his door. He called, "Come in," and Peter entered the office.

"Hi, Bodo. You asked for me to come over?"

"Yes, Peter. I wanted to get an update about the FDS interrogation. Don't get me wrong, I understand he is a hard nut to crack, but I would love to have at least something to present to the CC when I attend the meeting in about an hour."

"Bodo, you have no idea how you affect people when you threaten them, do you? After you left the room, the FDS asked me if you would really do what you had said. I asked him back, do you know me? And he said yes, I have known you for many years. So I asked him, do you believe me when I tell you that I know Commander Bodo very well and know that Commander Bodo never makes an empty promise? At that moment, he broke down in tears and started to talk."

"Peter, I had no idea I am so threatening when angry. Although I wasn't really joking, I thought it was compelling."

"Bodo, I am so glad that we have cameras and recorders running all the time because neither Officer Kenner nor I could write down as fast as he was spilling it out. We have all of it on one of the pocket memos, too, so you could take it with you and play it back at the CC meeting, at least in part. He is still confessing. He believes he may get away with a few years in jail if he comes clean. And I did not tell him otherwise."

"That is just great, Peter. Can you give me an elevator pitch of what you have so far?"

"Yes, we have nine bank accounts in several different districts under three different identities with a total of eight million Mark and five foreign accounts were are five million West Mark, and several more millions of other currencies, including dollars and Swiss francs, are hidden. And we are not finished yet. Just when you called me out, he started writing down a list of addresses of properties, including companies he owns in several Western countries."

Peter, explain how an FDS can own companies in the NSW (nonsocialistic economy)? Bodo was obviously shocked. "How is that possible? I am shocked!"

"Bodo, remember twenty-plus years of corruption, in the position where he was only controlled by those concerned with their own power and did not care about the country. There was a situation where a communist widow of a West German manufacturer entailed the manufacturing plant to the party and set the address of the SUP office in Rostock in the Will. Our FDS immediately grabbed that chance and signed the company to a fictive entity he had founded. From that moment on, nothing was too criminal for him. His goal was to retire, move to the Caribic, and enjoy the rest of his life after so many years of hard work for the communist cause."

Bodo was speechless for a while and sat there, totally amazed. This was such a level of impertinence that he was lost for words. Then after he had regained his countenance, he said, "Thank you, Peter, for getting this done, and let Officer Kenner know my specific thanks for being successful. I knew he was dirty and had stolen much money over the years, but I had never envisioned it as bad. I wonder how much human waste we must walk through to clean out the mess."

Peter confirmed the tragedy of this and, taking his notes, said he would go back to finish the FDS and prepare the interrogation for the FCS for tomorrow. He was explicitly eager for that piece of human savagery because he had suffered under his leadership for years.

A few minutes after he had left Bodo's office, Giesela came in and brought the pocket memo, saying that she had copied it to her device to type it into the file software on her computer. Bodo started to pack everything into his briefcase and, when he was done, walked out into the front yard. It had rained again, and he did not even notice, but the sun came through the clouds and dried things up.

Right then, Gunther appeared out of the breakroom with a cup of coffee, and Bodo called him over. "Gunther, are you ready to go? We must get on the road to be at the CC in time?"

"Yes, Commander, I am ready when you are." They entered the car and were on their way.

CHAPTER 20

A Memorable Central Committee Meeting and Some Historical Decisions

On the way to the building of the Central Committee, Bodo sorted out the information he had for his report and typed up a short summary of the two significant discoveries of the day. Again he marveled briefly about the small wonder of technology he was using, his OmniBook laptop. While thinking about it, he was sure that the great engineers of the communist part of Germany would have been able to come up with such things and maybe even better if it had not been for the betrayal of some of their leaders over the last thirty years.

They stopped at the gate of the CC, and after the guards were satisfied that he was in the car and not some terrorist, they drove into the underground garage and parked. Bodo told Gunther that the meeting may take longer and he could drive somewhere to get dinner. Gunther appreciated that, and Bodo hit the elevator to get to the floor where the meeting room was.

Exiting the elevator, Bodo almost ran into the secretary of Defense, Army General Bode. "I am sorry, General, I did not pay attention to where I was going."

"Commander Zipper, no problem. I was in my thoughts too, so we may care about the guilt together. How was your day? Uh, we will talk about that soon."

"By the way, comrade Secretary, I would like to thank you for the great help getting those facilities for the OIR. That was a great help to get started. And since I have your attention now, I am interested in contacting my former commanding officer after I almost run you over. He was my platoon leader when I served and an excellent officer and comrade."

"Sure, Commander Zipper, give me your data, and I will see that we find him. He might not be at that unit anymore, not even at that regiment. But we will find him."

"Thanks, comrade Bode, and please, when we are not in public, call me comrade Bodo. I am not used to being called commander, for sure not by a general," Bodo said, smiling.

"Oh, come on, Commander, it is your rank now, and you must get used to it. You will get used to it soon," he said, laughing while padding Bodo on his shoulder while they walked into the conference room. That's the reason I am calling you that way. It reminds me of when I got promoted to general. I had no idea how to handle it when suddenly everybody I knew for years stood in attention when I entered and saluted."

Bodo sat next to Bruno as it seemed to have become his place in the assembly of the decision-makers with the fade of the nation in their hands. Bruno looked up from the paperwork he was studying, smiled at Bodo, and said, "Hi, Bodo. I am looking forward to your first report. I heard you have the first two heavy hitters in your facility?"

"Bruno, you won't believe what I have to report. All secretaries will feel the same as when I heard the first two cases, partly because the interrogations and investigations have just started."

The secretary-general entered the room and took his place at the head of the large and impressive table, and all chatting fell silent.

Looking up from a stack of papers before him, he started, "Comrades, thanks for being here and on time. We have much to discuss today and a report from our military about the invention. We shall have a first brief report about the work of the OIR. Before we begin, I would like to announce that I, in cooperation with comrade Tecker as the secretary ICC decided to elevate the membership of comrade Bodo Zipper to the level of a member with full voting rights. Are there any comments or statements we need to hear about that decision? No? Okay then, let's begin. First, I would like comrade Pieker to give us an overview of the counterrevolutionary events and the preparation for the May 1 ceremonies."

"Comrades, after we finished the investigation of our own ranks for traitors, of whom we found a total of seventy-five throughout all ranks and positions and eliminated them, we can now focus with a clean and concentrated force to secure the eternal leadership role of the Communist Party in our nation. One of the most critical events to demonstrate this position and social cohesion with the workers' class is the demonstration of that role on May 1.

"The party has planned and organized May demonstrations in all cities, even in the smallest towns, are the leaders of the Communist Party engaged in organizing those marches. To ensure that these marches of unity of the worker's class and the Communist Party, which cannot be destroyed, are peaceful and without counterrevolutionary interruptions, we have ordered the arrest of all known subversive elements and those who are suspects of being sympathetic to that subversive elements.

"Two nights before, meaning this coming Saturday night, the SSP will arrest thousands of people of which we have documented data for a potential interruption of the May ceremonies. We are currently moving all necessary SSP forces and equipment into place. Zero time for the action is 11:00 PM Saturday night. With the deactivation of the members of the counterrevolutionary Monday demonstrations, we shall have a really great May 1 ceremony. In addition to the arrest, we will have large numbers of SSP officers in civil spread out through the cities and towns of the country to crush any spontaneous development in its beginnings."

"Comrade Pieker, how long do you consider keeping these elements under arrest, and do you believe we should prepare some kind of a communique about the issue?" the secretary of Information asked.

"Good question, comrade Kurt. My commanding officers think it would be wise to hold them past the following Monday, meaning to release them on Tuesday, May 8. That could put a considerable damper on the Monday demonstrations since we are sure that most of the savagery we consider arresting is part of the organizational leadership of those groups."

Bodo cleared his throat and said, "Comrade Jürgen, I know you at the SSP have a lot of experience with these bastards destroying our society, but I think you should rethink that decision. You are right to arrest them over the time of the May ceremonies, and I believe that comrade Kurt can come up with very acceptable explanations for why it needed to be done. The vast majority of the people enjoy May Day as the celebration of the victory of the working class in our nation and would not understand if we let them be interrupted. But keeping them much longer than Wednesday morning could turn them into martyrs. Just a thought, but the decision is definitely yours."

"Comrade Bodo, who is a valid point. We don't want to turn these bastards into martyrs. Why do you think that could happen? Do you have any indications?"

"No, nothing specific, but when you look at the masses running around those churches every Monday, they are like sheep. I would guess that 70 percent to 75 percent would not be there if they were not attracted by curiosity or friendship. What do we want to achieve by cleansing the party of corruption and showing those people, which is precisely that part of the demonstrators, that we mean business, correct?

"That means they need to hope that the party is willing to hear their cries and act accordingly. Suppose you cut off the head now, and I know it is a huge IF, and if the head becomes a martyr, all the efforts to silence the masses and isolate the counterrevolutionaries will fail."

Silence followed the analysis done by Bodo for several seconds, then comrade Pieker spoke again, "Comrade Bodo, your analysis is brilliant. I believe you are right. Comrade Kurt can prepare a communique that the safety of the May Day parades requires us to act before riots interrupt the May Day and put children in danger. If we overdo it now, we may lose that attempt to draw the masses back to us and separate the initiators. I agree we should hold them until Tuesday evening."

Several comrades nocked their heads, and comrade Werner said, "Okay, comrades, that is settled then?" All answered positively, and the secretary-general went to the next issue. "Comrade Frank, please update the committee on the efforts to create an increasing stream of exchangeable currency for the coming challenges."

Comrade Frank, secretary of Defense, cleared his throat and said, "We have excellent news to report about the top secret project. With the great support of the SSP, we have been able to increase the manufacturing capacity of the missile guidance system to approximately two thousand pieces per month. In addition, the Secretary of Economy and the Secretary of Finances have helped us contact decision-makers in the military of Russia, Syria, and China. We have demonstrated our promise of universal usage to those top military by mounting the guidance system on the two air-to-air missile systems, and all tests were positive."

"You named three countries you have contacts with, but tests were only made with two?" Secretary Kurt interrupted the presentation of the secretary of Defense.

"The Syrians are using Russian missiles, comrade Kurt. After we could demonstrate that the guidance system could function with all of their other missiles, ground-to-air and air-to-ground also, we tested it against NATO-style defense systems, as far as those were available. Also successful 100 percent. We were asked if the guidance system could distinguish between a Russian or Chinese fighter aircraft and a NATO-type aircraft.

"Last week, the Russians were presenting an F16 brought in from Alaska by a deep sleeper who had been recalled to get the test done. It was a total success. Although the pilot trained and one of the qualifications, Top Gun, tried everything to escape the missile fired from a MIG-31, he failed. We expect the Russian, Chinese, and Syrian military to begin conditional negotiations within May. We are not considering licensing the system soon since we are prepared to produce the amount they can pay for in Swiss Francs. The secretary for Economy, comrade Alexander, has already set up his best collective of international contract lawyers, which have been cleared by comrade Jürgen's office for the case."

"We are ready to start the negotiation but will hold back a bit to make them hungry. That will give us the leverage we need to get the best results." Comrade Alexander closed the presentation on the issue. And all the members started to praise the initiative of the small R&D department of the military.

Comrade Werner took over. "Comrades, let's have brief information from comrade Bodo so that we can go back to work we have to do. Comrade Bodo, please."

Bodo looked around the men at the table and said, "Comrades, we have just started to interrogate the first delinquents today, and I am shocked. We have the confession of the former FDS from Rostock on tape, and I will play at least some of it for you. But before, I need to tell you about another issue today. Our office in the north, ROS, under the leadership of my CO Reiner Worser, went to arrest the director of the yacht manufacturer in Rechlin. After the director, including his whole band of corrupt sewage, tried to bribe comrade Worser offering him an account with ten thousand West Mark in his name in West Berlin, the OIR officer became active, and within a few hours, they had discovered one of many foreign accounts with 2.5 million West Mark. He asked for a finance expert familiar with data analysis of foreign bank accounts. I believe comrade Walter can provide those." Turning directly to Walter Reichmann, sitting on the other side of the table several seats to the left, he said, "Comrade Walter, can we have one of your experts at the ROS facility tomorrow before lunch? I try to avoid any delay because we don't know what safety nets these savages have installed."

"Comrade Bodo, this is both excellent and sad news. Sad that we have leading members of our economy who struggle daily to have the appropriate amount of exchangeable currency for businesses stealing it without hesitation, and great that your agency can get the information we need to get it back. I will establish a task force under my direct leadership with experts in that field, and they will be at your disposal. Can you transfer two of my experts to your office in the morning?"

Jürgen said, "Walter, I will have a car at your facility at 9:00 AM tomorrow. Does this give you enough time to get the guys prepared?"

"Yes, that would be very great, comrade Jürgen."

Bodo continued with his information, "Now since this is out of the way, let me play the record of the confession of the man I had arrested immediately after I took over the assignment for the OIR." Bodo placed the pocket memo device in the center of the table and adjusted the loudness to the maximum. The voice of the former FDS Rostock was clearly understandable, and it took only a few of his words for many of the CC members let out a deep sigh.

The confession was a seemingly endless list of misappropriations, stolen money, blackmailing, and to the surprise of Bodo since he hadn't heard the tape himself, he confessed the order of two murders to cover up the theft of the property where he had built his vacation home in the hills near the Fichtelberg.

Bodo stopped the recorder after about twenty minutes, believing it was more than enough evidence for his coming suggestion. "Comrades, as you have heard and we will have this confession in written form added to his file on OIR computers, he is not just a thief and corrupt, he is a murderer, and his best companion is the FCS from the Island Rügen. We will have that confession by the end of tomorrow, and I will present both cases to you in our next meeting on Thursday."

The silence in the room was tangible. All that was to hear for several minutes was the heavy breathing of the secretary-general, who had to work on himself not to explode. When he had regained his countenance, he slowly began to speak, "Comrades, I have had some suspicions about the Old Guards' corruption, but in my wildest dreams would I never have believed what we just heard one of them confess. And addressing Bodo directly, "Comrade Commander Bodo, if you used so-called inappropriate methods and tactics to get this scum to confess, I approve of it, and I encourage you to have no hesitation. Whatever is necessary, do it."

"Comrade Secretary General, I will not stop. I will do whatever is necessary, even physical torture, to get the information necessary to regain what is ours. As I at the meeting stated, when you all assigned that task to me, I would not rest until the last one of these scums was eliminated. You have to be aware that these two, and probably the director of the yacht builder in Rechlin and maybe his sales manager, are on the pathway to be executed."

Again, for a while, nobody said anything. Then Bruno spoke and said, "Comrades, what we have heard here within the last half hour, confirms everything we had suspected. Suppose we want to get the trust of the people back. In that case, we have to place those cases in public, and we have, as Bodo requested from the beginning, show the execution life on TV."

"Comrade Pieker, I understand that your troops are busy getting all the preparations for the preemptive arrest of these elements done, but would it be possible to have a general arrest action done of all the suspects the ICC has fished out of the pool of potential traitors. I suspect they, seeing the preemptive action on Saturday, might get nervous and destroy the evidence. We need to get them all secure before they start to get suspicious. Do you have the resources to get that done?"

"Commander Zipper, I agree with you. That needs to be taken care of now. I will check our resources with operations and if we have some units of the Riot Police commanded by SSP officers to help."

"Please start the arrest ASAP and let me know when you need more information. But I think the files from ICC should be enough."

"Yes, indeed, we can work with those."

Comrade Werner finally spoke and closed that point of discussion. "That means that we have our tasks assigned and will meet again here on Thursday at the same time. All agree, comrades?" There followed a general "Yes, Secretary-General," and the meeting was closed.

On their way out, several members tapped Bodo on the shoulder and thanked him for being diligent. Bruno stopped at his side and said, "Bodo, do you understand now that the members of the Central Committee consider you one of us? You have more than earned the place and the money you are getting paid. Don't ever forget that."

"Thanks, Bruno. I am increasingly aware of the extreme economic damage these traitors have caused for the first socialist country on German soil. Until now, I considered the ideological damage more dangerous, but that is not the case anymore. The ideological damage we can get under control, even if necessary, with the power of the gun. But the economic damage is much worse."

They entered the elevator, and Bruno answered, "You are correct, Bodo. Just thinking of the money, we could have used to import some coffee or fruits and vegetables not growing here, people might have been calmer and not run behind the counterrevolutionary attempts of some provocateurs."

"Agreed, Bruno. I wondered how far we could have been in technological development and engineering. Just the project, our special R&D unit in the military, proves that we can develop systems second to none if we have the resources to place where it counts. I will be on the road tomorrow and on Wednesday, but we will be in touch if something comes up where I need your input, Bruno."

"Don't worry, Bodo, you will get it all straighten out. These first few weeks have proven that. And Annabelle has told me that she is going shopping with Sarina tomorrow after they have the kids in school."

"I knew something was brewing," Bodo said, laughing, and turning to his car, he said goodbye to Bruno, and soon Gunther had them on the way to the office.

CHAPTER 21

An Unexpected and Unappreciated Promotion Surprising Experience with a Chief Engineer and a Strange Invitation from a Powerful Man

When Fritz entered the breakroom at the shipyard the next day, several colleagues grinned at him, and only after he asked, "What is it? Do I have the breakfast egg I did not eat in my beard I do not have?"

They all started laughing out loud, and finally, Hannes, one of the master electricians with whom he often worked together, said, "Fritz, we are all so thrilled that you talked yourself into a new position. A position we know you would deny at all cost, but you can't anymore."

"Hannes, what are you talking about? I have no idea." Fritz looked from one to another, and all kept their grinning faces."

"You have been promoted to project manager, and we have been instructed to send you directly upstairs to the boss, Molly, when you arrive. Because we all know how much you 'love' that position, we are so happy that you have worked it all out." Hannes could barely finish the statement and laughed again so much that tears ran down his cheeks.

"They can't do that," was all Fritz could get out, totally perplexed by the statement, "They can't promote me to a position where I could destroy the achievements of the 'Paradise of the Workers' class. I am the

'Main Brake on the Golden Carriage toward Communism' in the nation. I have that in written form from the STASI case officer."

Now the group of colleagues turned to roar with laughter, and Fritz just waved it aside and walked out, the roaring laughter still behind him. He knocked on the door of Molly's office, and when he heard the "Come in," he entered. To his surprise, there was another person in the office, the shipyard's director of production, Werner. Fritz thought he had interrupted a meeting between the two and was about to turn and get out when Werner called, "Mr. Zipper, please stay with us. You are the reason I am here, and we need to talk with you."

"Oh, what did I do now to get your attention?"

Werner smiled and said, "We want to offer you a promotion. Please come and sit and let us explain what we want to offer you."

Fritz turned and slowly walked toward the table where they were sitting. "I am curious how you would argue with the Watchdogs because, as far as I remember, I was told I would never be allowed to walk in a leadership role again."

"We wouldn't call this a leadership role, Mr. Zipper. It is more like a specialist role. We believe that you are the best choice. We want you to be one of the project managers we need for the electronic equipment installed on our vessels. Your suggestion on Friday was the best solution to the problem. I admit I was totally against it until I took the time to think about it. When we finish this meeting and you go to your vessel, you will see that we are already preparing to place the new controller cabinet into the room through the opened side panel."

Bodo looked at Molly and then at Werner and said, "What if I have a condition to agree to be promoted against my will?"

Werner laughed aloud, and Molly grinned at him and said, "I told you, Jens, he isn't easygoing."

Then they both became serious, and Werner said, "Okay, Mr. Zipper, What is the condition?"

"I want to get one of the three-room apartments to which I know the shipyard has been assigned a contingent. I will only accept that new "position" if I get it in a written statement, signed by you, Mr. Werner."

"Do you have an idea what you are asking for, Fritz?" Molly asked with some anger in his voice. "That's almost blackmailing the shipyard."

"Oh, come on, Molly, you know as well as I do that these apartments are reserved for improving the shipyard's production. You guys in the ivory tower of power always believe that you can hold secrets, and they are none before you even decide them among yourselves. All shipyard employees know that ten apartments, eight three-room, and two five-room apartments were explicitly reserved for that." And turning back to Werner, he adds, "Mr. Werner, it isn't really a big deal. I want the apartment if you need me for that position, and you will guarantee it. If you can guarantee it, you really don't need me. You just want to use me."

Jens Werner, the most powerful man of the shipyard, and based on the size of it, of the whole city, turned to Molly and said, "Give me a page from that notepad there."

Molly looked at him as if he had just swallowed a stone, walked over to his desk, and ripped off a page from the notepad, saying, "Jens, I hope you know what you are doing. He is a rebel and an enemy of the party. He may use that to sabotage our economy at a critical production line."

"Molly, now you are getting ridiculous," Werner interrupted a beginning litany; both Jens Werner and Fritz knew well enough was just to begin. "Mr. Zipper has done more for keeping the timeline of the vessels going on a trial journey since he is here than anyone working in your whole company. When we can't use the knowledge and skills of people, we have to educate them with the money of the worker's class to benefit the worker's class. Why would we even send them to universities and get them educated?"

Molly returned to the table with the page and handed it to Werner. Then looking at Fritz without sympathy, he said, "Maybe we should not send them to universities at all."

Jens Werner was finishing his writing, handed it over to Fritz, and said, "Molly, I knew you have some strange idea, but this one is just stupid. And turning to Fritz, "Mr. Zipper, is this sufficient for you? If so, Molly and I will sign and date it."

Fritz was still baffled by the rebuke of Molly by the production director, looked at the paper, read the two sentences, and answered, "Mr. Werner, this is sufficient."

Molly and Werner signed and dated the paper, and Werner handed it to Fritz. "I suggest you get your personal stuff out of the collective room and move it over to the project management office," Molly said, already a little friendlier now, after he had realized that there was nothing he could do to stop the occupation of one of the most precious goods in the country, a newly built apartment by somebody how considered a traitor.

Although he was early impressed by Fritz's ability to fix issues by combining his education and experience in his electrical and electronic studies with the work, he had no sympathy for what he called a betrayal of the cause. Fritz stood and walked out of the office, knowing he had to watch his back because he knew Molly was not his friend. There weren't many friendly people even in his collective. With that thought, he actually appreciated the promotion and the pay raise that came with it. The promise to get an apartment for his family was the icing on the cake, which may not even be coming through.

But he accepted that as a punch in the face of the arrogant STASI officer who had promised him to shovel coal into a heating system at a crumbling facility rather than ever being able to work with modern technology. He moved his few belongings to his new office space, which he now shared with Willi. It was large enough to even have some privacy. There were three desks fully equipped as office workplaces. The third place would probably not be used for a long time.

Fritz chose the one farthest away from the door, which allowed him to sit to see who would enter, and had Willi's desk in front of him a decent distance away. After he had placed all his stuff where he wanted it, he grabbed the folder for vessel number 37 and walked out to investigate the status of the repair efforts.

When he entered the control room for the winches, his two colleagues were already working on terminating all the many wires they had to disconnect from the system to remove the defective control cabinet.

The older one of them, Manne, with whom Fritz had often worked together some months ago before he entirely concentrated on the issues with the computer-controlled power system, looked up, greeted Fritz, and said, "Hi, Fritz, we are about three, maybe four hours away to start the load cycle test. Can you ensure we get the water resistors to broadside the ship?"

"Sure, Manne, I will take care of that. Assuming the load test goes positive, how much time would you consider necessary to run the winch setup cycles until you can start six hours continuous 100 percent test? I know you may have some adjustment issues since the controller is from a different series."

"Yeah, Fritz, that might take some time to adjust all the timing relays and current controllers, but let me be careful and guess about two hours, if nothing else breaks."

"Okay, Manne, that sounds reasonable." I will see that you have the water resistor bank broadsides in about two hours."

Fritz left the room and climbed the stairs to the command bridge deck. The crew of radar specialists was just about closing their adjustments to compensate for the replaced transmitter, which was the last point on his punch list besides the winch controller. After a few words and an almost cynical gratulation for his promotion, they all laughed together, and one of the technicians said, "We actually like that is you, Fritz. We know you have the necessary knowledge to estimate the work needed." Fritz thanked them for their trust and said he would try not to disappoint them, as far as the conditions allowed, and left the bridge.

The punch list meeting and the water resistor load test went uneventfully. Fritz was satisfied with how the day ended for him, and he decided to use the last train to get home tonight, even though it meant getting up at 4:00 AM the following day. Arriving at the railway station, he used the only working pay phone. He called home to arrange to be picked up at the station since the local train connection did not run after 8:00 PM, which would actually have a stop at the village he lived now.

Karola was already there when the train stopped at the station, and within twenty minutes, they arrived home. He had told her about the promotion and the condition he connected his exception with. Knowing it would be a touch seal to his mother-in-law, he did not look forward to telling her. Without any hesitation, Karola told her Mom that Fritz had received and accepted a promotion combined with an apartment in the city which would allow them to live as a family again. Although it was evident that her Mom did not enjoy living by herself again, as she had for several years before, she understood this was the only way for them.

There wasn't much time to talk about all ins and outs of that change because Fritz had to get out very early. He enjoyed a few minutes to look at his children, deep in their dreams, and they went to bed. He was up early the next morning, and even though Karola was up too, he brewed a coffee while he got ready; Fritz had to run to the train station to catch the train at the last minute.

The day started actually very well because all the test runs they had done overnight had been finished, with positive results, and the protocol was ready for the commission. With the last point on his list finished, he went to find the chief engineer of the Soviet crew to set a time for the transfer of the equipment that was not signed off because of the punch list.

He was told that he might be in his cabin, and when Fritz knocked on the door, a sound "Заходи" was announced. Astounded that the thirteen years of education in the Russian language had left something for him to understand, Fritz entered the cabin and said, "Доброе утро!" The chief engineer, approximately in his fifties, looked up from a hill of papers on his small but convenient desk and, with a smile, said, "Кто ты? Как тебя́ зовут? Где Вилли?" Fritz was now at the end of the ability to answer correctly and switched to German with an excuse, "I am sorry, Chief, my Russian is somewhat rusty, and I would prefer to speak German or, if necessary, to get a translator."

The chief engineer laughed deeply. "We don't need a translator, and your Russian seems to need just a little training. What is the status of the remaining issues we have?"

"We have all points cleared, and I have the test protocols here, all signed by your department heads. All I need is for you to review it and sign the final commission statement. I can show you each item we have fixed if you like, Chief."

The chief engineer looked Fritz directly in the eye, and Fritz held his look until the chief engineer broke eye contact and said, "I don't think it is necessary. You're one of the few men I ever met who can hold eye contact. I trust you," he said, opening a drawer under the bench he was sitting on and pulled out a bottle of vodka, three-quarters full, and a box with dark bread made from coarse rye crops and a large junk of bacon.

He placed two plates on the table and cut a slice of bread and a thick slice of bacon on each. He grabbed two glasses from the shelve behind him and filled them to the brim. Pushing one of the glasses and one of the plates with the bread bacon over to Fritz, he said, "Nu, every good business needs to be sealed. We seal it with a sto gram and a slice of bread together. That's Russian tradition."

Fritz had known from others that this would happen and thought about ways to avoid it, but to finish the job and get the signatures, he had to bite the bullet. But he decided to do so by letting the chief engineer know he disagreed. "Chief, just to let you know, I can't digest hard liqueur very well, and I have always avoided that wherever possible to drink that stuff. But I will drink that one with you to finish the deal and not offend you and the Russian tradition. Fritz lifted the glass carefully, not to spill any of its content, and said, "Sto let!" Which was answered by the chief engineer with a grin and "Sto let, comrade Fritz!"

They both set down the empty glasses and took a big bite of the bread with the bacon. While chewing on it, the chief engineer began putting signatures on the many protocols and confirmation certificates. Since there were two copies of each, it took a while to get them all signed. After a few minutes, Fritz started to feel the effects of the vodka already and hoped the chief engineer would just finish the signing and let him go. He had heard stories about colleagues from other branches of the shipyard who had been carried off the vessel they had commissioned for their trade, wholly drunk and almost unconscious. He knew that would not happen to him, but risking an insult was not really good either.

The chief engineer finished the signing, looked up at Fritz, and said, "I can see you are not doing well with the vodka. I understand. You are a good man, Fritz, because you are honest, and as I said before, I trust you. He filled another glass for himself and, lifting it, said, "Sto let to you, Fritz!" They ate the bread, which Fritz enjoyed eating because it tasted natural, and talked about family and some personal things. Politics never entered their conversation because they both felt the same. They disagreed with what was going on and, at the same time, knew there wasn't much they could do, sitting on that fishing trawler.

When Fritz left the cabin of the chief engineer, he was a little tipsy, and he knew that that feeling would go away soon. He was very satisfied because he had gotten the complete commission paperwork for his company on this vessel signed and ready to deliver to his boss, Molly.

Fritz despised Molly, not for being a defender of the Communist Party ideology, but because Molly did so only when it was opportune. He was one of the opportunists who had the party membership book in their pocket because it helped them to crawl up the ladder.

He decided to play a little game with Molly and would deliver the document folder directly to Jens Werner. He knew that that was the wrong way to do it, but he had that great excuse, which he was planning to use for some time during the next few days. He was new in the position of project manager and did not know how everything was handled. He climbed up the stairs to the production director's office and asked his secretary if he could briefly meet with him. The secretary looked at Fritz briefly and said, "Wait here, let me ask him."

She knew exactly who Fritz was because she attended the same church Fritz had attended for several months until he found out the pastor wasn't watching out for his sheep, more likely for his wallet. A few minutes later, she exited Werner's office with a package of folders on her arm and said, "Sit down for a moment, he will be ready in a few minutes to call you in."

It was just a few minutes, as she had said, when a voice, subdued by the thick doors, yelled for him to come in. Fritz thanked the secretary and went into the office of the most powerful man of the shipyard, again considering why everyone was so afraid of him. The production director stood up from behind his desk, pointed to a seating area with a small coffee table, and asked, "Do you like a cup of coffee, Mr. Zipper?"

Fritz was surprised by that offer, but feeling still the vodka circulating in his system, answered, "That would be great."

Werner opened the door and told his secretary to brew them a coffee. Then he returned to the seating area and sat on one of the comfortable chairs across from Fritz. "What can I do for you, Mr. Zipper? You know I am pretty busy, and a project manager from an external company usually doesn't comes to my office to talk with me personally. That is the privilege of the station manager, in your case, Mr. Mollenka."

"I know all of that, Mr. Werner. I thought I would personally bring you the commission binder for our company's part on vessel 37. I just got the remaining signatures from the chief engineer. If all the other trades are finished, you could have the change of flag ceremony organized for tomorrow. If I had given the binder to Molly, excuse me, Mr. Mollenka, you would probably not see it until tomorrow afternoon."

Werner's facial expression changed, and he asked with a slightly disappointed tone, "What is that supposed to mean? Do you suspect Mr. Mollenka to sabotage our economy by willingly withholding information?"

"Oh, I don't believe he is thinking along that line. He hates me for what he calls the betrayal of the Communist Party and the cause of building the 'worker's paradise' on German soil. He believes I should be in prison, and the key should be thrown away. If he could still do anything that this would happen, he would do it. If the delayed delivery of the Binder would cause the delay of the flag ceremony for a day, and he could blame it on me, he would do that."

Werner was looking out of the window where they had a great view over the kay where several vessels lay tied to the pier in different stages of completion, then looked back at Fritz and said, "I am really interested to know and understand your reasoning for what you did. You must have been aware of the consequences. Would you accept my invitation for dinner at my home, let's say next week Wednesday night at 7:00 PM?"

"Mr. Werner, I am not sure this is a wise step to invite me. I might be still, or even again be, on the radar of our beloved SSP, and they may not appreciate you inviting me into your home."

Werner laughed out loud and, standing up, indicating it was time to leave, said, "Let that be my problem, Mr. Zipper." They shook hands, and Fritz was on his way to his office. Looking at his watch, he realized that it was already time to quit for the day.

CHAPTER 22

Regional Office South Established and Trusting a Young Comrade

Gunther arrived about half an hour earlier than they had agreed, but Bodo was already prepared to jump into the car and get on the road. He entered the car and greeted Joachim, sitting in the passenger seat. "Good morning, Joachim. Are you ready for this fantastic and exciting day?"

"I am, Commander Zipper, I am. I look forward to starting my work as an important part of the agency and will do my best."

"Okay, Gunther, get us there and see to it that we are not wasting time. I want to be at the ROS property before the officers arrive."

With a "Yes, Commander," Gunther moved the car, and soon, they reached the Autobahn 10.

Bodo took out the OmniBook, extended the work desk, and began writing the indictment for the two inmates of the headquarters holding cells. It took only a few minutes, and he had blended entirely out of Gunther's and Joachim's conversation had, talking about their service in the military, which was very different. Bodo had received the complete written and signed confessions of both the FDS and the FCS, accusing each other of being the leader of the crime.

Since he also got the voice recordings, he was baffled by the chutzpa with which they accused each other of having ordered and paid for the murder of the man who owned the piece of land where the FDS had built his blockhouse in the Fichtenberg area. And how they finally got rid of the guy who drove the dumpster with seven tons of sand and ran over the landowner. They killed him by telling him they had opened a way through the border for him. He believed them because of their power in the district and ran straight into the minefield, stacked with personnel mines.

Bodo's investigators had pulled out all the documents of those incidences, and everything lined up. There was nothing to debate. All he had to do, was to present a seamless stream of crimes committed by these two people and ask for the death penalty. Based on the increasing activities of the mass demonstrations in many more cities, now even smaller ones, he would insist that the executions would be transmitted in real-time on TV.

He was nearly done with the first file when he noticed the car slowed down. Looking up, he saw that they were entering a rest area, and Gunther, seeing in the mirror that Bodo looked up, explained, "We need to fuel, commander. It will only take a few minutes. Maybe you want to use the break o get to the restroom?"

Bodo thought that was a good idea and closed his OmniBook and placed it aside. He left the car and walked to the restroom. When he was done, he bought some Wiener Würstchen with rolls and walked back to the car, where Gunther and Joachim were standing outside, enjoying the warms of the last few April days.

They tanked Bodo for the meal, and soon they had eaten the Würstchen and rolls and were on their way. Not even two hours later, Bodo realized that Gunther slowed down again and was amazed that they had already reached the forest road leading to the somewhat hidden property where their future ROS would be.

He had not noticed when they had left the Autobahn, which indicated to him two things, first that Gunther was really the best driver he had ever experienced. Secondly, he was intense in file number two, writing the indictment thoroughly. After about two miles, the last buildings left and right way behind them. They reached a barrier with a sign telling that this was a restricted military area and trespassers would be shot without warning.

Joachim got out of the car and unlocked the barrier with the key he had gotten from Karl, which, in turn, had gotten it from the construction crew, who had returned on Monday night, reporting all done. Gunther drove through, and Joachim closed the barrier but did not lock it. Turning to Bodo, he said, "Commander Zipper, I will send one of the officers back with the key to lock it when they all have arrived."

"Good idea, comrade Joachim."

A few minutes later, they arrived at the property. Bodo was surprised at how great the whole assembly was situated. There was actually a complete house set back about one hundred yards that was built as a block house. It was only one story, but rather large and, for sure, an excellent place for Joachim to live in. There was a two-story building on one side of a paved place with a paved road and several parking spots in front of it. On the other side of the paved place was another building almost as high as the two-story building but was only one story with a relatively high roof and looked like a barn.

Joachim exited the car again, unlocked the gate, and waved Gunther to drive through. He then closed the gate but left it unlocked. Gunther parked the car on one of the parking spots in front of the two-story building, and all got out. Bodo stretched and then looked around. The property was fenced in the same way as the RON property. He missed the safety guards, which the SSP should have provided. He would call Jürgen after they had finished the tour.

The two-story building had sufficient office rooms downstairs for at least four teams working on different cases simultaneously. The second floor had twelve similarly equipped bedrooms, with beds, cabinets, a table, and a bathroom sufficient for two officers to live comfortably.

The barn was another surprise for Bodo. It was almost a mirror of what he had at the headquarters. When they entered it, Joachim looked immediately at Bodo. He said, "Commander Zipper, did you send the barn drawings at Headquarters to the construction crew?"

"Not that I know off, but we know Karl has coordinated all the construction efforts and used the same architect for the facilities. Let's go over and have a look at your new home, comrade Joachim."

They walked to the blockhouse and found the key was in the lock. They opened it and walked in. It was a very nice and open design. After passing a powder room on the left side and a small office room on the right, the space opened to a large eating, sitting, and kitchen area. The cooking area on the right-hand side was comfortable and separated from the open sitting space by a breakfast bar similar to that Bodo had in his house. Straight to the back was a large patio door leading to a terrace with an extensive grassland behind it, bordered by the forest behind a fence at least twelve feet high, crowned with barbed wire.

Inside on both sides of the sitting area, was a door leading to hallways with a door on each side. Three doors opened to well-sized bedrooms with an enclosed bathroom and walk-in closet. The fourth door opened to an extensive master bedroom with a large bathroom and an equally large walk-in closet. The bedroom also had a patio door to a terrace on the house's small side.

When they had seen everything and walked back out of the house, Bodo asked Joachim, "So, comrade Joachim, do you think you could live here for a while?"

Joachim was still speechless from what he had just seen and thought would not exist in their communist nation; he hesitated and then answered, "I am just blown away. Who lived here before we took over this facility? This is a family's dream home."

"All I know is that the forest here is a restricted military area and was used by the long-range scouts for training. The military stopped using it last year in the fall when they opened their joined special forces training center on Dänholm." The soldiers must have built it as part of the training program, something like forming a solid collective."

They all returned to the car, and Bodo told Gunther to get the stuff they brought for the ROS operation into the office building. He told Joachim to take his personal stuff and make himself comfortable at the house, which was gigantic for him as a single. Still, he hoped it would soon be filled with children's voices. Joachim laughed at Bodo and said, "If I ever find a girl that would enjoy sharing my enthusiasm for the cause, you, commander Zipper need to be my best man."

Now it was Bodo laughing. He answered, "I would gladly be that man, but I guess many others would fill that position better than me."

Bodo decided to call Jürgen, and they went into the office building looking for the CO's office. They found it on the far right side of the building, and it was complete and ready to be used. It had all the gimmicks they had at all the other properties, and even the short dials for HQ, RON, and the mobile numbers for all CO and Bodo's were already programmed and labeled. Bodo read his number from his mobile and dialed it from the office phone. Jürgen took the call after the second ring. "Hello, who is there?" His curious voice was clear to hear.

"Hello, Jürgen, it's me, Bodo. I am at the new ROS property, and it would be great if you could call back when I hang up and test the connectivity… Sure," and the line went dead.

A few seconds later, the office phone rang, and Bodo took the call, "Hello, Jürgen, that works just fine. Another reason I called you is the security guard for the ROS property. I remember we talked about it, and you said it would be arranged the same way as you did for the RON, but there are none."

"Bodo, my apologies, but I believe the responsible officer has not been informed yet that the property is going operational. I need to call him and let him know that this is the case. Are you guys operational now, or when will you be?"

"We are operational in a few moments when my officers for the ROS arrive. But, Jürgen, nothing to apologize for. It was such short notice that I had no idea until Friday night. And I actually expected that the construction team would still be here today, finishing up some final tasks, but they must have been finished last week."

"Okay, Bodo, they should be at the property within two hours at the most since all is set up to start on a call. I will inform the officer now, and the ball will get rolling."

"Thanks a lot, talk to you later," and Bodo hung up. He turned to Joachim and Gunther and said, "Gunther, I want you to keep an eye on the gate. The officers should arrive any moment." While Gunther walked out, Bodo turned back to Joachim and explained the security guard agreement the OIR had with the SSP for all of their properties.

"Why do we have that agreement< could you not have just taken more officers from the SSP, integrated them into the OIR, and have them on security duty?" Joachim asked.

"Good thought there, comrade Joachim, but I didn't on purpose. I want to keep the agency as small as possible. That guarantees that we can react flexibly and focus on the task of eliminating the ulcer from our country. Having to organize the security for the properties would have added an additional autocratic level to our organization that may hinder us when we have to react on a moment's notice."

"Oh, yes, Commander, I understand. It is easier to have it this way." Suddenly, there were engine sounds to hear, and they walked out of the office building. Gunther had opened the gate, and one car after the next flooded into the property and parked at the marked parking lots. Bodo turned to Joachim, who was definitely enjoying the parade, and said, "Comrade Joachim, this is your show now. Get the officer lined up, report, and then report to me. We are a semi-military organization in our structure and hold more power than any other organization. We need to keep the discipline from the first second. You served as a sergeant, you know to command a unit, and you need to see this office here the same way. Is that understood?"

"Yes, Commander, I need to learn a lot, but I know everything about commanding a fighter unit."

Joachim went to the car's plot, where all the officers were assembled, and when one of them noticed him, he commanded, "Attention!" Bodo watched them, listening to Joachim's instructions, and within a few minutes, they were all lined up in three rows; when Joachim walked over to the lined-up officers, one stepped forward and reported.

Now, Bodo slowly walked over to the group and stopped when he was at the proper distance. Joachim turned, made three steps in his direction, and saluted with his report, "Comrade Commander Zipper, I report twenty officers of the Regional Office South of the Office of Investigation and Recovery lined up for duty."

Bodo responded, "Thank you, comrade Lehmann. Let them be at ease."

After the command was given, Bodo addressed the officers directly, reminding all of them that they had a massive task in front of them, that they had a young but very competent commanding officer in Colonel Lehmann, and that the slightest form of disrespect would lead to their immediate termination. Bodo emphasized the punishment for disrespect by repeating it.

"If there is a valid point to criticize an action or command of Colonel Lehmann, Colonel Lehman has to be addressed directly, privately, and respectfully. If Colonel Lehman disagrees with the critics, the subject has to be written down and handed to Colonel Lehman. The copy has to be sent to the headquarters. I wish you all success and enjoy the environment you are living in now. You are dismissed."

The officers took all their belongings from the different cars and SUVs and moved into their rooms. Joachim walked over to the cars just before the officer who had driven the car assigned to Joachim was about to leave. He asked for the keys, and the officer said it was in the car. Joachim thanked him, and he walked into the building. While Joachim adjusted the seat in his car and started it up to drive it over to his new home, Bodo heard the sound of a large truck coming closer.

He looked at Gunther, who stood with some of the officers at the entrance to the office building, and when he got his attention, Bodo pointed to the gate and his ears. Gunther understood immediately and took two of the officer with him, running to the gate. They arrived in time to see the truck turning the corner of the curve from the main forest road toward the gate. The truck stopped, the passenger door opened, and a uniformed soldier approached the gate. Bodo could not understand what they talked about. When the soldier presented a piece of paper and an ID card, Bodo knew it was checked out that they were the security guard.

When the truck was parked, and the engine stopped, the soldier in the passenger seat walked up to Bodo, saluted, and reported, "Commander Zipper, twenty-four officers for the security guard duty at your disposal."

"Thank you, Sergeant. Colonel Lehmann will be the CO of this property. He is currently at his home and will be back any minute. Ah, there he comes already. Please make all arrangements with him. And on a side note, have you been instructed that the guards have no accommodation?"

"Yes, Commander Zipper. I have been advised about that, and we have brought tents and all the equipment needed to live appropriately until the living containers are delivered."

"Great, Sergeant, you are dismissed."

The sergeant turned and met Joachim right at the door of the office building. They shook hands and walked into the building. A few minutes later, they returned while having a map of the property in his hand, the sergeant pointed to a space in the back of the barn, and Joachim nodded.

The sergeant went to the back of the truck and gave some commands. The soldiers jumped off the truck and marched back to the area beside two of them, grabbing their rifles and magazine pouches and marching to the gate. The driver fired up the truck's engine and backed it toward the area Joachim and the sergeant had pointed out.

Bodo went into the building and to Joachim's office. He passed several offices with open doors and noticed the officers were all busy settling into their new workspaces. Joachim's office door was open, and Bodo knocked at the frame, which caused Joachim to look up from some papers he had in front of him. "Commander, sorry, I was just looking at some of the files we have to work on here in our area and completely forgot that you are out there."

"Nothing to apologize for, comrade Joachim. Great to see that you are going right to it. I just wanted to let you know that you have done great so far and should not hesitate to command according to your position and rank. These are officers and soldiers, and you are now at the rank of a colonel. Never forget that."

"Thank you very much, Commander. Your support helps me face this enormous challenge I have in front of me. And I will try my very best not to disappoint your trust in me."

"I guess we are done then here. We will be in touch, don't forget that all my numbers are programmed on our office phone, the mobile in your car and your home phone too. I repeat, comrade Joachim, hit the button whenever you need to talk to me. And always remember, the right time is when you think the first time, "I should call the commander!"

Bodo turned and left the building looking for Gunther. He saw him at the place where the soldiers of the guard were setting up four large tents. After a few minutes, Gunther noticed Bodo's gesture toward the office building. He said goodbye to the soldiers, turned around, and jogged toward Bodo.

"Gunther, are you ready to get back home?"

"Yes, Commander, I thought me may stay overnight?"

"I was prepared to do so, but since everything is as it should be here and they have already started working on some of the cases they have, we can get on the road."

They entered the car, and Gunther started the engine and started toward the gate. The two guard soldiers saluted. One of them walked to the driver's side, and when Gunther lowered the window, he told him that he needed to unlock the barrier at the end of the forest road. Bodo and Gunther had all but forgotten about it. While they drove slowly down the forest road, a guard soldier passed them, and when they arrived at the barrier, he had already unlocked and opened it.

After several minutes, they entered the Autobahn and were on their way back to Karolinenhof.

CHAPTER 23

Unjustified Arrests

Bodo was amazed at how the two days in office after his return from the ROS was running by. He had worked with Poeter and Giesela to finetune the indictments and the sentence formulation for the first two death row inmates. Ready to present to the members of the Central Committee, he wanted to ensure that there was no hesitation by any of them to vote yes. It was already Wednesday later in the afternoon when they were sitting together in Bodo's office, reading through the final version of both documents. To ensure it was as perfect as possible.

Now, Bodo and Peter and Giesela knew that there was no court of law this had to be presented. That door was closed when these criminal elements—traitors—decided to work against the Communist Party, damaging the cause of creating a victorious communist Germany. As Bodo went through the copy he had in front of him, he smiled briefly as he remembered their faces when he told them, "You have no rights! You wasted your legal rights the same second when you abandoned the communist ideal!"

After a few more minutes, Bodo was finished reading and leaned back in his chair, satisfied with the result of three hard days of work by Peter and Giesela, especially the interrogator of the cases. Peter and Giesela finished their proofreading and looked up at Bodo.

"Do you think it is sufficient?" Peter asked.

Bodo thought for a moment, looked back at the paper before him, and returned his look to Peter. "If this is insufficient to shoot these bastards, I will drag them out on Alexander Platz and shoot them myself. Even if it is the last thing I can do! You all have done an incredible job getting this information together. Please, Peter, express my personal thanks to the collective for their diligence in turning over every stone during the last two days to reveal all this."

"I will definitely do so."

Bodo thanked both of them for proofreading the final version and instructed Giesela to handle the necessary copies as before. He told her to use Gunther to hand them to the members personally, as with other documents. She needed to instruct Gunther again about the importance that nobody else could get the sealed envelopes but the members of the CC personally.

Giesela left the office, and Bodo and Peter talked about the developments of the investigations in the four additional cases they had the delinquents in their holding area. Peter explained that they had made some progress. But there was one guy, the general director of the shipyard industrial complex, who would not believe that they had the power to arrest him nor that they had the right to question him.

Bodo thought about his reaction and said, "Peter, let's get over there and talk with the king. I will tell him my rights and maybe show him I mean what I say." Bodo stood, and Peter followed him out of the office into the barn. They went through the security procedure, which had not been softened to Bodo's satisfaction and walked into the interrogation room.

The interrogator of this case greeted Bodo. "Commander, we are not making any progress here. I was about to meet with you to talk about the next level. We are now at twenty-eight hours, and he still believes that we are breaking the law and will all end up in prison because he has connections and a very powerful position."

Bodo looked at the former general director, smiled, and said, "He looks pretty good for twenty-eight hours of sleep deprivation."

The former general director looked at Bodo, full of hatred, and used all his remaining strength to place that hate in his response, "You don't know what awaits you, oh, oh, Commander, oh, oh, what a joke! You are a criminal, and as soon as the authorities realize that I am abducted by your thugs, you will feel the full power of me. You will never see the light of the day again."

Now Bodo laughed and answered, "You don't get it. I am the authority! I am the law, and you don't have any rights. We will get the information out of you one way or the other. If I must pull your fingernails individually, I will do it personally. I am sick and tired of you assholes telling me you have rights. You lost those rights the same second you decided to betray the Communist Party!"

Bodo walked to the corner behind the guy where the stainless-steel table was with the instruments he had personally selected to be used. He took one of the pliers and walked back to the table in front of the traitor. Holding the pliers before his face, he said, "I will start with your fingernails. If we are done with them, and I still believe you are holding back information, I will start cutting off fingers, each at the joint, by joint. I guarantee you will tell us everything, even stuff we don't ask for."

The general director's face had turned white. It wasn't the whiteness of sickness. It was the whiteness of fear. He stammered, "You...you can't...no, that's torture!"

Bodo smirked and said, "Torture. Oh yes, I like that. I will torture you until you spill the beans or die. Because if you don't talk, all that you stole from the worker's paradise to be built by the Communist Party you swore allegiance to will be lost anyway."

The expression on the face of the traitor changed from fear to defeat. Again, Bodo had been convincing enough to do what he said to avoid what he would love to do to these bastards he hated with all his heart. Throwing the pliers on the table, he said, "Start talking. The tape is running. We will have you sign the written confession later. I will leave this friendly little tool in front of you as a reminder not to lie. I will come back and rip you apart piece by piece if I hear that you are not cooperating." And moving his face very close to the face of the traitor and added, "Believe me, I mean it. In my eyes, you are nothing more than a piece of shit that needs to be wiped off!"

Bodo left the interrogation room, followed by Peter. He checked with the security sergeant on duty that the video and audio taping worked and returned to his office. He finalized some paperwork, called Giesela to take it, and instructed her to send Gunther to him as soon as he returned. Then he called Reiner at the RON and got a comprehensive report about the cases they were processing. Bodo made some notes about the main facts and told Reiner to send the reports tonight by courier. They talked briefly about family and how Corinna had changed the house into their own home. Bodo promised to visit them with Sarina and Nick as soon as the bulk of the cases was taken care of and ended the call.

He hit the button for the ROS, and after the second ring, he had Joachim on the phone. "Hi, comrade Joachim, How are things developing down in the south today?"

"Hello, Commander Zipper. We have filled the arrest cells, and our officer collectives are collecting evidence and surveilling relatives. The interrogators are working overtime to get the interrogation going. I may have a preliminary report for you tomorrow morning. Written confessions may take till next week, so."

"That sounds promising, comrade Joachim. Is everything else okay? How is the security guards work? Are you satisfied?"

"Yes, Commander Zipper, they are very determined, and their NCO is beneficial with keeping them busy when they are off duty, keeping the yard in order, moving the grass, and doing little improvements and repairs here and there."

"That is great to hear. I wish you a nice evening and call me if you have anything for me I could use for the meeting tomorrow." Bodo finished that phone call. Just then, there was a knock on the door. Bodo called, "Come in," and Gunther entered the office.

"All the envelopes are delivered, and here is the signature list of the recipients, Commander."

"Thank you, Gunther, I am about to close up for today, and you can get me home in a few minutes."

"Yes, Commander. I will be at Maria's office. Please call me there."

Bodo raised an eyebrow and smirked, "Oh, there? But I hope the door stays open?"

Gunther blushed and walked away without saying a word, closing the office door behind him.

Bodo was about to shut down his OmniBook when the phone rang, and he saw Jürgen's number button flashing. He picked up the phone, and after saying hello, Jürgen started with a sigh, "Bodo, I just finished reading your paper. I have to say, excellent work there. There is no doubt in my mind that this goes straight through. So congratulations. But that's not the reason I am calling. I wanted to let you know that we, at the SPP leadership, have decided to start the arrest tomorrow night. We could not finish everything to secure the May ceremonies in all cities. We just don't have enough commanding officers to get it organized."

"Okay, Jürgen, I understand. It must be a nightmare seeing what needs to be done and don't have the resources. Do you have a plan to keep it unnoticed as long as necessary?"

"Yes, we have that all figured out. We will start with the most connected ones in the Monday demonstration movement and then down to the second and third layers. We believe if we cut off the head, we may gain enough time to get the other two layers before they can go underground."

"Sound like a good plan. Best of luck, my friend."

"We can definitely use that. We will discuss the details tomorrow in our meeting. I just wanted to let you know upfront. I suggest you inform your officer about it because they might be surveilling one of these subversive elements and wonder what is happening."

"Yes, Jürgen, that's a must. We may be on some of their tails, which could cause confusion. I will do it now. Have a great night, and see you tomorrow." As soon as Bodo hung up, he called Giesela through the intercom and instructed her to connect him first with Reiner and then Joachim. The phone rang immediately, and she announced Reiner on the line. "Reiner, the SSP is starting tonight with the preventive arrest action to secure the May ceremonies, as we discussed on Tuesday. Inform all your surveillance collectives that they may witness the arrest of one or the other of their subjects. Do not interfere. Not even try to help. Have them stay back, and if the subject can escape the arrest team, have them follow professionally and stay on their trail."

"Why are they starting so early? They must keep them for seven nights and feed them and the stuff?"

"It all comes down to manpower in the officer corps, Reiner. They just don't have the resources."

"I get it. I will see to get my guys all addressed tonight before we close the office." Bodo hung up, and immediately the phone rang again, and Joachim announced himself, "Comrade Commander, Joachim here."

Hello again, comrade Joachim. As we discussed on Tuesday, I needed to call again to inform you that the SSP is starting tonight with the preventive arrest action to secure the May ceremonies. Inform all your surveillance collectives that they may witness the arrest of one or the other of their subjects. Do not interfere. Not even try to help. Have them stay back, and if the subject can escape the arrest team, have them follow professionally and stay on their trail.

"Oh, that's a surprise. I will get the message out immediately, Commander."

"Great, comrade Joachim. Just ensure we stay in the dark and don't get discovered. Your collectives must be undercover. Otherwise, we can't do our job."

"Understood, commander." And he hung up.

Bodo leaned back in his chair and thought about the implications of starting the arrest action that early. Would it negatively affect his own objectives? Actually, it would not. Bodo thought about possible different developments and concluded that they could be positive for his agency. It would certainly scare the traitors who had not yet been officially discovered, but at the same time, they would feel safer since they were not targeted by that action.

And for the underground movement, he suspected was active in the country, avoiding any connection with the Monday Demonstrations movement, it would confirm their suspicion that the Monday demonstration organizers were infiltrated. They would see which of their guys was tinted or not. It could mean they would probably go even more profound and maybe even dark for a while.

But since only he suspected the existence of such an underground network, and his only reference for that was his brother, Fritz, he decided to stay silent until after the May ceremonies. Then he would use one of the collectives to place an "OPS" (Operational Personal Surveillance) on Fritz. And he would not stop until he was sure he could nail that bastard to the wall and shoot him.

He called Gunther via intercom, and Gunther dove him home.

Joining his family in his now beautiful home, he was soon in his family mood, laughing and kidding and pushing all the ugly thoughts about his hated brother into a different part of his brain.

The next morning, when he entered the office, Giesela, as usual, handed him his cup of coffee and read the most critical issues of her list. It wasn't much besides the confirmation that the arrest action of the SSP had started last night, ceased during the day, and would restart at night with the next layer.

"And," she added, expanding the pauses between the words, "there is this. Both offices, RON and ROS, and Peter got reports from their surveillance collectives that individuals they had under surveillance were arrested last night." Peter is in the interrogation room but said he would like to talk with you when you come in."

"Okay, Giesela, send Peter in when he comes from the barn and connect me with ROS and then RON."

A few minutes later, he had the call from ROS and talked with comrade Joachim, "Commander, as you suspected, two of our surveillance collectives were watching relatives of traitors we have here and working on them to get all the information we need, as they were arrested by the SSP yesterday night."

"Okay, comrade Joachim, calm down. We did expect that there might be connections. We need to increase the pressure on the traitors you have in custody and make them sing. Use all tools, including physical ones. I want you to have a comprehensive report next Tuesday, which we may have to use to stop the SSP from releasing them from arrest."

Yes, Commander." With the firm confirmation that Joachim understood the seriousness of the situation, Bodo hung up and had the phone ring a few seconds later, Giesela saying that she had Reiner on the line.

"Hi, Reiner, I heard your guys witnessed some arrests last night?"

"Yes, Bodo. We had three of our surveillance collectives out there last night. These are relatives of high-ranking police officers we have in custody. We believe there is some connection and potential weapon transfer. Two of the surveillance collectives called the night shift operator and reported arrests of their subject.

They were ordered to stay in place, and one of the collectives could follow the wife of that arrested subject. She drove to a small village about eight kilometers away and went into a house we have now under surveillance too. We have no defined understanding of the connection yet, but I hope to have more by the end of the week."

"Man, Reiner, that whole thing was planned as a preventive action to avoid any disturbances during the May ceremonies, and it turned into a door opener for us. We did expect that there might be connections. We need to increase the pressure on the traitors you have in custody and make them sing. Use all tools, including physical ones. I want you to have a comprehensive report next Tuesday, which we may have to use to stop the SSP from releasing them from arrest.

"Okay, Bodo, I will bring you all I can to the meeting on Tuesday morning. It's still 10:00 AM?"

"Yes, Reiner, still 10:00 AM, no sleeping late after the May 1 celebration. Just drink one vodka less." Bodo laughed and hung up.

Soon it was afternoon, and because of the overall situation, the meeting of the Central Committee had been moved to 2:00 PM instead of 4:00 PM. Giesela called via intercom, reminding Bodo that he needed to get going, and he packed his stuff in his briefcase and walked out of his office. He went over to the office of Maria, the secretary who was now fully involved in the daily organization of the work plans of the collectives and directed by the head of the interrogators.

The office door was open, which brought a grin to Bodo's face, and he knocked on the door frame to get their attention. Both looked at him, and Bodo asked Maria how she felt after a few days of working with the collectives. Maria smiled back at Bodo and said, "Comrade Commander, I am incredibly thankful you rescued me from that hostile environment at the district headquarters. I understand there is new leadership, but the general atmosphere probably needs years to clean up."

"I am glad you are here, Maria. You are doing great work, and I can see that even Gunther seems to be impressed." Bodo said, grinning and enjoying Gunther's face turning a shade deeper red.

"I don't know what I did that I deserve this," Gunther said, looking at Maria. She turned her face to Gunther and answered his question, "Gunther, everyone in the office has realized you have a crush on me. Why don't you just ask me out on a date."

Gunther was clearly shocked. He started to say something, but his voice failed. He cleared his throat, finally got his voice back, and said,

"Maria, I would love to invite you for dinner, but I wasn't sure you would like me. And you definitely did not need to say that in the presence of the Commander."

Bodo looked at Maria, noticing that she turned a shade redder, then back to Gunther and said, "What, Gunther, am I inhuman now? Okay, I need to get out of here, or we will be late for the meeting."

Yes, Commander," Gunther said, jumped off his chair, passed Bodo, still standing at the door, smiling at Maria, and finally said, "Maria, I hope he understands." She smiled back at Bodo and said, he just needs a little time, Commander."

Bodo entered the car, and Gunther drove off the property, heading to the city to get his boss to the critical meeting. Bodo read through his bullet points for his presentation. When he was done, he said, "Gunther, I did not want to embarrass you, but a woman like Maria is not waiting forever to be invited, especially not in a city like Berlin. Here is what I offer you; you can take it or leave it. I will call the Bulgarian restaurant and make a reservation under my name for you. The bill goes to the OIR because I consider it a benefit for your willingness to be ready at any given time. All you have to do is to get Maria to go with you. What about tonight?"

Gunther was silent for a while, and taking a deep breath, he answered, "Commander, that would be just too good to be true. I can't imagine how I earned that after the RON screw-up, but I appreciate your offer. What is the limit at the restaurant, I know it is pretty expensive, and I do not want to have to pay more than I can afford."

"Gunther, I know I am not really expressing my appreciation for your service as I should. But be assured I do. Even if I don't say so. You can eat whatever you both like there. The agency can afford it if you are eating the whole menu up and down twice."

Gunther thanked Bodo wholeheartedly, and just then, they arrived at the CC building.

CHAPTER 24

Great economical news: A Unanimous Decision for a Public Execution

When Bodo arrived at the conference room on the top floor of the Building of the Central Committee, most members were already present. They were standing in groups, talking about things. They greeted Bodo, mostly nodding, but Jürgen walked around the table, shook hands, and said, "Hi, Bodo, good to see you. Do you have any unusual incidents to report about the last night's action?"

"Hi, Jürgen, yes, I have some indeed, and I will explain what I have later in the meeting. But so much upfront for you, there are several of the arrested elements on which we had surveillance established."

"Good to know. We need to have the cases, not to let these elements go on Wednesday next week."

"That's exactly what I told my Cos. They will collect as much information as possible."

Jürgen walked around the table to take his seat and read some of the papers there. Bruno walked in when Bodo went to the place that had become his usual place and unpacked his briefcase. He joyfully greeted Bodo, congratulating him on the comprehensive papers supplied to the CC members the day before. They were chatting about the families when the secretary-general walked into the conference room through a door on the small side of the room. The door was almost invisible, and if Bodo had not noticed that he had walked through it before it automatically closed behind him, he would have had no idea that it existed.

The secretary-general cleared his throat and called the meeting to order. First, he asked the head of the SSP for a report on the execution of the preventive arrest of the subversive elements last night. Bodo was impressed by the perfectionism with which the action was executed, and it reminded him that the German people had a specific advantage in corporate skills before all other people.

Jürgen then pointed out some overlaps with the OIR investigations, and comrade Werner turned to Bodo, "Comrade Bodo, could you give us a brief conclusion of those overlaps? We will go into your first two completed cases later."

"Sure, comrade Secretary-General, I have." At that point, Werner Tauscher interrupted Bodo. He said, "Comrade Bodo, it is sufficient to address all of us as comrades and the first names." He looked around the table as if he wanted to say, "Anyone disagrees? You are one of us, and thinking of the work you have delivered so far with your brand-new organization definitely lifts you to the top level."

Bodo was surprised and considered this a great honor and appreciation of his work. He swallowed and then said, "Comrades, while the preventive arrest of the subversive element was executed, our agency had several surveillances current. Three surveillance collectives monitored the subjects of interest because they were relatives of the case subject in our custody.

When they noticed the execution of the arrest by the SSP, they stood back as ordered and kept the surveillance active even after. On one occasion, they experienced that a woman of one of the suspects drove to a neighboring village and went into a house where we are currently trying to get all the necessary information. We will work closely with the SSP forces to unravel the connection to the surveillance suspect."

"Outstanding, comrade Bodo. Do you think we need to do something with the subject SSP arrested while your collectives had them under surveillance?"

"I spoke briefly with comrade Jürgen before we started. Yes, we will handle these cases together. I just thought about combining our forces for these cases, comrade Jürgen, and forming a task force. It would be interesting to see the connections between the Monday demonstration organizers and the traitors in custody that may exist."

A general nod was around the table, and Jürgen said, "Excellent idea, comrade Bodo."

Bodo continued, "Since we know that many of the bastards we have in custody have transferred stolen money to foreign accounts and have, in many cases, several accounts with foreign currency, and I am talking about West Marks, dollars, Swiss franks, and British pounds, it might be possible to prove that they have financed the counterrevolutionary activities with foreign money."

Comrade Kurt Kreuger suddenly jumped into the discussion. He said, "Comrade Bodo, if you can prove the flow of foreign money into the Monday demonstration organization, that would give us an enormous advantage when crushing the demonstrations, which we need to do sooner or later."

"You are correct, Comrade Kurt. I have no proof yet, but we will find out. And if not, if we find foreign accounts in possession of the traitors of relatives in the counterrevolutionary movement. We can just assume that there is a link. And I am sure you can create an official statement as good as proof." Bodo said with a smile, and comrade Kurt took that sentence as a compliment.

After that, comrade Alexander briefly reported that they had closed the deal with the Soviet Army for a preliminary delivery of five hundred rocket guiding systems per month in exchange od twice as much oil and natural gas they had supplied so far, compensating the difference in official gold from the Russian Central Bank. At the current price per ounce of $ 950, locked in for twelve months, that would mean that they would get approximately 475 million dollars in gold per month. The Soviet Army is interested in getting a total of ten thousand guiding systems. If they can get enough gold produced, they might order more."

There was great joy among the comrades because all their money problems dealing with imports necessary to keep their economy running were suddenly wiped out. All of them went over to the general comrade Frank and congratulated him for the wonder of development of his exceptional development department.

After the excitement had calmed down, the secretary-general, with a serious look around the table, stated, "Comrades, we shall now come to the last, but even though, unfortunate and severe agenda point of today's meeting. You all have received the indictment and sentence paper from comrade Bodo. I suspect you all read them very thoroughly."

Comrade Bodo has presented the results of interrogating the delinquents, including the results of investigations and interrogations of relatives and witnesses. His paper paints a comprehensive picture of the criminal and treasonous activities of the two individuals. For almost twenty years, they collaborated to commit many treasonous acts, stealing money from the party, transferring foreign currencies to hidden accounts, and committing endless acts of misappropriating limited resources for their own benefit.

To crown their criminal activities, they organized the murder of a citizen. Then they sent the man they used for that heinous crime into the minefields which secure our borders from the attacks of our class enemies." Comrade Tauscher stopped reading sections of the indictment paper and looked at the comrades at the table. Even though they had already read the papers, most were again shocked by the criminal energy the delinquents had to achieve their objectives.

In continuing, comrade Tauscher moved to the sentence request Bodo had formulated the night before in his home office, trying to be as precise as possible. "Comrade Bodo requests that the former FDS and the FCS be convicted of High Treason. Both are sentenced to death by hanging, and both executions are publicly conducted. I understand this is hard to swallow, but let me read the reasoning out loud. It reads:

"Both former comrades used their powerful positions as a party and political leader to compromise other comrades, to blackmail other comrades, to enrich themselves by stealing foreign and national money, and to initiate murder and to cover it up by murdering the hired murderer.

"Thus, they created and supported a situation in their area of influence and power that destroyed the trust of the workers' class in the Communist Party as their eternal leadership force. The damage has led to counterrevolutionary movements and brought the nation to the edge of collapse.

"The death sentence, publicly executed, shall be a first step to show the people that we mean business and should reduce the sympathy for the counterrevolutionary movement."

There was silence in the room, and for several minutes nobody even dared to breathe loud. Then, comrade Frank, Secretary of Defense, spoke, "I am in total agreement with comrade Bodo. And I am sure we have enough volunteers to join a firing squad, but hanging, I don't know. Isn't that somehow middle age?"

Jürgen joined in and said, "Comrade Frank, how would you do a public execution by a firing squad? That may create a lot of safety hazards for the public."

Comrade Karl, secretary of Education, usually very silent and seldom saying anything, spoke shallowly, "I think public execution is too much. The shock for the people might be too much. I suggest shooting them by a firing squad in a facility and transmitting them via TV. That would be as effective, I think."

Bodo had difficulties keeping his temper, and with a restrained voice, feeling a calming touch from Bruno on his Arm, he said, "Am I the only one here who knows Lenin's writings? Do you really believe you can calm a counterrevolutionary movement, such as destroying the remains of the party's power, by showing a TV transmission of something that happens, or in the eyes of the doubters, doesn't? Do you believe the class enemy would not immediately cry foul that the communists are lying?

"This is for all of you comrades if you don't have the guts to drag these bastards out on a public square, where they face the gallows and hang them in front of thousands of our citizens to see that we mean it when we say we are cleaning the mess if you don't do that with all of the top level criminals, you have already lost. You can as well call in the leaders of the counterrevolution and start negotiations under what conditions they will keep you alive in prison for the rest of your existence. That's my opinion, and I can prove that I am right. All you need to do is to ask comrade Jürgen how many subversive elements the SPP arrested last night preemptively. And if that is not enough, disguise yourself and attend a Monday demonstration next week. You will feel deep hatred for the betrayal of the cause."

At that point, the secretary-general said, "Comrade Bodo, my deepest thanks for this explicit statement. I am convinced you are correct. We must do it to make it believable. The traitors know we mean it.

Who votes for the execution as described in the sentence developed by comrade Bodo?"

To Bodo's complete surprise, all hands went up. And more so when comrade Tauscher suggested using the May 1 ceremony in the capital to exemplify it. And again, all comrades voted yes.

Comrade Jürgen was ordered to organize the execution, and comrade Kurt was asked to create the speech for the secretary-general to be held at the event. Both comrades said that they were honored to be part of the process to cleanse the party from the ulcers of betrayal and corruption. With that, the secretary-general closed the meeting.

On the way out, several members padded him on the shoulder, positively confirming his stand on demonstrating toughness and showing the people that things have changed, not just saying it.

Jürgen and Frank caught up with him at the elevator. Frank said, "Comrade Bodo, what about Jürgen and I come out to your office tomorrow and we discuss the details of the action? What would be the best time?"

Bodo looked at both, grinned, and said, "You both are curious what great nest I have built me? Okay, what about 10:00 AM? Gives us all enough time to fix things that need to be taken care of in the morning, and when we are done, we may have lunch together?"

Both agreed, and they reached the garage, said goodbye, and entered their cars to drive back to their homes. Because it was already after 6:00 PM, Bodo instructed Gunther to drive directly to his home. Again, Gunther's special license plate and driving skills overcame all rush-hour obstacles of the rush hour already in full blow. After just a little over twenty minutes, Gunther hit the opener for the gate and drove to the front of the house. Bodo instructed him to pick him up at eight the next morning, and Gunther was on his way out.

It was a quick dinner with the family. Bodo used the chance to read a little story from Nick's favorite book and said good night. He had a glass of wine with Sarina, talking about the reflection of the people about the arrest action the SSP had executed. Bodo learned that the average citizen wasn't really concerned. At least, that was what Sarina had heard when she was out with Nick, for his school and afterward with the sailing club. None of them realized that they lived in a bubble. The agreement with the Monday protesters was very low in an area where primarily government employees in high-ranking positions lived.

The following morning after a quick breakfast, Sarina was out bringing Nick to school because she had decided to do that for the first two weeks. Then they would try to use the bus in coordination with the Tecker children. Shortly after, Gunther arrived, and they drove to the office. The SSP had the two already sentenced traitors transferred to the SSP prison, and a new transport of two additional ones was expected during the day.

During the morning meeting, which slowly became a fixpoint, Bodo was briefed that the interrogation of three more of the arrestees was going forward. As with the previous criminals already discovered, these had also developed pathways to transfer goods illegally into the NSW and got paid by their brothers-in-crime for it into Swiss or West German bank accounts.

Maria had already written complete confession statements from the writing of the delinquents and the tapes into the legal software they had started to use, and Giesela had begun to create transfer files for Bodo to get them onto Bodo's OmniBook. Bodo could therefore begin to write his conclusive indictment and sentencing statement for the next week's CC meeting. Both Cos from RON and ROS called in and reported the results of additional confessions and surveillance activities.

When the meeting closed, Bodo started to look through the data Giesela had transferred to his laptop. Again, he was shocked by the audacity of the people the party had entrusted with the administration of enormous resources, who had betrayed the trust and stolen millions of hard currency from the country. It should be easy for comrade Kurt Kreuger to write a speech for the SG to convince the nation that the harsh measures were necessary. And it should give them the people's trust back to calm the situation.

His thought was interrupted by the intercom call from Giesela telling him that comrade Pieker and Bode had arrived. Bodo walked out and saw them both already in the hallway with Peter and Giesela. He greeted them and asked them into his office, telling Peter to join them. Giesela brought coffee and left the office.

"You have a really great facility here, Bodo," Jürgen stated. Peter added, "I used the chance to give the comrades a tour before I told Giesela to interrupt you."

"Thanks, Jürgen, but most of it results from Karl's unbelievable engagement to get this organization up and running. Without him, we would not be where we are today."

"I think he is the coming replacement for Bruno if he ever decides to retire," Frank added. "There is an enormous love for the cause in that young man."

"You are correct, comrade Frank. The two death row candidates are already at your facility, Jürgen. And we need to finetune the action on Monday. How did you think you would proceed with the execution?"

Frank and Jürgen looked at each other to decide who would start to speak. Then Frank nodded toward Jürgen, who began, "We will shield off a large part of the Alex on Saturday night and secure it with troops from the Guard battalion. We are already building the structure of the gallows. It will be made to hang three at the same time. The area will stay covered until Monday at the approximate time the demonstration arrives at the Alexander Platz."

Frank jumped in and continued, "We already have over a dozen high-ranking officers who have volunteered to press the button to release the trap doors. It has been decided to have the man be drawn by lot. We have a platoon from the corps of engineers building the gallows, and we are well in time with all the preparations."

"That is great, comrades. I can't wait to see the faces of these pieces of worthless human flesh swing in the breeze. What about the TV broadcast system? Any arrangements done there?"

"Yes, the information department has all equipment ready to be transferred to the place, and comrade Kurt has personally taken responsibility for having the right people behind the camera and the commentator, ensuring that none of them is fainting." Jürgen added with a laugh.

Giesela nocked and opened the office door telling Bodo that the restaurant had called and the lunch would be ready in about ten minutes. They all walked out, and Gunther drove them into the small town to the privately operated small restaurant next to the sailing club. It was usually only open on training days and weekends. Giesela had developed a relationship with the wife of the owner. They would serve them whenever they needed something for particular situations by delivering or opening it for their guests.

It was a great ambiance, and they enjoyed a great lunch. When they were back at the OIR Headquarters, Jürgen and Frank thanked Bodo again for the great work and said they looked forward to seeing him on Monday. Bodo looked at them and said, "I am sorry, comrades, but you won't see me even near that event on Monday. My job requires me to stay in the background, and I will make sure that Kurt does not name me in the speech he is writing for the SG." Both confirmed his decision and said it was a shame he could not earn recognition for his work, but they understood.

The time flew by with much work and coordination with the RON and ROS. They were at the point where they had several additional death sentence candidates, as the phone calls during the Friday morning meeting revealed. Bodo asked to send all the information to the headquarters ASAP for Maria to get it sorted so that Giesela could formulate the files correctly.

One surprising fact was that the surveillance revealed additional people involved in money laundering for the traitors and would be sentenced to many years of hard labor for that. At the end of the week, Bodo was ripe for the weekend. Not so much because of the many hours he was working on the files, instructing Peter and the other Cos how to focus on specific details he had discovered, but because of the sewage he had to deal with. Those people had once been trusted with the treasures of the Communist Party. They had misused that trust for personal benefits. Doing so wasn't really what angered Bodo. What really made him angry about these people was their actions. Undermining the people's trust in the eternal leadership role of the Communist Party for the worker's class.

They had a great weekend. Nick participated in two competitions with the new pirate sailing boat, which he owns now personally, and his friends as a collective with four boats. The collective won the gold medal for the district competition in their age group, and Nick won the silver medal. Sailing this class for about two weeks and making second place among thirty-two sailors was a fantastic achievement. They were all celebrating with a great dinner in the restaurant next to the club when they returned later Saturday evening.

Monday morning was the First of May, and this was one of the most celebrated days in any communist country, called the Worker's Day. It was about 9:00 AM, and they had finished breakfast when Bodo turned on the TV. Nick questioned why they would not be in Berlin at the most significant demonstration. With Bodo's position, he would surely be at the main grandstand with all the other leaders.

Bodo took the time to explain to his son the delicacy of his position regarding what his work included and that it was necessary to stay under the radar. "I want you to pay close attention to what will happen and to understand that your dad had a decisive part in that, Nick. You will see history before your eyes and know that your dad has been part of it. But because of his part in it, I cannot be known as being that person under any circumstance. The enemy would immediately try to attack me, and with that, you and your mom."

"I understand that, Dad, But could you not be in Berlin at the place to experience what is happening in life?"

"I could, but it would not be wise, and you will understand when you see what we, the leadership of the Communist Party, have prepared for the people."

CHAPTER 25

Publicized Executions and an Address to the People

In the meantime, with tens of thousands of people, the demonstration reached Alexander Platz. It assembled in front of the grandstand on which the members Central Committee were assembled. The secretary-general moved over to the forest of microphones, and after a few minutes, the crowd became silent. Clearing his throat, the secretary-general began his speech, written by comrade Kurt, a genius in propaganda.

"Comrades, honored guests, fellow citizens. Today we are celebrating the fighting and holiday of the working people. We celebrate the huge accomplishments of the workers in their own country, a country free of oppression and exploitation. We have done that since this nation was formed as a free country. But things changed over the years. Comrades became lazy, complacent, and yes, some of them corrupt. A few months ago, a group of comrades saw a great danger that the workers could lose everything. All they had worked so hard for over the last forty-five years."

Some heckling confirmed the statements, but the crowd was silent and listened. They wanted to hear what the new leader, at his first public appearance, was telling them.

"Our nation is struggling with counterrevolutionary protest and inner turmoil. There is no unity. We seem to have forgotten the common goal that united us in 1949. And we, a small group of leaders inside the Communist Party, understood the signs of the time and convinced the old guard, the outstanding leaders of the party of the last decades, to retire. This was the first step."

A vast applause interrupted the speech of Werner Tauscher, who was obviously enjoying the people's reaction and let it go on for some time.

Then he continued, "But the demonstrations of the counterrevolution did not end. It increased. We knew that the average worker was frustrated. We understand that. And we understand that most demonstrators are not part of the counterrevolutionary movement. The vast majority see those Monday demonstrations as a way to express dissatisfaction with the situation. We decided that we must stop the corruption inside the Communist Party and the leaders of the economic locomotives of our nation to ensure the average worker that we mean what we promised when we took over from our predecessors."

Again enormous applause interrupted the speech, and the secretary-general stood silent until it ebbed away.

"Several weeks ago, we installed a new organization and made their objective public. Thousands of citizens have since that day indicated their approval by sending in complaints and evidence of wrongdoing by leaders in the highest positions. We had an incident where the first district secretary of the Communist Party, Schwerin, tried to avoid his arrest by using a weapon and was deadly wounded in the shutout with the SSP officer. We have arrested many former leaders of the Party and economic leaders under severe suspicion of misappropriation of vast amounts of money, domestic and foreign, and the first two of them have been indicted and sentenced."

There were hecklers calling, "Show us those bastards!"

And others, "Hang them high, but get the money back first!"

The secretary of Defense walked to the microphones. When the crowd had become silent again, he spoke, "Fellow citizens, I have been chosen by the members of the Central Committee to read to you the indictment and the sentence for the first two of a line of traitors who will face the result of their betrayal of the Communist Party and the people of the nation."

While he was reading Bodo's complete indictment paper and the sentence, the visual barriers around the gallows were removed. The two death candidates were suddenly at the center of the attention of tens of thousands of people. With a loud murmur of the masses, all their eyes were on the gallows.

Comrade Frank Bode continued, "Based on the undeniable proof of high treason, murder, and incitement of murder, theft of domestic and foreign money of several million from the people of this nation, the former FDS and FCS are sentenced to death by hanging. The sentence might be executed."

At that moment, somewhere behind the gallows, the officer who had won the vote pushed the button, and the trap doors under both delinquents fell away. The additional weights bound to their legs, invisible to the crowd, ensure that their neck break immediately.

After the multiple sounds of fright and horror and some applause vanished, the secretary-general returned to the microphones, "Fellow citizens, we do not enjoy doing this. Many of the indicted former leaders began their carrier as good comrades. But the moment they started to place their own interest above that of the people, they lost everything, including their right to mercy. We promise you today we will no longer tolerate the destruction of the great achievements of the first state of the workers and farmers on German soil. Everyone who betrays the Communist Party and its objective will face the same fate."

Bodo was satisfied when he experienced the enormous cheers of the masses. But he knew another force growing underground that would not be impressed by today's demonstration of power and will.

He looked over to his son and, realizing that this experience might have been somewhat heavy on his developing brain, he started to say some words of explanation when Sarina laid her arm around Nick's shoulder and said, "Nick, are you disturbed by seeing the traitors being hanged?"

"No, not about that," Nick answered without hesitation. "I understand these were traitors to the communistic cause, and they need to be dealt with in no uncertain way. I am just astounded how easy the secretary-general was turning the mood of this massive assembly of people, "and looking to Bodo, "What do you think, Dad, over a hundred thousand?"

Bodo thought momentarily and answered, "You might be close, son. I would say maybe ten thousand more."

And Nick continued, looking at his parents, "I would say, whoever wrote that speech, is a master of influencing the masses to follow his line of thinking. They followed every single argument going from a questioning mood to total agreement."

Bodo and Sarina looked at each other and were obviously positively astounded about the comprehensive understanding and knowledge their son, at the age of just not eleven years, had about how propaganda works. He seemed to have understood entirely that the correct mixture of some facts with some emotional reasoning can twist people's minds in any direction when correctly applied.

After the end of the demonstration, the centralized TV switched through reports from other cities, reporting about the general joy and appreciation of the thousands of people celebrating the holiday of the working class. There were several reports about the positive response to the execution of the traitors, and several interviews were done with people on the street. These interviews were not staged because some interviewed people were slightly surprised by the reporters' approach.

They watched for a few more minutes and then decided to go out and see what their new hometown had organized for this great holiday.

"What do you think about going by bicycle instead of driving into the city? It would help us get faster in and out without needing to search for a parking spot, which is limited around the center anyway. That area might be closed off because of the festivities," Bodo suggested.

"Awesome, Dad. I wanted to use my new bike for a long time. This would be great," Nick yelled in excitement.

Bodo looked slightly dumbfounded since he did not know about Nick's new bicycle. Sarina laughed and said, "Bodo, you should have seen your face. That expression was priceless."

Bodo laughed back and said, "I did not know about a new bicycle for Nick, and I hope priceless wasn't the amount of money you had to pay for it."

"No, it was a special sale at the particular store where we have been several times with Anabella. He was grown out of the old bicycle, and it would have needed some repairs anyway. Since you could not do the repairs, and this one is an awesome sports bike for his age with a reduced price, I just bought it. We can surely afford to spend a couple of hundred Marks, right?"

"Sure, no problem with the money. I was just surprised that you would buy a new bicycle for Nick. You are always hesitant about such things."

They walked into the attached garage where the bicycles were, and after a check that all was in order and safe, they were on their way into the city of the small town they called now home.

After about ten-minute ride, they arrived at the waterfront near the sailing club, where most of the activities of the day were taking place. They met several parents who had kids at the sailing club, and the discussion about the execution was the central theme of the conversations.

While Nick, who had met some of his new friends from the club, of whom two were in the same school class, had asked for some money and was at the shooting booth, Bodo listened to the conversation of the people who were sitting at the outside tables of the privately run restaurant, Sarina and he had joined.

Bodo was satisfied that most people at that large table responded positively to the event earlier in the morning. Many had ordered a beer, as did Sarina and Bodo, and some had non-alcoholic beverages. Sarina suggested getting a late lunch or early dinner there and saving the hassle of cooking when they got home. Bodo agreed, and they waved Nick over to sit with them and chose what he wanted. Astounded by the variety of meals offered, they finally decided and ordered.

As soon as Nick had finished his meal, he asked if he could get more money because Nick wanted to use some temporary rides there for the festivities, and he was gone. Although both had an eye on Nick's location, they listened to the discussion, and soon, Bodo realized that most of the people at the table were actually in total agreement with the public execution.

One of the men at the table, referring to the doubtful expression of another one about human rights and that we were not in the middle ages said, "Oh, come on Paul, you know as well as I know that 80 percent of our colleagues would not have believed the execution had really taken place if they would not have seen it with their own eyes."

And while Bodo was still in deep awe about how precise he had estimated the effects of the public hanging and how necessary it was to ensure the masses believed it was real, a woman in the round said, "I just hope the people get the signal and understand that the need for these Monday demonstrations is over. I can't tell you all how sick and tired I am of listening to the news every Tuesday night about the so-called counterrevolutionaries. Most of them are people like you and me, and many of them are friends and colleagues of ours."

And another one jumped in right after her. "You are right, Manuela, I was on one or two of those demonstrations, and I know for sure I am not a counterrevolutionary! Most of them just want to be heard. To have a voice and an end to the corruption which is everywhere."

Bodo was sitting there and was amazed at how the general public reaction was almost to the point as he had expected. But then, he thought about his years of training and work as a county secretary with his fingers at the pulse of the people's issues. He should have expected nothing else. He knew how the tools of propaganda worked, and he was sure he and the members of the Central Committee played those tools the right way and would do so in the future.

When they finally came home late, Nick was brought to bed immediately, having school the next day. Bodo told Sarina that he would switch channels to watch the Western propaganda TV station to see how they would fume at the mouth about the justice finally brought to bear in the only legitimized republic on German soil. That is what he said, and it was precisely what he meant.

He was surprised by the hateful commentaries from several politicians of the West German parties. All of the member parties of the West German so-called parliament and the traitors in the West Berlin mayor bashed the Socialist United Party of the German Democratic Republic for the decisive action they had done against the criminals. Bodo was laughing about the commentaries because he knew that if they were under his jurisdiction, they would hang within a week because of how corrupt they were, as he knew. And Bodo was sure he knew only the tip of the iceberg based on the few lines of the confessions he had seen so far.

They had enabled the stealing of most of the money his investigators had discovered so far. He had not only the confessions from three or maybe even more of the traitors now that several of the lying bastards in the West German TV stations running their crocodile tears over the "murder" of those precious and reasonable leaders in the GDR had been bribed with thousands of West Marks for allowing them to open hidden accounts and squandering the money of the Workers for their own luxurious demands.

Sarina joined him in front of the TV, and after a few minutes of watching the spitting of hatred, she said, "It looks like you stirred up a hornet's nest, Bodo. How much damage might it create to our international reputation?"

Bodo smiled at her and said, "No worries there, Sarina. At first, if we would not have done this, we would have lost the complete trust of our people. We could not lose any reputation with these bastards," pointing at the TV showing a round table talk group of politicians, "Because we never had any. Secondly, as you have heard with your own ears today, the average citizen approves of the execution, including the public version of it. And thirdly, I will have all the documents we have secured during the investigation of these two crimes, and the FDS of Schwerin handed over to the Secretary of Information first thing in the morning. Those documents will open the involvement of several of these bastards sitting there and lying their lives away. Those documents prove that they have been part of laundering our money into West German and Swiss bank accounts by getting a cut of it."

Sarina was baffled. "How much of that money can we get back? Do we know all the accounts they have used?"

"We know many of them, but we have scratched the surface. There are at least another sixty traitors whom we are sure to have had the opportunity and have used to funnel money from export businesses or bribe for either hindering the export of goods or for reducing the price of exported goods and cashing in part of the increased profits."

"Okay," Bodo closed the conversation. "Let's go to bed. I have a hard week in front of me. We will have some more executions, and I need to get a handle on that Underground Resistance Network. I am feeling it is growing its tentacles across the nation."

While walking up the stairs to their bedroom and getting ready to lie down, Sarina asked, "You believe there is something else trying to destroy the power of the party?"

"No, Sarina, something else, and somebody else. And that something else is led by my brother, is one of the most dangerous men our party has ever created in her existence."

All Sarina could get out was a fearful "Oh, man!"

EPILOGUE

What is in Part 3 of this fictional history story?

Is the strategy the Communist Party has started to implement successfully? Can they subdue the protesters marching around the churches every Monday night and chanting, "We are the people?"

Does the hanging of so-called traitors who committed high treason in public in the eyes of the newly established oligarchic powerful men turn the citizens back to believing the rhetoric about the workers' paradise on German soil?

Or is the analysis stated several times by Fritz to his friends and co-conspirators correct, and the communist oligarchs, fearing to lose their grip on the people and, with that, the absolute power, are taking the fight for survival to a whole new level?

How will the Underground Resistance Movement get better organized, becoming a power to be recognized, and how is the Office of Investigation and Recover reacting to that new and secretly growing danger to the eternal power of the Communist Party?

Especially considering the abysmal hatred of the powerful man in charge against his brother.

Is it possible that they will decide to do what the Chinese communist leader did to keep their power and order the military to use deadly force against the demonstrators they call counterrevolutionaries?

And probably the most challenging question to answer upfront is whether the military is indoctrinated enough to shoot and kill their own people?

The Chinese did! But will the East German National People's Army do the same?

And is it the last part? Honestly, I am not sure yet how the whole story ends. It might be too much for three parts and require another one. But that remains open and might be heavily influenced by the reception of the book by the readers.